A TEMPTING RISK

I turned to look at him and snatched up my cup, deliberately displaying my more than human speed. I expected to see fear, but only admiration crossed his gorgeous face. His eyes took on that feral look that all men get when desire takes possession of their minds. He wasn't observing the creature in me. He saw only the woman: soft, sleep-tousled, with luminous eyes and a pouty mouth. And he wanted to kiss me. I could tell.

Boy, did I want him to. I'm not going to deny that the thought of seeing him naked and in my bed left me feeling a little more than flushed. But I didn't mix business with pleasure for a reason. The last thing I wanted was to put Tyler in danger, no matter how well he could handle himself.

SHAEDES
of GRAY

A SHAEDE ASSASSIN NOVEL

AMANDA BONILLA

A SIGNET ECLIPSE BOOK

SIGNET ECLIPSE
Published by New American Library, a division of
Penguin Group (USA) Inc., 375 Hudson Street,
New York, New York 10014, USA
Penguin Group (Canada), 90 Eglinton Avenue East, Suite 700, Toronto,
Ontario M4P 2Y3, Canada (a division of Pearson Penguin Canada Inc.)
Penguin Books Ltd., 80 Strand, London WC2R 0RL, England
Penguin Ireland, 25 St. Stephen's Green, Dublin 2,
Ireland (a division of Penguin Books Ltd.)
Penguin Group (Australia), 250 Camberwell Road, Camberwell, Victoria 3124,
Australia (a division of Pearson Australia Group Pty. Ltd.)
Penguin Books India Pvt. Ltd., 11 Community Centre, Panchsheel Park,
New Delhi - 110 017, India
Penguin Group (NZ), 67 Apollo Drive, Rosedale, Auckland 0632,
New Zealand (a division of Pearson New Zealand Ltd.)
Penguin Books (South Africa) (Pty.) Ltd., 24 Sturdee Avenue,
Rosebank, Johannesburg 2196, South Africa

Penguin Books Ltd., Registered Offices:
80 Strand, London WC2R 0RL, England

First published by Signet Eclipse, an imprint of New American Library,
a division of Penguin Group (USA) Inc.

First Printing, December 2011
10 9 8 7 6 5 4 3 2 1

PUBLISHER'S NOTE
This is a work of fiction. Names, characters, places, and incidents either are the
product of the author's imagination or are used fictitiously, and any resemblance
to actual persons, living or dead, business establishments, events, or locales is
entirely coincidental.

The publisher does not have any control over and does not assume any respon-
sibility for author or third-party Web sites or their content.

For Juan, because you looked me in the eye and made me promise not to quit

ACKNOWLEDGMENTS

Some people think writing is lonely business, but I have never felt such a sense of friendship and community as I have since I began this endeavor. I don't think my words could ever do justice to the love and gratitude I feel for everyone who has stood by me, believed in me, and supported me in my journey.

To Juan, Jacquelyn, and Drew, you endured my absentee status the past few years as I hid behind a computer screen. You've been patient with my writing marathons, midnight scribbling by the light of the refrigerator, and late—sometimes burned—dinners. You've allowed my brain to be where it needs to be, and I couldn't love you more for it.

Mom and Dad, God knows I've put you through the wringer, and since we all know I'm Murphy's Law incarnate, you both deserve some kind of medal. Or award. Or both.

Niki, you're my partner in crime. There's no one I'd rather get lost with or talk books with.

Suzanne Hayes, Sarah Bromley, and Windy Aphayrath, how your eyes aren't bleeding from the number of times you've read this book, I'll never know. But I wouldn't be half the writer I am without you guys. You've listened to me whine, talked me off of ledges, and offered me constant support. I owe you all a hundred times over.

Cole Gibsen, your advice when I had doubts carried me over many a rough patch. Michael J. Pollack, you were my first "writer friend" and read the very first draft of *Shaedes of Gray*, and assured me that it didn't suck. And to Nancy Smith, Cassidy Winter, and Jess Ellis, your enthusiasm and love of reading are contagious! Through your eyes, I saw what could be.

To my Magic and Mayhem sisters: Sandy Williams, Shawntelle Madison, and Nadia Lee. Sandy, thanks for bringing us all together. Shawntelle, my Web site would be drab and lifeless without your expertise. Nadia, you are indeed a marketing guru. I've learned so much from you guys!

Suzette Saxton, Elana Johnson, and Mary Lindsey, you gave me the confidence I needed to get myself out there. Christine Fonseca, and Michelle McLean, thank you for bringing me out of my shell while I negotiated the waters of blogging, and social networking. And to Kimberly Minter and Joy Denisoff, thanks for lending your artistic talent and services and helping me look more glamorous than I really am.

I wouldn't be writing these acknowledgments at all, though, if it weren't for several fantastic people. Thanks to my agent, Natanya Wheeler and everyone at Nancy Yost Literary Agency. Natanya, you are made of awesome. You believed in me and this book, and you put up with my neurotic insecurities, which has to be a full-time job in itself. I also owe a huge thank you to Laura Cifelli, who went above and beyond for me when she didn't have to, and to my amazing editor, Jhanteigh Kupihea. The Army's got nothing on you! You totally know how to make someone be all they can be! Thanks also to Kathleen Cook, my production editor; Robin Catalano, my copy editor; and Cliff Neilson, my cover designer, for all their hard work.

And for anyone I might have missed, I apologize for my lack of functioning memory. But I trust you know who you are and you know how I feel!

Chapter 1

I live in the gray. It's a wonderful place, free of account-ability, bereft of conscience. I've lived in the black and white, but that was before, and I don't worry about how I used to be.

I hate the cold, and yet there I was, standing on the roof of the Cobb Building, looking out across the Metropolitan Tract while the dark, cloudy sky spit snow on my face. I wouldn't have been there at all if I hadn't needed the money. Okay, that's not exactly true. I didn't need the money. I *wanted* the money. I also wanted the action. That, I needed.

"Could you have picked a weirder place to meet?" a man's voice spoke from behind me.

Marcus. *Lovely*.

"Where's Tyler?" I demanded, a little on edge that Ty had sent an errand boy instead of meeting me himself.

"Had an appointment that ran late." His thin lips turned up in a twitchy smile, and I palmed the dagger at my thigh, feeling a bit twitchy myself. "He said to tell you he's sorry and he'll call you later."

Great. It was bad enough I had to wait out in the cold. Now I had to do business with this clueless idiot. Not many of Tyler's contractors enjoyed the privilege of an in-person visit from him, but since day one, I'd been the exception. I looked Marcus over, from his dirty black hair to his soft middle and right down to his worn, secondhand army boots. Where did Tyler find these guys?

"Let's get this over with," I said. "I'm freezing my ass off out here."

"Seventy-five percent," the lackey said. My eyes narrowed and I felt again for the dagger at my side. As if it made everything okay, Marcus quickly added, "Tyler promises he'll get the rest to you after the job's done."

I jerked the envelope out of his hand. I didn't stand out in the cold for seventy-five percent. I didn't have to. "Ty knows I won't do shit until I get the rest." I tucked the money into my coat and waited.

Marcus stared at me, shifting his weight from one foot to the other. He looked like he was trying to keep from pissing his pants. I can come across scary when I want.

"Look, Darian. I'm just the messenger." I quirked a brow and he faltered. "Y-you have a problem with what's in that envelope, you take it up with the boss man. I'm out."

He turned his back on me, and I fought the urge to laugh at his carelessness. The tip of my blade pressed into his back before he could face me again. "You know what they do to the messenger—right, Marcus?" He swallowed, and the sound was like a stone dropping into a fifty-foot cavern. "I want the rest of my money," I whispered close to his ear, and he shuddered. "Tell Ty to call me when he gets it."

I disappeared before he could open his mouth again.

A gust of wind hit me full in the face as I walked, blowing back my hood and causing my hair to billow out in soft strawberry waves. I locked eyes with a man who brushed my shoulder as I passed him on the street. He studied me for a fleeting moment before averting his gaze. Perhaps he'd picked up on the faint glow of my green eyes that betrayed my lack of humanity, or maybe it was simply the solemn black clothes and deadly expression that seemed out of place on an otherwise innocent-looking girl.

Most nights I felt comfortable roaming the streets of

Seattle alone, but tonight something didn't feel right. I suppose it could've been the cold or the wind that stole my breath. Or maybe the fact that Tyler sent Marcus to meet me instead of coming in person. We'd been avoiding each other lately, and not because of our business relationship. It didn't matter that Ty had shorted me money for the first time in a long time. The only reason I'd threatened Marcus at all was because I knew he'd tell Tyler about it and he'd be forced to call me up. I didn't like distance between us, despite the fact that I needed it.

I walked, my face protected by the high collar of my duster, deeper downtown and skirted two guys and a girl hailing a cab. "Dude, you're four-oh-four if you think you've got a chance with her," one guy said to the other before climbing in after the girl.

"Four-oh-four," I whispered under my breath, committing the phrase to memory. I wanted to find out what it meant, add it to my mental dictionary. I was always careful to use the vernacular of the times.

As the cab pulled away, I thought of the many instances I'd watched from beneath lowered lashes, listening in on conversations. I have perfected the art of imitation. Mannerisms, slang, modes of dress change every day, let alone every year. I don't miss a single trend. My looks are enough to make me stand out; I don't need another excuse to draw unwanted attention.

The sleet began to accumulate, and I shuffled my boots through the muck, making narrow paths behind me. I tucked my fists into my pockets and picked up my pace, no longer patient with the weather. Hustling along, I tried not to dwell on the fact that I was alone in this world. I hadn't encountered another of my kind in nearly a century, and when I had known one, I'd been too green to ask the right questions.

Azriel. As shrewd as he'd been secretive. Answers didn't come easy. He'd kept me right where he wanted me, under the guise of love and devotion. Even as I forced the memories down, they resurfaced.

"I don't want your kisses." I looked into his handsome, ageless face. A face that would never change, despite the passing of years. "I want answers."

"As long as you're with me, there's nothing you need to know."

"Why do you seem like a mirage once the sun sets, and I seem more solid?"

"I am born, and you are made." He tried to stop the questions with another kiss.

"But you can look more solid if you choose," I said.

"Glamour for human benefit. It's nothing for you to worry about."

"You don't need glamour during the day," I pressed, eager for information.

"Neither do you," he said in an offhand way.

"What about the others? Are there others like us wandering the earth?"

Azriel let out an exasperated sigh. "No. We are the last. The only ones of our kind."

"Tell me something else," I begged. "Anything."

"Really, Darian, you are like a whining babe." His dark eyes turned cold, but he softened the cruel edge by taking my hand in his. "'Why, why, why?' It drones in my ears. Why don't I ask you some questions?"

"Such as?"

"Are you deadly?" he asked.

"If I want to be."

"Are you strong and quick as the wind?"

"As strong as you and just as fast," I replied.

"Can you pass as shadow during the night, and are you confined to corporeal form during the day?"

"I can, and I am," I said, almost pouting.

"Then do not worry about what you do not know. We are immortal. The only weapon that can kill us is a blade

forged with magic, and even I don't know where one might be. We are alone in this world, and you have nothing to fear." His mouth hovered close to mine. "Ask me no more."

I broke free from the unpleasant memories and cursed myself for thinking about him. He was long gone. Though I'd never been able to prove it, I figured he'd wound up on the pointed end of a magic blade. Dead. It was the only explanation; he'd never have left me otherwise. But that part of my life was best forgotten. My focus needed to be on the money I was owed and Tyler's absence tonight. Not a long-lost lover who'd disappeared ages ago.

Thoroughly annoyed with my nostalgic moment and chilled to the bone, I arrived at my studio apartment near the center of Belltown, the northern district of downtown Seattle. The densely populated area suited me—too many people paying too much attention to themselves to worry about me or what I might be.

I stepped from the lift that opened to the apartment and was greeted by a gust of warm air. Every muscle in my body relaxed. I kept the thermostat at a toasty seventy-five degrees, sometimes warmer.

Falling onto a chair, I drummed my hands on the armrest. I hated having my time wasted, and Marcus was a *huge* waste of my time. My cell phone rang, breaking the silence. Since I didn't have any besties calling to gab about their hair appointments and desk jobs, I knew it was Tyler.

"Speak," I said into the receiver.

"Darian?"

"Were you expecting someone else to answer my phone?" I smiled, enjoying the way my name sounded like a soft caress when he said it. "Do you have the rest of my money?"

"Yeah. I had to guarantee it, though." His tone sounded put out, but I knew the truth: Tyler could afford to guarantee my work. "What did you do to Marcus to-night anyway? He said he'd quit if I ever sent him on an errand that involved you again." The laughter in his voice put me at ease. He knew I'd been messing with Marcus, and he didn't entirely disapprove. That guy needed to grow a pair if he was going to play with the big boys.

"You should have come yourself," I said. "I don't like meeting with your errand boys."

A long silence stretched between us, and I couldn't help but wonder what Tyler was thinking. "Snow's com-ing down pretty hard out there." His words were stilted—definitely not what he'd planned on saying, as if the weather were a safer topic than what was really on his mind. "I'll bring the rest of your money over myself. Be there in ten minutes."

I snapped the phone shut. He knew me down to the smallest detail, and the fact that he was willing to come over so I didn't have to go back out in the cold warmed me from the pit of my stomach outward. Avoidance wasn't going to work. Not when we both made excuses to continue to see each other.

I twisted the ring on my left thumb—wide, worn silver with an antiquated carving. I'd never been able to iden-tify the animal; it looked sort of like a bull or maybe a buffalo. Too much like a cave drawing for me to tell for sure. Tyler had given it to me after I'd completed my first job for him—said all of his people wore one. In the event a job went south, the ring would identify the wearer even if dental records couldn't. And if anyone happened to cross me? Well, according to Tyler, the ring would guar-antee my protection. Apparently, one look at that bull . . . buffalo . . . whatever would set stone-cold killers to shak-ing in their boots. It hadn't mattered to him that I wasn't so hard to dispatch. He'd insisted I wear it, and who was I to turn down free jewelry?

I met Tyler five years ago. He's like a temp agency for

the underbelly of society—a problem solver in the basest sense of the word. Tyler makes them—*poof!*—disappear. He's known in a lot of circles, and he gets paid a nice chunk of change for his services. Working for him had been a no-brainer. I'd needed a new benefactor, as my previous contact had met an untimely end at the hands of the Russian mob. Tyler needed someone apathetic and discreet. He knew I was a killer the first time he laid eyes on me, and I knew he was the type of guy with connections.

Tyler was known for his hard edge, but when his eyes met mine, they held a depth of emotion that caught me off guard. It sparked something in me I'd thought long buried. "You're not just a good-looking daddy's girl, are you?" he'd asked.

I laughed. I'd *never* been a daddy's girl. "Nope. But I've got skills, and from what I hear, they're the kind you need. The kind of skills that could earn us both a lot of money."

"What do you know about my business?" he asked, a smile in his voice.

"I know people pay you to solve their problems."

"And how do *you* solve problems?"

I pulled a dagger from the sheath at my thigh and drove the point into the bar's thick wooden tabletop. "I take them away. Permanently."

And with that, I was hired.

As promised, the elevator whirred to life ten minutes after his call.

Tyler never disappoints. He's never late.

I didn't greet him at the door. Cordiality wasn't one of my strong suits. Instead, I stood at my kitchen counter, pretending to be anything but preoccupied by who had just stepped into my apartment. It's hard to ignore that level of gorgeous, and Tyler had it in spades. My heart raced at the sight of him, and it suddenly felt like my mouth was too dry to speak. *Damn.* I hadn't seen him in a couple of weeks, and just watching him walk toward me was enough to make my stomach do a backflip. And that was a huge fucking problem. I couldn't afford to feel anything for him. I'd learned the hard way that love is nothing more than the sharpest blade, and it can easily be turned against you. I refused to let anyone have that kind of power over me ever again.

"Is there anything in your wardrobe that isn't black?" he teased as he walked toward the kitchen.

I resisted the urge to smile, unwilling to let him see the trace of warmth his nearness caused. "I like black." I almost always wear black or white, depending on the job and the circumstances. Tyler only saw me in black. The work I did for him wasn't exactly on the sunny side.

"Don't get me wrong," he said, coming closer. "You look great."

So do you, I thought as he shrugged off his heavy wool peacoat. Ty never overdid it in the clothing department. He was a jeans and T-shirt guy all the way, but he knew how to make the simple garments complement his lean, muscular body. Tyler's not even a notch below Calvin Klein underwear-model physique, and has a tousled mop of gold-and-bronze-streaked hair and strange hazel eyes—green with a brownish star surrounding the pupil. A garbage bag would've looked like an Armani suit on him. He reached around to his back pocket and produced an envelope containing the rest of my money, and a slip of paper. "Is that for me?" I asked, reaching out.

"Yeah, the information's on the paper."

I leaned over the bar and he pressed the envelope and paper into my hand, grazing my fingers as he pulled away. Though his skin was cooler than mine, Tyler's touch left me warm. And wanting more. My skin all but burned where he'd touched me, a brand that reminded me I'd have been better off dealing with Marcus. Tyler must have felt it too, judging by the way his lids became hooded and his chest rose and fell in a quick rhythm. I took a tentative step back, irritated at my own stupidity for orchestrating this visit. *Shit.*

He ran his fingers through the thick tangles of his hair and dropped onto a stool at the bar. His jaw clenched, the muscle at his cheek flexing. "Look, Darian. I want you to be careful on this job. Something doesn't feel right."

Ty's instincts were usually right on. But I never gave much thought to things like caution. "I can handle it," I said. "You don't need to worry about me."

"I know you can handle it." Ty gave me a level stare. "That's not the point. Maybe I should take this one myself."

"No way." This job paid double my usual fee. I had no intention of giving up that kind of money. Or the kind of action a double fee usually indicated. "I've got this one. Period."

Ty shifted in his seat, and I knew his pensive attitude had nothing to do with the mark. "You ever think of a change in venue? Maybe a new line of work?"

"Sure, because I've always secretly wanted to pursue my dream of becoming a kindergarten teacher. Please. I'm good at what I do, and you know it."

Standing from the stool, Ty rounded the bar and leaned up against the sink beside me. I balled my hands into fists, more to keep them from shaking than anything. God, he smelled good. Comforting, like fresh-baked cinnamon bread or something equally delicious and loaded with rich spices. His unique scent swirled around in my head, and I wanted nothing more than to lean into him, feel the weight of his arms around me as I breathed him in. But then my common sense gave me a swift kick in the ass. There was a stack of reasons why I couldn't be with Tyler. He was human while I . . . well, I sure as hell wasn't. Plus, he deserved someone softer. A nice piece of womanly eye candy. Someone capable of giving and receiving love without considering it a bargaining chip. Someone who wouldn't stab another person with something sharp if he pissed her off. That someone wasn't me.

"How long are we going to keep doing this?" His tone, though dark, had a sensual edge to it. A yearning that mirrored my own. *Shit.*

"Tyler—" My gaze dropped to the floor. I couldn't look up because he'd see the emotion written all over my face. "We're not going to talk about this."

"Maybe I want to talk about it." His voice became softer still. He reached out, his fingers caressing me, shoulder to wrist. A jolt of excitement shot through my core, and I cursed my weakness and my susceptibility to his touch. I wanted him, and not just for the night.

"We work together." The excuse sounded as lame in my head as it did coming out of my mouth.

"Then you're fired," he murmured, brushing his fingers against my palm.

My cheeks flushed and it had nothing to do with the temperature in my apartment. These moments between us were becoming more frequent—and harder to resist. I put my palm against his chest, my entire hand tingling with excitement from the contact. He felt solid, rock hard, under my hand, and I wondered what his skin would feel like without his T-shirt between us. I pushed him gently away, severing our contact and allowing me enough space to take a decent breath. I couldn't focus with him so close. And we needed to talk business.

"So," I said, shaky, "I take it the mark's a real bastard?"

Tyler took an extra step back, his smile turning almost sad. "You know me," he said with a sigh, and the sound mirrored my own disappointment. "I don't take money to kill just any asshole. Only the scum of the earth will do."

That's why I worked for Tyler. He shared my disgust

for the morally bankrupt, and I could count on him to flush them out of their holes for me. Be it a drug dealer, pimp, or worse, Tyler hated abusers just as much as I did. And each and every one of them abused their victims in one horrible way or another.

Talking business was like a gust of fresh air. It cleared my head, redirected my focus. This job was the only thing keeping me from violating all of my self-imposed rules in regards to Tyler. I'd spent decades polishing my armor, and now was not the time to let it tarnish.

I leaned back against the stove, but still, the distance between us could be closed by an arm's length. Even the air seemed thinner, as though there wasn't enough of it to share. Tyler sealed the gap, his eyes trained on my face, drinking in every detail. He reached out, his fingers feather light against my cheek, and tucked a stray strand of hair behind my ear. Time to take this conversation out of the kitchen. I needed some space, and the current cramped quarters weren't doing anything for my will-power. I tapped the envelope of money against my palm, paced away from Tyler, and rounded the far end of the polished concrete countertop. I flopped down on the overstuffed chair in the living room that bordered the kitchen. Unfolding the slip of paper, I read the mark's info with more interest than the situation called for. "I'll get ahold of you when it's done," I said.

Tyler stiffened, his shoulders square. "You can't keep avoiding this—*us*—Darian."

Who says? As far as I was concerned, I could keep avoiding it until the end of time. "If it's not broke, don't fix it. Right, Ty? We work well together. And I'm not going anywhere anytime soon. Why can't things stay just the way they are?"

"Change is the only constant, Darian."

He always said my name with care, as if the word were fragile. The sound of it made my chest ache. "We just can't ... *be* together."

His eyes burned into mine. "Why not?"

Why not, indeed? "It's not a good idea. Trust me, Ty. I'm not what you need."

He threw his coat over his shoulders and headed for the elevator. "Why don't you let me worry about what I need? Be careful tomorrow. I'd hate for you to trip on your boulder-sized pride before you get the job done."

The elevator whined its way to the ground floor, leaving me alone.

Way to go, I thought. *You wanted things to cool down. Looks like you got your wish.* He'd forget about his fascination soon enough. It wasn't really me he wanted. More likely it was the idea of me. The exotic, preternatural creature. Tyler would find someone worthy of his adoration. The thought of his arms around another woman made me want to scream. I sat for a moment, absorbing the quiet and the hollow ache in my chest that only his absence caused. Fuck if I knew why, but the torture of having him near was almost better than the anguish of watching him leave.

Rather than continue to stew in my misery and obsess over emotions best left unrealized, I locked the envelopes—both the seventy-five percent and the remainder of my fee—in a safe tucked behind a false wall. Tyler wouldn't dare cheat me. I trusted him with my life; the money was a no-brainer.

I unfolded the paper once again and reread the name and address scrawled on it.

Xander Peck, 1573 East Highland Drive

His name rolled off my tongue a couple of times. Not exactly a Tom or Josh or Steve. But I guess Darian wasn't exactly a Becky, Suzie, or Jennifer either.

Poor bastard. I wondered who Xander Peck had pissed off to deserve a visit from me. Whatever he'd

done, it must've been pretty bad. People paid through
the nose for my services, and I wasn't exactly listed in the
yellow pages. You'd have to have connections, and not
the normal kind, to hire a Shaede to mete out your punishments.

Chapter 2

The next night, a light rain misted the air and the snow from the previous day melted away in the gutters. The city teemed with activity, restless and anxious, just like me. I carried, tucked inconspicuously beneath my coat, a dagger and a short saber slung across my back. I never use guns—too impersonal.

I could have traveled unseen, but that night, I wanted the attention. It kind of revved up my engine, got me ready for the job. I wore my signature black—tight pants, low on my waist; long-sleeved black nylon turtleneck that clung to every curve of my body; black boots (of course); and, to top it off, a long black duster. I admit, the coat was a little over the top, but I love dramatics. Especially when I'm on a job.

I went without an umbrella, and my hair coiled in soppy curls that dripped over my shoulders. I walked with my chin high, shoulders back, and my stride long. And I made sure to direct my glowing gaze at anyone who dared to look.

A group of guys passed me. One of them ran right into a streetlamp, he was so busy staring. The man to his right seemed much more confident. "Hey, baby. Lookin' for a little company?" he shouted, turning to watch me pass.

I stopped dead and turned to face him. He must have thought himself a real ladies' man, because he went so far as to urge his friends on their way.

I flashed a wicked smile. A dumbstruck look crept onto his face. Weak. Easy. Not even a challenge.

"You must be this tall," I said, leveling my hand well above his stocky height, "to ride *this* ride." I blew him a kiss and kept walking.

The light drizzle became a downpour as I made my way toward East Highland Drive. I could no longer remember what things sounded or looked like through my human ears and eyes, but with my heightened senses, a simple rainstorm became a symphony of sensory overload. I heard every drop as it made contact with the ground, exploding from one into several, dissipating into the collective body of water that ran in a sheet along the concrete sidewalk. I felt sorry for humans sometimes. They missed out on a lot.

As I neared lucky Mr. Peck's address, the city melted away and the neighborhood became more residential. Apartment buildings morphed into town houses, and retail spaces disappeared into grassy parks. The neighborhood looked richer than I'd expected. Usually the kind of people who ended up on the sharp end of my knife took up in a decidedly seedier atmosphere.

I found the place with little effort and took a seat, watching, on a bench across the street. Tyler's visit the previous evening still had my head spinning. The set of his jaw, the way he'd thrown his shoulders back as he walked toward the lift . . . Maybe I'd put the final nail in the coffin of our almost relationship. A pang of regret shot through my chest at the thought, even though I knew it was for the best. Sure, it would have been fine in the beginning—all groping, greedy hands and hours of sex followed by sweet affirmations and professions of love. But that would only last so long. The moony-eyed-lover crap would turn to resentment, power struggles, and manipulation. He'd grow to hate me, and not just because of my less than gracious personality. Then something would happen. He'd want me to quit this line of work, or move away, or he'd expect me to go June Cleaver and marry him or some shit. And when none of that happened, he'd resent me. Or he'd use my affection against me like Azriel had. He'd use love to control me, keep me nice and subservient. And wouldn't that just be the fairy-tale ending. No, I had to be strong. I couldn't let Tyler worm his way into my heart. He was human and he'd age and eventually die. He needed to forget about me and find himself a pretty human woman to grow old and die with. And then I'd be truly alone. Wouldn't I?

Rain pattered against the round toes of my thick-soled boots, and I watched the drops splatter like the tears I refused to shed. The town house loomed before me like a voyeur, its windows curious eyes that drew my attention away from the empty ache in my soul. The place looked pretty much like every other generic town house on the street, except for the fact that the curtains were open wide and every light in the place was on. *Maybe he's afraid of the dark,* I thought as I felt for my dagger.

"Xander Peck," I said, popping the "P" as I tried out his name again.

As if he'd heard me, the man in question strolled in front of the largest window on the second story. He was a tall one—muscular, late twenties, maybe, with flowing blond hair that brushed his shoulders.

From the looks of him, he wasn't expecting company. Wearing nothing more than loose cotton pajama bottoms, he stretched for an inappropriately long time. *Give me a break.* I'm sure the show supplied more than a few suburban housewives with enough fantasy fodder to get them through a tedious night or two.

Damn it. Discretion might be a bit of a problem if telescopes all over the neighborhood were dialed in to that window. I'd been paid a pretty chunk of change for this job, and I wanted it neat and tidy.

Standing from my perch, I fluffed out the duster. Raindrops scattered from its black surface, sounding like wind chimes and steel drums. I wrung the water from my hair as well. Didn't want to add insult to injury by dripping all over the poor guy's floor.

I reached to my right thigh. The sheathed dagger waited to be put to good use. Stretching my neck from one side to the other, I looked up at the balcony to the side of Xander Peck's picture window, and with as much concentration as it took to bat an eyelash, my body became one with the dark night air.

In the next second, I stood on the balcony. I didn't need to break in; I simply glided through the glass. Shadows don't worry about things like doors, windows, bars, gravity. I appeared in the next room—the bathroom, to be exact. I could hear Blondie moving around his bedroom, probably flexing and posing for his audience.

A faint smell lingered in the air, and at first I thought I'd imagined it. The aroma of warm spring flowers, stream water, grass, and pitch. That fragrance hadn't touched my nostrils in at least a century. It threw me off my game a little, but I brushed it away like a buzzing mosquito and focused on the job.

His presence was harder to pinpoint than a human's should be. Usually I can feel where they're standing, as if I have a built-in thermal imager. But my senses felt askew and I couldn't quite get a bead on him.

Oh, well, I told myself. *You'll just have to be quick.*

I passed through the wall, feeling no hindrance from the solid structure, to where I thought he'd be standing. He'd moved beyond the large window, just as I'd predicted. Dagger poised and ready to strike, I took a steadying breath and prepared myself for the kill. Muscles rippled beneath flawless, creamy skin. His spine straightened. I couldn't get my arm around him; he was too broad for my shorter reach. So I decided to sever his spine at the nape of his neck. It wasn't my usual MO, but beggars can't be choosers.

The smell that I'd tried to ignore hit me hard, choking me with its sweetness. I stabbed and then cut with the sharp steel blade, but all I managed to slice was thin air.

My target, vulnerable only a moment before, vanished just as effectively as I had. I spun around to guard my own back when a large, strong hand seized me by the throat.

"Who sent you?" Xander Peck asked, a little too calm for someone who'd almost lost his head.

I should have been more shaken, but his voice distracted me, draped over me like a red velvet blanket. I wanted to wrap myself up naked in that voice. The next thing—and it should have been the first thing—I noticed was the way his form quavered in the artificial light. He was almost . . . transparent.

I hadn't encountered anyone like me in close to a century. In fact, I'd been sure I was the only one left. But there he stood: tall, blond, and angry, and a natural-born Shaede.

"Who sent you?" he asked again, his grip tightening on my throat.

"I'm hired," I rasped in a flat, icy tone.

"Then who hired you?"

He almost sounded amused, but he wasn't going to be when he got his answer.

"I don't know," I said. "I never meet the clients."

"Well, then, you're not much use, are you? Maybe *I* should kill *you*."

"You could try." I didn't have to pretend to sound defiant or confident. Even a born Shaede would need a special blade to kill me.

He laughed, and the sound of it caused a spasm of pleasure to ripple from the top of my head right down to my toes. His grip on my throat disappeared with his body, and in a waft of dark air, he reappeared on a small sofa, very much at home.

"What's your name?" he asked.

"Darian," I said, throwing it out there like I had nothing to lose.

"Darian," he repeated. "So, Darian . . . who do you think would want me dead?"

"How the hell should I know?" I asked, maybe a little more indignant than I ought to have been considering the circumstances. "I guess you must've really pissed someone off."

"You think?" I couldn't blame him for mocking me. Hell, I *was* there to kill him. "Now, why would anyone send you to kill someone that you couldn't kill?"

I hadn't thought about that. Didn't care. Thinking wasn't part of my job. The client had to have recognized something inhuman about Xander Peck. Born Shaedes did have the ability to dazzle, glamour—whatever—a lot better than I could. They could convince humans that they're made of something more solid. Still, the "otherness" that exists in us has a tendency to set a person on edge.

"My guess," he said, resting an arm over the back of the couch, "is that you were set up."

That thought knocked the breath right out of me. Adrenaline pulsed in my veins. My heart hammered against my rib cage. Who would set me up? And why? Who, besides Tyler, knew—truly knew—about me? And, more importantly, who *knew* I wasn't the only one of my kind? I choked up on the dagger, the guard digging uncomfortably into my hand for a brief moment before I slid it into the sheath at my thigh. I'd been alone. The only one. *Only. One.* God, it didn't sound convincing even as I thought the words. Had Azriel known? He couldn't have. He never would have kept it from me. Or would he? His words, spoken long ago, haunted me. *We are alone in this world, and you have nothing to fear.* My head swam, feeling as though all the blood had rushed from my brain to my pounding heart. Not alone. *I am not alone.* The situation demanded a little more thought and a lot more caution. If anything, I needed answers from someone, and there happened to be only one someone on my list.

For the first time in my long existence, I left a job unfinished.

I sought the shroud of my shadow self for a stealthy escape and fled the town house. But when I gazed up at the window, Xander Peck stood at its center. He bowed his head deeply and vanished.

Chapter 3

"Meet me at The Pit in thirty minutes," I growled into my cell, "and if you're even fifteen seconds late, I'm going to slice you open like a Thanksgiving turkey."

Tyler was five minutes early.

The Pit isn't a prize to behold, but it's my favorite haunt. The stale smell of beer never went away and mingled with hundreds of different perfume and cologne samples into an olfactory nightmare. But the dim lighting and the warm air made me feel safe, no matter how bad it smelled or how many times I had to send an over-eager guy on his way.

Lucky for me, I like the heat. And the club happened to be seven different kinds of hot that night. But I couldn't take the duster off; it hid my saber and covered the dagger. I'm sure I looked like a Goth kid's wet dream, sitting in my black sex-kitten outfit, sipping a rum and Coke, exuding little to no emotion on the outside while my insides writhed like angry vipers.

Despite the fact that I'd all but shut him down the night before, Tyler gave me one of his lusty once-overs, and if I hadn't been so jacked up I would have smiled or even welcomed the attention. Ty was easygoing and had a tendency to bounce back even when things didn't exactly go his way. Apparently, he wasn't willing to give up on me quite yet. But my encounter with Xander Peck had been more than a message, and more like a slap in the face—just what I needed to keep my mind focused on the business at hand. And I wanted answers.

"Who's the client?" I shouted over the thumping club music that tuned out the private conversations I couldn't help but overhear.

"How should I know?" he shouted back, giving me his most charming smile.

I reached across the table and grabbed him by the collar, drawing him as close to my face as I could without biting his nose right off. "I'm not playing fuck-around, Ty. Who is it?"

His eyes narrowed, fixing me with a shrewd and calculating stare. But then his eyes softened as he studied my face with an expression of . . . could it be . . . concern? My stomach churned as I fought a wave of emotion, and I hate to admit that I dropped my gaze first. Ty glanced down at his shirt and slowly back to my face. I released my hold and he sank back in his chair. He ran his fingers through his thick coppery hair and continued to study me as if trying to crawl right into my thoughts. Maybe he was wondering if I was still thinking about what had happened between us last night. Right now, though, I didn't have the luxury of mulling over my love life. And, really, at this point, neither did he.

My nerves hummed, wound as tight as a trampoline spring. Though I'll admit to being arrogant at times, I realized now I wasn't the *only* unnatural thing on the planet. Of course others like me existed! I wanted to bang my head against the table. How could I have been so blind? I probably couldn't even pick one out of a crowd, though once or twice I'd sensed a different kind of energy surrounding someone who, for all intents and purposes, *looked* human. I'd let Azriel's words lull me into a false sense of security. I minded my own business and they minded theirs.

But now I truly worried that someone hadn't read that same memo. Someone who knew me as a Shaede had chosen to put me in a very precarious position.

"I never met the guy," Tyler said after a passing silence. "I talked to him on the phone and we arranged drops for the money. He called me, but his number was blocked."

"Did he ask for me specifically?" Tyler had a tendency to hire freelance professionals, even though we both knew I was the best.

"Yeah. Said he'd heard about you. Said you were the only one for the job."

I'd been set up. At least now I knew why the client didn't want to pay up front.

But that also prompted another interesting question. How had the client known what I was? If he knew about Shaedes, he would know we aren't so easy to kill. Food for thought.

"I want you to set up a face-to-face with this guy." I didn't care that it wasn't the norm. I wanted to look the bastard in the eye, let him see that I wasn't a helpless target.

"Are you crazy?" Tyler's voice rose above the din of the music. "That's a huge liability!"

"Can you arrange the meeting or not?"

The muscles in his jaw flexed. "This isn't a good idea." His voice strained as he fought for control of his temper. "I'm the middleman for a reason, Darian. Your anonymity protects you. If you meet with a client, it puts you in danger."

"I'm not worried about that." I could handle myself and Ty knew that. "Please. I want up close and personal with this client. See the whites of his eyes."

Tyler's jaw flexed and his brows came together, crinkling his forehead. Again, I got the feeling he wanted to get cozy with my private thoughts. "You think this is necessary?"

I nodded once.

"Fine," he said, as if the word left a nasty taste in his mouth. "I'll see what I can do."

I stood up and stretched my too-tight muscles. Extending my thumb and pinkie to my ear and mouth, my lips moved in a silent *call me*. I left Tyler staring after me as I wound my way through the gyrating dancers to the exit.

"Goin' home, Darian?"

The bouncer's nickname was Tiny, and he was as big around as a California redwood. I thought Killer or Skull Crusher might have been a more appropriate term for him, but, oh, well, it wasn't my job to give him a name.

"You know it," I answered as he put his body between me and the line of enthusiastic patrons salivating at a chance to get into the packed club. I shook my still-damp hair forward to hide my luminous eyes and sauntered down the street, fading into shadow as soon as I knew curious stares no longer followed me.

I stepped out of the lift into the vast, open square of my apartment. The only room closed off from the studio was the bathroom. The bed sat in one corner, the living room in another, and the kitchen and bathroom at the opposite side. High, vaulted ceilings gave me a good twenty feet of space, and windows showed a cityscape dotted with skylights. The frequent Seattle rains played a symphony on those skylights, and I usually lay stretched out in bed, staring at the ceiling until nature's music put me to sleep.

I discarded the wet duster, flinging it across the flat-screen TV to dry, and returned the saber to its resting place on the wall above my fireplace. I set the dagger on the mantle, wondering at Tyler's show of protectiveness. I liked to think he cared enough about me to be concerned, though now was not the time for him to get all personal bodyguard on me. One of the things I liked about Ty was the fact that he didn't coddle me or treat me like I was made of glass. He thought of me as an equal, and I thought of him the same way. But my inner damsel did swoon—a little. Dislodging one boot and then the other, I kicked, sending each to a different corner of the studio. After peeling off my wet pants and sweater, I stayed in the living room, allowing the balmy heat floating down from the vents to air-dry my body, clad in nothing but a black bra and matching lace underwear.

"Now, that's a sight to behold," said a red-velvet voice from behind me.

I cursed under my breath. Xander had been following me. Anger pulsed hot and welcome in my veins. I shouldn't have let my guard down—especially now that I knew someone like him existed.

Instead of turning to face him, I strolled to my bathroom to retrieve a fluffy white fleece robe that I draped over my body and cinched tight at my waist. Then, with murder written on my face like tomorrow's lunch special, I turned around. He sat relaxed in my overstuffed chair, looking very much at home.

Even from across the apartment, his eyes held me captive. Melted caramel flecked with gold, possessing the bright glow that I knew mine had, though his were more brilliant. The smell of him permeated the air, filling my studio with a sweetness that would put a field of wildflowers to shame. His lips curled up at the corners, hinting at an arrogant smile.

"You look even better in that robe," he said.

The sound of his voice sent a spasm of chills over my skin. I tried to shake the sensation and moved to the kitchen to pour myself a tall glass of juice. It's not like I could throw him out, but I wasn't going to be hospitable either.

His voice cut through the silence. "Who is your maker, Shaede?"

I bristled. After all, I'd told him my name—he should've at least tried to use it. "His name"—I paused to sip my juice—"was Azriel, and he is dead."

He rolled that comment over in his mind for a moment. "I've heard the name," he said. "How did he die?"

"I don't know," I said indignantly. "I know only that he's dead."

I didn't leave the kitchen. For some reason, I didn't want to be too close to him. You don't often drop in on the assassin who's been hired to kill you, and I didn't think he'd stopped by for a cup of tea.

"From whom did you acquire your skills?" he asked.

"From myself," I snapped.

A deep, rumbling laughter erupted from his chest, and another round of thrilling chills trickled across my skin. Shaedes are alluring by nature. Azriel's eyes, voice, and laughter often had the same effect on me. I wondered, though: *Could it be something more?*

"I've come with a message," he said.

"Oh yeah? What's tha—?"

Before I could finish, he appeared in front of me in a wisp of darkness. His form became solid and his face demanded my attention.

"You are summoned to the king's guard," he said.

"Whose king?" I asked. Certainly not mine. I was my own woman, and I had no country or master to swear allegiance to.

He brought his hand up to my cheek. I could feel the heat before he touched me, but when he did, I felt as if he'd laid my skin against one of those electric heating pads that humans use to ease their aches and pains. Wonderful.

He brushed his thumb across my cheek before dropping his hand to his side. I couldn't break his hold on me, and my eyes didn't leave his. I swallowed. Hard.

"*Your* king," he whispered, and vanished.

I let out the breath I hadn't realized I'd been holding. *Well, this has been a shit-tastic day,* I thought, leaning against the kitchen counter to steady my quaking body.

I had been alone for so long—the only one for years. I'd developed a comfort zone and lived my life within its boundaries. Well, that was shot to shit now. I turned toward the picture window, staring out across the dark city peppered with random white lights.

The rain had started up again and pounded on the skylights like it wanted in. I watched the water bounce and land, running in rivers down the pitched glass. Making my way to the bathroom, still watching the rain on the skylights, I shucked my robe and started the shower. I never used the cold water; I like my showers *hot,* and the temperature didn't damage my preternatural skin. Within moments, the room filled with glorious steam, and I joined its company for a single second as I glided under the water. I could have taken the extra couple of steps, but why exert the energy?

The steam was welcome as I inhaled and held it in my lungs. I gave off a perfumed aroma like any Shaede, but mine smelled like summer blossoms in the late-afternoon sun. Sitting on the tiled shower floor, I let the scalding water pour over my skin until it ran cold. I passed through the steam again—lazy, I know—and ended up next to my robe. After running a comb through my hair, I collapsed into bed and drifted off to sleep, wrapped like a mummy in fluffy white fleece.

Xander's visit prompted me to dream about Azriel that night. His perfect image floated nearby, just as I remembered him. With olive skin and black hair, he looked like someone of Middle Eastern or Indian descent, though he'd been cut from an entirely different cloth. His eyes were nearly black—cold and devoid of emotion. But when he smiled, a spark lit in them and they danced to life with a mischievous gleam that rendered me helpless. He was neither kind nor cruel; he simply was.

He made me, left me, and taught me nothing.

My eyes were thick with sleep but I pried them open, fighting against the dream. My heavy breathing filled the air, though I lay still as death on the bed. Banishing every thought of Azriel, I closed my lids and forbade myself to dream.

*   *   *

The next morning, I sat at the table, working on my second cup of coffee, when I heard the lift. My apartment, which used to be old warehouse space, occupies the entire top floor, hence the lack of an actual door. No locks, no security code. Just an old freight elevator protected by an iron gate. Some people might have been put off by the lack of security, but I'd never worried about my personal safety. A proper visitor would've thought about ringing the bell before coming up, but this guest didn't have a problem with barging in like he owned the place.

Tyler.

He had a recognizable signature for a human, and my unique senses had no problem picking him out, even in a crowd. His smell was different from most of theirs—homey and comforting with a dark, spicy edge. I'd wondered about it, but it's not like I lost any sleep over it. Maybe it was his aftershave. I loved the way he smelled. One breath of him could make me feel almost normal, but I would never tell him that.

He helped himself to a cup of coffee, knowing that I wasn't going to extend any kind of Martha Stewart hospitality, before taking a seat next to me. I didn't look at him. For some reason, Xander's visit made me feel as if I'd betrayed Tyler somehow, though the Shaede's invasion of my privacy left me more rattled than enamored. I hoped Ty couldn't sense my leftover discomfort, and I prayed he'd come this morning because he had good news.

Tyler never disappoints.

"It's set up," he said. "Tomorrow at midnight."

My scalp prickled and the chill continued down my arms. Something didn't add up. "How'd you get him to do it?" I asked, still not making eye contact.

"It took some coaxing, but I convinced him."

"*You* can't even get face time with the guy. But suddenly he's warmed up to the idea?"

"More or less," Tyler said. "I told him there was a complication and you wouldn't do the job without seeing him in person first."

"How do you know I didn't get the job done?" My suspicion of Tyler grew by the second. But every instinct in me screamed that he'd die before allowing any harm to come to me. Still, no matter who'd orchestrated it, the whole situation reeked of a setup.

"Look, Darian. We've worked together for a long time. When you called last night, you didn't say the job was done, and you've never given a passing thought to the identity of a client before. What happened? Was the mark a kid or an old man or"—he paused to sip from his cup—"something else?"

As a rule, I never take jobs that involve innocent people. It rests a hell of a lot easier on my conscience to know I'm being paid to clean the streets of one more asshole, and Tyler felt the exact same way. Thugs, criminals, thieves, drug dealers. The dregs of society were *this* assassin's cup of tea. But I never forgot that equally nasty people paid me for that service. They'd get theirs eventually. Shit always had a tendency to roll downhill.

Tyler hit one nerve and then another by implying the mark may have been anything but human. We didn't usually discuss my otherness. He knew more about the supernatural than a human should, and he brokered in things far from my scope of business.

I turned to look at him and snatched up my cup, deliberately displaying my more than human speed. I expected to see fear, but only admiration crossed his gorgeous face.

His eyes took on that feral look that all men get when desire takes possession of their minds. He wasn't observing the creature in me. He saw only the woman: soft, sleep-tousled, with luminous eyes and a pouty mouth. And he wanted to kiss me. I could tell.

Boy, did I want him to. I'm not going to deny that the thought of seeing him naked and in my bed left me feel-

ing a little more than flushed. But I didn't mix business
with pleasure. The last thing I wanted was to put Tyler in
danger, no matter how well he could handle himself. I
looked across the table as he brought the coffee mug to
his lips, a frown marring his normally unworried forehead. Something wild and sweet bloomed in my chest,
and it scared the hell out of me. I'd been burned more
than once, and for that reason, I just didn't do love. Besides, I cared about Ty too much to let him get dragged
into whatever mess I'd landed myself in. Xander had
popped in and out of my studio with ease, showing that
if he could find me, anyone could. And now the mystery
client wanted to meet with me.

In my line of work, nothing happened that easily.

Chapter 4

Tyler agreed—well, demanded, actually—to accompany me to the meeting that night. He told me he'd pick me up at eleven thirty, and since he was never late, I knew my timing would be perfect.

He pulled up to my building at eleven twenty-nine, probably allowing the extra minute to come up to my studio. But I had prepared to give him a show, hoping to demonstrate to him that meddling in the affairs of the nonhuman variety could be hazardous to his health.

I appeared as soon as his foot hit the sidewalk. A trace of dark mist trailed out behind me, and he nearly bumped into my body as it became corporeal. I had never let him see me pass from shadow before, and I hoped I'd shaken him up.

Abandoning my signature black, I was decked out in white from head to toe. My white-on-white striped blouse buttoned up to the swell of my breasts, with my white bra visible underneath. I'd tucked the shirt into a white pencil skirt that reached to my white satin heels and hugged my hips perfectly. Business attire, to an extent.

I could almost hear the rhythm of his heart increase as he devoured every inch of me with his eyes. He showed amazing restraint as I fought my own urge to reach out and run my fingers through his hair. Tonight was for Tyler as much as for my own peace of mind. I had to do something to cool the slow burn between us before it raged into a fully involved fire. I'd take care of this mystery client and slap Tyler with a dose of reality, and, hopefully, myself as well. Perfect. I'd be killing two birds with one stone.

"We'd better get going." He breathed close to my face and ventured toward the car door.

He moved to open it for me, but since I was going all out to shake him up, I slid through the solid metal like a warm breeze and appeared in my seat, staring serenely out the window at him.

Tyler stood on the sidewalk, gaping. His hands hung limp at his side, resembling the wax figures you see in museums that depict a Cro-Magnon man.

Good. I'd gotten my point across. It took a minute for him to snap out of it, but he regained his composure and took the driver's seat. He didn't utter a word after that, which suited me just fine because I'm not what you'd call a conversationalist.

At five minutes to midnight, we pulled into the parking lot of an old warehouse. This place looked more like what I expected in my line of work. I suddenly longed for a nice pair of stretchy black slacks and my boots.

I was unarmed. Stupid? Maybe. Arrogant? Absolutely. But I didn't need a blade to be deadly.

I left the car the same way I'd entered. My shadow form slid through the metal, plastic, and glass that made up the door, and I gathered myself into a solid form right outside the vehicle. I waited for Tyler with my back turned to him, to show him I wasn't afraid.

He took my arm this time. Desire rolled off him like sweat. His fingers tightened against the gauzy fabric of my shirt, and the contact sent a thrilling pulse through my bloodstream. I kept my distance, knowing anything besides a work relationship would crash and burn. But my heart jumped in my chest every time he touched me, and I wanted more. I took a deep breath and focused on the task at hand.

But, damn, he smelled good.

Just before the warehouse entrance, he stopped. I kept walking, but he pulled me back. I recoiled and ended up face-to-face with him. His nostrils flared and he gripped my other arm, not cruelly, but with enough purpose that I could sense he was about to do something rash, spoiling all of my well-thought-out plans in the process.

"I know my timing sucks," he said in a ragged voice, "but I have to do this."

Even though I was substantially stronger, I let him pull me closer. He slid his hands from my arms and placed one at the small of my back. The other wound through my hair. He dipped his head to mine, his tongue tracing his bottom lip. My stomach clenched as I was hit with a longing I'd been suppressing for far too long.

"Darian." He paused a fraction of an inch from my mouth, and my breath came heavy as I waited for him to follow through.

His mouth tasted just as delicious as I'd imagined it would, cool compared to my warmer temperature. Like a tall glass of ice water after a five-mile run. His arms tightened around me. My tongue darted inside his mouth and he returned the gesture, a moan escaping from deep within his throat. His head slanted, urgency playing out through his mouth, lips, and tongue, and his arms wrapped tight around me in a way that made me feel both protected and possessed.

The echo of footsteps on concrete made its way to my ears through the haze of desire fogging my brain. Tyler couldn't hear it, but I could. That cooled my jets as effectively as a cold shower. I didn't want to get caught with my pants down, as it were.

I broke from his embrace. His breathing came in ragged gasps. The spark of passion in the depths of his eyes raged. A guttural, almost growling sound bubbled up from his throat and he lunged at me, taking me once again and bending to resume where we'd left off.

"Take it easy, tiger," I said, putting my hand on his chest, pushing him away. He tried to pull me back, but I used my real strength against him, and he might as well have struggled against a boulder. "Someone's coming to the door."

A trace of sanity crept back onto his face. "I've wanted to do that since the day I met you."

Thankfully, I didn't get the opportunity to reply in kind. The door swung open, and I couldn't believe my preternatural eyes.

Ho-ly shit.

A woman, most assuredly Shaede, greeted us, and I rolled my shoulders to release the sudden tension that had settled there. It seemed Shaedes were coming out of the woodwork like carpenter ants. Where had they come from? Surely I would have picked up on something, their scent at least, if they'd been in the city for long. Xander's scent had stunned me from the moment I'd entered his town house. If Shaedes had been running willy-nilly through the city, I should have noticed. My lips spread into a wry smile as I looked her over. If Tyler had been worked up by me, this one should have sent him into an absolute lather.

She looked like hot sex wrapped in leather. Literally dressed from head to toe in red leather pants, boots, and a bustier, she gave the impression she'd be quite at home in a dungeon, whipping a desk jockey into submission once or twice a week. Her sleek, dark hair was pulled into a severe ponytail that sat at the topmost part of her head and cascaded down to her ass.

Tyler looked her over and his smiled faded, leaving an expression that was a strange mixture of controlled anger and shock. He placed an arm in front of me, tried to shove me behind him. "Wait," he said, becoming serious. "Stay here. I'll go in alone."

Okay. I hadn't expected such a strong reaction. Tyler's level gaze reminded me of that of a wild animal, like a wolf protecting his mate. My nerves ratcheted up a notch as I considered my circumstances. I trusted Ty; we'd worked well together for five years. He never took money for a job that didn't involve ridding the world of a drug dealer, flesh peddler, or worse. And, believe me, there was a whole hell of a lot "worse" out there. Something had him on edge, and I didn't like it. He'd be an easy target for a Shaede who wanted to do him harm—badass reputation or not. For once, I was going to take the lead with a client. "Ty." I gently pushed his arm away. "Don't be ridiculous. I'm going in there."

An exasperated sound escaped from under our hostess's breath before she settled her gaze—which looked like she'd just scraped something unsavory off the bottom of her boot—on me.

Violet eyes, gorgeous and fringed by thick black lashes, locked with mine. Hers glowed even brighter, glittering with an adversarial edge. "You don't look like much." Her disgusted tone told me we wouldn't be braiding each other's hair at a slumber party anytime soon. "I don't see what all the excitement is about."

I'd pushed Xander's talk of kings from my mind, focusing instead on the very real danger of the identity of the client who'd hired me to kill him. But now, in the presence of yet another Shaede, I wondered if I should have taken his speech so lightly.

With a curt inclination of her head, she moved aside so we could enter. Her lips stretched in a proud sneer, and she snorted, shaking her head as she walked just in front of me. I may not have been acquainted with my own kind, but that didn't make me some unsavory outcast either. I could tell just by her bitchy swagger that this Shaede thought she was better than me. And if there's one thing I hate, it's a snob.

The space was vast, dark, and empty, save an ornate chair at the very far end. Blue-dyed concrete floors gleamed beneath our feet, and the high beams of the trusses were crafted from large logs that had been shaved, burned, and varnished. Even the windows lining the high walls were not the industrial sort typical of a warehouse, but framed cottage style in rich wood.

The Dungeon Mistress led the way, and as we walked deeper into the warehouse, I sensed the presence of others I could not see. But I smelled their unique aroma and felt the weight of their eager stares.

As I drew closer to an unoccupied chair, I realized it looked too much like a throne for my taste. I turned a wary eye on Tyler, who shuffled next to me with a very human lack of stealth.

"Did you set me up?" I asked, fearing the answer.

"No." His tone was low, seriously on edge. The look he gave me spoke volumes about his own surprise. "Why would I set you up?" His gaze flicked from me to the entrance and every darkened corner in the place. Ty's stance shifted, one foot in front of the other, slightly crouched, as if ready to defend in the event of an attack. His body, so relaxed before we'd entered, was rigid, wary. And he looked flat-out pissed.

For a moment, I felt bad about my plans to scare him out of his infatuation with me. I hadn't given a passing thought to his safety, only guarding my own heart. If I'd been more in touch with my softer emotions, I might have done something to make sure he'd be safe. Those tender feelings had sure picked a shitty time to rise to the surface. Too late now. I threw back my shoulders, my attention focused on the throne, a mysterious king, and the possibility that this would be my last night of existence.

Our escort stopped short of the throne and genuflected, an act that caused laughter to bubble up like carbonation from my stomach. The bowing tickled my funny bone—and I don't have much of a sense of humor. But bowing to an empty throne? That sent me over the top. Hilarious.

Until I realized the throne held the assembling form of a man.

"High King Alexander"—she looked at me with disdain—"the *girl* is here."

The leather-clad Shaede's humble voice betrayed her outfit and her previous attitude, as far as I was concerned. But he wasn't my king, so I couldn't judge her.

Silence followed, and the air around the throne stirred, becoming thicker and more substantial. Shadows gathered around the seat, swirling and finally coming together to form a very real creature.

My jaw took on a stubborn set, and my eyes narrowed like a hunting cat about to pounce. The high king smiled at me, and his golden eyes glinted with a calculating and mischievous light.

"*You're* the king?" I asked in the most disrespectful tone I could muster.

The woman hissed—actually *hissed*—at me, and before I could close my mouth, she stood behind me, holding a very old, jewel-encrusted dagger, point up, underneath my chin.

"What the hell is this?" Tyler shouted, reaching for the Glock he kept tucked in his waistband. He looked ready to jump right out of his skin, pulse pounding at his temple, jaw flexing. The Shaede jerked the tip of her blade toward my neck, and Tyler froze. His eyes blazed with an angry fire.

"You should be killed for your disrespect," she seethed in my ear. "You are nothing—less than nothing—and I won't need much of an excuse to cut your throat."

"Try it," Tyler's voice came as a growl. "I'll fuck you up if you draw even a drop of her blood."

"That's enough, Anya," the high king said. "Let her go. I'd hate to see anyone . . . *fucked up* tonight."

I felt her become little more than a whisper, and she reappeared behind the throne, glaring at me with her dangerous purple eyes. She kept the dagger visible, twirl-

ing it against her palm as if silently daring me to step out
of line again. I had a problem with being treated like a
second-class citizen, and Anya was pushing all of my hot
buttons. It might have been because of my solitary existence or my reputation in certain circles, but in my book,
you had to give respect to earn it. And neither Anya nor
her king had earned an ounce of mine.

Tyler moved in close, his body touching mine in more
places than was appropriate, considering the circumstances. He wrapped a hand around my wrist as if ready
to drag me out of the building, if need be. The other hand
he kept wrapped around the Glock, his finger danger-
ously close to the trigger. I'd never seen him on high
alert like this. Then again, I'd be willing to bet he'd never
been in close proximity to so many supernatural beings
before. For that matter, neither had I. His stress was
making my blood pressure rise. I couldn't help but feel
flattered, though. Here he was, a hell of a lot more breakable than anyone else here, and ready to throw himself
in the path of danger to protect me.

I pointedly ignored my leather-clad antagonist, as
well as Tyler's manacled grip on my arm, and stared at
the Shaede who'd been in my living room just the night
before. "You hired me to kill . . . you?" I asked incredulously, because, well, who *does* that?

"Yes," Xander answered, like that was the sanest
thing in the world to do.

"Wanna fill me in as to why?"

"Would you have answered the Summons?"

I wanted to say "hell, no," but I thought that might be
something Anya would use as an excuse to skewer me,
so I opted for, "Probably not."

"But you certainly *would* want to meet the man face-
to-face who endangered your existence?"

"I don't like to be played with." An answer and a
threat, to an extent.

I had the distinct feeling that this guy—king, Shaede,

whatever—was full of shit. There was something else; I could feel it. His story held as much water as a rusted-out bucket. If he'd merely wanted me here, the ruse he'd concocted with the fake assassination would have been enough. Why even bother to show up at my apartment later?

Tyler's grip loosened and tightened again on my wrist like a pulse, reminding me that I wasn't standing alone in the presence of my own kind. "My friend should leave." I made the suggestion hoping Tyler would be regarded as inconsequential to the goings-on. All I could think about was keeping him alive and in one piece. "He delivered me, held up his part of the bargain. He should go."

The king looked at Tyler as if he'd only just realized he was standing there. He tilted his head as if pondering the fate of the world, and with a wave of his hand said, "Fine."

"Bullshit!" Tyler stared down the king and took a protective step in front of me. "I'm not going anywhere. You're insane if you think I'm leaving her alone here with you."

Xander laughed. His mocking tone did nothing more than stoke the flames of Tyler's indignation. "Stay, go—it matters little to me. I know who you are, and don't think it worries me in the slightest. You're not the one I need."

Not good. Tyler was the human in a vat of supernatural stew, and he'd seen too much already. Xander's reaction meant whether he stayed or left, he'd be dealt with in due time. Where would he be safe? I couldn't handle the threat inherent in the king's tone. I had to protect him, whether it offended his tough-guy persona or not.

"Tyler, go to my place," I whispered in his ear. "Wait for me there and don't go anywhere else."

"Not a chance, Darian."

Okay, so I should have known he'd puff out his chest and beat on it. *Shit.*

My eyes delved into his, and I nearly lost focus on everything else around me. I could see the resolve etched on every line of his face, and I wondered how in the hell I'd get him out of here without an argument.

"Darian, I'm not leaving you unprotected," he said in a soft but stubborn tone. "So don't even bother."

I repeated my request, adding a sweetly spoken "please." Kind words from me were rare, but my feelings for Tyler made me a little more sentimental than usual. "Unless you know something I don't, there's no danger here. Right? So if you didn't set me up, he's just a regular paying customer." I jerked my head toward the throne. "Right?" He nodded, his gaze trained on the Shaede king. I couldn't tell if he refused to look at me because of a bruised ego or if it had more to do with asserting himself to our host. I sighed, realizing I might have to bash him over the head just to get him out of here.

A still silence fell on the warehouse, as if everyone waited for his response.

"Ty," I said, low. "I wish you'd quit being so stubborn and leave. I'm doing this to keep you safe. I can handle myself. Don't worry. I'll be fine."

A faint stirring in the air seemed to brush against every nerve ending on my body. Tyler shuddered as if he'd felt it too, and his jaw clenched so tight I thought I heard it pop. "All right," he finally said, his voice strained. "I'll go. But if you don't show up in a couple of hours, I'm coming back here to get you."

"Fair enough," I said. "I'll see you then. Now go."

He cast a warning glare in Xander's direction before he turned his back and walked to the door. I gave the king a look of my own, as if to say, *You're a dead man if you touch him*, and waited until I heard the door close and his car pull away.

"Is he your lover?" the king asked.

I pondered that question. More every day, I wished he was, but I couldn't have a relationship with him, no matter what had happened outside the warehouse earlier. Too many variables stood in our way. "Who I take to bed is none of your business."

I could almost see the flames shooting out of the top of Anya's head, but I didn't care. Now that Tyler was safely off the premises, I could talk to Xander however I damn well pleased. "So, what should I call you?" I wondered aloud, pushing her a little further. "Your Highness, King Alexander, or"—I dropped my voice a few decibels—"can I call you *Xander*?"

That did it. She tackled me before I could even crack a grin.

I knew she'd go for the bait. Anya's reaction didn't disappoint as she plowed into me and knocked me backward. I dissolved, and her face met the floor, sounding a lot like a melon dropped from a two-story balcony. Without giving her time to react, I reappeared, standing over her dazed and startled form.

I hadn't been prepared to fight, and I was really pissed that I'd dressed up, because I couldn't kick anything while I wore the tight white skirt. I braced my legs apart and the seams ripped, giving me movement above the knee. While I still had the upper hand, I brought my high-heeled foot up in the air and stomped down on Anya with lightning speed. She was fast and rolled to the side, but despite her best effort to evade me, my heel made contact with her leather-clad back before she vanished into mist.

Fool, Darian. You should've at least brought a dagger. Moreover, I longed for my saber, because even though I knew it wouldn't kill her, I would have liked to have sliced through her midsection. She would have been laid up for a couple of days, and the mere thought made me smile.

Anya appeared behind me, and before I could turn to face her, she gave a sharp kick square to the middle of my back. I flung off the damn heels and spun like a top, swinging my fist and making contact with her jaw before she could evade the punch.

I hadn't fought anyone so fast in a long time, and though I was certainly rusty, it came back to me in surprisingly quick degrees. A good, long exchange of jabs and kicks—on her part—followed. I could only imagine what we must have looked like—two shadows shifting and blowing in a nonexistent breeze, becoming solid only long enough to strike a blow.

Anya drew her dagger and I knew she was finally tired of dicking around. I was unarmed, and though it didn't make for a fair fight, I would have done the exact same thing if I'd been in her position.

She took a couple of wild swings, missing me by miles. Retaliating, I turned into a wisp of nothingness, reappeared behind her, and swiped the back of my fist against her head. But I wasn't used to fighting an equal, and she vanished and moved to the side of me before I could react. She swept the dagger in a downward motion and I heard it rip through my blouse, felt the blade slice into my skin. Blood issued from the wound and drew her attention from the fight.

Liquid fire burned from the cut, oozing down my side, and my anger blossomed into full-fledged rage. I used the opportunity to unleash the force of hate-fueled strength on her pretty face. My fist made contact and her nose popped as the cartilage broke. Blood spewed from her nostrils and splattered across my face and the once-pristine white blouse.

In an action too fast to see, I pulled back again, determined to break her jaw with the blow. As I moved to throw the punch, my progress stalled as a hand squeezed mine with such strength that my own seemed like a child's in comparison.

Screaming, I allowed the fury to scald all the way up my throat. I wanted nothing more than to beat that high-and-mighty bitch to a pulp. I fought against the hold on me, and even though I shifted into my shadow form, the figure held me still.

A strong arm wrapped around my waist, and Xander's velvet voice spoke in my ear. "You've made your point."

"What in the *hell* is this about?" I screeched through clenched teeth.

I twisted and fought, but he tightened his grip until he had me sandwiched against his body. Heat poured from his skin. His scent swam in my head. Intoxicated by his nearness, my anger abated.

His grip tightened despite the fact that I'd quit struggling. Anya stood, wiping blood from her face, giving me a look that should have killed me without the aid of a magic blade. Her eyes darted to her king, and she went down on a knee.

Oh, how I wanted to kick her while she bowed. But in my pencil skirt it wouldn't have been very effective, ripped seams or not. I'd have my chance, though, and the next time it would be her turn to taste my steel.

"Anya, you are the most loyal of all my subjects." The sound of his voice, coupled with his warm breath in my ear, caused a shiver to trace down my spine. "But now you should tend to your wounds and leave me with our guest."

"But, my liege," Anya said, her head snapping to attention.

I rolled my eyes. *Ugh.*

"No," Xander commanded.

Anya bobbed her head, looking a little like a goose. I made sure to give her a superior glower before she vanished into shadow.

"If I let you go, will you behave?" he asked when we were alone.

I relaxed completely, and by slow degrees, his grip loosened. When at last he pulled away, he let his fingers linger against me, pulling back from my stomach, around my waist, to my back. I didn't appreciate these games, and rather than turn to meet his eyes, I dissolved and reappeared to face him.

He'd done a little vanishing act of his own and was seated in his throne by the time I became my solid self.

"Why am I here?" I asked, my voice echoing in the empty building.

"I need your services," he said simply, as if he were commenting on the weather.

That was laughable. He looked like he had plenty of help from his red-leather girlfriend.

"I don't know what you have in mind," I said, deciding that puckish was the attitude I was going for, "but some of my services aren't for sale."

He erupted into a round of robust laughter that only sparked my ire. "Although I'm sure it would be worth every penny," he crooned, "that is not the service I'm after. You have been called to serve your king. In fact, you've been paid in advance, if I'm not mistaken," he continued in a much more formal tone. "And you must obey."

Obey. Another word that didn't exist in my vocabulary. "You're not *my* king," I reminded him.

His eyes took on that thoughtful look again, as if he were contemplating the fate of the world. "You are very ignorant, Darian."

I raised my chin a notch.

He ignored my show of indignation and continued. "Your maker failed you, left you alone and believing there were no others in this world but you. You know nothing of your people, your true nature and skills. You are lost."

If I'd raised my chin any higher, I would have been looking at the ceiling. I stared right through him, neither acknowledging nor ignoring his words.

I'd always believed I was alone.

I'd taught myself how to fight, how to survive, how to *be.*

I'd never needed others of my kind to give me a sense of who I was.

And if Xander thought he could march in and change my entire universe with a snap of his royal fingers . . .

"I know you hear my words," he said like a father to a stubborn child, "and you have much to learn. But know that you *are* summoned to *your* king's service, and you *will* do the job I have *paid* you to do. You may go, and we will speak again."

I stood, gaping for a moment at his casual dismissal, before I turned my back with neither a bow nor a word of parting. Throbbing heat pulsed from the gash in my side, and I drew in shallow breaths to control my anger as much as the pain. I refused to show Xander any weakness. With a sweeping motion, I retrieved my soiled shoes, walked with as much dignity as if I were myself a queen, and pulled open the heavy metal door.

"Darian," Xander, the King of Shaedes, called from across the building.

I paused, halfway out the door.

"I enjoyed watching you tonight."

I passed into shadow and became one with the night.

Chapter 5

Tyler was waiting up for me like a dad on his daughter's first date. He paced the small space of my living room like a caged animal, one hand raking through his hair, the other clutching a beer. A dark expression clouded his handsome face as he picked up his pace and the amber brew sloshed around in the bottle. His cheeks puffed out as he exhaled a great gust, and he muttered a curse under his breath. When I stepped into view, he stopped dead in his tracks, relief showing in the way his shoulders suddenly sagged.

Dead on my feet and pissed to boot, I wanted nothing more than to discard my bloodied clothes and tend to my wound, which had already begun to heal.

"Hey—" He cut off when he caught sight of my blood-spattered and torn shirt. *Great.* "What the hell happened?" he demanded, rushing toward me with an urgency that didn't exactly mesh with the moment. "Did they hurt you? I never should have left you there alone. Damn it!" His hands balled up in tight fists at his side, and the muscle at his jaw ticked. The anger rising from his body was so intense I could smell it, and I fought my own reaction to his protective attitude. To think of him worrying about me in that way sent a warm tingle through my body that made itself at home in the traitorous nerves below my waist.

He surged forward in a rush, his face flushed with rage. "Don't," I commanded, holding him at arm's length.

"I'm fine; the wound's already healing. Don't go all mushy and try to take care of me."

"What happened?" he asked.

"I sort of picked a fight."

His expression softened, but only a little. "Wow, that's really out of character for you. The dominatrix?"

His little attempt at sarcasm put a smile on my face, and I had to admit I was grateful for the levity. "I broke her nose." Despite his outrage, Tyler knew I was no delicate flower. In fact, once he'd said that I could probably take on an entire company of Navy SEALs and kill them before they knew I was there. He was right, of course.

He wanted details, but I wasn't saying anything until I'd cleaned up. "I need to shower," I said. "But answer me one question first. Did you know he wasn't human when you set up the job?"

"No," he answered, dead serious. When it came to business, Ty didn't mess around, and I trusted him.

"Okay. That's all I needed to know." I started toward the bathroom, unbuttoning my shirt as I went. Ty's gaze burned a hole in my back, but I didn't dare turn around unless I wanted a repeat performance of his earlier ardor. I didn't know how I felt about what he'd done or how I'd reacted, but I wasn't ready to think about it.

I took a quick, screaming-hot shower. The gash left by Anya's knife looked a little worse than I'd expected, but the wound puckered where the skin had begun to fuse. It hadn't completely closed up yet, but the flesh looked healthy and clean. Soon there wouldn't even be a scar left to betray the injury.

After toweling off, I stepped into my robe and ventured out to check on Ty. He was asleep on my couch. *Convenient.* I was about to kick him out and send him on his way, but he looked so peaceful. I stood over him for a minute and found my thoughts drifting to how he'd look in the morning, with the sun's first light on his resting face. I snapped to and realized I was obviously exhausted and delirious. So I left him alone, and, slipping out of the robe, slid between my cool sheets and let the warm air of my apartment lull me into a much-deserved slumber.

"Darian."

Cool breath trickled over my cheek. I didn't try to make myself wake up.

A hand brushed at my hair, sweeping it away from my forehead. A deep sigh and another wash of cool air. "Darian."

The whispered voice spoke more clearly, and fingers traced over my bare arm, up and around my shoulder, grazing the skin at my collarbone. Shivering from the skin-on-skin contact, I rolled onto my back to give those fingers a wider canvas to paint on. This was a dream I didn't want to wake from. Lips brushed my forehead, tracing a line down my temple to my jawline. I arched my back, and my nipples hardened as my breasts strained against the sheet. A sharp intake of breath that wasn't mine brought me to awareness. I wasn't dreaming and I wasn't alone in my bed.

Tyler.

Even if I wanted him close, it couldn't happen now. My life had taken an unexpected turn down a dangerous road. I couldn't risk Tyler's safety. A new world unraveled around me—and he had become a liability by association. I could hope Xander would leave him alone. But I couldn't be sure. Whether I wanted it or not, distance was what we both were going to get. He needed to be taught a lesson, and I was more than happy to oblige him. I feigned a languid stretch with the arm not anchored by Ty's fingers and absently slipped my hand beneath the pillow. My fingers found the hilt of the dagger and I paused, waiting for the right moment. I didn't want to kill him, after all; I just wanted to reaffirm some boundaries.

Bending low, he took a huge whiff of my hair. Seriously—*smelling* my hair. I sensed him shift on the bed, straightening, and I struck.

I brought the blade around in a movement so fast that it must have been a blur in his slow human vision. The steel winked at me, the tip glinting against the hollow of his throat, and I pressed gently against his tender skin. Propping myself on the other elbow, I glanced down at his hand still touching me.

He didn't make a sound. Actually, he didn't even jump. I had to give him credit: The boy had balls. His mouth spread into a slow, sheepish grin, like a kid caught with his hand in the cookie jar.

Giving a gentle shake of my head, I pressed the blade deeper into the recess of his throat. "May I ask what you're doing?" I didn't move the blade. Not an inch.

"Admiring you," he said. "You look different when you're asleep. Softer."

Had he known I'd been watching him last night? Rather than push him away, my actions were only drawing us closer. I wanted to slap myself for being stupid enough to let Tyler kiss me outside of that warehouse.

"You know, it's not advisable to molest a dangerous woman while she sleeps. You might find yourself bereft of your head."

"I would never hurt you, Darian," he said.

Here we go again. I'd just told him that if he didn't take his hands off me I was going to give his head a permanent vacation from his shoulders, and he said *he* wouldn't hurt *me*. "Ty, you couldn't hurt me if you wanted to," I said in a voice gentle as falling snow. I wondered why he hadn't pulled away from the dagger. All he'd have to do is sit up straighter, but he seemed to delight in leaving his life in my hands. *Sick.* I fought the urge to smile.

"Tyler." I spared what little patience I had to offer. "Being as I'm naked under this sheet, it would be a good idea for you to take your fingers for a walk and give me a little privacy."

His eyes widened, like he'd never actually considered what might be under the sheets, though I knew he'd gotten a nice, long look. He leaned in, pressing against the dagger as if he'd forgotten I was still holding it there. It pricked the skin, and a crimson drop bloomed and forked as one path followed the curve of the blade.

"Do you have a death wish?" I asked, watching the other trail of red make its way down the peachy flesh of his throat.

"Something like that," he murmured, adding to the utter weirdness of the moment.

I pushed myself upright and felt the sheet give way, revealing a generous portion of my breast. Tyler's eyes shone like someone had lit a candle behind each of them. I expected a thin line of saliva to trickle from the corner of his mouth at any second. The hand that he'd rested at his side twitched.

"Yesterday . . ." he started to say.

"Was yesterday," I finished for him. "And today is today. We work together, Ty. That's all. I shouldn't have let you kiss me."

"You liked it," he said, pushing himself against the blade again.

Maybe Ty was less of a tough guy than I'd given him credit for, or maybe he was simply like all men—one thing on the brain.

"What I would or would not *like* to do with you is immaterial." I argued my point in the most logical way possible. "We work together, and I don't blur the lines between my personal life and business."

Dismissing my argument, he reached out, ran the backs of his fingers across my cheek. "You don't have a personal life."

He did have a point. I didn't have friends, family, or acquaintances. And there was a reason for that. My pulse picked up as his fingers left my face in favor of my arm, trickling slowly across my skin from shoulder to wrist. I wanted to return the gesture and just trace his skin with my fingertips.

His hand continued to wander as slowly as if he were approaching a hungry tiger, coming to rest on my thigh. A thin cotton sheet was all that separated our skin, and I can't say it wasn't exciting. The touch of his cooler skin permeated the fabric and left a trail of chills as he ran his hand along my thigh and up over my hip, curling around my waist.

I lowered the dagger. It wasn't doing any good, and I found I didn't feel much like threatening him anymore. When had my mouth gone dry? God, he was ridiculously beautiful. Tyler's chest rose and fell with his breath, and I imagined what he'd look like without his shirt, his muscled chest beneath my hands. I gathered my bottom lip between my teeth. He took the action as consent and swooped down to lay his mouth to mine. I came to my senses just in time and rolled, taking the sheet with me. Tyler fell to the mattress, getting nothing but a mouthful of pillow.

By the time he sat up, I stood at the bathroom door. As I passed through the threshold I said, "Time for you to go, Ty. I'll talk to you later." I closed the door behind me and turned on the shower, determined to ignore him. Through the sound of rushing water, my keen hearing didn't have to strain to hear the gate slam down over the lift. I leaned my forehead against the cool tile wall and let out a deep breath. The unique scent that was all Ty swirled in my memory, and I was less than relieved to be alone with my thoughts. No doubt Tyler was pissed.

He'd get over it.

I lay across my bed, arms and legs splayed out like a starfish. Clouds chased each other across the skylight.

Patches of blue peeked between the fluffs of gray and white. Xander's words played on a loop in my head, messing with me as I tried to comprehend all that I did not know.

I would have made a great poker player. I could bluff like nobody's business. What Azriel hadn't taught me could fill an Olympic-sized swimming pool, and what I did know might have filled a tumbler, if I were lucky. Maybe if he'd done his job and given me some basis for my existence, something to define who and what I had become, I might not have been so hard. I might have actually given a damn about something.

I'd never tried to seek out another inhuman creature. Azriel told me there were no others. I believed him too. Stupid, blind faith. He'd never given me reason to doubt him, and I'd never seen proof to the contrary. What an idiotic notion. Had the Shaede population purposely stayed away? Had they known about me all along and silently spied as I lived my life? Jesus, the thought made me sick. Why show up now and ruin the illusion Azriel had so easily crafted? And if more Shaedes roamed the earth, what else existed beyond my scope of reality? I shivered at the thought.

For too many years I had simply existed. Going through the motions, making more money than I could spend, eating, sleeping, drinking, killing, finding pleasure when I wanted it. But I had not lived in a very long time. I had not known companionship, tenderness, camaraderie, and a sense of duty or purpose. I had not known love.

Xander said I was ignorant. He said I knew nothing of myself, my people, or my skills.

And he was right.

So it was no big surprise that I went out looking for him as soon as the sun went down.

I traveled as my shadow self for both speed and cover. I don't know why I thought he'd be at the warehouse, sitting on that damned throne in the middle of an empty building. So I shouldn't have been put out when I didn't find him there.

After that, I checked the town house. Not a single light illuminated the lonely windows, and though his scent lingered, he hadn't been there for at least a couple of days.

Beleaguered, I went to The Pit. I didn't want to sit in my apartment and stew, so I decided to seek out diversion in the crowds of humans who went out night after night, trying to define their fleeting lives with even more fleeting encounters.

The club was packed with humans celebrating the end of the work week. They played their usual games, rituals that centered on flirty gestures, suggestive conversations, and the occasional flash of skin. I leaned against the bar and watched, trying to remain as inconspicuous as possible. It would be only a matter of time before someone homed in on the faint glow of my eyes or my flawless porcelain skin and decided to throw their hat in the ring.

Levi, the bartender that night, slid a bright blue drink in my direction. The first one of the night was always on the house. Cute, preppy, and completely out of place, Levi looked like an Abercrombie ad. He also struck me as a good guy. He never came on to me and always flashed a friendly smile when I walked in. If he had any idea about my otherness, he never asked. He didn't stare and gave me space, one of the main reasons why I favored The Pit.

The bar seemed to be the lake that most lonely single men fished from, so I left with my drink and gave Levi a silent toast as I walked away. I found a nice dark corner, and, with the help of my black clothes, melted right into the scenery.

Tyler showed up after I'd been there an hour. He must have had some kind of internal Darian tracking system, because he made a beeline for my table.

I looked away, watching the humans on the dance

floor as if I were totally engrossed in their gyrations. Another thing I didn't do. Dance.

I didn't acknowledge him when he slid into the seat next to mine, and I tried not to pay attention to how great he smelled. Like an antsy kid, he fidgeted silently, waiting for me to look at him. I wanted to—those hazel eyes of his had a tendency to suck me in—but I'd learned pretty quickly that if you gave Ty an inch, he took about five miles. *Oh, man, he smells good.*

"Aren't you going to talk to me?"

The sensation of his breath in my ear sent a zinging rush right through my center. I refused to admit that Tyler had the most delicious mouth I'd ever tasted, and I banished the memory of our passionate moment to the farthest recesses of my mind.

"If Xander always called you, how did you get in touch with him to set up the meeting last night?" I stuck to business. Business . . . business . . . business.

"He called me right after you left here. I guess he knew you'd be fired up to meet him."

My jaw clenched like a vise. Xander's recent disappearance really rubbed me the wrong way. I did not wait at anyone's beck and call, and the least he could offer for the inconveniences he'd caused in my existence was a few answers.

Turning away from Tyler, I centered my focus on the dance floor again. A very young woman pulled up her shirt and tucked it underneath her bra. She stroked her belly like it was a magic lamp. The guy next to her rubbed himself up and down her body. It might have been sexy if either one of them had been more coordinated—or sober—but as it was, they just looked ridiculous. I cracked a grin as I watched them bump and grind, thinking wryly to myself that at one time, the Charleston had been considered lewd.

Tyler's hands moved up my back by small degrees, creeping against the thin fabric of my T-shirt and over my shoulders. His thumbs rested at the nape of my neck, and he wrapped his fingers around my throat. As soft as a spring breeze, his cool fingertips caressed my skin, fanning out toward my collarbone. I found the contact so completely erotic that I had to stop myself from throwing boundaries to the wayside and laying him across the table.

I didn't have it in me to explain why this thing he wanted between us was not a good idea. And so I passed into shadow, not caring about the other humans scattered around the club, and moved silently through their masses to the exit.

Tyler wasn't the only one with boundary issues.

I returned to my apartment to find Xander in my living room. For an oh-so-important king, he seemed to come and go as he pleased with little thought to security. Maybe I was spoiled by my heretofore solitary ways, because I wanted to knock him across the studio for the calm expression on his face.

"What are you doing here, Xander?"

He gave me the same treatment I'd given Tyler at the club, basically ignoring me to get some sort of rise. It worked.

"Is that how you address your king?" he asked, staring at the wall.

My king? My ass. I still wasn't excited by the idea that someone could hold dominion over me, no matter how much he insisted he could. I gave a quiet but derisive snort.

"My liege," I began in my most regal voice, copying Anya's from the previous night. "I am both humbled and honored that you have graced my hovel with your imperial presence. I am yours to command and wish nothing more than to serve you."

The air in my apartment changed. Charged with energy, like a coming thunderstorm. Xander's body became insubstantial, scattering in a violent pepper of black dust.

In a waft of sweet, fragrant heat, he reappeared to stand in front of me face-to-face, or, more to the point, face-to-chest. He stood so tall that I almost got a crick in my neck from looking at him. But I didn't cower in the presence of anyone.

"You were looking for me tonight?" he asked.

With a movement so fast even I had a hard time tracking it, he ran his hands along my side, lifting up my shirt along the waist. My breath caught in my throat as he passed a warm palm along the gash in my side— almost completely healed, save for a thin white line.

"You're healing well." The sound of his rich voice lulled me, banishing any trace of anger. He pulled the shirt down and flashed a very unkingly grin. "What do you want of me?"

At that moment, I could have made a list a mile long and comprised of the different things I *wanted* of him. And then I came to my senses. I thought about Ty, sitting alone at the club, the things he'd said, the way his mouth pressed against mine, and my feelings for him, despite the rules I'd laid down for myself.

"I want to know," I said, swallowing my considerable pride, "about who I am."

"I can't tell you who you are," he said. "But I can tell you *what* you are."

"*What* am I, then? How did I come to be this way, and why did Azriel leave me without teaching me anything? Why have I thought that I was alone for a century and that there were no others like me?" I paced as I rambled on, trying to form the questions my arrogance didn't want me to ask. "What is it that I can and cannot do, and why do I do those things? Am I immortal or something else? And where is the magic blade that is the only thing that can take my life? Who has it? Do you?" I asked, remembering Azriel's words to me.

I left Xander gaping after me and settled down in a chair, too flustered to continue. I suppose those were a lot of questions to bombard someone with. I hadn't intended to let them all tumble out of my mouth like marbles rolling out of a sack.

He didn't come to my side, and I was glad for it. His voice floated on the air, and I listened with my eyes closed, out of shame more than anything else.

"You . . . are . . . nothing," he said. "A creature that lives between the realms. You are made of twilight and shadow and move as the wind through the trees. You are Shaede."

I reluctantly admitted to myself that his speech sounded eloquent and kingly. *If only Azriel had been a millionth of that,* I thought as bitter memories taunted me. Though he'd shared the king's flair for dramatics (maybe it's a Shaede trait), Azriel had never been one to lend me words of comfort. Merely a force of nature, he'd existed like the wind: fickle and unconcerned with the obstacles in his path.

"You won't wither and die the way humans do," he continued. "And even if your physical form is damaged beyond repair, you will only fade into shadow for eternity, never recapturing your solid self."

Xander appeared before me, his eyes studying my face, right down to each individual pore. "If I had known about you, I would have come for you decades ago. Only a very powerful Shaede can make another, and Azriel was a fool to have left you."

That didn't exactly bolster my spirits—or answer *any* of my questions.

"How was I made?" I asked, *needing* to know the answer to this question.

"I told you last night that I require your services." He changed the subject, I think, because he could tell I was becoming agitated by his lack of a straight answer. "You are an assassin by trade, and that's what I need. What I hired you for."

"Why me?" I asked. "Anya appears to be able to hold her own."

"You'll find out," he said, standing. "Come to the warehouse in two nights' time."

My mouth twisted into a smirk. He sure snapped back into king mode pretty damn fast. "Why?"

"You need to begin your training."

I opened my mouth to challenge him, but he had already left.

Chapter 6

I stripped down, changed into some comfortable clothes, and found a nice spot on the shag rug in front of the TV. Using the couch as a backrest, I pulled my knees up against my chest, hugging my body into a tight ball. I wasn't thinking about Xander or the job anymore. He hadn't answered any of my questions, more or less giving me the runaround. As if finding out after all these years that I wasn't the only Shaede roaming the planet wasn't enough of a shock, I had been assured by Xander that had he known of my existence, he would have come for me. The thought of knowing others like me, the freedom of being released from anonymity, frightened me. Truth be told, I only pretended to want nothing more than to be alone. Solitude was not what I wanted, though I'd been alone for nearly a century. And I had Azriel to thank for that.

I'd been human once.

I met Azriel in another age. A gentler age—a bullshit age, really. Women hadn't learned how to empower themselves yet. Of course, there was a growing faction of females who were big into the suffrage movement. They were the first real feminists, ready and willing to embrace their true power. I think I could have been one of them.

According to my family, I was a sad excuse for a girl. Though I was winsome and lovely, my mouth could sometimes be my greatest flaw. My father had been fairly successful, a banker in a rising industry. And he wanted his daughter's marriage to echo his financial status. They tried to peddle me off to every guy with a buck. None of the matches ever worked out ... until Henry Charles. He was an up-and-coming doctor, upstanding and well liked by everyone. He made a decent living, and he seemed to adore me. So, of course, my father pushed me to accept his proposal. I was already twenty-one—old by marriage standards—and my family was dying of embarrassment that I had yet to find a suitable husband.

They were so anxious that they allowed for an unusually short courtship and married me off to him just weeks after our initial meeting. "Charming" didn't even begin to describe Henry. I had high hopes for me and one of the city's most eligible bachelors. I wanted to be loved, adored, and paraded on someone's arm. Only my sharp tongue hinted that I was a less-than-docile female. But fiery or not, a girl wants affection. I dreamed of an equal partnership full of passion and tenderness. Life would be perfect.

In reality, our life was as far from perfect as one could get. Henry never wanted me; he'd actually never wanted any woman. His tastes ran a little more on the masculine side. Now, in this day and age, Henry would have had a better chance at happiness. The modern world isn't perfect, but he would have found some of the acceptance he assuredly deserved. He lived a double life, slinking around, finding pleasure under the cover of darkness. And I was left to take the brunt of his anger at the card he'd been dealt.

I was a human punching bag. His drunken antics always ended in a beating. I suppose he was mad at me for being lovely and soft—all of the things society dictated he should love and yet didn't. And so I took the abuse, day after day, week after week, until the years sort of faded into obscurity. My parents, glad to see me gone, never visited. They'd never truly understood me. I was the product of a blossoming female society, a generation of women who were finding their voices. But despite my intelligence and need for independence, I couldn't find my voice when it came to my husband. Henry didn't keep me prisoner. But thanks to the constant bruises, my own shame kept me safely at home lest some concerned community member question my routine injuries. Let's face it: No one's that clumsy.

I didn't hate Henry; he was a product of his time and environment just as much as I was. I could've done without the verbal and physical abuse. Who knows? Maybe he didn't treat his boyfriends any better. The fact of the matter was, no matter whom Henry loved, he was a lousy, abusive drunk, and an asshole's an asshole no matter your creed.

The days bled into one another, and I wanted a new life so badly I could taste it. I wished every day that I would go to sleep and awake to a better existence.

Azriel gave me that gift.

"Darling, I want you to meet a friend of mine." Henry had been just as shocked as I was when the knock came at the door. But he could be all grace and charm when the situation demanded it, and his new friend's surprise visit required all of that and more. "Azriel, my wife, Darian Charles."

No doubt Henry met him and fell head over heels. Azriel was something to behold. Dark, curly hair, dark brown eyes—beautiful despite their cruel edge—and russet skin that glowed in the firelight. He looked like a Roman god come to sit in our living room, and little did we know, it wasn't too far from the truth.

"Mrs. Charles," he said, bending over my hand. "I'm so *very* pleased to meet you."

The touch of his lips on my skin sent a river of chills flowing across the landscape of my body. Of course, I sensed something different in him. And yet, I was as infatuated with him as my farce of a husband. "Will you join us for dinner?" I asked, glad to have Henry distracted for the evening. If anything, it would keep the abuse at bay.

Azriel stood, his eyes roaming over what I hoped he couldn't see: traces of yellowing bruises that had not quite healed. I didn't want this stranger to see the physical proof of my weakness. But he noticed. Azriel never missed a beat, and his pained look instantly tore at my heart.

"I'd love to join you for dinner," he said. His fingers lingered on my palm as he pulled away. "Henry, let's sit with your beautiful wife and enjoy her company while we eat."

Polite and attentive, he hung on my every word. It made Henry jealous beyond description, but I didn't care. I was falling in love by the second, hypnotized by his exotic beauty and soft yet intense voice asking me questions I didn't feel worthy to answer.

Azriel seemed interested in the story of my life, my day-to-day activities, the goings-on in the city. Seldom did he address Henry, except every now and again when my husband would interrupt to gain Azriel's attention.

I knew the consequences of my actions, but at that moment, I didn't care. I didn't care if Henry beat me to a bloody pulp, because it would all be worth it for a few moments of Azriel's undivided attention.

"You stupid bitch!" Henry railed hours after Azriel had gone. "You just had to get in the way, didn't you?"

His fist landed squarely against my jaw, the popping sound making me sick as I crashed to the floor. The metallic tang of blood lay thick on my tongue, and I tried to shake the fog from my addled mind.

"Henry, I—" Words stalled in my throat. My head felt too heavy for my neck to support. God, why couldn't he just kill me and get it over with?

His boot made contact with my ribs and I heard more than felt the crack. I wanted to curl up in ball, protect myself, but I didn't have the strength for the simple act. "Do you even think you'd be here if it wasn't necessary?" A sob broke through his chest. "I hate you!" His fist came down, bashing my chin. Another pop, blood welling from the split in my lip. The smell of the blood made bile rise in my throat.

Henry hauled me up by the collar of my dress and slapped me with his open palm. "He was for me!" he shouted. *"You ruined everything!"* He followed through with the back of his hand, striking my other cheek. "I should wring your scrawny, ungrateful neck!"

I looked up at the panes of the French doors leading from the parlor to our garden and caught a reflection in the night-shrouded glass. His dark and lovely form slid through the solid structure as if the doors hadn't been there at all. An apparition. An angel come to take me to heaven.

"Get off of her, you coward!" Azriel shouted, pulling Henry away from me. "You have no idea what you're doing, who she really is!"

Henry screamed in a maddened rage, and he must've been surprised as hell to see Azriel pop in out of nowhere. Floating in and out of coherence, I listened as he beat Henry to death. He paid him back for every single time in our five years of marriage that he had laid his fists on me. When Henry's screams died with his body, Azriel took me in his arms, and I thought I'd die from the pain of it. He lowered me to the bed and whispered in my ear, "You're mine now."

Mine.

For some reason the word felt right. I wanted to belong to this beautiful stranger, this man who had rescued me from the clutches of death. He wanted me when no one else ever had, and I remember feeling like I wanted to crawl right inside him and stay there forever. It seemed hard to believe, his wanting me. I was so blinded by pain and grief that nothing made sense, least of all Azriel's motives for killing Henry and taking me away.

But I didn't care. I wanted him too. As I was his, he was mine.

There is a space of time afterward that I don't have any recollection of. I don't even know how long it spans. It could have been days or even weeks, but when I finally woke, I was in an unfamiliar place and forever changed. As though I'd been swathed in fine silks, I felt the shadows flow over my skin, entreating me to join with them. *I am no longer myself,* I thought, bringing my hand before my face. My skin seemed to quaver, shrouded by darkness and becoming solid once more. Like a contented feline, I stretched my limbs, aware of the fact that I no longer felt the pain of my many injuries. In fact, I'd never felt so invigorated or strong.

The lamplight flickered in the corner of the room and I sensed Azriel nearby, his life force pulsing like a beacon through the fog. A sweet scent, like a field of pansies beneath the summer sun, permeated my senses, and I breathed deep, holding the aroma in my lungs.

"What's happened to me?" I whispered, my heart hammering in my chest.

Dark mist stirred at my bedside and Azriel materialized from shadow. I stared in wide-eyed wonder as he sat beside me and brought my fingers to his mouth, bestowing a gentle kiss on my knuckles. "Fate has claimed you, Darian. No mortal will dare harm you again."

Being whisked away by a handsome stranger had been exciting. A touch romantic, even. But I knew virtually nothing about the man who'd saved me from my life of abuse. I learned very quickly that Azriel wasn't a creature to be ruled by his emotions. He simply existed, and was unapologetic for his nature. It never mattered to me one way or another. I think maybe part of me died with Henry.

The town gossips murmured that Dr. Charles and his wife had been the victims of a violent robbery gone wrong. The good doctor had been beaten to death, and his young wife had vanished. The police suspected a kidnapping, and they were fairly certain she'd been raped and dumped in the river or tossed into the bay. They held little hope of finding the gentle girl.

We'd left California and moved north to Seattle. Azriel was very fond of port towns, and he kept close to the water at all times. He said it calmed him to be near the water, and I didn't question his desires. We never wanted for anything. Azriel's wealth surpassed even that of Henry's. Assuming the guise of the leisurely affluent, we spent our days shopping, sightseeing, or simply enjoying the local culture. Our evenings were spent under the cover of shadow, and more nights than not ended with us enjoying each other's bodies until the sun rose.

Though we didn't need the money, Azriel had a restless spirit. He craved excitement like he craved my flesh, and it wasn't long before he went out in search of diversion. He found employment easily enough. Killing for money satisfied his cavalier spirit. And he was all too eager to bring me along. If the humans he worked for noticed anything about us that was more than human, they never mentioned it. One deadly glower from Azriel was enough to stifle even the most stalwart of humans.

I'd never been angry with him for what he'd done to me. Just like I'd never blamed Henry for his treatment of me. I'd welcomed the change, as I was done with humanity. I was curious about what I'd become, though, and I questioned Azriel often, only to be silenced by soft kisses. And if I pressed him further, he silenced me by taking me to bed. On and on it went for years, until one day I would not be silenced.

"Please, Azriel," I said. "Tell me something, anything. What am I now? How is it that I cannot die? How do we become one with the darkest shadows? I want to know."

"There are no others," he said as he unbuttoned my dress. "I have been alone for so long. My people were killed, eradicated. We are unique, alone in this world.

And it will be better for us to keep to ourselves. I was the last, and I needed a companion, so I made you. We cannot die unless we are struck down by a magic sword. It's the only thing that can kill us. It will be better if we hide—for a while, at least. If we avoid them, stay to the night, the humans won't notice our differences. We'll soon be forgotten, and no one will care. You and I will live together, forever, and I will taste your flesh for eternity."

"But—" I protested, and he covered my mouth with his to silence me. I let him, of course—he was a marvelous lover. He never allowed me to broach the subject again.

Maybe in the end, Azriel was just as bad as Henry. Where Henry kept me subservient through violence, Azriel kept me through ignorance. But I allowed it. He never once told me he loved me, but he didn't beat me either. And so I guess, in the long run, I thought I'd traded my life for a more tolerable existence.

He taught me very little about combat, but he did help me to become a very stealthy Shaede. We meandered through the night together, and he indulged my desire to watch the humans, living their lives, from afar. I believed I'd found happiness.

The cloudy skies and rainfall in Seattle brought a darkness almost as welcome as the shadows we inhabited. Azriel had been more partial to the weather than I. He never missed an opportunity to walk with his face tipped toward the sky as droplets caressed his dark features.

We'd abandoned the city in exchange for a walk in the woods. Abandoned the city sounds as well, exchanging the industrial noise for the *pitter-patter* of drops striking the leaves and needles of the trees. The bustle of the blossoming city dissipated into the surrounding green, lush and quiet and ours alone.

Ever the obedient companion, I dragged the long

hem of my dress through the tall, damp grass. In fact, he rarely left my side or allowed me to leave his, as if frightened I'd run away in search of more entertaining distractions.

"Do you believe we are creatures of nature?" he asked me.

"I believe we are creatures of darkness," I said.

Azriel's cool laughter mingled with the tinkling sound of rain. "We are born from air and black earth," he mused before leveling his gaze on me. "And some of us are born from nothing at all."

His tone was as dark as the darkest shadow, and his words confused me. But Azriel always talked in circles, so I wasn't surprised by the cryptic nature of our conversation. But I was not immune to the ominous feeling that accompanied his speech. Dread and foreboding congealed in the pit of my stomach. I reached out to take his hand, but he moved quickly forward and slid from my grasp.

"I'm tired," he said as he walked. "I am tired of all of this."

"All of what?" I said, pulling up my sopping skirt so I could run to catch up to him. "Of me? Are you tired of me?"

He stopped, and when he turned to face me, the absence of emotion on his face sent me stumbling back a pace. I knew that look of detachment. I'd seen it a million times from Henry. But I pretended it wasn't there. I dismissed Azriel's look, and instead defined it as exasperation with my silly, girlish questions.

"Who could tire of you?" He stroked my cheek, wiping droplets of rain from my skin. "I have plans for you."

The next morning, I woke alone. Azriel had gone out the night before, the first time in decades he'd left my side, tucking me into bed with a promise he'd return by dawn. I'd assumed he'd taken on a job too dangerous for me to tag along. For days I searched the city, wandered alleys under the cover of shadow. He had to be dead. He'd promised we would be together forever—the only two of our kind, bound for eternity. No one confirmed that he'd died. I didn't get a visit from the police telling me, "Excuse me, ma'am, but we found your Shaede lover dead in an alley this morning." He simply did not come home, and that fact alone was enough to convince me he'd died. Who had killed him and how never crossed my mind. He'd told me to lie low, and I did. I had no intention of sharing his fate, and by his own words, I knew that I'd be forgotten soon.

He'd stayed with me for twenty-five years before he disappeared. *Eternity, my ass.* What an eternal fool I was.

Industrious, I wasn't, but I learned fast. Employment opportunities weren't great for women in the 1930s, and I wasn't about to become anyone's maid. Azriel had connections; he'd been hiring himself out, taking money to kill. I'd been his apprentice of sorts, and thank God I'd paid attention. When the first letter arrived, I'd known what it was. Azriel used to receive a letter from a courier each time he took a job to kill. It outlined the mark's—or intended target's—name, address, and pertinent information. Sometimes the letters even came with a down payment.

I crumpled the paper, and as its sharp edges dug into my palm, I knew what I had to do. As soon as I made up my mind, it was easy. My first hit was successful. Clean. And I'd found my first contact. I bounced around after that, a freelance assassin, hired by word of mouth. For many years, I attributed my success to gender. My benefactors seemed to get a kick out of hiring a "lady" to do their dirty work. But I kept my standards high, refusing to take any job that involved an innocent. The men who paid me eventually met their ends. Once or twice at my hand. I'd worked for a Russian mob boss for years, and just like the others, his luck had run out. That's when I met Tyler.

I'd heard about him. His name had been whispered in

certain circles with a mixture of respect and fear. And, boy, when I met him, had I been surprised. He didn't look the part—that was for sure. Cute—*beyond cute*—with a quick smile and a charm that blew the competition out of the water. I knew that I wanted to work with him the moment I laid eyes on him. I felt safe with Tyler, and I hadn't felt safe in a good many years. Not since Azriel had taken me from Henry's home ...

And now eighty or so years since Azriel had left me alone, I was brought out of the dark by my own kind, hired for the skills I'd honed over decades, and dropped headfirst into the deep end of the supernatural pool. *Sink or swim, baby.* Isn't it funny how life can give you a good kick to the gut every once in a while?

But hired I was, and paid a mint for my services. I never backed down from a challenge, never left a job unfinished. And I wasn't about to start now.

Chapter 7

Not for a very long time, not since my human life, had I felt so lost. It pissed me off to no end.

I took a detour to the warehouse by way of Pike Place Market. I marveled at the people crowding the booths and breezeways, inquiring after the freshness of the fish or inspecting bouquets of dried and arranged flowers, all the while oblivious to one another in a way that comforted me. In a city the size of Seattle, people are packed together, inches from contact, all day. They pay as much attention to the human beside them as they do the speck of dust floating by on the breeze.

I am that speck of dust.

No one paid enough attention to see that quality in me that was other.

Except Tyler.

He *knew* me the moment he laid eyes on me. With a shrewdness that belied his usually casual nature, he studied me. And as if he could see every molecule that constructed me, he spotted the otherness and did not cower from it. His recognition of me never caused disquiet. Instead, I gleaned a certain comfort from the fact that I did not have to hide my eyes when they glowed against the backdrop of darkness, or pretend I was not fast and cunning and deadly. Ty was much more perceptive than I gave him credit for. It was only his human nature that prompted me to suggest he didn't always catch on.

I stood at the warehouse entrance, a moment of indecision making me pause. Should I knock? Walk right in? Shout *Anybody home?* I took a deep breath and held the air in my lungs. I hadn't been unsure for a very long time; it was a sharp thorn in my side.

Azriel had taught me to be arrogant, and, whether he ever realized it or not, to survive. "We are deadly creatures by our very nature," he'd say. "Why not put those skills to good use?" I couldn't disagree with him, not really. What else was there for creatures like us? An eight-hour shift at the local Wal-Mart? I don't think so. *I am a killer and I answer to no one. I am my own woman, my own kingdom, and I am afraid of nothing.* Letting the air out of my lungs in a rush of breath, I pushed open the door and strode in, a warrior.

Xander's throne had been removed. One row of lights illuminated a single trail in the dark, open space. My boots echoed eerily on the concrete floor as I passed through the threshold. The hairs on my neck prickled as I recognized another's presence somewhere nearby. Could it be Anya, or even Xander himself, who lurked in the darkness, watching me with invisible eyes?

I threw off my long coat and it drifted to the floor, allowing access to the saber I'd hidden beneath it. My steps were guarded. One foot crossing the other, I let my heightened senses guide me toward the disturbance I sensed in the air. Reaching behind me, I wrapped my right hand around the hilt of my saber, ready to rip it from the scabbard at a moment's notice. Tension thickened the atmosphere as it became fragrant with the sweet scent of my own kind. I should have noticed the smell long before I'd come in. Hell, I should have learned my lesson the first time I'd been brought here. Arrogance, again, superseded good sense. But it had been so long since I'd had to rely on such things that I was definitely out of practice. The air behind me became dense, and in a movement as fluid as a passing stream, I turned. I slid the blade free and faced my assailant, but froze before cutting down on the body that materialized before me.

The Shaede met my height almost exactly and had a lean and wiry build rippled with muscles. He looked lethal, and that was a huge thing for me to admit. His clear blue eyes glowed in the faint light. Hair the color of spun gold was pulled back at the nape of his neck and tied with a length of leather cord. Dressed in an antiquated getup, he looked like a cross between Legolas and Robin Hood—and was just young enough to pull it off.

A cold smile that would have surely frozen flames midflicker danced across his hardened face, showing a glimpse of the killer in him. Absent was any spark of humor, and in its place, only cruel calculation and intelligence. He was a frightening creature, and I instantly liked him.

"You're fast," he remarked. "But your stealth isn't much to brag about."

"I was asked to be here," I said, minding my p's and q's. "I didn't expect to be walking into a trap."

I relaxed my stance, slid the saber into the scabbard. A huge mistake. Before I could say *Screw me sideways,* I was flat on my back, staring at the laces of the Shaede's boot. They were brown, by the way.

"You should assume that every room you enter, whether invited or not, could be a potential trap." He pressed his boot tighter on my throat. "And *never* let yourself be seen."

"Point . . . taken," I said through rasps of breath.

With a reluctance that made me rethink coming here at all, he lifted his foot from my neck. He held his hand out. The smile faded, and from the look on his face, he'd just as soon eat a dog-shit sandwich than help me up. So, in an effort to rack up some brownie points, I declined the offer, and pushed myself up off the floor.

One corner of his lip twitched. A good sign.

"I'm Raif," he said.

"Darian." I used a tone to match his in its coolness. I decided he would respect aloofness more than he would a chummy greeting. I was right.

"So, you're what all the fuss is about?" The question didn't ring with Anya's condescension. Rather, humor, or at the very least, amusement. I really wanted to know what he meant by his comment, but I wasn't so stupid as to actually ask. "I'm told you are an assassin and your targets have only been humans. Is that right?"

Hmm. That got my attention. Apparently, my skills weren't going to be used to take out Joe Schmoe down the street. A challenge. Exciting.

"That's right," I said, wanting to finish with *So what*? But since I wasn't interested in tasting the sole of Raif's boot, I swallowed those two tiny words.

The cold smile crept back onto his lips. "This'll be fun." His blue eyes glowed bright for a fleeting moment. "You've got a lot to learn. I hope you're ready."

And with a movement faster than any I'd ever seen, even from Xander, Raif drew his sword and struck.

I spent the better part of five minutes in retreat. Raif pressed forward, and I parried his blows without striking a single offensive maneuver. His relentless pursuit had my back bent more than once as I tried unsuccessfully to throw off the weight of his sword. I fought with two hands wrapped around the hilt of my saber, while Raif needed only one.

He twisted and turned, dissipating into a breath of dark air. "You are a poor excuse for a warrior!" he shouted. "You aren't worthy of the name Shaede!" I ducked and jumped back as he swung his sword and followed with a fist. "You are slow, clumsy, and untrained! You are weak and pathetic; I wouldn't honor you with a warrior's death!"

I stumbled and rolled, coughed and labored, and never once had the presence of mind to make my body insubstantial. He had me against the ropes time and again. My mind raced to stay even a half pace ahead. In midswing, he paused, and lowered his sword.

"You're going to have to do better than that if you want any chance of success in your mission," he chided, taking an easy step back. His eyebrow quirked and he said, "I thought you were a fighter."

"So?" I said, through gasps of air.

"So . . . fight."

My temper surged and I rushed him. I pushed myself beyond my limits, thrusting the saber at his face and then swiping low at his knees. He deflected my attacks easily, but I wasn't moving backward any longer. Confident and strong, my second wind came faster than I expected. I mimicked his movements, learning as we went. I shifted from shadow to my solid form with fluidity, seeming to travel through time itself, popping in and out of thin air. I met him blow for blow and once almost knocked him off his feet. Refusing to quit, I pushed myself until I thought I'd break under the pressure.

Only when Raif stopped and lowered his blade did I know we were done for the night. "Not bad," he said with the barest touch of humor. "But not good either." He sheathed his weapon and left me standing alone in the dark with orders to return in two nights' time. There were no heartfelt words of congratulations, no offerings of a job well done. Not a whisper of who—or what—I was intended to kill.

I felt like I'd been run over by a bus, trampled by an elephant, and dragged behind a jet boat going Mach 10 over rocky river rapids. Until this point, I'd been self-trained in the art of assassination. I had no experience in combat. Common sense and my preternatural skills were what made me good at my job. Raif had thrown all of my arrogant misconceptions of myself on the floor and stomped them—hard. He'd worked me up one side and down the other.

Tyler showed up at my apartment just as I was dressing my wounds. I'd have to seriously reconsider my open-door policy with him. Since our impassioned kisses, he'd grown bolder, or at least more confident in his off-work-hours status with me. And Tyler was very stubborn.

I used my dining room table as a makeshift triage station. I'd already disposed of the torn spandex shirt I'd been wearing and tossed the pants as well. Perching on top of the table in a tank top and underwear was not a good way to get Ty to calm his libido.

His eyes looked like they were about to jump out of his head—like a cartoon character's after he's seen a pretty girl. But it only lasted a second once he noticed the bowl of bloody water and my sliced skin.

"Hell, Darian! What happened?"

Ass-tired and scored like a marinating steak, I wasn't sure I wanted to exert the effort to recount the details of my Ultimate Fighter training session. "It's no big deal. I'm fine; I'll heal. Our boy from the other night has arranged for me to receive some job training à la a medieval warrior. I guess I'm not up to snuff."

I grabbed the soaking rag and wrung the pink-tinged water from it. That's as far as I got. Tyler didn't waste a second to wrangle it from my grasp. He didn't speak. He didn't even look me in the eye. With gentle swipes, he tended each and every wound, rinsing the rag and starting all over. When he was done, he dried the excess moisture from my sliced skin and covered each cut with gauze, taping it in place. It took a half hour at least to dress the deeper cuts, and another fifteen minutes or so for him to check the various scratches that would be gone before I woke in the morning. I didn't protest or argue; just simply let him do what he had in mind to do.

"Where did you get the gauze?" He laughed gently.

"Drugstore," I murmured. "You should have seen the guy's face when I walked up to the counter."

As he worked, my eyes slipped shut. It had to have been somewhere around five in the morning, and I couldn't remember the last time I'd felt so physically spent. My head dipped forward a couple of times, and I snapped to attention, determined not to fall asleep on top of my dining room table. When Tyler finished, I felt his cool arm wrap around my shoulders. With his free hand, he pushed gently above my sternum. I fell back against him like a feather landing on a puddle, and he scooped me up in his embrace and carried me to my bed.

"This doesn't change anything, Ty," I murmured as he set me down. "So don't get any ideas."

My eyes didn't open again, but I felt a depression in the bed as Tyler lay down at my side. He wrapped his arm around my waist, careful not to touch the bandaged areas. For a moment I felt unsure, like I didn't know Tyler at all. His breath tickled the skin near my ear, and I relaxed against him. Cool and fragrant, his presence lulled me with all the things I liked about him. Taking my hand in his, he caressed the silver ring he'd given me years ago. "Everything's changed, Darian," he whispered. "You just don't realize it yet."

The next day brought with it a debilitating stiffness. Thank God Raif had granted me two full days of rest. Muscles I didn't even know I had ached. I could only hope he suffered a little in turn, but that was a pipe dream. I smiled indulgently as I imagined what it would be like to lay him flat out on his back and stomp my boot into his throat.

A seldom-heard buzz startled me. I realized it had come from my doorbell. I sighed, wondering why Tyler would think now, after everything he'd said and done, was the time to show respect for my privacy. I stomped to the intercom and pounded down on the button with a closed fist.

"Hit the bricks, Ty," I said into the speaker. "I don't have the patience to deal with the *us* issue right now."

"Um," said a tiny voice on the other end. "I have a

delivery for Darian . . ." He paused, and I could hear the shuffling of papers. "Sorry, no last name. I have a delivery for someone named Darian."

I sighed heavily and wondered what it sounded like on the other end. "Come on up," I grumbled.

After a couple of minutes, the grinding gears of the elevator lifted the delivery boy to my apartment. He didn't move to open the life gate, so I opened it for him. Taking two timid steps, he positioned himself at the edge of the entrance. The six-foot-by-four-inch case he carried was supported by both hands and held aloft, like he was holding out a steak for a cougar.

"A-are you Darian?" he said.

"That's me. What have you got there?"

"I don't know!" he exclaimed, like I'd accused him of something. "I didn't look."

I laughed, hoping the sound would put him at ease, but I noticed his shoulders slowly creeping toward his ears. "I'm sure you didn't peek," I said, wishing I knew some motherly phrases to calm the poor kid down. "I guess I'll just go ahead and take it."

I reached out, making sure to keep my movements as slow and human as possible. The exchange went smoothly. As I reached to shut the lift gate and send him on his way, he remembered I needed to sign for the package. I took the clipboard and scribbled my name. He was pushing buttons on the wall as I slid the clipboard through the wooden slats of the gate. Apparently, he couldn't leave fast enough. I laughed as he sank below my floor and out of sight. My charms didn't work on everyone.

I carried the long rectangular box to my table. Three silver latches and a handle adorned the shiny mahogany container. I stood in front of the case, realizing it had been more years than I could count since I'd received a mysterious package of any kind, be it present, payoff, or threat. Could've been a bomb, though I doubted anyone would use a box so big. It might've contained a dozen

long-stemmed roses. It was definitely too big for a neck-
lace or pair of earrings, and certainly not Tyler's MO. An
AK-47, maybe? Only one way to find out. I threw caution aside and flipped the latches in succession before
lifting the lid.

Wow.

Resting inside the black-velvet-lined case was an ancient katana. The preferred weapon of the long-extinct
samurai, as deadly a weapon as there ever was. It could
slice a body in half with surgical precision. I estimated
the blade at two and a half feet in length before the tang
disappeared into a hilt wrapped in old, oiled wood and
black fabric. It bore an impressive forging pattern, the
darker gray rolling like the ocean's waves along the
brighter and much lighter steel below it. I traced my fingers along the symbols engraved in the metal, obviously
the signature of its maker. A note, written in flourishing
script, had been placed inside the case.

> *Edo 1681—made by Yasutsuna. It is called*
> *Bright Death.*

This was no bouquet of flowers or twenty-dollar box
of chocolates. From the look and condition of the blade,
I estimated its worth somewhere in the range of tens of
thousands of dollars. I took the sword from the case with
reverence. A weapon worthy of its name, I was sure.
Warriors of the ancient world often named their swords,
a practice as out-of-date as sword use itself. I hadn't even
been a living human in the year 1681. My immortal existence began somewhere closer to 1910, but the ancient
weapon connected me to all those who lived and fought
before I had been made into what I am now.

My cell rang, interrupting the awe of the moment, and
I dug it out of my pocket to read PRIVATE NUMBER on the
caller ID. "Hello?"

"Did the box arrive?" Xander's smooth, smug voice said on the other end.

"How did you get my number?"

"That saber of yours is an unfit weapon." Then he asked, "Do you like the katana?"

Leave it to His High and Mightiness to totally ignore me. "Exactly what do you want in return for this ... token?" I'm not stupid; nothing in this world comes without a price.

Xander's answering laughter said, *Aren't you quaint?* "I don't want anything at all. If you're going to work for me, you'd best have the right tool for the job. Enjoy."

Before I could get a word in, he hung up. I stared at the sword, gleaming blue in the light of my kitchen. I wanted to keep it. It was the most magnificent sword I'd ever seen. I just hoped that by doing so, I wasn't biting myself in the ass.

I don't know why, but aside from feeling very manipulated, the katana made me feel very, very purchased.

Chapter 8

When I showed up at the warehouse, Raif examined the katana with jealous eyes. I couldn't help but show it off. I pulled it from the scabbard, savoring the ringing tone as the blade slid free. A wicked smile curved my lips as I pictured my teacher flat on his ass and me standing over him with the shining steel hovering over his heart.

"How did you come by that blade?" His almost accusatory tone belied his envy.

"Xander gave it to me," I said, giving it a few practice swings.

Raif turned, and with a swing that took two hands to maneuver, struck my back with the flat of his own sword, knocking me face-first to the floor. I cried out—the blow stung like hell. I pushed my palms into the cold concrete and tried to propel myself upward, but my progress was stayed by the sole of Raif's heavy boot.

"*Who* gave you the katana?" he asked in a tone colder than Death itself.

Several quips leapt to the tip of my tongue. But I thought better of putting my voice behind the words when I pondered the painful consequences. "The High King Alexander gifted me with the blade," I said, glaring at the concrete inches below my eyes. I hated humbling myself to anyone. Raif demanded respect, and I had no choice but to oblige or else learn respect the hard way. Considering his not-so-gentle tactics thus far, I didn't think I'd like the hard way.

Raif spent the better part of six hours teaching me a painful lesson. He used every opportunity to lay his blade against my skin. I paused to survey a new gash, realizing this was punishment. I would not be permitted to speak with a loose tongue in regard to Xander again. It didn't matter that I thought of him only as a client and didn't regard him as king of anything. He was Raif's king a thousand percent, and in his eyes, my king by virtue of my very existence. Let me just say that didn't sit well with me.

I ducked as Raif's fist swung for my face, turned and swept my leg in front of me. I managed to knock him off his feet, but he scattered in a cloud of dark air, reappearing behind me. His dagger at my throat signaled the end of another embarrassing training session.

"You're improving," he said. "But don't let your head get too big just yet. You're far from ready." Raif inspected the tip of his dagger before sheathing it at his waist. "He's stronger than you, faster than you, and a thousand times more deadly."

I opened my mouth to ask the million-dollar question: *Who's the damn mark?*

But he'd vanished, leaving me alone. Again.

As I stood in the shower, allowing the water to cascade down my battered body, I regretted having no real confidant. Ty could have filled those shoes, but he was human and probably couldn't relate to my unusual existence. But I needed advice, or, at the very least, an outside opinion. This *job*, if that's what it still was, had become a little more complex than what I was used to.

I thought of Azriel. He'd been my confidant, listened to me talk for hours on end. Though he'd never answered any of my questions. I hadn't become a proper warrior in his care, but he'd taught me stealth and how to slide a blade along a target's throat. He'd taught me how to lie low. It'd been his idea, killing for money, though he was

less discriminate as to our clientele and marks. In his
opinion, we were perfectly suited for that particular line
of work, and it paid well. Enough to keep us more than
comfortable. He'd lined up the jobs and did most of the
legwork. I'd been nothing but an apprentice, someone he
brought along for amusement. Until he vanished. Then I
had no one but myself to rely on. My mind wandered to
one of many kills.

*"Shh," he whispered against my ear. "He's nervous to-
night. Knows someone's following him. You need to wait
and pick your moment."*

"He's human," I whispered back. "Shouldn't be hard."

*His low laughter rumbled in his chest, making me
tremble. It never took much for him to get a rise out of me.
"True. But you won't be worth a dime to anyone if you
can't do a job without remaining completely unseen. Humans can be insufferably curious. You never know who
might be watching you—watching him."*

*I nodded slowly, tucking a stray piece of hair up in my
cap. I hated the fact that I couldn't just wear the pants,
button-up shirt, and vest, and leave my hair down. But
Azriel said it would draw too much attention. Women just
didn't wear pants, and there was no way I could work in
a dress.*

"He's coming this way," he whispered.

*Our mark for the night had been a poor slob who'd
gotten in deep with the mob. He'd raped the bookie's
daughter and gambled a little more than he could pay
back. Now his creditors were taking payment out on his
hide. And I was the debt collector.*

*Obviously a little on the drunk side, our man stumbled
and swerved, crashing against a trash can. Looking
around, he opened the front of his pants and turned to the
wall. Lovely. Just what I wanted: to kill the guy while he
took a piss in the alley.*

"Do it now," Azriel whispered.

Melting into glorious shadow, I appeared, poised and ready, the dagger gripped firmly in my right hand. I leaned toward my mark and whispered the words I'd been paid to deliver with the death blow: "Jimmy the Shark says, 'This is for Maggie.' Now he's paid in full." My movement blurred from speed, a merciful action, I hoped, and the blade slid across his throat.

He didn't even have time to be surprised.

"That's my girl," Azriel said, appearing beside me.

"Too easy," I complained. "It's not even interesting anymore. I want to learn how to fight, not how to sneak up on people and kill them like some kind of coward."

Azriel's cold laughter bounced off the brick walls of the alley.

"Have you ever fought another Shaede?" I ventured. "When there were others?"

He took the dagger from my hand and cleaned it on a rag before handing it back. "Of course. I was trained by the best. The fiercest warrior among us. No one could best me. Not even him, after a while."

"Teach me!" I exclaimed. "Please, Az. I want to fight. I'll do everything you say. I won't whine. I won't complain even a little bit. Train me."

He laughed again. "Then you'd be deadly, indeed. Wouldn't you?" He laid his lips to my temple. "Maybe someday, my love. Maybe someday."

Of course, that someday never came. The asshole left me high and dry, and wound up dead. Or so I assumed.

The way I saw it, I helped the world with the work I did. One less drug lord meant one less supplier for the dealers. And in turn, if I managed to take out the dealer before he could entice some stupid kid into trying his product, then little Sonny might not turn out to be a junkie. Let's face it: Criminals don't exactly enhance society. There's too many of the morally defunct running loose on the streets as it is. I don't mind taking out the bad guy, but I don't do it for free either. A girl's gotta eat. And that's where Azriel's philosophy deviated from mine. He never cared who we killed. Not me. I'd never take out a housewife for her life insurance or a witness to a crime just to keep him silent. I had standards. I refused to kill an innocent. But I have no fucking problem killing a man who beats his wife and sells meth to kids. The way this crazy world works, I am far too busy. Decent people are few and far between.

Which made me wonder about Xander's unknown target. Was *he* one of the bad guys? And in who's opinion? The thought of servitude left a sour taste in my mouth. Whether I'd been paid or not, Xander considered me one of his subjects. And the more I thought about it, the more I wanted him out of my life once and for all. I'd been seduced by the idea of what my training could do for me, the status it could bring me. What if Xander's motives were altogether more devious? Momentarily blinded by the dollar signs I saw whenever I thought about working for the king, I needed to consider the possibility that he wouldn't pay me for future services. Or, worse, use me and keep me as another one of his little pets. Just like Anya, bound in a sexy catsuit and purring for a bowl of milk. If Raif considered me simply another subject of his Lord and Master, wouldn't it stand to reason that Xander considered me in the exact same light? Had he perhaps wooed me with payment for services rendered, only to jerk the rug out from under me? I had to think past the job. What about after it was done? It made me sick to think of how fast I had fallen under his spell.

I would not, under any circumstances, become a pawn. I wanted answers to the questions of my existence, and serving Xander was one way to get them. Would he give them to me? Or just continue to string me along, keeping me in the dark, just like Az? My mortal life had been out of my control. I would never again allow anyone to keep me under his thumb. Xander was just going to have to make Raif or Anya or some other idiot do his dirty work, because this girl was taking herself off the market.

I returned the katana to its mahogany case, though it pained me to do so. Next to the sword, I placed the envelopes of money Tyler had given me. Returning the money wasn't as big as giving back the sword, but I did what I had to do. I couldn't spend eternity being Xander's ignorant strong arm. So I returned to the warehouse in the harsh light of day. I set the case inside the door, certain the right person would find it and return it to the king.

I expected to receive a visit from the High King himself. The sun sank into the western horizon, but he didn't come. Night came on the heels of twilight, and still my threshold remained uncrossed. Tyler stayed away as well. I was almost positive he'd make an appearance. He didn't.

Pensive, and maybe even a little insulted, I sulked around my own space. Where the hell *was* everyone? Xander obviously didn't give a shit that I wasn't interested in serving him, and Ty must have snapped out of puppy-love mode. I should have been relieved. Somehow, I wasn't.

After resigning myself to sleep, I lay in bed, tossing and turning and tossing some more. I wasn't used to staying in at night. I guess I didn't go out because I expected company. Since no one cared enough to stop by, I wasn't about to go looking for either one of them. After a few more angry tosses, I finally found a forced sleep that had about as much to do with rest as knitting had to do with swimming.

Something startled me awake. I lay unmoving to better listen, smell, *feel* the air for any distinct changes. Besides the scurrying sound of an insect across my floor, nothing betrayed who—or what—stirred me from slumber. The sound persisted; it must have been one hell of a busy bug. My eyes began to slide shut, and I allowed them to close all the way, thinking any danger was beyond me.

The sound of voices drifted to my ears sometime later. The strangest thing was not the voices, but the fact that they were all facets of the same voice. An echo of sorts, it called out to me in different tones, but spoke as if from one mouth, one throat, and one being. I would have thought I was dreaming if I hadn't felt its breath on my face.

"Darian."

The moment brought to mind Tyler stretched out beside me in bed, whispering my name while he stroked my hair. His words had been spoken tenderly, though, and the voice speaking my name now seethed with menace.

"Darian."

My eyes were closed, but my senses were as sharp as the katana I wished I still had. A suffocating pressure, like being trapped under a fallen log, pressed all around me. Since my night at the warehouse, I'd come to realize that in the presence of a Shaede the air becomes palpable, dense. I felt this other creature, just as I had my newfound brethren, though the sensations were like night and day. Aside from that, I didn't know who—or what—it was.

"Darian." Again, my name floated to my ears, carried by myriad tiny voices melded into one. I shivered at the whispering sound and wrinkled my nose in distaste as a foul smell reached me.

"Who's there?" I asked stupidly. I mean, it wasn't like the disembodied voice was going to answer, *Oh, sorry. I should have introduced myself. I'm George . . .*

The voice didn't answer—what a shocker—and I slowly inched the covers from my body, readying to defend myself if the need arose. The flutter of something touching my face sent my heart hammering against my rib cage. Like the kiss of sunlight or the stirring of air, I felt the microscopic hairs on my cheek move, sending a tingle deep into my flesh.

"I'd like nothing more than to suck your innards out through your nose. I bet you taste as sweet as honey." The words, whispered from the many-faceted voice, stretched my nerves taut, leaving a hollow ache I was desperate to escape.

"You can try," I said, cranking up the bravado. "But maybe I'll surprise you and make you sorry you ever stepped foot in here." The pounding inside my chest intensified. "If you're so goddamned tough, why don't you show yourself?"

"Perhaps after the eclipse," the voices sighed. "I wonder, will it change the way you taste? No harm is to come to you until then. Doesn't mean I can't have a little fun with you in the meantime."

Invisible claws, like shards of broken glass, scraped me from head to toe. I clamped my teeth together and pushed my tongue against them, determined not to cry out. I squeezed my eyes tight, feeling the moisture escape from my lids as I lay as still as possible.

The encounter lasted only seconds, though it felt like agonizing hours. By slow degrees, I unclenched my jaw, fingers and toes relaxing, followed by arms and legs, and finally my core. Again, I heard the scurrying, like mouse scratches in the wall, fading into silence. *Alone*. No one here but me, my heavy breathing, and *pain*. Lots of pain.

Early-morning sun shone in through the skylights, casting a lemon yellow glow on the white coverings of my bed. My pulse picked up its beat once again. What nature of creature could have come to me invisibly in the light of day? I wasn't going to burst into flames if I walked outside at high noon, but I was confined to my solid self. This creature didn't seem to share my restraints. No Shaede, that was for sure. And talk about creepy. What the hell . . . Eating my innards? Eclipse? Whatever it was, it had its Vincent Price impression down pat.

I plucked my phone from the table beside the bed. In a moment of uncharacteristic weakness, I dialed.

"Ty, can you please come over?" I said.

"Give me ten minutes," he said, and hung up.

Tyler never disappoints.

I don't know if it was the lingering fear that kept me marooned on the mattress, or some other, simpler reason. Weak and wary, I hadn't an ounce of energy I could devote to leaving the bed. The adrenaline rush had taken everything out of me.

"Darian," Ty called out. His footsteps echoed on the hardwood floor. Quiet steps, not his usual elephant stomps. I didn't answer him. Sick with shame and fear, I stayed immobile, huddled beneath the blankets.

He touched my cheek. Remnants of fear coated my mouth, and the words came thick. "Someone was here."

"Who?"

"I don't know. Not like me. Sun was already up. The thing was in the *air*, Ty."

He sat down beside me. I didn't turn to look at him; my sudden frailty was a disgrace to my nature. Embarrassment kept me from meeting his eyes.

"What happened?" His gentle voice soothed me, assuring me it was okay to be scared without having to say it out loud.

"The voice, I can't describe it. Like nothing I've ever heard before. It touched me, and it wasn't any tickle either."

Tyler tugged at the covers burying my body. I resisted at first, unsure of what his next move would be. Insistent, he pulled harder, and I finally relented, too shaken up to do anything about it. As he peeled back the blankets, he examined the skin that my tank top and shorts didn't cover. He rolled me gently from my side to my back. My eyes met his. The hazel orbs grew wide, and he sucked his breath in sharply. An angry frown marred his features.

"Welts," he murmured.

"What?"

"Your skin is welted," he explained, tracing a fingertip over the raised marks.

I have to say the news came as a relief. I half expected my skin to be ripped open. "I didn't see anything; only felt a presence." Fear was washed away by confusion. Anger approached on its heels. "When I find the creature that did this, I'm going to slice it into a million bloody pieces."

Expressing my anger felt good, as if I were reclaiming a bit of my flagging nerve. I put my palms down on the bed, pushed myself to a sitting position, and drew my knees up a little. Closer to eye level with Tyler, I read both worry and fury in his expression. His normally cool body temperature seemed to drop by a few degrees.

"They're only welts, right? I've healed from worse."

"Yeah." He ran his hands over the miniature roadways of raised flesh along my arm. "Do you think it has anything to do with this job you're training for?"

He stopped stroking my arm, and though his gaze didn't detach from mine, his hands continued with their exploration of the marks on my skin. He moved a palm under my calf, cupping the flesh before traveling up and over my shin. I shivered.

"I don't think so," I answered honestly. "If Xander had a creature like that in his service, he sure as hell wouldn't need me. I quit that job, anyway. It's a nonthing."

"What do you mean, you quit?" His fingers traced each one of my toes. "You never quit anything."

"I quit this," I said. "I was starting to feel like a possession, and I don't like that. And I still don't know who the mark is." I looked away, distracted by the warm, masculine scent that was one hundred percent Tyler.

Reluctantly, I met his face again. His soft, greenish eyes held a lustful hunger, and something sparked inside me. Teasing fingers stroked my bare skin, traveling from my toes, across my ankles, and up my shins. I tried to look away, but Tyler's gaze held me in place.

"Darian, I wish you'd let me protect you."

Good Lord, did he even *know* me?

From my knees, his hands spread out across my thighs, over and around, his fingertips grazing my butt at the hem of my shorts.

My voice caught in my throat. "How do you propose to do that, *human*?" It's not like I didn't appreciate the offer. But I didn't need to be taken care of. Strong, independent, not to mention indestructible, I wasn't exactly the damsel in distress. He squeezed my flesh—*Oh, dear God!*—gently but just hard enough. *A-maz-ing!*

"I might surprise you," he said in a calm, unsettling way. Inch by inch, he scooted closer, rising on his knees until our noses almost touched. "Bring it on." His voice, gruff and full of innuendo, sent a pulsing thrill straight through my core. "I can handle anything standing in my way. You'd be safe."

I snorted. Maybe he should stand against Raif sometime. That'd be interesting. I'd be picking up little pieces of Tyler from one end of the warehouse to the other. The mental image made me cringe.

Tyler graced me with a confident smile, abandoned my thigh, and worked his way up my waist. He knew how to use his fingers. A series of rippling chills traveled from my toes to the top of my head and back down. He grazed the sensitive skin exposed where my tank top had ridden up, and my eyes involuntarily drifted shut.

"Don't presume you know all about me." His fingers traveled upward, tracing my rib cage. Oh, man, it felt good. I'd almost forgotten the scare I'd had earlier. He kneaded my flesh with his strong hand. I did moan this time. I couldn't help it.

"I'll keep you safe."

"Tyler—"

Before I could pull away, his mouth found mine. Soft, searching, but full of purpose, his lips caressed mine, and I responded, unable to form a coherent thought with my senses full of Tyler. His thumbs brushed my nipples on the outside of my tank top and they rose to stiff peaks, wanting more than a passing caress. He opened his mouth, kissing me deeper, and I leaned in toward him instead of away, like I'd intended. Without considering the consequences, I reached out, dragging my hands down over his chest, enjoying the feel of his muscles through his T-shirt. Lower, my hands acted on their own, brushing the waist of his jeans and then his fly and the hard bulge that made my breath catch in my chest. Tyler moaned, and my heart sped to an unnatural rhythm. Just a pull here and a tug there and he'd be bare to my touch. I wanted to feel him, full in my hand, my mouth—

His proximity and swaying tactics had easily broken down my defenses. I forced my hands back up his chest, balling them into fists, forbidding myself from taking what I wanted. I tried to ignore his smell, his touch, his reassuring words, and gently pushed him away. It took more effort than I thought I could manage, because what I really wanted to do was pull him a hell of a lot closer.

"Tyler," I whispered. I had to stop this. Now. Before either of us was tempted to take it further, I steered his focus to the matter at hand. "I appreciate that you want to protect me, but there's nothing you can do. I'm a big girl and I can take care of myself."

"I know you think so," he said. He leaned forward and kissed me again, long and languid.

My body attempted mutiny, responding to waves of pleasure I knew I shouldn't want to feel. The moment ended all too soon, and when he pulled back, I opened my eyes. He smiled in a very self-satisfied sort of way that made me want to slap the expression right off his face. But since that might encourage him, I said, "Did it ever occur to you that *I'm* protecting *you* by keeping you at a safe distance from all of this nonhuman stuff?"

He moved in again, but I backed away. I sure as hell didn't trust myself to be a good girl. "Tyler, I can't do this. I have to keep my head on straight. Until things cool down, I'm still in way too deep. I have to think of *your* safety."

"Darian, I don't need protecting." He actually laughed, though his eyes shone with disappointment. "I'm more than capable."

My brain didn't have its usual get-up-and-go, so I ignored that little statement. He stood up, giving me a much needed moment to take control of my raging sex drive. I lowered my gaze and banished from my mind the thought of his scent and cool fingers. *Shit.*

"Ty, what do you know about the others?" Changing the subject would be best for both of us, or our clothes would be on the floor in a matter of seconds. "Am I the only one you've ever known?"

Backing away, he passed his hands through his hair and expelled a deep breath. He seemed to seriously contemplate my questions before answering, as if divulging too much would risk spilling a secret. "I know of other nonhuman beings."

Oh, wow, Ty. Thanks for the Encyclopaedia Britannica *answer.* I couldn't believe I'd been so turned on a moment ago, when all I wanted now was to throw something at him. "Do you know of anything that could have come into my apartment this morning? Something invisible, with a mean streak?"

"Meaner than you?" Tyler's frustrated smile drew a momentary twinge of guilt from the back of my ragged emotions. "Let me see what I can find out. I'll meet you back here later tonight."

"No!" I said with enough oomph to blow him across the room. I did not want to spend the evening deciding if clothes on or off was the best way to play with him. "Meet me at The Pit."

His face fell a little. *Well, too bad.* "Fine," he said. "I'll meet you there around eleven or twelve."

Eleven or twelve? Tyler was nothing if not punctual. Everything *was* changing.

Chapter 9

I never made it to The Pit. Strong arms, fast and stealthy, took me from the sidewalk, blindfolding me before I knew what was going on. I kicked and screamed and fought like hell, but I'd been bound by something that kept me nice and secure. The air around me became dense and fragrant as I recognized the presence of my kidnappers. Shaedes. Two of them. And from the tone of their voices, I got the impression that neither one of them was particularly fond of me at the moment.

"We should kill her now and do Alexander a favor." Anya flat-out hated my guts for some reason, so I guess her role in my kidnapping wasn't so surprising.

"Quiet, Anya. You're not here to pass judgment."

Raif? Seriously? I'd thought we'd grown closer during our nights of training. Since discovering I wasn't an endangered species, I'd considered the possibility of connecting with someone. Raif had become that someone. He got me. And aside from Tyler, I didn't have anyone else in my life. If he was party to this, I must've pissed him off, and that hurt. Returning the katana and disrespecting his king had clearly pushed his buttons just a little.

I couldn't move, which was yet another new thing for me. New experiences just didn't hold the appeal they used to. A length of cord bound me, the material of which I couldn't identify. Soft like silk, and at the same time almost rubbery. No matter how I fought, I couldn't wrench my wrists free. I focused on letting go of my corporeal form and becoming one with the shadows, but somehow the bindings kept me locked within my skin and restrained my unnatural strength. The cords had to have been woven with some sort of magic. They moved with even the slightest shift like elastic bands, yet were unyielding to my struggling wrists. They rendered me as helpless as a human bound with plastic zip ties or metal cuffs. *Perish the thought.*

I lay on the cold metal floor of what I assumed to be a van. Unable to see, I had only my senses of hearing and smell to aid me. The sweet scent of Shaede hovered around me, and it didn't take long to discover that Raif and Anya weren't the only ones there with me. Several scents I couldn't place, though they were unmistakably of my own kind. I'd learned since being exposed to these Shaedes that each of us has a unique signature, and I knew Raif's and Anya's. I heard virtually nothing. My captors grew quiet as doors closed me in and the vehicle pulled out into traffic. The only sounds were the hum of the engine and the vibrations of each tire as they rolled over the road.

I had no doubt they were taking me to Xander. I assumed he'd been a little fired up by my dismissal, but all-out kidnapping hadn't topped my list of possible retaliations. As we drove to who knows where, I tried to prepare myself for whatever punishments would be meted out. If Xander was mad enough—and I suspected he was—I could expect a severe ass kicking from Raif or Anya or both. I didn't think an encounter with either one of them would leave me feeling like we'd bonded from the experience.

My thoughts drifted unbidden to Tyler. I wondered if he was waiting for me at The Pit. I wondered how long he'd stay before he went looking for me at the studio, and how long after that before he'd start scouring the city. Ty *would* go looking for me. I wasn't wrong. Something had developed between us whether I wanted to acknowledge it or not, and he would track me down like a hound on the hunt. I just wished I didn't have to worry about him losing his fool head in the process.

After what felt like forever, the vehicle came to a stop, and I took in a great gulp of air to steady my quaking limbs. The thought that I might leave this existence and pass permanently into shadow sent a wave of anxiety washing over me. I prayed I would die with a sword in my hand. I hoped I would leave this solid form with dignity and with the respect of my adversaries.

"I wish I could kiss Ty one more time," I whispered.

The back doors of the van opened, and I was hauled out by several pairs of hands. My head bounced against the pavement, and my hips and legs followed suit as I was dumped on the ground. Someone standing above me snickered, and I connected the sound to Anya. Of course she'd be delighted to see me suffer.

Lifted as if I weighed nothing, they carried me through a door, and the familiar smells of a home drifted up my nostrils. We weren't in a musty warehouse or unused residence like the town house. This place had a lived-in scent that lingered everywhere.

My head knocked uncomfortably a couple of times as I was towed up a flight of stairs. Again, my captors did not make much of an effort to see to my comfort. I could hardly blame them. But that didn't mean I wasn't crazy-pissed because of it.

They threw me down on a soft, cushiony surface. The blindfold was removed, and I felt the air shift as my kidnappers departed under the cover of shadow. It took a while for my eyes to adjust, even though the room was relatively dark.

The surrounding space boasted rich furnishings. Sporting an enormous bed, couches, chairs, a table, and a desk, it was a suite unto itself. Antique dressers and vibrant oil paintings decorated the walls. Doors led from the central room to other unknown places, waiting like dark chasms branching off from the main body of a cave. The smell of Shaede permeated my senses. New, fresh scents, and old as well, wafted around me, but the most prevalent scent in this room belonged to *him*.

"What shall I do with you, Darian?"

He startled me with his velvety voice; it trailed out to wrap me in its embrace. I hated him for his voice, for the way it made me feel, what it sparked in me. For that reason more than any other, I despised him.

I bucked my chin toward the ceiling. *Screw you*. I locked my defiant gaze with his when he came around to sit on the edge of a wing chair and face me.

"What *are* you going to do with me, Xander?" I asked.

He laughed and the sound touched every square inch of my body. Reaching out, his balmy fingertips crossed one of the raised welts on my face that had yet to go away. He turned on every light in the room, and I tucked my head against my shoulder, squinting. Pulling up my long sleeves, he examined the welts with interest, a sound not unlike a growl erupting from his chest. In my incapacitated state, he left me little choice but to accept the appraisal as he continued to search, lifting first my shirt over my belly and then my pant legs, blazing a path across my skin as he surveyed the damage done.

"Lyhtan," he said through gritted teeth.

"Who?" I couldn't help but ask.

"Not *who*," he said, his voice soft. "What. A Lyhtan did this to you. When did it come?"

"This morning," I said, loathing myself for letting my guard down. "What is it?"

"The Lyhtans are creatures of the light," Xander explained, "and vicious, deadly beasts. But whereas you can pass into shadow at night, so can the Lyhtan move unseen in the day. They are confined to their corporeal forms once the sun sets."

Oh, goody, more surprises. What next—aliens living

among us? "They're like us?" I asked, chagrined that I even had to ask.

"More like us than I'd care to admit. We're cousins, in the true sense of the word. Both our lines were born to brothers, Artis and Rannan. They defied their father, as the legend goes." Xander paced the room, and a thoughtful expression graced his face. "Kreighton was a foolish king and let fear ruin his kingdom. The brothers took brides that displeased the king, and their descendants paid the price. Kreighton had favored Artis before his rebellion, and rather than exact the harsh punishment he planned, he graced Artis's children with Fae beauty so they'd blend with society, and cloaked them in shadow at night. Rannan was not so fortunate. Kreighton cursed his less-favored son's offspring, banishing them to the light, where they'd be forced to hide their ghastly forms, marking them as outcasts. They're uncivilized beasts. We're the lucky ones, I suppose. The Lyhtans"—he looked away wistfully—"are jealous. Vengeful. They despise all Shaedes for our very existence. A Lyhtan needs no excuse to attack a Shaede. They're dangerous. Especially to us." His gaze, burning gold flecks in melted caramel, pinned me right where I stood. "Especially to *you*."

I stiffened at Xander's words. What did they want with me? Which raised an even bigger question: Why hadn't the Lyhtan tried to kill me? Xander had just said they needed little to no excuse to kill a Shaede, and yet it had let me live. My nerves stretched taut and my pulse skipped. The damn thing had been playing with me. It had admitted as much. *But why?* "I've never seen one before," I whispered. "I had no idea anything like that existed. Didn't even get a look at the one that attacked me."

"They're solitary creatures," Xander said. "Lyhtans do not live in groups, and though they want for much, they need very little. They hunt like lone wolves, glutting on the weak, and do not seek prey for weeks afterward."

His warm gaze scorched over me again as he continued. "Lyhtan claws and teeth contain deadly venom. We're allergic to that venom. Those welts on your lovely skin are scratches. Because of the allergy, it will take longer for you to heal. You're lucky to have come away with only welts. This is . . . disconcerting, Darian. I don't understand why it didn't inflict more damage. By all rights, you should be dead. To your attacker's discredit, it must have barely broken the skin."

My attacker's discredit? Like he did a piss-poor job of trying to kill me? Well, the damn thing had said that no harm was to come to me. At least not until the eclipse, though what that meant, I had no idea. And at this point, I didn't trust Xander as far as I could throw him. No way was I divulging that little piece of info. "Are they allergic to us?"

Xander's lip curled. "Not really. There, they have the upper hand. Though shadow does have its effect on them. But deadly shadow is hard to come by. Lucky for you, I know just where to get it. The most stalwart Lyhtan can't defend itself against true shadow. Once extracted, the shadow becomes a solid thing, impervious even to magic. It can squeeze bones to dust and render an opponent immobile." His eyes roamed over me once again, his lips curving in a seductive smile that would have melted the resolve of any number of women.

I moved against my bonds and remembered that no matter how good he looked, I wanted nothing more than to flay the skin from his body. He *had* kidnapped me, after all.

"Untie me," I said.

He must have been mulling over his options, because he stood and paced about the room, tapping his chin with a finger. "I'll let you go," he said from behind me. "If you agree to not run away."

How many victims would agree to that demand? And how many times was he going to restrain me and then ask me to stay? But I agreed, knowing as well as I know myself that I would come to regret it.

He fiddled with the knots, and a moment later, the cord relaxed and drooped from my body. As soon as I was assured of my freedom, I dissolved, reappearing inches from Xander. I drew back my hand to strike him.

Rather than stay my hand, he wrapped his own around me, pulling me tight to his body, which exuded so much heat that I thought I would melt right into him. He buried his face in the strawberry curls of my hair and whispered, "Do you hate me that much?"

"Yes!" I shouted into his chest. "You wooed me by wrapping servitude up in a pretty bow. You gave me gifts only so you could use me, and when I turned my back . . ." I took a deep breath so I could really let him have it "You . . . had . . . me . . . kidnapped!"

A low rumble of laughter erupted in his chest. *Bad move.* It was like pouring gasoline on an already raging fire. I shoved at him, pounded a fist into his muscled chest, and screamed my frustration.

"You should stay here. For your protection," he said, as if I hadn't tried to punch my fist right through his heart. "I wouldn't wish a Lyhtan on *anyone.* The next time you encounter one, you might not live to talk about it."

Oh, great. Not that I planned on encountering one anytime soon. "There's no *way* I'm staying here with you. You got your money and your sword back. I'm done with you, *Your Highness.*"

"This is no coincidence, Darian." Xander leaned away, though he didn't let go of me, and tilted his head thoughtfully to one side. "I don't believe in coincidence. My enemy is now your enemy by virtue of association. And my enemy wants me dead. A Lyhtan is a skilled and thorough killer. It will tear you limb from limb if it gets the chance. It's a miracle you're alive." He brushed his thumb across my cheek. "I can't help but wonder why it didn't try to kill you. You have no choice but to be the stealthy assassin and do the job I've paid you for. It's the only way to guarantee your own safety."

"Bullshit." I was tired of playing his games. I wanted answers. "Who's the mark?" I asked yet again. Even Xander believed the Lyhtan's visit hadn't been a coincidence. Fucking thing was connected to the *job*. "It's connected. Is that what you're saying? The Lyhtan is connected to whoever you want offed?"

"I'm fairly certain," he answered. Reluctantly, he let me go, and his strong fingers lingered against me as if trying to savor every second of contact with my body. His thumbs were the last to leave me, and they climbed up my torso, stroking outward, brushing against my ribs.

Just perfect. Like I didn't have enough to worry about. Now I had to watch my back for invisible attackers. Attackers that might rip my arms right out of their sockets. Just because I'd decided to work for Xander. Some jobs just *suck*. I *so* did not need this shit. But I couldn't logically find any way out of it. I couldn't fight something I couldn't see, and I couldn't prepare for an attacker that I knew little to nothing about. Continuing with Raif, and thereby this job, seemed to be my best line of defense. "I'll do this for you," I said, feeling the manacles of slavery tighten. "Only because I'm interested in saving my own neck. But I will not, under any condition, stay here with you."

"What makes you think you have a choice?" He was the high-and-mighty king again, looking down his haughty nose at me.

Give me a break. "Because if you don't let me leave, you can take this job and shove it right up your—"

"My king . . ." Anya stormed into the room. I thought briefly about delivering a sharp kick to her gut while she wasn't looking. But I decided to ignore her instead.

"What is it?" Xander sounded a little less than gracious. Good. She needed to be put in her place.

Anya took to her knee. I wanted to gag. She wore hot pink leather tonight. I wondered how she even managed to move, wrapped up in that much tanned and dyed flesh.

"Her companion is here," she said with contempt. "He's demanding her release."

Xander laughed. The sound of it tickled my flesh like warm rain. I forced myself to disengage from the sensation and focused on my anger.

"And what does he propose will happen if I don't meet his demand?"

Anya's eyes widened for a moment. She rose and stood very close to Xander's side, whispering something in his ear that made him shake with another round of laughter. I shivered from head to toe at the sound.

He gave her a pat on the shoulder like she was a good little pet and sent her on her way. She shot me a furious glare before leaving, and I blew her a kiss. Someday I'd crack her skull open.

Xander gave me another of his contemplative stares and then let out a great sigh. If he was put out, I was glad. "You've drawn an interesting admirer. I don't know quite what to think of him."

Aside from his scent, Tyler was about as interesting as vanilla ice cream. Lucky for me, I'm partial to vanilla. But I wondered why she said *her companion*. What the hell was that supposed to mean? And how the hell had he known I was here? Had he followed us? "He's not *my* anything." I hoped that by showing disinterest in Tyler, it would protect him from Xander's interest as well. "I don't know why he's here. Get rid of him if you want. I don't need rescuing."

"I've decided to let you leave," Xander said, as if making a great proclamation. "But you will continue your training with Raif, and when you are deemed ready, you will perform the task I've paid you for."

"I want to know who the mark is."

"No. Not yet. It's too dangerous for you to know. When you're ready, Raif will explain everything." He turned his back on me. "Until I can give you a means of protection from the Lyhtan, you should guard your every move. You can go now."

Well, if this wasn't just a huge waste of time. The King of Shadows needed a lesson on how to properly kidnap someone. He'd wanted me to take up residence a moment before. Now he was throwing me out on the street. Not that I was upset. And as far as the Lyhtan was concerned, for the time being, I'd just have to watch my back. But Xander's ineptitude was to my benefit, so I didn't argue. I turned to leave, determined not to look lost, even though I hadn't the first clue how to get out of there. I stomped to the door and yanked it open.

"Aren't you forgetting something?"

Aren't you? I thought. *Like, oh, I don't know . . . how about some* information? God, I was tired of being jerked around. I wanted answers, damn it. Unknown marks and now Lyhtan attackers—and me, smack-dab it in the middle of it all. And if Xander thought I was going to bow or kiss his ring or anything like that on my way out, well, he was dead wrong. "Am I forgetting something?" I asked, turning to face him.

From the table at the far end of the room, he retrieved the case that held the katana *and* my money. "I don't appreciate having my gifts returned," he said.

I didn't hesitate for a second. I'd regretted my decision to give the sword back. I took the case and the cash from his hand and strode to the door without a parting word.

The house was full of creatures like me. I felt their presence though I didn't see a single one. The air stirred around me as the curious Shaedes brushed against me, too timid or else too good to show themselves.

I found my way out well enough. A long hallway led to a flight of stairs, and at the bottom was the exit. I didn't even warrant a good-bye as I opened the heavy oak door and walked out. My release wasn't exactly that. I'd be even more under Xander's thumb from that moment on. I ventured down a long walkway, past a sprawling lawn, and found Ty waiting for me near the street. He paced back and forth, fidgeting.

"Tyler, you really do have a screw loose, don't you?" I would have socked him if he hadn't smiled so brightly in my direction.

"Your wish is my command," he said in answer.

"What are you talking about, you idiot? You're lucky they didn't dismember you. How did you know I was here?"

Rather than give me the straight answer I wanted, he took me in his arms and laid a kiss on me that would have blasted the clothes right off my body if I'd been in my right mind. He trailed his fingers along my cheeks, down my neck.

"Do you have some kind of mental condition I don't know about?" I asked, breathless.

Tyler chuckled. "Come on." He wrapped his arm around my shoulder in a protective manner and glanced back toward the house as if declaring something to someone behind him. "I'm taking you home."

Chapter 10

My release from Xander's captivity had nothing to do with his ineptitude. Just as the actual kidnapping had nothing to do with him making me a prisoner. It did, however, have everything to do with teaching me a serious lesson. Taken with such ease, I hadn't stood a chance against Raif and Anya together. And if ordered to do so, they'd kidnap me again. Xander was telling me very plainly that no matter what I thought, I was his subject, his servant, and whatever else he wanted me to be. But more than that, it taught me I was far more vulnerable than I'd imagined.

In a rage, I took the katana and sliced clean through a watermelon. It rested on the kitchen counter undisturbed. If not for the juice bleeding from the line in the rind, you wouldn't have known I'd cut it at all. I flipped the top half over and dug through the juicy flesh with a spoon, shoveling the sweet fruit into my mouth while I continued to stew.

"Xander," I muttered under my breath. "Good-for-nothing pain in my ass." I shoveled another spoonful of watermelon into my mouth. "He's useless. All I want is a little fucking information, and he gives me the runaround." I shook my head and looked Tyler dead in the eye. "That Lyhtan should have killed me. Why didn't it? I'm tired of knowing absolutely nothing."

Tyler stared right back, a look of near pain flashing behind his hazel eyes. A crease marred the smooth skin of his forehead. As if he wanted to tell me something very important, but the words, for some reason, failed him. "If you want some answers," he began, "some *real* answers, go to The Pit and talk to Levi. Take plenty of cash; he won't talk to you unless it's worth his while."

"He's human!" I blurted, filling my mouth with more fruit to prevent another outburst.

"And he's got the information you need," Tyler said. "Just go before he closes for the night."

My mistrustful glare sent his gaze toward the floor. *That's right, Ty. You're being a little too helpful. What's up with that?*

"I'd like to go with you," he said, as if he could read my mind. "But this is probably something you should do on your own. Go. Before I change my mind and tag along. But after tonight, do me a favor and call me whenever you go out."

I stabbed the spoon into the melon I'd been gutting and secured the katana to my back. "Turn around," I said, and without asking why, Tyler turned his back. I retrieved a wad of cash from my safe and secured the false bricks back into place on the wall. If Levi had answers to my questions, he'd be worth every damn bill. "Thanks, Ty," I said as I headed for the elevator. "You can show yourself out, right?" Without waiting for a response, I ran toward the lift, scattering into shadow and disappearing from his sight.

Two a.m. saw the last of the die-hard partiers slowly winding down. Another hour, and Levi would have Tiny kicking them to the curb to find fresh venues for their nonstop drinking and revelry. It was the perfect time to talk. A small group of people lingered in the darkest corner of the bar, probably hoping their presence would go unnoticed for a while longer. Levi restocked the condiment containers with lemons, limes, cherries, and olives before stowing the tray in a refrigerator for the night, while a cocktail waitress counted out her tips. This early in the morning, Levi still looked college-boy fresh.

"It's a little late for you to be here, isn't it?" he asked with a smile.

"Or a little early, depending on your perspective," I said.

Levi laughed, poured me a gin and tonic, and slid it across the bar. "What's up?"

Ah, the quintessential bartender. Always ready and waiting with a willing ear. How to start? "Tyler sent me," I said, taking a tentative sip of my drink and settling onto a stool at the bar. "He said you're the question-and-answer man. And I'm in need of some answers."

Levi seemed to contemplate my statement and fixed me with a pointed stare. I fished a fifty-dollar bill from my pocket and slid it toward him. When I lifted my hand, he palmed the bill and shoved it into his pocket. "I know some things, Shaede girl. What do you want to know?"

Son of a bitch! That wily little bastard! I looked at Levi with a scowl. I'd always appreciated how comfortable he'd been with me, how he turned his head from my unusual nature and treated me like everyone else. Of course he did. It didn't have anything to do with him being a genuinely good guy. He was just in the loop.

"What are you?" I asked.

"Wow, that was a waste of a fifty," Levi said with a laugh. "You'd better be more careful about what kind of answers you're willing to spend your money on. I'm human. Nothing more; nothing less. Just a guy who knows some things. There aren't many humans who have the knowledge I'm privy to, but I'm not the only one. Anything else you'd like to ask?"

I fingered the hilt of my dagger. *Smart-ass.* I slid another fifty across the table. If I didn't watch out, this was going to be an expensive meeting. "Lyhtans. What do you know about them?"

Levi pocketed my money and smiled. "For starters, I wouldn't want to stumble across one of them unless I

was heavily armed and escorted. They're nasty, dangerous bastards."

"Why have I never seen one before?"

That question earned me a strange look from Levi.
Maybe he was just as blown away by my ignorance as
everyone else. *Fantastic*. "They can go around invisible
during the day. And if you ever saw one, you'd know it.
They don't look like any human or animal. At night, they
stick to the shadows. Lyhtans don't live in large groups.
They're pretty solitary. I don't know for sure, but I think
they live in the forests, parks—places where they can
hide above human eye level. Trees, bridges, cracks, and
crevices. Lyhtans stay above your head and well out of
sight. Honestly, though, I'm not surprised you haven't
seen one. It's been quiet around here for a while—as far
as the supernatural community goes. But a month or so
ago, there was a bit of a population explosion. Seems
Seattle is the new hot spot."

Well, that explained why I hadn't noticed Seattle's
nonhuman inhabitants: Until recently, there hadn't been
many. "How do Lyhtans make a living if they're so obviously not human?" Levi looked at the counter, and I
sighed, slapping down another fifty.

"They don't need money." Levi laughed. "If they
don't look human, they're not very likely going to be
shopping at the Gap. Lyhtans are more like animals than
people. They hunt for their food. They don't live in
houses. I don't even think they wear clothes, for that
matter. Hence, they don't need money."

Lyhtans might not shop at the Gap, but Levi sure did. I
had a feeling I'd be fronting the cash for his new wardrobe
too. I drained the gin and tonic and handed the glass to
Levi, along with another folded bill. "What do they eat?"

"Anything they can get their hands on," Levi said. He
paused to take a tray laden with discarded glasses from
one of the waitresses, and handed her an empty one.
"But they prefer fresh meat. Human or other."

"Sounds lovely."

"Yeah," Levi scoffed. "You know how spiders inject their prey with venom? Well, Lyhtans can do that too. It's in their teeth. Paralyzes the prey and dissolves its insides and bones into goo. Then they slurp it out like a smoothie, leaving an empty husk behind."

I thought of my Lyhtan visitor commenting on how it would like to suck my innards out through my nose, and my stomach heaved, threatening to send my gin and tonic back the way it came. I took three fifties, folded them in half, and handed them to Levi. "Can they be killed?"

"Yes, but don't ask me how to do it. I have no idea."

"Anything else I need to know about them?"

"They can compel a victim if they want to," Levi said, and I wondered if I imagined the shudder that seemed to shake his body. "I've only heard stories, so I don't know for sure. Maybe through their venom. Whatever it is gives them some sort of mind control over their prey. The ones they don't eat, that is."

"For what reason?"

Levi shrugged. "Who knows? Protection. Slavery. Meals on wheels. What would you do with a walking, talking zombie? One ready to do whatever you asked."

Hmmm. I wonder. "What else creeps around out there, Levi? If Shaedes and Lyhtans are running loose all over Seattle, there have to be more. Who are they? What are they?"

Levi plucked the bill I'd thrown him off the counter and pressed it back into my palm. He reached up and rang a bell above the bar, giving the lingering patrons a start, and hollered, "Last call!"

Grumbling replies answered, and Tiny stepped through the entrance, ready to send any hostile stragglers on their way. Levi grabbed a bottle of imported beer from the fridge and popped the cap before sending it rattling down the bar toward Tiny. He scooped it up in his paw of a hand and tipped it back, nearly draining the bottle in one swallow.

"Keep your money," Levi said, low. "You can't afford for me to answer *all* of your questions. There are more things in heaven and earth than are dreamt of in your philosophy."

Cheeky. College boy knew his *Hamlet.* "Horatio," I said in response.

"Huh?"

Well, well. Maybe I should be asking for a partial refund if I had to answer any of his questions. "'There are more things in heaven and earth, *Horatio*, than are dreamt of in your philosophy.' Hamlet is speaking to Horatio in that scene."

"Oh!" Levi smiled, his face glowing like an ad for high-end cologne. "Gotcha. Don't worry about what you don't know, Darian." Boy, did those words hit a nerve. Azriel had said that to me more times than I could count. It's easy for someone armed with knowledge to tell the ignorant one to relax. He offered me another refill and I took it gladly. A whole bottle of gin wasn't going to be enough to get me over this night. He checked his watch and grinned. "Just enjoy the ride."

I downed the drink in a single swallow, slamming the glass down on the bar. *Enjoy the ride.* Sure. Whatever. No one was trying to kill *his* ass. Or tell him bald-faced lies. But I couldn't deny that Levi was a fucking fount of supernatural information, and I wouldn't forget it. He was worth the cash.

"Thanks for the drinks, Levi," I said, pushing off my stool. "You're a good guy."

He flashed me a flirty smile, saluting me with my empty glass. "It's been a pleasure doing business with you, Darian."

Smart-ass. With a tilt of my head and a parting smile to Tiny, I left a little more informed and a lot more angry.

Chapter 11

The pristine blue sky graced Seattle with a shining sun. I took the beautiful weather as a sign, and decided to see if I could get myself into a little trouble. Ignoring Tyler's urging that I call him *whenever* I went out, I walked the sun-drenched sidewalks, hoping my Lyhtan friend would pay me a visit.

I'd passed the corner of Pike and Fourth when I noticed the *snick-snick-snick* like tiny insect legs scurrying on the sidewalk. Then I recognized the disturbance in the air around me. I tried not to let it see how the sound of its many facets of voice unsettled me. For a block or so, it merely called my name, taunting me with its nearness. I felt a waft of breeze now and again and recognized the dense air where it traveled beside me, unseen. Its stench sickened me, hanging over me like a cloud. I don't know how the Lyhtan would have smelled to a human or if it would have smelled at all. But I found its odor foul, sour, and nothing like the sweet scent of my own kind, or the delicious aroma that clung to Ty.

"My master wants you," it said in my ear.

I pushed the image of my insides melting into a slurpable goo to the back of my mind. Who was its master and why did he want me? I swallowed the fear threatening to overtake me. "Your master?" I goaded the thing. "I wouldn't boast about servitude. It makes you pathetic."

"As pathetic as you, Shaede?" Its grating voices used my own words against me. "Aren't you a slave yourself?"

"I am my own," I said.

"NO!" A blast of wind whipped at my face. "You belong to that scum of a king!"

"I am employed." I kept my voice steady, my gaze straight ahead, even as the other pedestrians on the sidewalk gave me a wide berth. I must have come off as batshit insane.

"You are purchased," it seethed. "You are a king's whore and nothing else."

Now, I've been called a few names here and there. Most of them didn't even cause me to bat a lash. *Whore* was not one of them.

I stopped dead in my tracks. "You are a cowardly piece of shit," I said in voice dripping with malice. "If you were half as tough as your talk, you'd show yourself so I could kick your ass and send your soul into the light forever."

The Lyhtan's many voices laughed in my ear, and I felt its presence close to me, like a bulldozer pressing against my body. "You speak with the arrogant supremacy of all Shaedes. But the eclipse will see to the end of your conceit."

Again with the eclipse talk? I guess this particular Lyhtan was an astronomy buff. I looked straight ahead. I didn't blink. I didn't breathe. My hand twitched as I thought of retrieving the katana from my back. Another gust of air pushed at me and then dissipated, followed by the familiar scurrying sound, only to leave me standing alone, trembling with rage.

The Lyhtan—and its master—*had* to be connected to the hit. Even Xander thought so. But the question was, Why would the mark want me? *The plot thickens,* I thought as I picked up my pace, walking the adrenaline out of my system and waiting for sunset to release me from pathetic uselessness.

When I made it back to my studio, I was unsurprised to find a note from Raif stuck to the wall beside the elevator door. The long knife he'd used to secure it there was a nice touch. He wanted me at the warehouse as soon as the sun set. I was almost excited for a night of training, despite my apprehension that he was going to kick my ass.

I showed up at the warehouse precisely at sunset. I didn't want to give Raif any excuses to be unduly rough. Though it went against my nature, I vowed to behave myself. The epitome of humble, I kept my gaze cast down, my ears open, and my mouth shut. And I worked my ass off for him.

By the end of that night's session, I was doing acrobatic maneuvers that would have made an Olympic gymnast jealous. "That was a sweet move, right?" I asked an indifferent Raif, who merely answered with a raised brow. "Come on. You have to admit, I'm much better than I was."

"I suppose it's good for a warrior to be arrogant or, at the very least, confident." He turned and swung. I parried the thrust, no longer needing both hands to stay his progress. "You're far from ready, though."

I leapt high and became nothing but a mist of dark air. Twisting in midflight, I became solid just as my boot made contact with Raif's arm. He spun away, deflecting my momentum, grunting as he gained his bearings. I landed and held the katana high.

"You're not big on compliments, are you?"

"I'll give you one when you deserve one," he said, jabbing at my midsection.

But my swordplay was impeccable, my speed and precision without flaw. Buckets of sweat ran down my back and my toes squished in my black boots. *Yuck.* I didn't give Raif one single excuse to punish me, and he didn't. He worked me raw. No one could say Raif wasn't thorough. It didn't matter to me that he was doing this more out of duty to Xander than out of any concern for my well-being.

I cleaned the blade of the katana before sheathing it. The sun would be rising soon, and so our session had come to an end. I sensed Raif's approach and I stiffened, waiting anxiously for him to make his move.

His voice was gentle in the empty warehouse, no longer barking orders, goading me, ridiculing me like a deranged drill sergeant. "Your wounds from the Lyhtan attack seemed to have healed."

Is he actually trying to be nice? Maybe I'd gained some ground with him. "I have a few on my legs, but for the most part, they're gone." I shrugged, acting tough for his benefit. "Xander thinks the Lyhtan is connected to the job. You have an opinion on that?"

"I think it's possible. More than possible, in fact. They are formidable," he said, reminding me of an ancient warrior, which he assuredly was. "And you're not anywhere near strong enough to go up against one yet. But if you train with me, you will be. When I'm done with you, only a fool would rise against you. In the meantime, do not let your guard down if you should come across a Lyhtan again."

"Too late," I said, guiding the katana into the sheath and driving it home. "It's got a crush on me. Followed me around for a while today."

Raif looked taken aback. That was new. "It didn't attack?"

"No, it was all about the name-calling today." I kept my demeanor calm, even. "I think it's building up for a big show."

"What did it say to you?"

"That its master wanted me. What do you think that means?" I wished to hell I knew. Up until I'd met Xander, I'd lived well under the radar. No one besides Ty had known anything about me. Suddenly, I'd become *very* popular. "Xander said under normal circumstances, a Lyhtan would try to kill me on the spot. Why the games?

So far, it's just playing with me. And why, exactly, does its master want *me*?"

Raif's eyes widened a fraction of an inch. But for him, it was as good as a gawking stare. "Don't go anywhere alone," he said after a moment.

Oh, great—another guy looking out for me. If I'd been any other girl, I might have been flattered. But I was *not* any other girl. "Raif, please. I can handle it. I don't need backup or bodyguards. What I'd rather have is answers."

"You can't handle *it*," he snapped.

Christ. Mr. Sensitive.

"Lyhtans are dangerous creatures. You'll need protection."

"I can protect myself," I said. "Just tell me how. Do I need a special weapon—kryptonite? Holy water?"

"I'll take care of it," Raif said, distant and thoughtful. "Lyhtans are usually quite predictable. I don't like that this one isn't. They don't take Shaede prisoners. They kill us. In the meantime, if you insist on going out during the day, take the Jinn with you."

"Um, the *what*?" I said.

"Your friend. What's his name—Tyler?"

"Oh, Ty. Well, I doubt he'd be much help. What's a Jinn anyway—some kind of Shaede slang for *human*?"

Raif gave me the strangest look. Like he wanted to say something. Instead, he graced me with a benign smile.

"What do you want me to use Ty for if I get in a pinch?" I really wanted to know what made Raif think he'd make a decent protector. "You want me to feed him to the Lyhtan or something?"

Raif laughed. It sounded foreign coming from him, like a bird meowing. He was too hard for laughter; it didn't suit him. "Let's say I'd be willing to bet Tyler would give you anything you want."

"O-kay," I said. "Whatever. Listen, Raif. I'm tired of being led around by a ring in my nose. I want in the loop. Otherwise, why the pomp and circumstance? I'm working my ass off, not knowing why or for whom. I don't want to fly blind anymore. I'm done guessing. Who's this guy Xander wants dead so bad?"

Raif sighed. "What if I told you he wants you to kill his son?"

Words stalled in my throat. *Jesus.* Xander didn't dick around, did he? "He wants me to kill his . . . son?"

"Yes," Raif said, his voice hinting at disappointment. "It's become . . . necessary, I'm afraid. It was a fact he wanted withheld until the last possible moment. He didn't want your conviction to waver."

Well, it wasn't going to win him any Father of the Year awards, but that was his business. Mine was killing. "I guess he's got his reasons. But why would it matter to me?"

"We agreed that the fewer people who know, the less the risk that it gets out. He doesn't want his people to find out, and I don't blame him. I've never met a better fighter than Alexander's son. Nor anyone more ambitious. Trust me when I say your training is necessary. I want you ready for anything."

Anything. Before I could ask him to elaborate on that, he was gone.

I made my way home in the hours before dawn. I took comfort from the fact that the Lyhtan would not be able to torment me until the sun crested the horizon. But after that, I was fair game. I opted to glide as a shadow while the waning light permitted. But as night faded quickly away, I wasn't strong enough to remain shrouded and was forced to walk in my solid form. I could have called Tyler or a cab to pick me up, but I wanted the time alone to think.

I spent the rest of the day in my studio, waiting for the

Lyhtan, which never came. The time spent anticipating an attack ticked by torturous and slow. Perhaps that was the plan. Mess with my head; keep me guessing; drive me crazy. It worked. I was going out of my fucking mind waiting for that damned thing to make its move. *Nothing*. Not even a whisper.

Tyler showed up later in the afternoon. It wasn't yet twilight; the sun had a couple of good hours left before it sank out of sight. I suppose he'd picked that opportune time to come for a reason. He wasn't alone.

He'd brought a girl with him. *Interesting*. I might have been jealous if she'd been his type, but she obviously wasn't. Meek, thin, and sallow, she shuffled her feet beside him, keeping her shoulders and arms hunched close to her body as if protecting a secret. Her mousy brown hair, stringy and not even a little lustrous, hung around her childlike form. Totally unremarkable. Only her blindness made me take notice.

Her milky blue eyes gave her away and creeped me right the hell out. And they didn't move—ever. If she heard a noise or sensed movement, her head would jerk and tilt. The motion of a small creature, alert in the presence of a predator. She stayed close to Tyler, moving with every shift of his body as if tied to him with a length of rope, urging her to stir whenever he did.

"You should have called first," I said. I didn't like company. Especially weird company.

Tyler shrugged, leaving *his* guest in *my* living room and following me into the kitchen. "I wanted you to meet Delilah," he whispered.

"Why?" I adopted his quiet tone, ignoring the girl. "What makes you think I would want to meet her?"

"Well, if you don't want *me* around during the day, I thought Delilah could give you a hand."

"Really?" I said. "Sorry, Ty, but she doesn't look good for much. What am I supposed to do with her?"

"I'm standing right here!" Delilah snapped. Well, she

had more-than-decent hearing and a fiery temper. Good. It was a bit of a shock, really, to hear such a strong, snarky voice come out of a weak and fragile body. I'd expected something much more demure.

"Sorry, kid," I said. "So . . . you tell me: What good are you?"

"I have a gift," she said. "I can see things you can't."

"Oh yeah? Like what?"

"I can see the Lyhtan during the day when it's invisible."

Okay, that got my attention. Not even Levi had supplied me with that little tidbit of information. "How do you know what they look like? Have you seen one before?"

"Yes."

A real conversationalist. We might get along after all. "Well, what did it look like?"

"Ugly," she said. "Ugly as sin."

Her assertion seemed to match Levi's. Maybe I'd finally stumbled across a couple of people who weren't intent on bullshitting me to death.

"They can't pass as human?" I asked, waiting to see if once again her answer would match Levi's.

"No. Not even a little."

"Can you see me right now?" I asked her.

"No. But if you were to take your other form, I could." *Hmm. More food for thought.*

"So, again, what help do you think you'd be to me? I can hear the Lyhtan. And I can sure as hell smell it. That's good enough."

"Is it?" she asked. "How do you fight a voice?"

Damn. She had a point. Even if Raif was successful in getting me something to defend myself with, I didn't want to hack away at the air, hoping I was getting a piece.

"You might be worth keeping around for a while," I admitted.

"I don't work for free," she said.

A woman after my own heart. "Fine. Ty can negotiate your fee."

A stiff nod sealed the deal, and Tyler led her back to the lift.

"I have to take her home," he said. "But I'll be back later."

"Don't bother," I told him. A suspicious glance was all he was going to get out of me tonight. I guess I wasn't the only "interesting" person Tyler hung out with. "I'm meeting Raif in an hour."

He turned and, without another word, left with weird little Delilah in tow.

Chapter 12

Raif stood in the center of the warehouse, staring at an empty bottle. I approached him slowly, wondering at his strange behavior, and wary that he was trying to trick me into distraction. His body looked too relaxed for a fighting stance, his concentration centered on the vessel. I paused a couple feet away, and Raif's eyes drifted shut. He brought the wide mouth of the bottle to his lips and expelled a slow, long breath. My own halted in my chest as I watched his breath become visible, dark and glistening. Thick like black mercury, the substance crept into the bottle, and when he had no more air to expel, he shoved a cork into the opening, trapping the murky sludge inside.

"Holy shit, Raif!" I said. "What in the hell is that?"

"A means to defeat sunlight." An unguarded smile dawned on his face, and I couldn't help but smile back.

I looked at the sludgy black goo in the bottle and back at his face. I didn't know what sort of expression I was wearing, but Raif looked back at me, his smile faded. He couldn't stand my lack of knowledge—and I didn't blame him.

"How did you do that?" I asked.

"I'm only one of a few of us who can produce that little bit of magic." Raif sounded proud of himself, and he had a right to be. *Damn.* "*Anam Scáth.* Soul Shadow." Raif shook the container of bottled shadows, presumably extracted straight from his soul. Must have been the deadly shadow Xander had been talking about. Amazing.

"I had no idea—" I bit back the words. No shit I had no idea. I didn't have a fucking *clue*. "I can't do anything like that," I said, still amazed. "Who else can do it?"

Raif raised a challenging brow. He had no intention of spilling that little secret. "Our individual abilities are connected to our lineage. Those of us closer to the roots of our family tree are blessed with certain . . . gifts. But you"—he gave me an appraising stare—"are nothing more than a leaf on that tree, twisting in the wind." I sensed a touch of Xander's arrogance in Raif's tone. An almost royal superiority that hinted of bias. He'd been spending a little too much time with his king.

"Well, aren't you special?" I drawled. Did I mention that I *hate* being treated like a second-class citizen? "So, tell me: What's that little parlor trick for anyway?"

"There are only two times in a day's cycle that Lyhtans and Shaedes can face each other as equals and you won't need this. Can you guess when that might be?"

I thought about the question for a moment. My brain kicked in to high gear; I didn't want Raif to be disappointed in me. Understanding dawned, and I couldn't believe I hadn't thought of it sooner. "Twilight and dawn."

Raif smiled his deadly smile. "You're catching on a little quicker, aren't you? We are both vulnerable to any attack in the gray hours and much easier to kill. We won't heal as quickly, and any wound could end up being fatal. In full day—or night, for that matter—we're each much harder to kill. I'd suggest beheading if you should come across a Lyhtan after twilight. A quick and effective kill. Necessary too. They're fast on their feet—faster than you could imagine, no matter the hour. If you should be attacked in full day, however, use the bottle."

I wondered how I should use it. Pour the contents on to the ground? Drink it? Bash it over the head? Ask the Lyhtan to drink it? But I didn't think such an evil and calculating creature would simply take the offering and swallow it down. I laughed.

"What's so funny?" he asked.

"How do I use this?" I took the bottle, swirling the contents before I stuffed it into my coat pocket.

"Just pop the cork." Raif drew his sword, tested the sharp edge with his thumb. "The shadows will do the rest."

Okay, so play-by-play instructions weren't exactly Raif's thing. Sounded simple enough, though.

One: See a Lyhtan.

Two: Pop the cork.

Three: Watch the shadowy action go to work. Kind of like a shampoo ad. If shampoo were deadly.

"Delilah told me that Lyhtans are ugly as sin," I said, shucking my coat and tossing it over a bench near our practice area. No need to mention Levi. I didn't want to expose him to any undue scrutiny. "And in my opinion, we're all pretty good-looking. I've been thinking of the whole, good-guy, bad-guy, beautiful-ugly, light-dark thing. Which are we? Good or bad?"

Raif snorted. Definitely disgusted. "We are nothing but what we are," he said, very enigmatic. "Who's Delilah?"

"A friend of Tyler's . . . or something. She's blind, but she can see things—invisible things. Like the Lyhtan during the day."

"So he brought you this Seer to help you spot your attacker during the day?"

"I guess so. I could break her with one hand, she's so tiny. I don't think she's good for much else."

"You do keep strange company, don't you?"

I didn't have much time to contemplate his question because his sword was swinging toward my face.

My skills improved. I'd become faster, stronger, more adept. A warrior Shaede, Raif had made me a killing machine—lethal and unapologetic. And, in my opinion, ready for anything.

"No, not yet," Raif said.

"Why not? You're keeping something from me, aren't you?" I shouted in the empty building.

Raif shook his head. "Your lack of patience is what's going to get you killed," he said in his dead-calm tone. "You can't charge ahead like a young bull on this one. You are an assassin. Let your stealth be your greatest weapon. Be patient, and your prey will come to you."

"When?" I asked.

"Soon," he said.

"You know what, Raif?" I said, my anger boiling, "I wish you'd—"

Raif clamped a hand tight over my mouth. "*Shhh.* Don't you *ever* mutter that word in my presence."

"Wha wrd," I mumbled behind his hand.

"Wish."

He slowly removed his hand from my mouth, as if afraid I'd actually say it. "You want to elaborate on that?" I asked.

"No. Just watch your mouth."

Again, I walked home in the hours before morning with a thousand questions, the least of which being the strange weapon that was supposed to protect me from the Lyhtan. Why not a sword—a magic sword? Wasn't there supposed to be a magic sword that kills us? Why not one for the Lyhtans too? And now that I thought about it, when was I going to get a magic sword? I'd need one if I was going to kill Xander's son. Instinctively, I reached my hand to my back and caressed the hilt of the katana. Maybe I'd had a magic sword all along. . . . But would Raif let me train with something that could actually kill him? I was a walking question machine, spitting out queries faster than my brain could fathom an answer. I made it to my building and found Delilah on the sidewalk, waiting for me.

"Delilah," I said in greeting.

"Hi!" she said in that self-assured voice that was an oxymoron to her appearance.

"See anything creepy hanging around?"

"Not yet," she said. "Can I come up?"

I grabbed her hand and helped her to the apartment. But truth be told, she didn't need much help. She didn't suffer from her lack of actual sight. First impressions can be misleading.

Delilah had a strange sense of the world around her. I guess I should have anticipated as much. After only a single tour of the place, she knew her way around my apartment as if she'd lived there for years.

"Have you known Ty long?" I asked, setting the bottle of shadows on my kitchen counter.

She took a seat in front of the TV, listening to one of those cheesy court shows. I pretended not to mind. "I've known Tyler for *ages*," she said.

"Huh." *Ages* couldn't have been too long; she looked barely old enough to be out of high school. "How old are you, Delilah?"

"Older than you'd think."

God, how I hated cryptic answers. It seemed as though everyone around me had taken a class in beating around the bush. "And you're not a run-of-the-mill psychic human, right?"

"Nothing gets past you." Delilah laughed, and I sent a glare her way that would have given anyone else a moment of heart failure. But she didn't flinch. My dirty looks were a wasted effort.

So Tyler had at least one more supernatural friend than I'd thought. Not counting the very human, *very* informed Levi. How many more did he have stashed away for a rainy day? Thinking of the way I'd wandered the city, ignoring all of my better senses, made me sick. I'd been surrounded for years and stuck my head in the sand. *How very smart of you, Darian. Christ.* "When did you see the Lyhtan?"

Her lips curved into a slight smile, making her look even more waifish. "I've seen them more than once.

They're not very agreeable characters. They like to create havoc wherever they go. And they're nasty too. Mean, masochistic beasts. When I see one, I run the other way."

"Run?" I couldn't picture her running anywhere.

"I'm not weak," she said. "You should know looks can be deceiving."

"I guess you're right," I said. I didn't exactly look like your average dangerous killer, though how she knew that, I have no idea.

"What do you have planned for today?" Delilah asked.

"I've been up all night. I *plan* on sleeping."

"Do you care if I hang around while you sleep? Tyler insisted that I stick to you like glue during the day."

Tyler. What an annoyance he was becoming. Annoying and somehow . . . endearing. "Suit yourself," I said, heading for the bathroom. I wasn't going to be responsible for her. If she got herself into trouble from hanging around, that was her problem. "I'm taking a shower. Then I'm going to bed."

Delilah cranked up the volume on the TV. I didn't give two shits what she did, as long as she stayed out of my hair.

I didn't linger in the shower. I staggered into the single room of my studio, ready to hit the sheets and say good-bye to this miserable excuse for a day.

"Hey, Darian . . ." Delilah said.

"Hey, what?" I grumbled as I fell facedown on my bed.

"What's in the bottle you brought with you? It sounds like it's full of tar."

Blind, schmind. Delilah didn't miss a beat. "Raif gave it to me," I said. "It's supposed to be some kind of anti-Lyhtan serum or something."

"Cool," she said, just like an enraptured kid. Then asked shrewdly, "Who's Raif?"

"My teacher, sort of."

"Hmm. Well, I hope I get to see that stuff in action."

"Delilah," I muttered, only half paying attention. "You are one weird chick."

I heard her giggles mingling with the raucous court-show guests cheering for the verdict. I blocked her out and found a restful sleep.

After weeks of the same boring routine, I decided to skip class, so to speak. A training-free night was what I needed. I called Raif—it always cracked me up to call his cell phone and think of him standing there, talking in his Robin Hood–meets-Legolas outfit—and requested the night off. He let me off the hook easier than I expected. Maybe he was sick of me. The sun had set, Delilah had left, and I wasn't under house arrest. So I went to The Pit.

I walked the darkened streets, my sensitivity to everything around me heightened. I paid more attention to the smells lingering on the air and the way the breeze felt against my skin. At one point, I'd felt a presence near me and whipped around, only to see a flash of golden fur duck into an alley across the street. But the creature was much too large to merely be another stray dog. I chalked up the sighting to an overeager imagination and continued on my way.

The usual crowd of hopefuls had queued up outside the door. I greeted Tiny, who stood at the head of the line, holding the fate of their social lives in his hands. He was on a total power trip. Cute.

"Hey, Darian," he greeted. "Haven't seen you in a while."

I flashed him my most earnest and sexy smile, and he pulled the red velvet rope aside to let me in. Grumbles filtered from the line behind me. I ignored their complaints, sliding into the packed club to lurk in the shadows for the night.

I ordered a drink and took up my place in the farthest, darkest corner. Sipping from the glass, I watched
the humans come and go, hooking up, getting shot down,
dancing, flirting, drinking. Their actions so normal, it
made me feel a momentary sorrow for my own lost humanity. But I shook it off. Even when I'd been a regular
human girl, I hadn't enjoyed the freedoms women had
now. All the *boo-hooing* in the world wasn't going to
change the fact that I wasn't one of them anymore, and
I never would be.

I faded into my shadow self, blending with the hazy,
dark air. No one noticed, too wrapped up in themselves
to pay attention to my corner of the club. I felt better this
way, maybe a little more voyeuristic. I didn't go there for
any other reason, so what did it matter if I watched in my
solid form or under the cover of darkness? A woman,
laughing and swaying in the arms of her date, leaned in
to bestow a kiss to his cheek. He smiled and squeezed
her tight against his body before swooping down to return the favor. Wrapped up in each other, they kissed
and laughed, talked and swayed. A stab of jealousy shot
through my gut as I watched them. The building could
have fallen down around them and they wouldn't have
noticed. I would never have that. I was too hard, too
cynical, and too deadly for soft emotion and affection. I
was fire and passion, but not love.

I'd had enough, so I passed from shadow to my human form and made my way to the door. Tiny watched
me go in; he'd wonder if I never came out.

"Goin' home, Darian?" He asked me the same question every time. What would he say if I answered with,
"Nope, going out to assassinate some asshole, Tiny"?

"You know it." What else was I going to say? "See ya
later."

"Be careful," he said. "I heard there's been some people go missin' around here the last few nights. Stay away
from dark alleys."

"Promise," I said, flashing a reassuring smile. What he didn't realize: Dark alleys were *exactly* my thing.

I traveled in shadow form, crossing the darkest places I could find. I didn't have anything to fear; I was safe in the dark. At least, that's what I thought. The sounds of a struggle traveled to my ears, and I remained shrouded, approaching the source of the scuffle with caution. At first, all I noticed were a pair of legs jutting out from behind some battered metal trash cans. But as I allowed myself to take in the scene, I realized this was not just some homeless person asleep in the alley.

A long, lanky body hovered over the poor guy, its wide mouth fastened on his waist near the stomach. Devouring its meal with indulgent grunts and moans, the creature pulled away, only to paw at its bloody mouth before dipping down and resuming the feast. *Shit.* Levi hit the nail right on the head. Sounded just like a goddamned smoothie being slurped through a straw. Too horrified to do anything but stare, I watched as the Lyhtan brought its head up from its dinner.

"I feel you, Shaede," an unsettling set of voices said.

I froze. Through my fear, I forced myself to become corporeal and face the source of those grating, seething voices. And let me tell you, Delilah wasn't kidding about ugly.

The Lyhtan couldn't have looked farther from human. It couldn't even pass as animal. Tall, at least seven feet by my estimation, it resembled a praying mantis more than anything. Long, lanky arms and legs connected to a thin, elongated torso. It hunched at the shoulders, giving it a stooped appearance with a distended stomach. It was naked as the day it was . . . born? Made? Created? Slimy greenish drool leaked from its mouth, tinged with its victim's blood, causing its sharp, pointed teeth to glisten in the dark night. Glowing amber eyes bulged from its pale and drawn face. A shudder of revulsion passed through me. I reached for my pocket, for the bottle that was home on my counter. Could I have even used the bottled shadows at night? Fuck if I knew. I was unarmed, with not even a container of magic sludge to help me. *Shit.* Shit.

But a coward I'm not, no matter how on edge I felt. Making sure to keep my distance from the creature, I took a step back; I didn't intend to be its next liquid snack. I had no idea if this Lyhtan was my personal tormentor, but I figured I'd find out soon enough.

"Who are you, Shaede?" it asked in its many voices.

Well, this one wasn't mine. I didn't know if I should be relieved or not. "What do you care who I am?"

"I don't know you," it seethed. "Are you one of his?"

"One of his . . . who?" I asked. "I don't know you either, but what difference does that make? Who do *you* belong to?"

The creature laughed, and my spine seemed to lose some of its starch. I reminded myself I was the stronger opponent. It was night and he was the weak one. The Lyhtan crept closer.

A menacing hiss issued from its jagged-toothed mouth, and it crouched, looking ready to strike at any moment. It edged toward me. I stood, virtually defenseless, with only my stealth to aid me. I could have passed into shadow and left the Lyhtan behind me, but my curiosity burned. "I wish I had a sword right now," I said under my breath.

Something moved behind me, and Tyler's voice murmured close to my ear, "Your wish is my command."

I didn't have time to think about the hows and whys of what happened. The handle of the katana slid into my hand. I struck in a flash, passing into shadow and reappearing feet from my attacker. I spun and swung the samurai sword with all of my strength.

A screeching gasp burst from the Lyhtan's mouth, like a great swarm of people crying out in agony. I sliced through its midsection as if it were made of butter. It doubled over, clutching at its gut, which oozed a thick, orange-tinted blood, and screamed words in a language I couldn't understand. The wound began to heal as I watched, and the creature looked up, the drool running in a stream from its ugly mouth. Drawing a rasping breath, it turned and jumped, using the buildings of the alley for momentum as it bounced from wall to wall, ever upward, and fled into the dark with a speed that belied its clumsy form. Another grating scream pierced the night, echoing and then dissolving into eerie silence.

Tyler's footsteps shuffled behind me, and I swung the sword around, its tip barely brushing his chest as he stopped dead in his tracks. He smiled at me.

"How did you get here?" I asked.

His lazy smile grew, and he tried to take a step closer. I pressed the sword's tip closer to his heart. "No," I said, staying his progress. "No more games. I want an answer. Now."

"I told you: Everything is changing."

Some explanation. The Lyhtan's blood glistened like wet rust on my blade. I paused to look at it, disgusted, confused, and angry. I looked back at Tyler's unchanging face. "What does *Jinn* mean?"

"It roughly translates to 'genie,' " Tyler said.

Fuck me. Genie? "Like the kind that lives in a lamp?" I asked.

"Yes and no." He shrugged. "I grant the occasional wish."

I couldn't take it. One more shock and I would have fallen down dead without anyone's assistance. I became one with the darkness and left Tyler where he stood.

Chapter 13

Delilah waited by my building, looking like a potted plant wilting under the morning sun. Maybe she was getting as tired of our little arrangement as I was. We rode the lift in silence, but she cocked her head in my direction. Perhaps she sensed the questions forming on my tongue.

"Spill it," I growled. "Everything you know."

"If I tell you everything I know, we'll be here for a year," Delilah said, plopping down in front of the TV. It drove me crazy the way she talked and channel surfed at the same time.

"I'm not in the mood for your smart-ass answers," I said. But she was right. Good Lord, between her and Levi it would cost a year of my time and a million dollars in fifties to properly educate me. "Tell me about Tyler. When you said you've known him for ages, you weren't kidding, were you? Exactly how old are you?"

"Older than you by about ten centuries," she said.

"And Tyler?" I asked, dreading the answer.

"Older than me."

My cheeks flushed with anger and humiliation. Here I'd been, so superior in my otherness, boasting and tossing casual threats, demeaning Ty with *human* this and *human* that. And he literally had *lifetimes* on me. He'd let me make a fool of myself over and over again, never letting me in on his little secret.

"What about the wish granting. How does it work?"

"Well." Delilah paused to listen to the verdict on her

court show. "It's not like the stories. You don't come across a lamp or bottle and give it a good rub. He's not a slave, per se. But he can tie himself to someone if he wants to. Once he's chosen the bond, he becomes that person's sworn protector, and he only grants that person's wishes. No others until you break the bond. His loyalty is uncompromising."

"How do you break it?" Delilah's attention drifted back to the television, but she heard me.

"There are no magic words or rituals, Darian. You simply end it."

Kind of like a breakup, I guessed. "So if I say, 'Tyler, I don't want you as my genie. Go away,' he has to do as I ask?"

"Pretty much," Delilah said. "But why would you want to? If it's in his power, he'll help you any way he can."

"Are there restrictions?" I asked. "I mean, could I wish for world peace, a billion dollars, or a new car—and just get it?"

"There are restrictions," Delilah said, "but you'll have to ask Tyler about that. I'm no Jinn, and I don't know the rules."

"What are *you*?"

"I'm a Seer, plain and simple. More to the point, I'm an Oracle, but as few can afford that service, it goes unused for the most part."

"So . . . you see the future?"

"Sometimes."

"Can you tell me mine?"

Delilah laughed. "Sorry, it doesn't work like that. You have to make a sacrifice. Like I said, few can afford the price."

"You've been around the block a few times. You know all about *us*, don't you?"

Delilah turned her attention from the TV and threw

down the remote. "If you're talking about Shaedes, sure, I know about them."

I hated feeling vulnerable. And this moment proved no less unsettling. I had once been strong, confident, and self-assured. Now I was weak, self-conscious, and unsure. I had no sense of identity. A creature without race or allegiance. Even more of a nothing than I was by my very nature.

"Delilah," I ventured, "how do you kill a Shaede? Is it with a magic blade?"

Her head jerked in the avian fashion that made her look so wild. Pity poured off her like rotten honey, and it made me sick. I didn't want pity. I wanted answers.

"There are stranger and stronger bonds than the one you have with Tyler," Delilah said. "A bond with one of your own is what gives you power over life and death."

Fear congealed into a sour lump in the pit of my stomach. I could barely comprehend the words as she spoke them. Here I was, nearly one hundred years since my making, and tiny, strange Delilah was laying out who I was more plainly than Azriel or Xander ever had.

"A parent and child, husband and wife, maker and made: These are all the strongest of bonds, and the only thing that will lend you dominion over one of your own. It's not that strange. These bonds are strong no matter your creed."

"No matter the time of day?" I ventured.

"Anyplace, anytime, anywhere," she said.

Xander. That son of a bitch. He'd known all about me; he hadn't stumbled across me. My skills weren't impressive or unique. I held power over someone he wanted dead, and I was the only one who could deliver the blow. No magic blade would do the job, no weapon designed specifically to carry out our executions. *I* was the weapon. Me and me alone.

"Azriel," I whispered in disbelief. "He's alive."

"Who's that?" Delilah asked.

"My maker. I can kill him after sundown. Even in his shadow form. No one else. Is that right?"

"Yep," she said. "No one else. Well, that's not exactly true," she said, tapping a finger on her bottom lip. "His father, mother, or maker could kill him as well. A wife, if he'd been sworn to one. It's a real tangled web when you get right down to it. Like a family tree of death." She giggled, which put her weirdness factor through the roof, and then she turned up the volume on the TV.

"And the Lyhtan?" I spoke over the noise. "Raif said we are equals in the gray hours. Can we kill one another then?"

"As far as I know," Delilah said after some consideration.

I slumped down on my bed, dead tired and emotionally spent. I'd let Xander play me like a fiddle, all because the words sounded pretty coming out of his mouth. I'd never thought of him as anything more than a man. But he was, and had always been, the king, and I was simply his pawn. Not a subject, not even a woman. Just something to use. I could be discarded as easily as I'd been picked up.

The sour feeling of betrayal in my stomach bubbled up and lodged near my sternum. Without thinking, I let out a primal scream. It felt good to vent the rage trapped in my chest. I ached a little less by releasing that scream. Delilah didn't even flinch. She watched her shows as if I weren't there, oblivious to my display of temper.

I jumped from the bed like it was on fire and tucked a dagger into my belt. Swinging a black jacket over my shoulders, I stalked toward the kitchen.

"Where are you going?" Delilah asked, saccharin sweet.

"Out." I didn't have the patience for more than the one word.

"I'm supposed to go with you when you go out," she called after me.

I paused at the counter and stared at the bottle of anti-Lyhtan goo, wondering if I should stuff it in my pocket. I didn't. "No. I don't need you tagging along right now. Stay here, Delilah," I said. "I'll be back in a while."

"Tyler's not going to be happy," she said.

I stalked to the lift and shut the gate in front of me. "Do I look like I give a flying fuck?" I asked.

"I don't know how you look," I heard her say as the lift began its descent. "But you sure don't sound like you do."

I stared from the street toward the iron gate of Xander's place. It looked less menacing in the light of day. The house sat deep in Capitol Hill, which was a better place than Belltown to remain obscure. The area reminded me of the Haight-Ashbury district of San Francisco. Grunge met grandeur, and the seedy, dirty, and half-crazy mingled with the haughty, spiffy, and wealthy every day. Of course, wasn't that the case almost everywhere? Old cities were the perfect melting pots. Ever expanding, always making room, modern architecture never steamrolling over classic elegance. Flashy condos felt right at home next to early-1900s Victorians. A twelve-million-dollar mansion could sit beside a run-down motel and it didn't bother anyone. Well, maybe except for real estate agents. But social variety made it easy to hide, and I had no doubt Xander had picked the area for its eccentricity.

The winding driveway was bordered by manicured grass and tall shrubs, and the entire property had been barricaded by a tall stone wall. I bypassed the iron gate, complete with guard station, scaled the wall, and dropped to the lawn on the other side. I didn't exactly want my presence announced. If I'd been bolder, I would have stomped right up the driveway. But since meeting Xander, I'd lost a little of my pluck.

I found a set of double doors toward the back of the house and used them to gain entrance. The house wasn't quiet or noisy; it just bore the normal sounds of day-to-day bustling. And though I was sure I'd be outnumbered if it came down to a fight, somehow I didn't care.

A daytime wraith, I crept through the many rooms of the ground story with an assassin's stealth until I found what I was looking for. Xander sat at a desk in a large office, his head bent low over something of interest. I moved to the doorway and took the dagger blade side in my hand. With speed and precision, I pulled back and threw. The point buried itself in the wood inches from his head. How I missed, I wasn't sure, because I aimed for the middle of his high-and-mighty forehead.

I pitched forward as a heavy foot made contact with the back of my knee. I twisted as I fell, landing facing my assailant. Reaching out, I grabbed the offending foot and turned it sharply. Anya's startled form flew in an acrobatic roll before she crashed to the floor beside me. I reached an arm to the ceiling and jerked, bringing the full force of my elbow down on her chest. I owed her a hundred times over, and payback is a bitch.

My training finally proved useful. I rocked back and kicked hard, propelling myself from the floor to a standing position. Dragging her sorry-ass, leather-covered body beside me, I brought up my knee and sunk it into Anya's stomach, eliciting a grunt, before I threw her back and kicked again, this time at her ribs. It was when I reached to pull at a hank of her long, flowing hair that I felt a soft touch at my shoulder.

"Stay your hand, Darian." *Raif. Damn him.* "You won't get what you're after by beating her."

"Maybe not," I said, "but it sure feels good."

I had forgotten about Xander, having become so enthralled with giving Anya a proper beating. But I noticed from the corner of my eye that he stood. As Raif asked, I refrained from further damaging Anya's not-so-gentle form. That's not to say that I didn't accidentally stomp on her instep when I brought my foot down.

"Who's the mark?" I shouted at Xander. "I want his name."

"Darian . . ." he said in his infuriatingly soothing voice.

"Who?" I screamed this time. My chest heaved with my breath, and I felt the sting of angry tears behind my eyes. The rush of rage through my body was tangible; I heard it in my ears and tasted the gall of it on my tongue. "Azriel!" I shouted. "It's him, isn't it? There's no magic weapon but me! *You* are a liar!"

I didn't care what Raif thought of me at that moment, and I sure as hell didn't care what Anya thought. I was too pissed to care about anything. "Azriel isn't dead, is he?" So many lies . . . first from the very one who made me, and now from a king, his *father*. I couldn't breathe, I was drowning in lies. "He's alive! All this time, you knew and you said *nothing*?"

"Leave me with her," Xander said. Raif helped Anya from the floor. The door closed behind them, and I was left alone with the King of Deception.

Rounding the desk, he came to stand before me. He looked deep into my eyes and laid his hands on my shoulders. He sighed.

"Don't," I said, bringing my arms underneath his, brushing his hands from me. "I know what you're doing, and it's not going to work this time. I don't care how beautiful you are or how sweet your voice sounds in my ears. I'm done with you, and I refuse to allow you to seduce me into doing anything for you. Magic blade, my ass."

He took a step back. "I never told you there was a magic blade. That was Azriel's lie. My only sin is that I withheld information. I never played you false."

A lie by omission was still a lie in my book. My anger boiled to the surface again. "Pretty talk," I said, "and nothing else. You never played me false, but you played me, all right. Not anymore, though. You can go to hell."

"I need you," he said.

"Fuck you," I answered.

"He's banded with the Lyhtans and is gathering an army. He plans to overthrow me, and if he succeeds, it will be the end of our existence as we know it."

"So what?" I said. "I've existed for a century without *any* of you. Nothing will change for me."

"Oh no?"

"How was I made?" I asked the question, determined to get an answer this time.

Xander looked to the floor. It was the first time I saw him truly uncomfortable. "Those of us who are strong enough can make another. I know of only a few that can do it, Azriel being one of them. An exchange is made between two souls, creating an ethereal connection that changes you forever."

"How," I said. "Tell me how."

"In essence, he would have taken a part of your soul into himself, and in return, given you a bit of his own to replace the empty space."

"In essence?" I shrieked. "Bullshit! I want details."

"He might have seduced you. It usually happens during moments of passion, such as love, longing, or even anger. It would have been a simple act, though not simple to perform. With just the joining of your mouths, bodies, spirits, you would have opened your heart to him, and that's all it would have taken. A window of opportunity for him to extract that small piece and replace it with something of himself. It is not only physical in nature, but metaphysical as well. It would have taken a moment of strong emotion for the exchange to happen."

"That's the dumbest thing I've ever heard," I said, turning my back on him. "You're trying to tell me an exchange on a spiritual level effected a physical change. It's impossible." I would have fallen for a bite or drinking blood. Hell, an STD would have made more sense than soul exchanging.

"I understand your skepticism," he said. "It's a very rare occurrence. I know of only three who have been made, including you. You must have been particularly receptive to the change."

"Receptive . . ."

"Receptive, meaning that maybe your life wasn't a wonderful thing and you longed for a new life, a different existence. Or maybe you were truly in love with him."

I snorted in disgust. "You still didn't tell me how it was done."

"At night, in his shadow form, he would have passed through your body. The exchange is made at that moment. What do you remember from the last night you were human?"

"Not much," I said. "I remember him, the brief time we were together before it happened, and the time we were together afterward. But of the actual transformation, I remember nothing."

"There must have been a shadow on your soul, Darian." His voice slithered around me in false, empty warmth. "You were a shadow of a human; that's why it was so easy for you to turn. You were one of us before you ever realized it."

I turned to face him. I hated him more now than ever. He'd managed to draw me from obscurity, connect me to others like me. And I'll be damned if I didn't, in some deeper part of me, crave to belong to something. Because of that I knew—against my better judgment—that I would stay this course.

"Will you do this terrible thing for me?" he asked, taking my hands in his.

I looked away. "I'm leaving now," I said, low. "I'll meet Raif tomorrow night, and I want *double* my fee. And after this is done, I don't want to see you again."

Xander drew a deep breath. I cut him off before he could speak, saying in a strong and determined voice, "I wish Tyler was here to pick me up."

Tyler never disappoints.

Delilah was gone when we got back to my studio. Tyler must have sent her home. It's not like I missed her. I'd never thought her skinny ass would have been much good for anything anyway.

The ride up the elevator had been nearly intolerable. Ty's gaze flitted back and forth from the floor to my face and back again. Though he didn't say a word, I had the feeling volumes of prose sat on the tip of his tongue. I'm sure he wanted to talk—share oodles of feelings, clear the air. But I didn't have it in me. I'm not big on sharing or feeling, for that matter. Plus, I was still mad that he'd kept his true nature from me for so long. So the last thing I expected to do was go after him like a carb-starved dieter after cake.

Which is exactly what I did.

He waited in the lift and stepped out right after me. His delicious smell floated on the air, his body close enough for me to feel a static tingle in the space between us.

My mind raced with almost incoherent thought. Memories flooded my consciousness, some from my human life and others from my Shaede existence. I thought of Azriel more than anything, and a hole opened up where my heart should have been, threatening to swallow whatever was left of my soul.

I couldn't stand it. The pain, the memories, the heartache were too much. I'd gotten used to my gray, stoic self. I'd been unfeeling for so long, the walls I'd put up began to crumble, and I thought I would start screaming and never stop.

My gaze absorbed the cold, unwelcome studio. Everything about it spoke of detachment. The white furnish-

ings and cold brick walls. The polished concrete
countertops, sparsely covered and shining with an anti-
septic quality that made me shudder. It was more than I
could take. To see what I had become, what I had reduced myself to . . .

I turned, and Ty beamed at me. It was one of his huge,
unguarded smiles that usually made me want to slap his
face and then strip off all his clothes. The joy of that expression seeped into my pores, and all I wanted was to
be taken away from my cold, unfeeling nature for a little
while, at least.

I rushed to him, twining my fingers through the thick
locks of his hair, and kissed him. My mouth pressed hard
against his, and I ran my tongue along the cool skin of his
parted lips. His arms hung limp at his sides, and I guided
them around the small of my back so I could press my
body closer. Slowly, I traced my hands up his arms and
shoulders, and my mouth tasted the flesh at his neck. His
scent, the delicious smell that had no comparison, intoxicated me, and I inhaled deeply at his throat before
biting at the skin there. He sucked in his breath between
his teeth, and I felt his hands leave my back to wrap
around my arms just above my elbow. He gently pushed
me away.

"No, Darian," he said.

I lunged toward him, determined to have my way.
"What do you mean *no*? You've been after me for
months, and now no?"

"You're angry and hurt, and I don't want to be some
kind of revenge screw so you can feel better about something."

"Why are you saying this?" I demanded. "Revenge
screw? You're acting like I'm using you to get back at a
boyfriend or something."

"Isn't that what you're doing?"

His calm answer pushed me closer to the edge.
Couldn't he just shut up and *act* like a selfish, sex-starved

man for an hour or so? "You think I'm doing this because of Xander? You think I'm trying to make him jealous or something?"

"No," he said, too calm. "I think you're doing this because of Azriel."

"Get out!" I yelled at the top of my lungs.

I didn't even have to wish to make him leave. He turned, gone before I could beg him to come back.

Chapter 14

Raif didn't say anything to me about my outburst at Xander's. We trained like we usually did, but Raif decided to quit early, which was out of character for his never-say-die attitude. He looked uneasy. *Great.* Apparently, he *was* going to bring up my outburst.

"War is serious business, Darian," he said. "And we are at war."

"I'm not at war," I insisted. "I'm hired help. I have only one job to do."

Raif laughed, and it always sounded strange coming out of his hard-lined mouth. "You are a very stubborn woman. Do you know that?"

I shrugged. "I've been called worse."

"I want you to know I was never in favor of information being withheld from you. It was my king's decision. I must abide by his ruling."

Touching. Raif was reaching out, albeit a little stiffly. "I appreciate that," I said. "But I don't like being played with. I'm not just going to sit here and pretend that it's all water under the bridge, because it isn't. I've been lied to long enough, and I don't want to be lied to again."

"I'll level with you," Raif said, "because I believe a soldier must know what he is fighting for if he is to commit to battle. Azriel *is* Alexander's son. He's been in exile for almost a hundred years. That was the last time he tried to rise against his father. Obviously, he didn't succeed, and his punishment was banishment. He was kept comfortable, as was his due—under guard, of course."

Sure, of course. Why the hell not?

"A few months ago, he managed to evade the detachment Xander had assigned to watch over him. He came straight to Seattle, so naturally we followed. Curious as to what might have drawn his interest, we came to only one conclusion: He came for you."

If he'd kicked me to the curb all those years ago, leaving me convinced he'd been killed, I couldn't imagine he was looking for a lover's reunion. "Maybe he just missed the city? He always loved it here. Besides, it's not like he came out of hiding to take me out to dinner or anything, Raif."

Raif shrugged as if he weren't interested in my opinion. "Either way, he must be dealt with."

"So why kill him now?" I asked. I couldn't imagine a father signing his son's death warrant, but Xander had done it easily enough. "Why not lock him up, keep him under house arrest like you did before?"

"How do you suppose we do that?" Raif asked. "He managed to escape once. He'd do it again."

"What about the rope you used on me?" I suggested. "I couldn't move or transform. We could tie him up with it."

"Lyhtan hair," Raif said. "That's what the rope was made of. He's become much too dangerous to be simply restrained or imprisoned. No. He's crafty. Deadly. The best student I ever trained. And you'll have to be better than him if you want to beat him at his own game."

I *got* deadly. In fact, I considered myself a tad deadly. But *dangerous* is never good. "Dangerous how?" I asked, banishing the image of being bound with Lyhtan hair from my mind.

"Three of my best men were ambushed just before dawn yesterday," Raif said. "They were torn limb from limb."

"By Lyhtans?"

Raif nodded. "I assume so. We're tracking them now,

but they're not so easy to find. Elusive creatures"—he almost spat the word—"and violent to an extreme."

"And you're *sure* Azriel commands them?"

"Yes. He sent an envoy a month ago."

"What was the message?"

"'Surrender the throne,'" Raif said.

"Nothing else?"

"Nothing."

I had to admit, it sounded like Azriel. He didn't mince words. "What does he want with Xander's throne?"

"What does any usurper want?" Raif asked. "Power. Think, Darian: Kingdoms are not often inherited in our world—not when the king might live for millennia. Azriel would be nothing more than Xander's son for what might as well be an eternity. A crown prince, of course, but an impotent figurehead. Azriel craves that which he might never have: a king's crown upon his head and the power to command those under his rule. And who better to help him in his endeavors than an army of Lyhtans? Vicious killers"—Raif paused and massaged his temples between his thumb and fingers—"and easy to control."

"But why would he want me?" I asked. Did he, perhaps, hope to kill me before I could kill him? I wondered what death would be like for a Shaede. Would I wander like a spirit, confined to shadows for all eternity, insubstantial and unrecognized?

"You are his weakness," Raif said, taking me by surprise. "His Achilles' heel."

"What makes you say that?" I said.

"I would have killed you decades ago," Raif answered with a frankness that told me he wasn't kidding, even a little.

"Who are the three who made others?" I needed to know, in some perverse way. Who were these Shaedes that had taken human lives and transformed them into something else altogether?

Raif contemplated his answer. I think he wrestled

with whether he wanted to tell me or not, but he finally spoke. "Anya, who made Dimitri, her mate. Azriel, who made you." Raif paused and looked at the floor. "And Alexander, who made Azriel's mother."

"Holy shit," I said. "Who? How? Why?"

"Padma," Raif said with a harsh laugh. "And I don't know why. I would never ask. That is my king's business, and his alone."

"So what do you want to know, Raif?" I was tired of beating around the bush. "If Azriel is my weakness as well? Do you want to know if I'll be able to seal the deal?"

"I suppose yes, that is what I want to know."

"You want to be sure that I'll kill Azriel before he can kill Xander."

"Yes, I want to be sure," Raif said.

Let's see. In the time I'd known him, Azriel had used me, lied to me, and abandoned me. He'd seduced me, and I'd loved him. And his only gift had been leaving me with just my wits to survive by and a farce of an existence to guide me. And now he'd sent his Lyhtan lackeys to threaten me. "Don't worry. It's in the bag." And I wondered if it could really be that easy.

Delilah wasn't waiting in front of my building. *Strange*. She'd become such a permanent fixture that her absence sparked a small amount of concern. I stepped from the lift and found Tyler sitting on my couch. Probably why Delilah wasn't here.

"What're you doing here, Ty?" I tried to sound normal, not like a jilted woman, even though I was.

Tyler didn't make eye contact. His shoulders slumped and his forehead fell to rest in his palms. "Delilah is missing."

All I could think of was poor, skinny, helpless, and blind Delilah being knocked around, bound and gagged, and dragged away with nothing but her smart mouth for defense. "Who did it? Do you know?"

"I think it was a Lyhtan. There was a pretty foul odor surrounding her house."

"Why would they want her?"

"Maybe for the same reason we did: to use her as a scout." Tyler looked lost, guilty, and angry.

"No." I doubted they needed her for something as trivial as that. It had to be something else, something she hadn't been used for in a while. "How many other Oracles are there wandering around the world?"

"A couple maybe, including her," Tyler said. "Oracles are rare in this world. She had a sister, but someone killed her two or three centuries or so ago. I don't know much about it. Delilah may be the only one. You don't think—"

"Why not?" I said. Wouldn't it be handy to know the outcome of a war before you had to shed any blood?

"But why kidnap her? Couldn't they just hire her to do the job?"

"Tyler, she said no one could afford to pay the price. She said it takes a sacrifice."

His face snapped into an expression of awareness. "What about you?" he asked.

"Me?"

"Darian, the kind of sacrifice necessary to pay an Oracle is a high price because it's something you can't bear to be parted from. What if that sacrifice is supposed to be you?"

"That doesn't make any sense. Azriel is leading the Lyhtans, and if he needs an Oracle, I'd be the last thing he couldn't bear to be parted from. Trust me—if I meant anything to him, he wouldn't have abandoned me."

Tyler paused. "But what if it isn't Azriel who took Delilah?"

The politics of war made my head spin. I couldn't wrap my mind around the various intricacies. "Ty, I'm tired. Don't be cryptic."

"If Azriel is shacked up with the Lyhtans, maybe

there's a displaced leader. Maybe he's the one who wants
you dead."

It sounded far-fetched, but I was willing to pursue any
angle if it meant getting Delilah back. "What do we do,
then?"

"Find out if there's a disgruntled leader out there and
arrange a meeting."

Oh, fabulous. That sounded like a ton of fun. "Ty," I
said. "How fragile is Delilah? I mean . . . could they—"

"Don't worry," he said, a sad smile offering assurance.
"If we're right, they don't want to hurt her, just use her
as a crystal ball. Besides, she's not as breakable as she
looks. Meet me at The Pit tonight around ten. Okay?"

That didn't seem like the best place to start looking
for a Lyhtan king, but I wasn't about to question Tyler
anymore. "I'll be there."

The typical throng of people hadn't yet lined up outside
the door, giving Tiny little to do. Inside, the club wasn't
much busier; only a few regulars hanging around, drinking their evening away. Tyler sat waiting for me, in my
usual corner, but tonight he wasn't alone. Levi sat with
him.

I took a seat next to Ty. He brushed his hand along my
arm, squeezing as he settled on my hand. I pulled away.
There was no such thing as PDA at a business meeting.

"So, what's up?" I asked.

Ty looked a little crestfallen. I sighed. I was sure we'd
have it out later. For some reason, he had a hard time
differentiating between us in public and us in private.
They were all one and the same to him. It might have
had something to do with the bond Delilah talked about;
he had been a lot more touchy-feely lately. In fact, I felt
a little more tuned in to him as well. He put me at ease
just by being near. Had we been bonded all along these
past five years? He'd made me feel safe since the night
of my first job when we sealed our business relationship

with a handshake and a silver ring. I hadn't thought about it, but perhaps something as simple as skin-to-skin contact had prompted Ty to bind himself to me. Or maybe it had been that first kiss outside Xander's warehouse, because I hadn't felt the same since that night. And like every other piece of knowledge I'd had to fight for these past weeks, I was going to make Ty spill his knowledge as well.

"Levi is what you might call a liaison," Tyler said, breaking me from contemplative thoughts. "He's a go-between for the natural and supernatural worlds."

That's the understatement of the century, I thought. Levi was a walking supernatural encyclopedia. "Well, Levi," I said. "What's the word?"

He smiled at me, a very genuine expression on his frat-boy face. I fought the urge to ask him if he was late for a kegger.

"There's a lot going on right now," Levi said. "There's talk of war between the Shaedes and Lyhtans. Many beings have their eye fixed to the outcome. It could mean change for more than just the parties involved."

"What about the Lyhtans?" I asked. "Do they have a leader who's been kicked from his throne or something like that?"

"They don't generally live that way," Levi explained. "Lyhtans are wild, lawless. They're solitary. Every once in a while you'll find them moving in packs, groups not much larger than ten. There's no real leadership hierarchy, no pecking order. They don't follow."

I looked at Ty and gave a silent shake of my head. We weren't getting anywhere.

"Have you heard of a Shaede who is banding the Lyhtans together?" I asked Levi. "Named Azriel." *And did I mention I need to kill the bastard?*

"I have," he said. "Like I said, they don't usually follow, so this Shaede must be promising the world to get them on board for his campaign."

"What do Lyhtans want?" I asked. "What could he use as a bargaining chip?"

"They're tired of hiding," Levi said. "They want to be more like you."

Acceptance. That's what the Lyhtans wanted more than anything. They wanted to blend in with the human population and pass as something close to normal.

"How?" I asked no one in particular. "How could he promise that? How does he think he'll give that to them?"

"Who knows?" Tyler chimed in. "It could be just a bunch of lies he's telling them to string them along. Otherwise, we're in for a shit storm of trouble."

"Because they're nasty fuckers," Levi added. "If they can come and go as they please, blend in with the general population, they'll cause all sorts of chaos."

Tyler and I exchanged a knowing glance. "Is there any Lyhtan who might not like that?" I said.

"I'm not sure," Levi said. "I can look into it—for a nominal fee—but I would think they'd all be pretty excited by the prospect. If there's anything to find out here, I'll find it."

We left, no better informed than we'd been when we entered. Frustration built up inside me like bubbles against a champagne cork. I wanted to *kill* something, just so I had an outlet to vent my anger. Ever the voice of reason, Tyler discouraged me from violence, convincing me it would only be counterproductive. It would've been in his best interest to keep his mouth shut. He was still pretty high up on my shit list, and I could just as easily release my anger on him as anyone.

Tyler made himself at home on my couch while I changed for another training session. My anger had been mounting, and I'd continued to suppress it. Much easier to do when we weren't alone. But, damn it, it pissed me off that the one person I trusted had pulled the wool over my eyes. The more I thought about it, the more my blood began to boil. Now was as good a time as any to broach the subject of Ty's true nature. In fact, I'd put it off for far too long.

"How does this work?" I asked, lacing up my boot. *Keep it nonchalant. Don't bite his head off.* "Delilah said you're bonded with me. What the hell does that entail?"

The twinkling light faded from Tyler's eyes and his mouth tightened into a fine line. Apparently, he wanted to discuss this just as much as I did. "Can't you just accept that I want to protect you and leave it at that?"

Um, no. If one more person tried to keep me in the dark, he was going to lose his head. "You mean just eat every spoon-fed bite of your bullshit? No, thanks. I think I've had my fill."

"Darian—"

"Do you think I'm stupid? Weak? Incompetent?" My ire rose with every word. "Do you have any idea how humiliated I feel? Five years! Five fucking years I've known you. And you let me act like a complete fool. You knew there were others. Shit, you were *one of them*! Why didn't you just tell me? Did you get off on seeing me alone and disconnected from everything? I threatened you, for Christ's sake! I called you *human*, like it was a dirty word or something."

Tyler's eyes held mine, showing a depth of emotion I was afraid to believe. "I was trying to protect you."

"Oh, really? From what? And did you ever think about asking if I *wanted* your protection? No. You just *bound yourself to me*."

"Darian, with Jinn, the urge to protect is like instinct. But with you, I feel the need twice as strong. And you, being the tough girl you think you are—there's no way in hell you would have submitted to the binding and let me become the protector that I *had* to be. You've always thought you could take care of yourself with no help from anyone. So I hid behind a normal-guy persona. I did what I had to do. It was beyond selfish of me, but I refuse to apologize. Yes, I kept the supernatural world from you. There are bigger and more dangerous things than Lyhtans and Shaedes in the world. And you would've taken them all on. Single-handedly. I couldn't risk your safety. I knew if I kept you focused on humans and human business, you'd be relatively safe."

I wanted to hate him right then but I couldn't. I did feel safe and protected when I was with him. And something deeper still. He'd been my lifeline to the world, even though Azriel's teachings had dictated I remain detached. Tyler had my back, no matter what. And I knew he'd never disappear in the middle of the night without a word. That was worth more than my anger and frustration. He didn't deserve an ass-chewing, but he took it— because he knew it would make me feel better.

"There are rules to this binding." All the fire had left me, and nothing remained but smoldering embers. "I know that much. And I want to know what they are."

"Okay." Tyler's voice, soft and husky, sent chills dancing across my skin. "In my lifetime, I can only choose to form a bond three times. I can choose to create the bond, but you have to choose to break it. Once it is broken, it can never be remade."

Three times. I wondered if he'd done this before. He was older than Delilah, and she'd been walking the earth for at least a thousand years. Could I perhaps have been lucky number three? "What about the wishes?" I abandoned my humiliation, the anger. We'd had it out and it was time to move on. Besides, Raif was going to kill me if I was late. I slid a dagger into the sheath at my thigh and another into my boot. "How do those work?"

"There's a moral code, more or less. Even I can't change some things. You can only wish for something you need, never for something you simply want." Tyler stretched out his hand, counting points on his fingers as he spoke, "You can't wish someone dead—or alive. And you can't wish for wealth. Extra abilities are out of the question as well, like flying or breathing underwater. I can't alter the paths Fate and nature have chosen for you."

That little statement earned a snort of derision from me, but Tyler continued, ignoring my sarcasm.

"You are forbidden from wishing away the bonds between others, and I cannot grant you love." His eyes burned into mine when he said it, and I averted my glance, afraid of what else he might say. "The timeline can't be altered, but I suppose that falls in line with fate. You could never wish to change the outcome of any event. And I can't give you what someone else has. But I can swear to do my best to help you if you need it, and vow to protect you until you no longer need my protection."

"Why didn't you tell me? God, Ty, how could you do that?"

The look of shame that flashed across his face helped to further cool my fiery emotions. "I wanted to tell you. So many times. But I was afraid you'd bolt if you knew the truth. I didn't want to be the one to disillusion you."

"You did, though," I said. "Just like the rest of them."

"I know." His voice was barely a whisper.

"How long?" I asked. "How long have you been bound to me?"

Tyler's lips hinted at a smile. "Not long after I met you. Almost five years."

Sonofabitch! For five years, Tyler had been secured to me like a snail on a rock and I didn't even know it! Was I the most clueless woman on the motherfucking planet—or what?

"How?"

"The binding is a gift," Tyler said, his voice as smooth as cream. "And it's not one I give lightly. Please just accept it and leave it at that."

I worried at the ring on my thumb, twisting it in a full circle. I traced the engraving on its surface, the hulking beast whose form I couldn't identify. This binding wasn't the first "gift" he'd insisted I accept. I took the katana from where it was mounted above my mantel and flung it across my back. "I'm going to be late meeting Raif, and, frankly, my brain fucking hurts. Don't lie to me again. Ever. Please."

His eyes answered for him, his expression honest and full of emotion. *I won't,* it said. *I promise.*

I left Tyler at my studio—he refused to leave—and met up with Raif shortly after midnight. He tapped the flat of his sword against the sole of his boot. My tardiness was sure to spark a beating. I saved my neck by convincing him to bypass training for another Q and A. Like Levi, he didn't have any more information or insight. I was ramming my head against a brick wall.

"So much to worry about," he muttered. "Like I don't already have enough on my plate."

I assumed his plate was full of me, but I didn't ask.

"There's a Summit to take place in a few days. The timing is inconvenient, but it might work to our advantage. Xander will more than likely ask for help if this situation becomes . . . uncontrollable."

Summit? Huh. "What kind of Summit? Like a Shaede Summit?" Then Levi's *Hamlet* quote sparked in my memory, and I rolled my eyes. I. Am. Such. An. *Idiot.*

"There's more, isn't there?" I asked. "More than Shaedes, more than Oracles and Jinn. The world is crawling with other supernatural creatures, and we're not so few in our numbers. Are we? We are not alone," I said in a spooky sci-fi voice.

"Alone?" Raif said. "Whoever filled you with that rot?"

Azriel.

"There is a large and thriving supernatural community. For the most part, we get along just fine," he continued without waiting for my answer, thank God. "Just like any human political body, we meet, talk, bring our concerns to a public forum. Vote. We're not uncivilized, you know."

"I know," I said like a schoolkid being scolded by her teacher.

"At any rate, this information about your Oracle and the Lyhtans is helpful. Thank you, Darian."

Raif had become extremely interested in Levi's theory. He wanted to bring it to Xander's attention before the Summit. He'd never considered the possibility that simple jealousy had been the motivation behind this political coup. He was actually a little smug about it.

"Our lives are so much easier because of our looks," he mused. "We do not have to hide in the daylight hours when we are restricted to our humanlike forms. We can pass through society virtually unnoticed, and it allows us to live a life of ease and prosperity. Wouldn't you agree, Darian?"

"Sure, whatever. It makes sense anyway. But it doesn't answer my questions. Does Azriel want me dead or not? And did he take Delilah?"

"I think he wants you dead. I don't agree with the Jinn's assumption. From a warrior's standpoint, you are a liability. And liabilities must be disposed of. I do not believe Azriel is harboring any tender feelings."

"Wow, Raif. You're a true romantic," I said. I agreed with Raif, for what it was worth. I believed Azriel wanted me dead. *Kill or be killed.* But something else stuck in my craw. We appeared so hard to kill, and yet so easy. There were rules that governed our deaths, but we weren't as invincible as I'd always assumed. Fathers, sons, mothers, daughters, husbands, wives, the maker and the made . . . all of these relationships intertwined to form an intricate web of death. The more you tied yourself to someone, the more they held dominion over your existence. Azriel sat between Xander and me. Either one of us could deliver the blow that would send him into the shadows for eternity. And as for the gray hours ... I still couldn't wrap my head around those boundaries.

I put the matter of death's silly rules on the back burner, and instead shifted my focus to Delilah. She wasn't a part of this war. Merely an unfortunate victim caught in the middle and used for the gain of either side. I'd used her as my own personal seeing-eye dog, and whoever took her had plans even bigger still. Tyler said she wouldn't be so easy to break. But I knew better than anyone that there are things in this world worse than dying.

Raif promised to look into the matter of Delilah's disappearance, but I didn't exactly think he'd stop the presses to do so. His first priority was keeping Xander in one piece, and he would be hard-pressed to weaken his king's defenses to investigate an Oracle's kidnapping. No matter what she might be or how his enemies would use her.

"I met an Oracle once," Raif said, offhand, as he stowed his battle gear. "She wasn't much to behold, but she was powerful."

"Did you ask her a question?" I said.

"No," he said. "I wasn't willing to make the sacrifice."

"What did she ask you for?" My curiosity piqued. I couldn't imagine what Raif could value so much.

"She asked for the death of my wife," he said gravely. "Our child had gone missing, and we were beside ourselves trying to find her. I went to the Oracle, and she requested my wife's life in return for information about our daughter's future. I refused. Illiana was the most precious thing in my world, and I would not give her up."

His story leaned farther toward the deep end than I'd anticipated. Poor Raif. I couldn't imagine him, so hard and proud, lowering himself to ask for help.

"What happened?" I whispered.

"Illiana could not forgive me for not making the sacrifice. She said she would have given anything to know our daughter's fate. She expected the same from me. She went to the Oracle and sacrificed herself."

Wow, Tragedy, party of one. No wonder Raif was such a pain in the ass. "Did you ever find out what happened to your daughter?"

"No."

"What happened to the Oracle?"

"I killed her."

An awkward silence passed. Comforting words seemed trite, so I kept my mouth shut.

"An Oracle is good for nothing," he said, piercing the silence like a sword thrust. "They are tricksters and deceivers. I don't think Azriel would want to kidnap yours. She has nothing to offer him anyway."

Raif grabbed his sword and slung it over his back. I let him leave. Once I was sure he was long gone, I turned out the lights and headed home.

Chapter 15

I walked back to my studio with memories of Raif's tragic story for company, alone and more confused than ever.

Careless, I'd stayed longer at the warehouse than I should have. Dawn approached, and I wasn't sure if I'd make it back to my apartment before the sun rose. Not that it would matter. I wasn't any safer there than I was here on the street. Delilah was gone, so I was down one set of eyes. My vulnerability wasn't limited to a set time or place.

I'd almost made it home when I heard the strange scratching sound of many sets of insect feet. The sun had just crested the horizon, a sliver of orange light. The sound followed me for a few blocks, and around me I heard the whisperings of a strange language, words that meant nothing to me. Quickening my pace, I tried to ignore it, at the same time trying desperately to manage a facade of calm. The scratching sound continued, coupled with a second set of voices to join the first. I turned, and my heart jumped up into my throat. Glittering in the morning light like perfectly cut diamonds, a horde of tiny insects scurried toward me. Beetles—no, miniature mantislike bugs—they zigged and zagged, quickly covering the distance between us. My tiny assailants sounded like an army, their outer shells ticking against one another while so many different tones of voice called out around me. No one had mentioned this little tidbit of info. Not only were they invisible in the light, but the fuckers could also reduce their bodies to tiny, innard-sucking bugs? Might have been nice to know! The sound of their many voices pressed on my ears, almost deafening. Lyhtans they were, for I couldn't mistake those voices. But I'd never seen them in the light of day, disguised for all intents and purposes like little exotic insects. Levi owed me a fifty. He'd left out this very important slice of information. One by one, their physical forms glittered into nothing and they became again the invisible foes I'd known. And as I reached into my pocket for what felt like the thousandth time, I found myself without the bottle of black sludge. Unfortunately, now wasn't the best time to find faith in its ability to repel a Lyhtan attacker.

Their presence harried me. They pressed their invisible bodies against mine, surrounding me in a strange bubble of pressure so tight I had to fight to keep moving. I almost missed their gruesome insect forms. The air around me became dense—I could barely breathe—and the stench of them caused me to choke. All the good looks in the world weren't going to do anything about that smell.

I wondered if I should wish for something. I didn't want Tyler to pop into the middle of a dangerous situation, though, and I still wasn't entirely sure how the whole wish thing worked. I wanted help, but did I *need* it? And who the hell was responsible for defining what I needed? Fuck. Maybe I could only wish for him specifically, and I refused to risk his life. I'd only just realized the extent of my own mortality; I had no clue as to the extent of Tyler's. The katana was useless against an invisible foe. And as for my theory that my life might be valuable—well, let's just say I didn't have much faith in that either.

The Lyhtan voices continued to taunt. Levi was right, though. They wanted the freedom to show themselves.

"Do you prize your pretty body, Shaede?" the many

voices taunted. "Can you charm the humans with your sweet voice, soft skin, and supple breasts? You don't live in fear of discovery, do you? You will, though! Soon you'll feel the pain of alienation!"

"Cry me a river," I said. I'd had it with their sad laments. I mean, give me a fucking break. "What do you want? To live like them? To amble aimlessly, playing foolish games and living meaningless lives? You want to appear weak and vulnerable and mortal?"

A thousand voices laughed in my ears. I fought the urge to cover them with my hands, to block out that evil sound.

"We will lure them with our beauty, and then we will rip their souls from their flesh! We'll have some fun with them!"

I brushed my fear aside and tried to decipher the nonsense from actual threat. I had to hope one of them would be stupid enough to identify the mastermind behind their little coup. Everyone suspected Azriel, but I had to be *sure*. Driven by basic instincts and simple emotions, these Lyhtans could be easily controlled by the right individual. They appeared to be brainless creatures with only base desires, though Raif had proclaimed differently.

"Who is your master?" I asked as I fought to keep moving.

I was answered by another round of cackling laughter. "Our master wants you," they said.

Ambiguous answers aren't my favorite. *Wants me what? Dead? Alive? Tortured? Stripped naked, doused with honey, and set on an anthill?* I was *so* over this unwelcome escort. "Look, ladies . . . fellas . . . *whatever.* Are you planning on doing something here, or are you just going to talk me to death? I'm pretty fucking tired, and I'm not in the mood for your bullshit this morning. So if you're going to do something, get on with it. If you're not, then get the hell out of here!"

I waited, my pulse pounding in my ears, for their next move. I was sure I'd invited an attack, and I stood ready to defend myself, no matter how wasted the effort might be.

Their laughter grew louder, and they pushed with their invisible forms, tossing my body this way and that. I tried to stay straight, but they were too strong and I listed, stumbling as they shoved. The sound of their mirth intensified until I thought I'd go crazy from the laughter. The density of the air changed, and I cried out as many clawed hands scraped against me. Blood oozed from the gaping wounds, and I fell to the ground. I reached over my shoulder, gripped the hilt of the katana, and ripped it free of the scabbard. On my knees, I held it out before me, ready to fight, though unsure how or where to aim the slice of my blade as flashes of light shone before me, too fast for the human eye to track, becoming solid for a split second before disappearing entirely.

Laughter turned to screeching. I felt the power of their screams deep in my chest, my heart threatening to explode at any minute. I swung the katana at the air, slicing and cutting down over and over.

The screams stopped. The laughter was gone. The air became easy to breathe, and I no longer felt the pressure of their presence. I fell face forward on the concrete, and I heard the metal blade ring as it struck the ground. Blood gushed warm and sticky from my many wounds, the pain almost unbearable, and there I lay, a mere block from my apartment.

Goddamn, I needed help. Needed it right fucking now. I tried to form the sentence that would save me, "I wish . . ." But I didn't get past the first two words. Darkness swept down on me, and it was welcome.

"Darian, don't move," Tyler's voice was soft next to my face. "This is gonna hurt like a bitch, but you can't move or you'll pull the stitches."

Stitches? What would I need stitches for?

Something cold and wet made contact with my skin, and a jolt of pain like liquid fire shot through me. I jerked but did as Tyler asked and tried to keep as still as possible. Dragging a ragged breath between tightly clenched teeth, I didn't dare open my eyes. I didn't want to see the damage that was so bad it would require my quick-healing skin be sewn together. A string of curses sat at my tongue, distracting me from the searing pain. For comfort, I visualized the many ways I could kill my Lyhtan attackers in the gray hours of twilight.

Soon the pain ebbed, and my breathing slowed. I allowed my tense body to relax by fractions of inches, slowly sinking into the soft comfort I recognized as my own bed. The delicious scent that clung to Ty drifted toward me, helping me to calm. I wasn't safe, but I felt better just being near him, my personal wish granter.

"How did you find me?" I croaked.

"I knew you were about to make a wish," he said as he propped another pillow beneath my head. "I get this tingly feeling that's a precursor to the actual wish. When you didn't follow through, I got worried and went to look for you. Luckily, you were close."

"Why do I need stitches, Ty? What the fuck?"

He brushed my hair away from my forehead. His touch felt cooler than normal. "Raif came by to check you out. He was pretty pissed—mentioned something about bottled shadows and your inability to obey an order. He says you'll heal, but the Lyhtan venom prevents your skin from closing up like it should. If I hadn't closed the wounds, you may have bled out."

"I thought they could only kill me during the gray hours," I mumbled, ignoring the *I told you so* Raif had delivered by way of Tyler.

"Are you dead?" Tyler asked.

"No," I moaned, "but that's not saying much."

He bent over and pressed his lips to my forehead. I

breathed deeply, taking in his scent as if I'd never smell it again. How many times had he gotten me out of a jam? How many more opportunities would he have to come to my rescue? Which of those times would kill him?

"Tyler." I worked to lean up on my elbows. It hurt like a sonofabitch. "You need to go. It's not safe for you here."

"Darian, I've dealt with nastier things than Lyhtans," he said, laughing. "Don't worry about it."

"What are you, Tyler?" I asked. Nearly delirious from the Lyhtan venom, I felt groggy, drugged.

"I'm yours," he said.

I mumbled a few incoherent words and lost consciousness again.

Angry voices roused me from a dark abyss. Two of my favorite voices, actually. Xander arguing with Tyler. I couldn't make out the words, but it was a heated discussion nonetheless.

I wanted to speak up, but my mouth felt like it had been stuffed with cotton balls. I tried to run my tongue over my lips, but it just stuck to the roof of my mouth like I'd glued it there. I wrestled with producing enough saliva to dislodge my tongue for a couple of minutes while Tyler and Xander continued to argue. I couldn't even wish they'd stop.

I abandoned trying to talk and instead let out a loud groan. I didn't need my tongue for that, and it managed to interrupt whatever was going on between the two men. I heard the shuffling of feet and maybe a shove or two, and then felt their presence beside me. I pried open my heavy lids, and the blurry room and occupants slowly came into focus.

"Hey," Ty said, obviously jumping in to be the first to speak to me. "How are you feeling?"

My tongue popped loose from the roof of my mouth and I parted my dry, cracked lips. "Water," I whispered.

The room blurred out of focus and I heard more commotion. Their voices low, they'd begun fighting again.

"Here," Xander said. I felt a depression in the bed where he sat beside me. "I'll help you drink."

I managed to clear my vision and caught sight of Tyler, arms folded in front of his chest. He snorted derisively.

Xander lifted the glass to my lips and I drank. It had to be the best-tasting water I'd ever had. Not too cold, not too warm, and it loosened up my dry mouth. Delicious. Xander pulled the lip of the glass away and I leaned back onto the pillow, exhausted from just the small task of drinking.

"I feel like shit," I grumbled. "When is this damn Lyhtan venom going to wear off?"

The bed shook with Xander's laughter. Tyler entered the fray and took a seat on my opposite side. He gave my hand a light squeeze. "Soon," he said. "It's already wearing off. It won't be much longer."

Xander grabbed my other hand. What was this—a battle for Darian's appendages? I didn't like it. "You're healing faster than we expected," he said. "We've already had to remove the stitches."

I clenched my stomach muscles and tried to sit up to see the extent of the damage. The cuts pulled and stung, piercing my side with a sharp pain. I sucked in a quick breath and eased myself back down onto the pillows.

"What were you two fighting about?" I asked.

Their voices answered in unison. "Nothing."

"Nothing, my ass," I said.

Tyler took the high road, just like I knew he would. "There was another attack just after sunset. Two more Shaedes were killed."

"And . . ." I said, prompting him along.

"And Xander thought that you should move into his house. I told him no."

"And I told him to stay out of matters that don't concern him," Xander interjected.

"Darian *is* my business," Ty said, gripping my hand a little too tight.

"No more than she is mine," Xander shot back.

"You're the reason she's in this mess," Tyler hollered.

"If you were more adept at protecting her, this never would have happened!" Xander yelled.

"Both of you shut up." I wanted to yell too. But I couldn't muster the energy; it only sounded weak. "You know, Xander, for *immortal* creatures, we sure are easy to kill, aren't we?"

I sensed his chagrin, but I didn't care. I'd been lied to. I had no clue what my true limitations were, the extent of my invincibility, and the actual length of my life. He could suck it up for a while and come clean.

"We'll talk," he said. "But not while the Jinn is here."

"I have a name, asshole," Tyler said.

"Stop it!" My voice had a little more to it that time. Good. I needed to kick my ass into gear. "Anything you have to say to me you can say in front of Tyler."

Gloat rolled off Tyler like a soft wave. Xander tensed, and I sensed another row about to begin. *Jesus.* I couldn't take the testosterone anymore.

"Tyler," I sighed. "Could you give us a few minutes?"

Hazel eyes widened and then narrowed. His body straightened, and I sensed the hardening of his form, his hurt at being asked to leave.

"Come on, Ty. Don't be like that." I wasn't strong enough to worry about his ego right now. "I don't have it in me to sit through another pissing contest. Just a few minutes."

He stood, his body still tense with anger, and he walked to the lift without a word. The gate slammed down in front of him and he left.

Xander relaxed beside me and smiled. *Great. Hurt one; encourage another.* Not exactly what I was going for. "Listen, Xander," I said. "This doesn't mean I like you better. In fact, you're at the top of my shit list. Just say whatever you need to say and get the hell out."

His smile grew. I really hated the way my anger encouraged him. He was a no-means-yes kind of guy all the way around.

"I hate to burst your bubble, Darian," Xander said, "but invincibility is a concept best left to comic books. There is nothing in the natural world that is *unkillable*. Including you. We heal incredibly fast; therefore, most injuries that would be fatal to another creature do not affect us in the same way. We don't succumb to illness, though as you can plainly see, toxins can weaken us and make us vulnerable. We hold dominion over one another when bonded by love, magic, or blood. Therefore, no matter the hour or the circumstances, we have the power to send one of our own forever into shadow. And we can live for generations, ages. Is that what you want to hear, Darian? Is this what you're so bitter about? The fact that it's not laid out for you in simple terms, black and white?"

"The natural world," I scoffed. "Do you really think we're a part of the natural world?"

"Yes." His answer was simple, definite, final.

Xander smiled and stood. No matter how much I hated him, I couldn't deny he was something to look at. His blond hair had been pulled neatly back and secured with a band at the nape of his neck. And his eyes sparkled against the darker backdrop of his face, which was angular and strong, a kingly face if I ever saw one. I wondered at his outfit—a silk T-shirt and slacks, both black. *Hmm. An homage?* Or maybe just a somber color for the somber tone of his visit. Oh yeah, he was something to look at all right, but he was Azriel's *father,* for chrissake, and my own personal tormentor. At the moment, I didn't think the line between love and hate was fine enough for me to feel anything for him but insufferable frustration, and no amount of beauty was going to change that fact.

"I suppose I'll leave," Xander said, as if leaving was the last thing he wanted to do. "Your slave is no doubt pacing the sidewalk right now and is eager to see to your care."

My slave? Laughable. "He's anything but a slave, Xander."

He raised a challenging brow. "Oh no?"

"What do you know about him?" I asked, my suspicions aroused.

"The Jinn has bound himself to you, Darian." He almost sounded sorry for Tyler. "Everything, even his own life, comes second to your wishes."

"Well, I never asked him to do that," I said, defending myself for something that wasn't my fault. "I don't need a genie."

"Oh no?" Xander said again, daring me to contradict him. "Don't be so sure. Heal quickly, little assassin. I need you."

The last traces of gray light must have been swallowed up by dark night, because Xander passed into shadow and disappeared from my presence.

Chapter 16

Xander's comments about Tyler left a sour taste in my mouth. I didn't want to think that by binding himself to me, Ty had given up his free will. It made me sick to think of anyone giving themselves over in that way, so completely, without reservation. I'd done that a century or so ago when I'd given my life over to Azriel, and look where that decision landed me. *Slave.* The word was degrading, disgusting, weak. Tyler wasn't weak. He was shrewd, handsome, and loyal. He didn't have to be flashy about his power; you could see it in his eyes. Tyler may have looked like a harmless sidekick, but only because that's what he wanted people to see. He wasn't weak— not by a long shot. And he was no slave.

I couldn't understand why Tyler had chosen this path. He'd known me for years. My personality hadn't changed in that short time; I wasn't charming or sweet or even remotely lovable. Why had he done this seemingly undoable thing? I didn't even truly know how to break the bond. And if I could, would I want to? Tyler's presence had begun to grow on me. I was tired of being alone, and he made me feel warm, protected, and almost normal. He'd sworn to keep me safe, but could I do the same for him? I was up to my eyeballs in danger, and I didn't want him anywhere near it.

I couldn't help but wonder why he'd hidden his true nature from me all this time. Did he think I'd care for him more as a hapless human? Had he worried that if I knew the truth, I'd send him away, or leave myself? I wouldn't have—left him, that is—no matter what. Now I wondered which one of us had been enslaved.

Daybreak brought with it a drizzling, somber gray. Storm clouds hovered low over the cityscape, brushing the tops of the taller buildings, hiding them like tall turrets in a medieval kingdom. I closed the drapes over my picture window. A kingdom in any form was a grating reminder of the harsh new reality of my existence.

Raif showed up just in time to make an already bad morning worse. Dressed to blend in, he wore a pair of khaki slacks and a dress shirt. He looked ridiculous. I was so used to seeing him in his elfin getup that to me he seemed more out of place than ever. I snorted into my coffee cup and took a seat at the dining table.

"How are you feeling?" he asked as he took a seat across from me.

"I'm not dead," I said in a flat, toneless way.

"No, you're certainly not that," he said. "But you are feeling . . . better?"

I shrugged.

"You are to report to the king's estate at sundown," Raif said. "Not a minute later."

I resisted the urge to douse his face with the hot beverage in my hand. Ty had it easy. *I* was the slave. "What for?"

"It doesn't matter what for," Raif said with a sneer. He tossed a thick manila envelope across the table. It spun twice, coming to rest by my cup. "Double your fee. I believe those were your terms. I think you've been paid enough now. And Alexander wants you for some . . . *freelance* work."

I guessed by his attitude that Raif wasn't exactly a morning person. I lifted a hand to my forehead and gave a crisp salute. "Yes, sir." I would have clicked my heels together, but that would have required standing up.

Raif didn't stick around to chitchat, but instead

headed straight for the lift. "Darian," he said as he pulled the gate shut. "Dress appropriately."

"What the hell is that supposed to mean?" I yelled as the lift disappeared below the floor.

"Work clothes." Raif's voice drifted up through the shaft.

"Work clothes," I muttered under my breath as I stalked up the winding drive to Xander's estate. Since I was fairly certain I wasn't being asked to Xander's to help with the gardening, I dressed in my usual ensemble: black pants, long-sleeve black V-neck shirt, and, of course, black boots.

I looked warily at a grouping of bushes, a rustling sound causing a burst of anxiety to rush through my bloodstream. Traveling in the gray hours of twilight had left me vulnerable. I'd been considerably shaken by the Lyhtan attack, and I didn't like being at a disadvantage. Not one tiny bit. I'd lived almost a century believing I was invincible. And now . . . now I was no more immortal than any other creature that roamed the earth.

An unusual amount of activity surrounded Xander's house. Guards had been placed strategically at every door, balcony, and gate. The glint of steel winked from each post, reflecting the artificial glow of the floodlights that had clicked on with the last trace of gray evening. I stood by the front door, observing the many Shaedes around me, feeling the weight of their glowing stares.

"You're late," a bitchy voice said from behind me.

I wondered what she was wearing tonight. Black studded leather with a whip to match? "Anya," I said, turning toward the open door. "Does PETA know about you? I mean, seriously. How many innocent cows had to die to complete your god-awful wardrobe?"

It wasn't black studded, but it *was* lime green. I don't know how she walked, let alone fought, bound up like that. She sneered and turned her back to me, leading the

way. Every movement of her body resulted in a squeak
or squawk of some sort, and even her gait was a little
stiff. Did she realize how impractical she looked? Maybe
she was planning on killing her enemies with bad fashion
sense.

I wasn't taken upstairs to Xander's suite, but instead
led into the bowels of the mansion, down a dark, wide
staircase, into a vast room that looked like the type of
place where war councils were held. The king sat at a
long rectangular table, and to his right sat Raif. He was
accompanied by eleven other Shaedes, all talking among
themselves while Xander bent over a stack of papers,
pen in hand.

"You're late," he grumbled without looking up.

Raif shot me a warning glare as if he'd already heard
the sarcastic comeback I was prepared to deliver. I rolled
my eyes, and in an unabashedly petulant manner, blew a
strand of hair from my face.

"Your Highness," I said, feeling utterly foolish. "My
apologies." If Xander thought I'd get down on a knee, he
had another thing coming. But I did incline my head—a
little.

The King of Shaedes paused in his work and looked
up. A corner of his mouth tugged upward, and his eyes
sparkled with a mischievous light. For that one moment
he was simply Xander. But the moment was fleeting, and
he returned to his stack of papers.

"Do not let it happen again," he said, scrawling something and then setting the paper to one side.

It took a real physical effort not to roll my eyes. He
was good at playing the king. I opened my mouth to
speak, but caught Raif from the corner of my eye, and
the slight shake of his head was good enough reason to
keep silent.

Anya stood beside me like she was trying to keep me
from bolting with something valuable. I *so* wanted to
reach back and catch her in the face with my elbow, but

from the looks of the seated council, they wouldn't appreciate the show. I rocked back on my heels, inspecting the toes of my boots as if I'd never noticed them before. The only sound in the room was the scratching of Xander's pen against the paper.

I stood there for what seemed like forever, wondering what Raif planned on using me for. A quick wish could've gotten me out of here in a snap, but as the thought entered my mind, I banished it. Tyler wasn't some convenience I could use as my own personal get-out-of-jail-free card. I sighed, and it drew the attention of a couple of disdainful Shaedes. Straightening from the slumping position I'd assumed, I watched Xander with as much enthusiasm as I could muster.

"You're to stay here in an official capacity tonight," Xander said, still scratching away on his parchment. "We have several meetings throughout the week, including a Summit for the governing bodies of the Pacific Northwest Territories, and I'll need you for that as well. As soon as we're done here, Raif will explain your detail."

Huh. I guess every governing body had to call itself something. It definitely had a ring to it. "Detail?" I asked.

"Yes. Security detail." Xander set the last paper on the discarded stack and flipped them faceup before tapping them on the table to straighten them out. He handed the stack to the Shaede at his left, a dark and brooding man with a somber expression. "I think I've paid enough to request your services."

The thirteen Shaedes stood, and twelve bowed to their king. Everyone but Raif took their leave in a strange, single-file fashion. I got a couple of curious stares and a few admiring ones. I smiled sweetly, at least sweet for me. I looked every last one of them in the eye, refusing to be demure for anyone's benefit. Xander dismissed Anya with a curt wave of his hand, and I gave her a little wave good-bye with my own sweeping gesture. Okay, so maybe giving her the finger *was* a bit uncalled for.

Raif's eyebrow cocked. I think he was waiting for an act of violence from Anya. She was a good and loyal servant, though, and I wasn't worried a bit as she turned and retreated up the stairs, her leather outfit squeaking with every rise of her knee.

I folded my arms at my chest and leveled my gaze on the two men left in the room. Neither one paid me much attention as they talked in hushed tones, their heads bent close to each other. My anger and annoyance quickly turned into a very real, very physical knot in the pit of my stomach. If I'd had something to chuck, I would have aimed right for Xander's regal head. I was so sick of his games, I wanted to throw up.

As if he could read my thoughts, I noticed him look at me from the corner of his eye. He smiled and continued his conversation with Raif. Who knows what they talked about? They could have been discussing the declination of hygiene among middle school students for all I knew or cared. Raif finally bowed and stepped to the side to allow his king to move past him. He followed Xander around the table to where I stood, tapping my toe on the thickly carpeted floor.

"You look much better," Xander said, pausing at my side.

"Whatever doesn't kill me, right?" I said.

He reached up and cupped my cheek in his hand. Before I could physically or verbally retaliate, however, he pulled away and started up the stairs. Raif shook his head and fell in step behind Xander as I took up the rear.

Raif spoke low as we walked. "I need you to serve as the high king's personal security. You'll answer directly to me."

Another ploy. Anya was more than capable, and I'm sure a dozen other Shaedes could have done the job. The King of Games and Deception was up to something—again. First, I'd been hired as an assassin, the only one of my kind fit for the job. And now? Now I was playing babysitter. "Why me? If Xander's looking to keep danger at bay, asking me to tag along might not be the best decision."

"His Royal Highness," Raif stressed, "paid for your services. That's all you need to concern yourself with."

"Well, if you ask me, *His Royal Highness* is inviting danger rather than dispelling it." I said. "Seriously, what's going on here?"

"I didn't give you the katana so it could go unused," Xander interrupted. He wouldn't waste an opportunity to hear his own voice.

We continued up a second flight of stairs, the ones that led to Xander's suite. The place was locked down; he wasn't in danger here. "I was under the impression you had a task laid out for the sword. You remember—I was hired to kill your enemy."

"Raif will explain your duties," Xander said, opening the door to his private suite. "I'll speak with you soon."

I stopped just short of the threshold, and Xander beamed at me before shutting the door in my face. I pulled back a booted foot, poised to kick right through the wooden planks, but halted before making contact. Raif chuckled under his breath, and I whipped around to face him.

I turned and leaned against the banister, staring at the wood-paneled wall. "What's so funny?" I asked without a trace of humor.

"My brother certainly knows how to push your buttons."

My jaw dropped and I promptly snapped it shut. *Come again?* "Your what?" Raif simply winked, and let me tell you, it wasn't an expression that suited him. Think of an alligator winking just before he snaps his jaws down on your neck.

"What's really going on here?" I asked.

Raif took a step closer and bent his face to mine. "War is coming, Darian. If you can't get to Azriel before he gets to his father . . ." His voice was smooth and frigid. "Xander's in danger, and we have no idea how far our enemies' reach is. We don't dare trust anyone."

"Why trust me?" I couldn't think of a reason. I was growing sick of Xander and his games. I might be more likely than his enemies to do him harm.

"I trust you," Raif said. "And so does he."

I raised a sarcastic brow. *Sure, he trusts me.*

"With his life."

I didn't argue with him. I was past the point of fighting in what was now a losing battle. I'd been drawn into the game that first night I'd entered the staged town house, dagger in my hand. "So, what am I supposed to do—sit outside his door all night?"

Raif laughed and turned toward the stairs. "Not exactly," he said, and left.

"Darian, come in here," Xander's muffled voice called through the closed door.

My shoulders slumped. *Shit.*

I stormed into the room without a knock. Xander lounged in a chair, bare to the waist. He kicked off his shoes one at time.

"So," I said, going for my best impression of casual disinterest. "You think there's someone lurking around who's even less trustworthy than me?"

He gave me a rather wan smile in response. For the first time, I noticed he looked tired. Exhausted, really. "Amazing, isn't it?" At least he wasn't too drained for a smart-ass remark. "I take it Raif filled you in?" He gave a wan chuckle. "You'd think he was the older brother, the way he watches over me."

I didn't exactly consider the small amount of information he'd provided as *filling me in*, but, to be honest, I was tired too. The Lyhtan venom had really kicked my ass, and no matter how much I wanted to, I just didn't have it in me to pick a fight. "You two don't look alike," I said instead.

Xander's brows inched up his forehead a bit. And then he smiled. "I'm better-looking, right?"

"I have a feeling you don't need me to offer confirmation of that," I said. "What's the plan? What do you want me to do?"

"Just stay close," he said. "For now, that's all I need."

He reached his arms high above his head and stretched his legs out toward the floor, showcasing each individual muscle on his well-built body. He closed his eyes and yawned, an almost exaggerated sound escaping his mouth before his body uncoiled and came to rest. He opened his eyes and looked me over from head to toe and back up again. An anxious shiver chased his gaze as it roamed over my body.

"Would you release your Jinn if I asked you to?" he asked out of the blue.

"Tyler is not mine," I said, the ire rising with the tone of my voice. "And you need to stop talking about him like he's some sort of stray I picked up on the corner."

"Did you know that by binding himself to you, he has essentially forfeited his life?" Xander stood and carefully draped his shirt at the foot of his bed. He turned to look at me. "His life is now tied to yours. If you die, he dies."

"Bullshit." The word shot from my mouth.

The look on his face said, *Do I look like I would bullshit you?* He settled back down on his chair and crossed his legs at the ankles before stretching out again. I could have sworn I saw him peek through one eye, checking to see if I was watching him. "The Jinn are an ancient race—older than the oldest Shaede. I'm not sure, but I think they come from across the sea—Europe, or some speculate the Middle East, which would explain the genie legends. I also know they possess a very powerful magic and can change shape and form, but only when their charge is threatened."

"Such as . . ." I prompted.

Xander shrugged. "I have no idea. I've heard tales that the shape they choose is the physical embodiment of their protection."

"Are they immortal?"

He shook his head and jumped out of his chair. "You don't listen very well, do you?" He took a few steps closer to me. "*Nothing* on this earth is immortal, Darian."

I looked away; his stare was too intense, and my emotions were becoming more ragged with each explanation. "Didn't you hear me say that his life is now tied to yours? He'll die if you die. He'll die to save your life. He's become entwined with you in a way you cannot comprehend." I still refused to look at him. "You can die. You can pass from this existence into shadow forever. Haven't I told you over again that you are more fragile a creature than you've thought?"

I felt an unfamiliar lump forming in my throat. It was like choking on a golf ball. The swell of emotion threatened to break from my chest and engulf me in a century's worth of sorrow, forgotten until this moment. Maybe it was an effect of the Lyhtan venom that lingered in my body. Maybe it was the realization of what Tyler had actually done. Maybe it was simply a long-overdue breakdown. *Keep it together, Darian. Christ. Just suck it up and keep your shit together.*

"Jesus," I said, snapping back into myself. "Why couldn't you have just left me the fuck alone?"

"I need you," he said. "And I suppose I must remind you again that you've been paid well for your services. I needed an assassin. And not just another killer off the street. I need *you* specifically."

Xander's smug expression did little to soothe my anger. How long had they been watching me, feeling me out and assessing my abilities? When did his little plan take root, and how had he known I was the only girl for the job? Of course, he could've killed Azriel himself.

Their blood bond made that possible. Then again, Xander would never risk his royal neck by getting close enough to Azriel to do the deed. Paid or not, I'd become a pawn in his little game. His sardonic smiles didn't fool me.

Resuming his place at the armchair, Xander regarded me like I was some sort of anomaly. Studying me like a cell on slide, his fingers in a steeple before him, his golden eyes probed right down to the pores on my face.

It wasn't pity, though my disillusioned state was undeniably pathetic. Made me easy to maneuver too. With Raif's help, he'd molded me like a hunk of clay, and if everything went his way, he'd have one dead enemy and one trained monkey. *Over my dead body.* Bile rose in my throat at the thought and I swallowed the bitterness down.

"We have a busy day tomorrow," he said. "And I'm ready for bed." His eyes twinkled behind a veil of calculation. "You can join me if you'd like."

Somehow, I didn't think Xander cared so much about social taboos. I'd slept with his son, for shit's sake, and I had no interest in making it a family affair. "Sure," I scoffed. "Wish in one hand, shit in the other. See which one fills up first." I spun on a heel and left the High King of Bullshit chuckling behind me.

Chapter 17

My phone vibrated in my back pocket, stirring me from restless slumber. Tilted back in a chair, my legs propped up on the banister, I caught bits and pieces of rest while Xander slept safe in his bed on the other side of the door. The vibrating stopped, and I sighed in relief just before it started again. I knew who was calling. No doubts there.

Stiff and numb, I lowered the chair onto all four legs. My knees buckled when I stood, and I shook out my blood-deprived limbs, bending at the knee and testing each leg before placing my full weight on my feet. Tiptoeing toward the door, I carefully opened it just wide enough to check on Xander. His peaceful countenance made him look like he didn't have a care in the world. *Asshole*. The vibration in my pocket stopped, but I was sure it would start up again as soon as Tyler could hit the redial button. A soft breeze stirred the drapes, and I quickly crossed the room. The French doors in the bedroom hadn't been opened the last time I'd checked.

Careful not to interrupt Xander's beauty sleep, I slipped through the open doors to check the balcony. Dawn had not yet approached. A lightening in the eastern horizon marked its coming, but I doubted it was visible to anyone other than a Shaede. I smelled the dew beginning to form on the leaves and grass below the terrace, and I drew in a deep breath to hold the heady fragrance of encroaching morning in my lungs. My phone vibrated in my pocket, and I fished it out.

"Where are you?" Tyler shouted before I could even say hello.

"Where are *you*?" I asked.

"Not funny, Darian," he said. "I've been sitting in your apartment for hours, waiting for you to show up. Is everything okay? Are you hurt? Why didn't you make a wish?"

"Calm down," I hissed into the phone. "I'm fine."

"Where ... are ... you?" The controlled ferocity of his tone made my skin prickle.

"Xander's."

There was a pregnant pause on the other end of the line. I hoped Ty was counting to ten instead of heading out the door.

"Why?" He let the single word hang.

I rolled my eyes. "Side job. Security detail."

"Security detail!" Ty exploded. "Security for who?"

"I'm Xander's personal bodyguard for a while." I cringed at the words, visualizing the incredulous look that was no doubt on Ty's face.

"I'm coming over," Tyler said.

"No."

Tyler just couldn't get it through his thick skull. I didn't need him charging to my rescue. I had my pride to consider. Sure, he'd plucked me up off the street after the Lyhtan attack. And he had shown up at just the right second with my sword when I'd needed it. Time after time, Tyler had proved his loyalty, his concern, his protectiveness. It wasn't that I didn't appreciate it. I did. My overinflated ego didn't.

"You can't always be my knight in shining armor," I said. "Ty, I'm obligated to do this. I can handle it."

"Since when are you *obligated* to be Xander's anything?" he said with a dead calm that was more frightening than anything he could have shouted. "You were hired for one thing only, and that one thing doesn't include following Xander around and acting as his personal live target! Do you have any idea what might happen if you get into anything dicey? You could die, Darian!"

The sky continued to lighten, and I sensed a presence somewhere above me. It could have been another Shaede, but for some reason, my instinct told me differently. I couldn't focus on my surroundings while bickering on the phone, and Xander was just inside the door, vulnerable to attack. If something were to happen to him while I was assuaging Ty's ego, I'd never live it down. In fact, I didn't think I'd live, period.

"Tyler," I sighed. How could I convince him I was okay when my senses screamed that danger was close? "As soon as I'm done here, I'll be home. Stay at my apartment and wait for me if you want. There's nothing for you to worry about. Nothing dicey here." *Liar.* "I appreciate your concern, and if I get into trouble, you'll be the first person I'll call. Promise. Wishes will rain down on your ears." The hairs rose on the back of my neck as the pressure in the air intensified. "But right now, I've *got* to go." I flipped the phone closed and slid it back into my pocket.

With steps as light as thistledown landing on the ground, I treaded back into the room. Xander was still asleep. I reached to my back, slid the katana from the scabbard, barely making a sound as it came free. And just as silently and quickly, I returned to the terrace.

The sky was illuminated in varying shades of gray. Before I'd discovered just how dangerous this hour could be, it had been my favorite time. A stillness hung in the air that wasn't present at any other moment, save twilight. What I used to consider a peaceful time had become fraught with unseen dangers. A Lyhtan waited somewhere close; I could smell it.

I didn't want to fight on the terrace. There wasn't much room. But I didn't feel like I should venture too far from Xander either. If it was an ambush, he'd be left unprotected while I fought from somewhere below—or above. The smell grew stronger, and I crinkled my nose in distaste. As the air around me became heavy, I looked up and froze in shock at what dangled several feet above my head. Hanging upside down, like a mutated fruit bat, the Lyhtan clung with its feet to the terrace above me. My enemy swung its elongated body, releasing its hold on the iron railing, and dropped. God, I hoped it was one of the Lyhtans that had attacked me. Gripping the handle of the katana until it felt like it was a natural part of my hand, the blade an extension of my arm, I waited.

"The Enphigmalé will see to the end of your kind," myriad voices said as the Lyhtan straightened to its full height. "Tell your king that."

"Come a little closer and tell him yourself," I whispered. "You'll only have to get through me to do it. Or are you afraid to face me in the gray hour, Lyhtan?"

A sharp and mournful shriek rent the peaceful morning. Poised and ready to fight, the Lyhtan dangled a jagged blade, rusty and neglected, unworthy of battle, from its hand.

I glanced at the sky, hoping I had enough time to kill my enemy before the sun crested the horizon. Bad timing, but I couldn't help but wonder where the hell I'd put the bottled shadows Raif had given me. Too late now.

"What's your name?" I asked the creature, which wiped at a trail of saliva running steadily down its chin.

"Why do you need it?" the Lyhtan said in its many voices.

"So I can engrave it into the blade of my sword after I kill you." It was big talk, but I needed something to hike up my confidence level. Memories of lying in bed, covered in welts and raw, seeping wounds didn't help bolster my courage. I had to win; I had to kill this thing before it could get to Xander. My pride demanded it.

"All you need to know, Shaede, is that I am Death."

The Lyhtan lunged at me, teeth bared and sword at

the ready. I parried the thrust and swung the katana wide toward the creature's head, missing by mere inches. Its cackling laughter only served to increase my determination, and I swung again, using all my weight as I came around, this time swiping at its knees. It jumped, easily avoiding the blade, threw its head back, and howled into the ever-brightening sky.

I'd never faced an opponent this way. An assassin doesn't go into battle or fight one-on-one. An assassin relies on her stealth and cunning and takes her victim's life before he is ever aware danger is present. My heart pounded against my rib cage, and though I tried to control my breathing, the air came into my aching lungs in heavy drafts. I needed a clear and level head. I needed to keep it together. I needed to focus.

It came after me and covered the space between us in one long stride. Swinging with wild abandon, it aimed for my waist and then my throat, slicing through the air with the jagged and rusty blade. The Lyhtan growled in frustration and swiped a clawed hand at my face. I pulled back just before its talonlike nails could dig into my flesh.

With preternatural speed and precision, it attacked. As fast as me, if not a little faster, its blade rang out against mine over and over as I parried each thrust or cut. The serrated metal made a clean break difficult. More than once I became hung up on the rusty barbs and had to move too close for my comfort in order to free the katana. I gave silent thanks to Raif and my training as I fought, glad to have the stamina required to stand against this much stronger foe. It hissed and uttered unintelligible words as it struck over and over again, hungry for blood and intent on my death.

I sensed a movement from inside the room, and my eyes darted to the side. The Lyhtan followed suit and looked toward the open window. The sky reflected off the glass, almost blue with hints of muted orange washing over it like watercolor. I used the opportunity and took a quick step forward, bringing the blade down with all I was worth. It sliced into the Lyhtan's chest and the creature screamed and thrashed, clutching at the wound. I pulled back and swung full circle, the blade singing as it cleaved the air, cutting across the creature's throat and severing its squealing head.

The vile thing rolled and came to a stop at my feet while the Lyhtan's body convulsed in a macabre display before falling over the railing. I heard it land with a thump, followed by utter silence. My sword hung limp at my side, covered with the rusty orange blood of my enemy. I turned toward the east and watched as an explosion of light was born out of the gray morning, coloring the sky with a brilliance that caused me to shield my eyes. The Lyhtan's head, which rested still at my feet, shimmered like it had been covered with a thin layer of early-winter frost. The effect intensified, and soon the disjointed orb glittered in a golden-red light and disappeared.

"It has gone into the light," said a voice from behind me.

I turned to find Xander standing in the doorway. He had a reverent expression on his face, and he bowed his head. If you ask me, not very fitting for a king. But I didn't bother to point it out as he paid me respect for services rendered.

The sound of frantic footsteps came rushing up the stairs, and Raif burst into Xander's room at a full run. He skidded to a halt just feet from his brother and looked from me to him and back again before sheathing his sword.

"Is everything all right?" he asked.

"Yes," Xander said. "The fight was over before I even knew it had begun. She's a credit to your training, Raif."

Raif smiled and inclined his head to his brother. Moments later, several Shaedes entered the king's suite, many of them dressed in the weird ancient costume that Raif was fond of. Anya came a few minutes after that, and in the commotion, Xander was led from the room, leaving a trail of nervous worshippers behind him. Only Raif and I were left to watch the sun rise to a giant yellow orb in the sky.

"Were you scared?" he asked me.

"Shitless," I said.

"Good. Fear is what keeps you alive in a fight. Was it alone?" he asked, looking over the balcony to where the Lyhtan's body had landed.

"As far as I know," I said, joining him at the railing. "I felt the presence of only one."

Raif raised a curious brow and then looked away. "You are full of surprises, Darian."

I didn't ask him to explain what he meant. He'd probably give me enigmatic answers anyway. "Raif, what's an En-fig-mal-ae?" I said, enunciating the word the Lyhtan had spoken.

"Some say they're an order of humans with too much time on their hands, but I'm not so sure. I haven't heard the name in centuries. The Enphigmalé are a legend, a rumor without detail started to incite paranoia among conspiracy theorists." Raif said with disdain. "Why?"

"The Lyhtan said the Enphigmalé will see to the end of our kind. What did it mean?"

Raif shook his head and looked away. "I don't know." He turned and strode back into the room. "I'm taking a team out to secure the perimeter. We need to make sure this place is locked down tight. I don't need another security breach like this one. Also, one of our point men didn't check in this morning. I'm afraid there may be a casualty. Will you be all right if I leave you here?"

I can't say I wanted to go with him on his scouting expedition, but it did sting a little that Raif didn't ask. I shrugged and nodded. "I can take care of myself."

His chest moved with silent laughter. "That was obvious the first time I laid eyes on you. Xander won't be back this morning. They'll have him under lock and key until it's time to leave. This may be an attempt to keep him from attending the Summit, or it may just be a coincidence. Are you rested?"

"Rested enough."

"We have a long day. You can use Xander's bathroom to clean up," he said, looking at my blood-spattered attire. "A change of clothes is on its way up for you. I'll have it left on the bed."

"What's on the agenda?" I didn't think Raif had a day of embroidery planned.

"Today is the Summit. Delegates from all of the ruling bodies will be in attendance. It's more or less a gathering of political blowhards."

I laughed. "Not much different from human politicians, I gather."

"True." Raif smiled. "It's a clearing of the air, I guess you could say. They come together once every three months, and Xander's going to use the opportunity to rally support, in the event our troubles with Azriel escalate into all-out war. It's best to line up our allies now, while we have the chance. And he wants you in his entourage."

Great. The fun times kept rolling. "How long do I have to get ready?"

"Thirty minutes," Raif said with a smile in his eyes. "Is that long enough?"

I answered with my first real smile of the day. "I'll be ready in fifteen."

Chapter 18

A change of clothes had been left on the bed, waiting for me, when I got out of the shower. Raif spared me the embarrassment of making me wear one of his *Lord of the Rings* outfits. Instead, he'd left a black ensemble draped across the coverlet of Xander's bed.

I left Xander's suite and met Raif at the foot of the stairs in the foyer. Again, he stood at Xander's right side, something I'd only just noticed, whispering in his brother's ear. A collective murmur ran through the small crowd as I stepped from the final stair. I got the impression I'd been the topic of conversation—the Lyhtan slayer, something new and exciting to discuss. I was greeted with plenty of approving nods and even a couple of smiles. However, the expression that made me take pause came from a pair of violet eyes.

Anya stood toward the rear of the entourage, her eyes narrowed into hateful slits. If looks could kill, I'd have been dead a million times over. I flashed my most winsome smile. She turned, her long braid whipping out behind her like a huge length of rope, and headed straight for the door.

I paid Anya's display little attention, and instead, focused on the King of Shaedes. Xander stood a few feet away, looking over the heads of his advisers at me with a fixed and serious expression. He didn't look like his cocky, carefree self. The weight of a kingdom sat atop his shoulders, and I could tell it was a heavy weight to bear. His drawn face looked too tired for having slept through the night. The sparkle was gone from his eyes, which now appeared dull and lifeless.

Several cars waited at the front of the house, and the king's entourage moved as a collective hive through the door. I took up a place at Xander's left shoulder, trailing behind him, hyperaware of my surroundings.

Something caused a traffic jam in the flow of moving bodies, and another murmur ran through the crowd. A few words reached my ears, such as *wish* and *Jinn*, and I said a few of my favorite curse words under my breath.

"Who is he?" Someone demanded from the front of the queue.

"He is my bodyguard's . . . bodyguard." Xander said in an exasperated tone.

Raif turned to me, a deadly expression planted on his face. I was in deep shit for this one. I shrugged; it was the only thing I could think of doing. I'd told Tyler to stay put, but I guess without the words *I wish* to precede the order, the command carried little weight.

The crowd parted, and Tyler stopped just to the side of the king, giving him a clear view of me. Without making eye contact, he bowed slightly in Xander's direction. But he locked his gaze with mine.

"You were in trouble this morning." It was more of a statement than a question.

I kept a stoic countenance. "Tyler." His name came out sounding a little strange because my teeth were clenched. "This is business. You remember *business*, right?"

"Your safety *is my business*," he said. "You remember that, right?"

A thousand acts of violence against Ty flashed through my mind. Embarrassed to the point of nausea, I wanted nothing more than for the ground to open up and swallow me whole. Heat rose to my cheeks, and a wave of anxiety—or was that excitement?—rippled through me. If he was this protective of me at the mere notion of trouble, I could only imagine how he'd behave if I were truly in danger. "Tyler, I'm fine. If I were in any real trouble, you'd be the first to know." I did nothing to correct the hard line of my lips. Exciting alpha-male moment aside, I was still *pissed,* or, more to the point, *embarrassed*, and I wanted him to be one hundred percent aware of it. "I have one more place to be today, and we're going to be late. We'll talk about this later."

Tyler smiled, a knowing expression, like he'd put me in checkmate. "It just so happens I'm representing my delegation at the PNT Summit as well. Mind if I ride along?"

Oh, great.

He turned his head in Xander's direction but didn't bother to look away from me. The king shared a silent exchange with Raif and sighed. He stepped through the parted crowd and climbed into his car.

I shouldered my way past Ty and ducked my head into the backseat of a sleek, black limo along with Raif and Xander. Before I could close the door behind me, Tyler jumped in and slid beside me, to make an already uncomfortable moment unbearable. He and I faced Raif and Xander, and not a single one of us spoke.

The king glowered at Tyler, and it should have burned a hole right through him. Raif seemed merely amused, while I opted to stare out the window and watch as we negotiated traffic. I'd been utterly embarrassed, and I didn't think I could look any of them in the eye again. The car rolled along the city streets, while its company sat brooding. I was having an internal argument with no end in sight.

I didn't know if I loved Tyler. At the moment, I didn't even know if I liked him. Aside from his constant proclamation of *I'm yours*, I had no clue whatsoever to his true feelings. What the hell was that supposed to mean anyway? *I'm yours*. My what? My slave, my guardian angel, my own personal pain in the ass? Of course he cared about me. You don't just give your life over to someone that you're not particularly fond of. But what was this between us? I knew about as much about tender feelings as I did about my own Shaede nature. Would I even recognize love if it slapped me in the face?

"Darian, did you hear me?" Raif asked.

Shaken from my thoughts, I looked at Raif. "Sorry. What did you say?"

Tyler snickered beside me. I wanted to punch him in the face.

"I will sit beside the king and you will be posted at his left shoulder. Most of the representatives present will have security personnel, and they'll be standing, like you. In the past, you would have been referred to as a shield bearer. It's a formality for the most part, a long-standing one, and not usually performed by a king's champion. But after this morning's near miss, I think it's better to be safe than sorry by having a formidable warrior stand at Xander's back."

"What near miss?" Tyler interjected before I could ask Raif what in the hell a king's champion was.

"Mind your own business," I said.

"You are my business."

"Darian killed a Lyhtan attacker this morning," Raif said, ending the discussion. "She stood like a true warrior and sent her enemy's soul into the light. I might add, with no help from *you*, Jinn."

I couldn't help but smile that Raif thought so well of me. Tyler sank into the leather seat, pissed and pouting like someone had taken his lollipop.

Xander didn't speak the entire ride. A couple of times I caught him staring at me, but when I met his gaze, he looked away. He might have been nervous about the Summit or upset that Tyler had tagged along. Whatever the reason, he was in a darker mood than I'd ever seen him, and I didn't like it at all. He tapped his foot impatiently and folded his arms in front of his chest. A deep sigh escaped his lips and he glared in Ty's direction.

We drove along the waterfront to the Industrial District, near Xander's warehouse. The heavy, sea-tangy scent of Puget Sound made me think of Azriel. He loved the almost-musty odor, too thick for a deep breath. Where had he been hiding these past few months? He could've been right under my nose the entire time, for all the attention I'd paid. Because of his lies and misinformation, I'd all but lost myself in the populace. A virtual ghost, wary of making contact with anyone or anything, lest my true nature be discovered. But thanks to Raif and his obsessive-compulsive training tactics, I was ready. And when I got my hands on him, he'd damn well wish he'd stayed hidden.

Chapter 19

Not far from the building where I'd trained for nights on end with Raif, we arrived at the location of the Pacific Northwest Territories Summit. The commercial-sized warehouse looked like it had at one time been a storage facility for the large metal shipping containers sometimes seen on tankers. A few of the steel boxes remained, stacked neatly to the sides and rear of the complex. A chain-link fence, topped with curls of razor wire, guaranteed the place would be left alone. A metal mesh gate slid open on electronically controlled wheels, and the limo crept through the entrance, depositing us just outside a gaping maw of a door.

Rows of lights illuminated the central space of the building, and four long tables had been set end to end, forming a large square. In the center of the square sat a great, round brazier. Inside the shallow bronze bowl, bright orange flames danced and frolicked. An assortment of bodies milled around the warehouse space, some with their own entourages hanging unobtrusively behind.

Tyler walked right past me, winked, and joined a group of delegates directly across from where Xander had decided to settle in. My jaw dropped and I quickly snapped it shut, hiding my curiosity at Ty's role in this strange meeting of mystical creatures. He inclined his head toward his neighbor and flashed a cheerful smile, then nodded to someone a few groups down. I'd never seen him look so comfortable, so immersed in his element.

"This is what you do?" I murmured as Raif came to stand beside me. "Walk around and bullshit?"

"Have you ever seen Congress in action? This is what the gallery looks like right before a voting session," he said.

"I've never been to D.C." I said. "Have you?"

His knowing smile was all the answer he'd give before he went to stand beside his brother.

As I contemplated the possibility that Raif had actually visited Washington, D.C., I fell into my role as a stoic man—well, woman—in black and tailed the king as he traveled from group to group. Raif was right; politics in the supernatural world were just like politics in the human world, with everyone jockeying for their views to be heard and backed up.

"Alexander!" A tall, drop-dead gorgeous woman approached, and I took a step forward, astonished at the protective instinct. Her red hair was streaked with gold and cascaded down her back in curling locks that shone with an unworldly light. Creamy peach flesh and golden eyes complemented a silk dress of peacock blues and greens. Her refined features were good enough for any fresco. Hell, Botticelli would have wept at the sight of her. My skin tingled as waves of energy emanated from her, the power seeping into my pores.

"Gods above!" she exclaimed, planting a kiss on Xander's cheek. "Your entourage reeks of gin."

Wait just a damn second! Indignation flushed my cheeks; I had not been drinking. Xander chuckled, and the blood drained from my face. Not gin. *Jinn. Oh, give me a fucking break!*

"Yes, well, my new security team leader has a little pet, my dear Luna. I hadn't realized you didn't favor the Jinn."

Luna pulled her eager gaze from Xander's face long enough to give me a sneering appraisal that would have made Anya proud. "It's not that I don't favor them. But have you heard what their delegation is proposing on the Shape-Shifter Initiative? Surely, you won't be voting ..."

I'd blocked her out once I realized Luna liked the sound of her own voice almost as much as Xander did his. Besides, if I'd had to listen to her disparage the Jinn delegation for a moment longer, I may have been persuaded to try out my fist on her perfectly shaped nose. But the king listened like a devoted admirer, nodding and hanging on every word. If it came to a vote, of course he'd consider her stance on the issue, and, yes, he would be honored if she'd return the favor to his issues as well. *Spare me! Next group, please!*

As if he'd heard my mental urgings, Xander kissed Luna's hand and continued on his stroll. "Shape-Shifter Initiative?" I asked Raif as he fell back to walk with me.

"Politics." He shrugged. "It never changes. The shifters are asking for the embargo to be lifted on their hunting grounds. The pheasant population in northern Idaho has diminished over the years, and the bird happens to be sacred in one of their coming-of-age ceremonies. They want to be allowed to hunt before the harvest moon and the autumnal equinox. It's up for vote in a few months."

"You mean the supernatural community actually makes environmental-impact decisions?" My brain reeled as it fought to soak up all of this new information. Levi would shit a brick if he could've been there to hear it all!

"Why wouldn't we?" Raif said. "We inhabit this world, just like the humans. We must make decisions to protect natural resources, enact laws and policies. This is not chaos, Darian. We are not ungoverned animals."

Hands tucked behind my back, I followed Xander as he paced from group to group. From the corner of my eye I watched as Tyler did the same, his hands flashing in animated gestures as he talked, sometimes emphatically with a stern expression on his face. I wondered as I watched, *What is his stance on the Shape-Shifter Initiative?*

"Darian," Xander said as we approached a small group comprised of men in tailored business suits, "I'd like you to meet Dylan McBride. He owns a consulting firm out of Portland. Though didn't I hear, Dylan, that you're considering moving your headquarters to Seattle?"

I tried to discern any pattern of energy coming from Dylan as I studied him top to bottom. Graying salt-and-pepper hair, fine lines at the corner of his eyes when he smiled. Dylan seemed as average as any guy walking down the street. "I am, in fact, planning a move. We'll be anchored here by spring." He turned his attention fully to me and took my hand. A firm but not unusual grip.

"What kind of consulting do you do, Mr. McBride?" I couldn't help but ask. Maybe he advised pixies on the best brand of magic dust to buy.

"I'm a financial consultant. I also manage business ventures for clients who have an issue with blending into normal society. Estate sales, acquisitions, stocks, bonds—I pretty much do it all."

Dylan's gray eyes sparkled, and I looked to Raif, who mouthed the word *human*. Sure, why not? Everyone else seemed to be here. Why not a human or two? I needed a drink.

"Nice to meet you, Dylan," I said, stepping back behind Xander. Dylan clapped the king on the back and moved on, smiling and chortling with his cohorts as they passed.

"Surprised?" Xander asked with a sideways glance in my direction.

"You have no idea," I said, sour and not afraid to show it.

His arrogant laughter sent chills down my spine. I hated the way he affected me, made me want to silence him for good. "What now?" I asked, my mood taking a

dive. "More meet and greet, or are we going to get this
show on the road?"

"I have one more person I'd like to speak with. By
then, I believe we'll be ready to start."

Xander plowed ahead, Raif beside him and me trailing behind, trying to look like I had my shit together. But
I so didn't. Not even close. *Son. Of. A. Bitch.* How in the
hell could I have been so blind? I was walking through a
supernatural pep rally with hundreds of attendees, by
my estimation. How had I never noticed them before?
Or was it like Levi had said, and the supernatural population had suddenly shifted their focus on Seattle and
the brewing conflict between Xander and his heir? I felt
like throwing up.

We approached a man and a woman, both tall and
unusually thin. Their pale skin appeared luminescent
against the warehouse lighting, an aura of pinkish light
hovering around them. With features too similar to ignore, they had to be related. Faun-colored hair, straight
and fine, trailed down the woman's back, while the man's
had been clipped short. Their eyes, the lightest blue and
hauntingly empty, only made their faces look more ethereal. As we came near, identical smiles graced their
mouths—a baring of teeth that could only be described
as predatory. They were a frightening pair, and I rested
my hand near my dagger, ready to defend if need be.

"Sidhe," Raif whispered close to my cheek. "The oldest living creatures in the Fae lineage. Older than re-
corded time. Do not look them in the eye."

Okay, easy enough. Just a glance in their direction
made my skin crawl. Literally. A powerful energy, greater
even than what I'd felt from Luna, crept out from where
they stood, slithering over my skin like rough-skinned
snakes.

"Alexander, I bring greetings from your father's father," the woman said. "To you as well, Raif."

Raif bowed his head, and Xander followed suit. My

own gaze I kept toward the floor, but I felt an urge to drop lower, as if invisible hands pushed me down. I looked up, just enough to see the man staring at me, his pleased smile telling me he was the one pushing my buttons. And I refused to let him. Without looking him straight in his eyes, I focused my gaze at his hawkish nose, fighting his influence with all I was worth. It felt like I was squatting five hundred pounds, but I resisted the power flooding from him as well as the urge to kneel at his feet.

His sneer faded into amusement, and still I would not meet his eyes. *I don't bow for anyone. Period.*

"I have matters to discuss with you," Xander said to the woman, brushing aside my silent power struggle. "You know what's happening in my kingdom."

"I do," the woman said, seeming disinterested.

"You will not intervene?"

"No."

The word carried enough finality to draw my attention. I looked at Xander; pain was written on his face. I knew that look; it was a reaction to betrayal.

"We will not involve ourselves in this matter," she continued. "Fate will see the victor."

"I'm putting this matter of war before the delegation today." Xander's tone had become more frigid with every word. "I will ask for aid if it comes to war. I cannot risk my kingdom."

With a slow inclination of her head, the woman rested a pearlescent hand on Xander's shoulder. "Then Fate be with you," she said. "I do not wish to see your kingdom in danger. Nor you or yours. But the die has been cast, and these events must be seen through to their end."

The sound of a gavel banging saved me from having to plunge my dagger into anyone's belly, and the siblings retreated toward the far end of the warehouse. The man cast a backward glance at me as they left, and I felt something in the invisible energy pulsing around him.

Nothing malicious or even taunting. But, rather, curious. As if he'd been testing me. His lips turned up in a soft smile that spread to warm the chill in his white-blue eyes. He looked pretty damn pleased, actually. I stumbled, my attention inexplicably drawn to the Sidhe. In turn, Raif snatched me by the elbow as we followed Xander to his seat. "I'm proud of you, Darian," Raif said. "He is an ancient, and *very* powerful."

"Does he have a name?"

"I will not speak it," Raif answered. "The older Fae will not be named. They believe that by giving someone their given name, they are giving up a portion of their power. Few know their true names."

Wow. Supernatural 101. I hoped there wouldn't be a quiz later. "What do you call them, then? You have to call them something."

"Moira, and her brother is Reaver."

Cheery names to go with their cheery faces, no doubt. "They mentioned your father." Or was it his grandfather? "I didn't realize he was still alive."

"Technically, he isn't."

Another round of gavel banging interrupted our conversation, and Raif and Xander promptly took their seats.

Curiosity burned little scorching paths through my brain as I rounded the rectangular table. *Technically?* What in the hell did that mean? I took my place at Xander's left side and used the moment of inactivity as an opportunity to take in each and every detail of the other beings seated along the tables.

I'd never known, let alone *seen*, such an assortment of creatures gathered in one place. Tall, short, fat, thin— and, for the most part, remarkably human in appearance. Everyone, that is, but Moira and her brother. They seemed to flaunt their otherness with brash arrogance. Beneath the facades of the delegates, I caught a glimpse of what these creatures really were. The glamour must've allowed them to pass for human. But a shimmer in the fabric of reality blew away as if on a soft breeze, and their true faces were revealed. A tiny girl sat to one side of Xander, her hair tossed in wild curls almost to the floor. She gave the impression that she could've crawled out from under a tree before taking her seat. Across the square from her, a pair of nymphlike creatures sat. A male and female, their skin glistened as if they'd just taken a swim. That wasn't all. Creatures with fur and some with feathers sat side by side with others covered in scales. And ignorant as I was, I couldn't even place a name with their shapes. Faeries, gnomes, werewolves; I wouldn't know a vampire from a shape-shifter, if either were present. And under the cover of their glamour, they appeared no different from the humans on the street.

My face felt hot all of a sudden as the embarrassment seemed to crawl right up my cheeks. *Damn Azriel.* I bet he was getting a good laugh over this right now. It must have been his goal to keep me in the dark, both literally and figuratively. His actions had become inexcusable, and the thought of his death not only acceptable but appealing.

Xander turned from his conversation with his brother and beckoned me. Like any good employee, I moved closer to see what he needed.

"What do you think?" he asked.

"I think I'm an idiot," I said, low, next to his ear.

Xander laughed and some of the spark returned to his eyes. I didn't miss the dark glance he shot in Tyler's direction, though. "Let me ask you this." He paused and traced his finger in a square on the table's surface. "What do you feel here?"

It was my turn to take a pause. *Feel? Like, my feelings?* I didn't know we were choosing this moment to open up about that sort of stuff. But then my brain actually kicked into gear and I realized he wasn't asking *how*

I felt, but *what* I felt. I'd noticed it before, as we walked among the other delegates, that the room definitely had the energy of many different creatures buzzing around inside it.

"I feel others like us," I began. "And"—my heart jumped in my chest—"I sense a Lyhtan somewhere here."

"What else?" Xander asked softly next to my ear.

"A hum, not like the pressure I feel in the air when a Shaede or Lyhtan is present, but something else. A vibration, almost."

"Faerie?" Raif asked, leaning to speak behind Xander. "I'm not sure, but I bet that's what you're feeling. It could also be a Sylph, I suppose." He pointed to the girl with the long, wild hair who was sitting beside Xander.

"Anything else?" Xander asked, ignoring his brother.

Raif shot his brother a murderous glare, and for a moment I could almost picture them fighting like children. A hint of a smile formed on my lips as the image of two boys arguing over a favorite toy popped into my head.

There were too many sensations to differentiate between them all. It felt like I was sitting in a hot tub, wrapped in one of those massage pads, with melting ice trickling down my back. Top it off with a buzzing in my ears, the hair standing up on my scalp, and a pounding pulse, and that just about covered it.

"I can't divide and identify all the sensations," I admitted. "And if I could, I wouldn't know what it meant or who to credit the feeling to."

Xander smiled and leaned farther back, studying my face. "You are remarkable."

I looked up to see Tyler scowling in my direction. I was warming up to the idea that the only way to settle their little grudge was to put him and Xander in a steel cage together and let them fight it out. *Two men enter; one man leaves.* I laughed.

"What's so funny?" Raif asked.

"I was thinking of Thunderdome," I said.

Raif gave me a puzzled look and shook his head.

"What about the Lyhtan?" I asked Xander, looking at the table to our left. Sure as shit, the nasty bastard lounged in its chair with, of all things, a human standing security at its back. I knew the guy was just as normal as Dylan McBride, though the glazed-over look on his face told me he wasn't all there. "That human," I said, jerking my chin toward him. "He's guarding the Lyhtan. Under thrall?"

"I would say so," Raif said, examining the Lyhtan's security detail. "How did you know?"

I wanted to shout with glee. Finally, I knew something that Raif didn't have to tell me first! *Thank you, Levi!* "I have my sources," I said, before snapping back into business mode. "Raif, it's obviously not safe to be here. Especially after the attack this morning."

Xander brushed the comment aside with a wave of his hand. "This is a diplomatic meeting. No violence."

"Then why am I here?" I asked.

Xander chuckled but didn't get the opportunity to answer. A man—not Shaede or anything else I'd ever seen—stepped to the middle of the square near the brazier and held his arms to the sky, palms facing up. He bore a striking resemblance to the Sidhe, Moira and Reaver, but at the same time, his features were different enough that I knew he wasn't one of them. A strange master of ceremonies, he tipped his head back and chanted something, his voice melodious and reverent, in a language that meant nothing to me.

The king and everyone else present bowed their heads. I took a step back and did the same, feeling a lot like a guest at a church I didn't attend. When the man was done with his prayer, or whatever it was, I studied him at length.

I sensed the hum coming from his direction, making me assume he was one of the faerie attendees Raif had mentioned earlier. Even beneath the surface of his glamour, he could've passed for human if he'd wanted to. He'd have to hide the slightly pointed ears and do something about the long, silvery-white hair, though. That might stand out in a crowd. An ageless quality graced his face; it seemed impossible to determine if he was old, young, adolescent. . . . His skin, smooth and fair, bore no wrinkles, even when his eyes narrowed at the corners.

The hum emanating from where he stood hit me like it was being funneled right into my chest. I concentrated on the sensation for a moment. It must have been magic; that's the only way I can describe it. I sensed power in him and felt it deep down in my bones.

He held a black velvet bag over the brazier and dumped out the contents. My breath caught as I watched the bleached-white hunks fall out. I expected them to tumble into the fire, but as if they'd been cast on a glass tabletop, the items rolled out like dice and settled on the air.

"The runes have selected the High King of the Shaede Nation, Alexander Peck, to speak first."

A corner of Raif's mouth tugged into a smirk, and Xander stood. "War stands at our doorstep."

"It stands only at your doorstep, Shaede," someone called out, eliciting nods of approval and shouts of encouragement. "Why should any of the other nations care about your coup?"

Xander placed his palms on the surface of the table and leaned down, eyeing the member of each delegation before he spoke. "If my nation is conquered, who's to say yours won't be next?" He pointed to the opposite table. "Or yours?" He pointed to his right. "Mine is only the beginning of a much larger problem."

A murmur ran through the seated delegates.

"We live on the precipice of discovery. The balance between our kind and the humans could be tipped by the slightest shift in power. Can we afford discovery? Are you willing to put your people at risk?"

"What do you propose, High King?" The faerie master of ceremonies asked from the center of the square.

With his palms on the table to prop him up, Xander slowly spread his hands outward, lowering himself into a humble position. He bowed his head to show respect for the delegates seated around him. I held my breath, my pulse strumming in my ears. He was magnificent—playing to the crowd, playing to their egos, sacrificing his own pride for the betterment of his kingdom. I felt as though I would drown in the aura of his presence.

"An enemy to one of us is an enemy to us all. We have lived peaceably these many centuries. I see no reason for our lives not to continue in peace. Consider our position in this matter ..." Xander continued to plead his case, and my gaze wandered to Tyler, who watched the spectacle with deep interest. In turn, I studied his facial expressions. And then he looked at me. He stared right at me, his hazel eyes pools of warmth and feeling that conveyed a thousand words without speaking. I saw in his eyes the words I hoped I'd never have to hear because I didn't know how I'd respond. *I'm in love with you.*

I broke free from the powerful hold of his stare, and the emotions that caused my own to swirl with uncertainty, to train my eyes on the other delegates seated at the tables. Xander was gaining ground; I read it on most of their faces. One by one, I recognized a change in their attitudes with the softening of their expressions. The Lyhtan delegate shimmered in the light of day, the many facets of dancing color almost grotesque as it mocked the ugliness of the creature itself. I shuddered as our eyes locked and a trail of spittle dribbled from its leering mouth. It would have been much more appealing as the tiny glittering insect I'd seen on the day of my attack. But all the beauty in the world couldn't mask the ugliness of their character. I continued to stare, and it snapped its strong jaws twice, the sound popping loudly in the mostly quiet building. It alone seemed untouched by Xander's humble act.

The Shaede King straightened and his smooth, wonderful voice boomed in the huge warehouse. "My friends, I would never ask you to fight a battle that isn't yours to fight. I ask only that if the need arises, you send aid."

As Xander's pomp and circumstance drew to a close, the growl of an engine announced its presence just outside. Tires squealed and came to a stop, and four figures dressed head to toe in red, complete with face masks, rolled aside the massive doors. Sunlight streamed in behind them, shading two more ominous figures.

"It seems a representative is missing from these proceedings!" one of them called out. They cast a tiny bundle to the concrete floor. It rolled once and landed like a sack of rocks several feet from where I stood. The hooded party crashers backed away from their cargo and turned to run. Car doors slammed in the distance before the screeching of tires signaled their hasty departure. We stood in stunned silence, listening as the sound of the fleeing vehicle grew fainter by the second.

A collective gasp broke the peace, and not a soul dared to move toward the bundle. I rolled my eyes. *What a bunch of cowards.* I drew the katana from behind my back and approached the object with measured steps. I heard a soft moan that wouldn't have been detected by human ears; mine barely picked up the sound. I rushed the last few feet, sheathing the sword and going to my knees. Quickly, I fumbled with the ropes tied around the rough burlap sack and pulled it off a tiny girl beaten so badly, she was almost unrecognizable.

Oh, my God. I sucked in a lungful of air, and milky blue eyes rolled in her head, which cocked very slightly, moving toward the sound of my inhalation. I'd found one thing I'd been looking for.

Chapter 20

Tyler slid down beside me on his knees and bent over Delilah's limp and almost lifeless body. His fingers glided to her throat and he sat, statuelike, while he searched for a pulse. I knew he'd found one when his body relaxed.

"We've got to get her out of here," Ty said, turning to me.

"Take her to my house," Xander said. His warm voice actually made me jump, and a moment later his palm came to rest on my shoulder. "Raif and Anya will take her in the other car. There's plenty of room." I could sense the reluctance in his voice when he added for Tyler's benefit, "You can come as well."

When Ty looked at me, his face was a mixture of rage and sorrow. Delilah had moxie, but her tiny little body couldn't have held out for long. And she'd taken one hell of a beating. As if he were lifting a newborn child, he took her in his arms. Her head lolled back, lacking even the strength to rest on his shoulder.

"Where?" he asked, and Raif led the way to the car.

Delilah's dramatic entrance brought the Summit to an abrupt end. The crowd of delegates dispersed in a quick and disorderly fashion. Only the Lyhtan seemed to take his . . . her . . . *its* time in leaving. It sauntered out into the afternoon sun with a strange confidence despite its grotesque appearance, flashing a jagged-toothed smile in my direction before its body dissolved. A shimmering insect dropped to the ground like a pearl where the Lyhtan had stood, and scurried away.

I hadn't noticed that I sat in the empty building alone until Xander's voice cut through the silence surrounding me. "Darian, we should go."

"Huh?"

He bent and wrapped his arms around my waist, gently pulling me to a standing position. I couldn't wipe the image of Delilah's battered face from my mind. It hit too close to home and reminded me of my human life, where I'd been weak, susceptible, abused. I compared her injuries to my own the night Henry almost killed me—the same night Azriel became my savior. The prickling of tears stung behind my eyes, and I fought the emotion with everything I had. Weakness wouldn't do me any good. I wasn't going to kill whoever had done this by crying in my beer. And I *was* going to kill the person responsible.

Xander's house buzzed with urgency. The very walls hummed with discord, and the air had become oppressive and grim in the wake of the day's events. Delilah's injuries weren't life-threatening, but she had a broken arm, two broken ribs, and a dislocated shoulder. In addition to the many cuts, bruises, and abrasions, I didn't think a square inch of her body had been left untouched by her attackers.

I don't know if it was the woman in me or simply the creature that thirsted for revenge, but I marched straight for Xander's suite and informed him of my intention to hunt Delilah's kidnapers.

"No," he said in a calm and simple way.

"No? Why not?"

"It's not your job to avenge her."

I couldn't understand how he could sit there, so calm and collected, after what had happened. I opened my mouth to assure him that maybe it wasn't my job to avenge the poor girl, but I *was*, in fact, still in charge of my own life, when Xander crossed the room and gently shut the door.

"I can't risk your safety," he said quietly.

Again, the words that tried to form died behind my lips. "What?" I finally said.

"You understand so little." He stepped closer and in a very deliberate way threaded his fingers through the curls of my hair, caressing my scalp with each of his fingertips. The contact sent rivers of chills along my flesh, and an exasperated sigh escaped my parted lips. Was I the only one here who thought there was something seriously wrong with this picture?

"I know what you're trying to do," I said, my tone laced with warning, "and it's not going to work."

Xander put his lips to my forehead and murmured, "What am I trying to do, Darian?"

My senses were awash with the most miniscule detail. The feel of his fingers as they raked through my hair, the smell wafting from his skin, even his warm breath as it tickled my temple. The air in the small space became almost heady, and my heart raced. I looked at his face, youthful despite the passing of years. He didn't look old enough to be any grown man's father. In fact, he had so little in common with Azriel, I had a hard time believing they were related at all. The soft glow of his eyes burned into mine. The heat from his gaze was unmistakable, full of passion and longing.

"I don't mix business with pleasure," I said. "And you're a little overconfident if you think I'm going to fall for this bullshit seduction. Xander, don't you think you're crossing some serious boundaries here?"

One of his hands came free of the tangle of my hair and, with deliberate precision, traced the side of my body to settle at my hip. The tension between us was palpable, like a big, thick blanket that wrapped our bodies together, suffocating me, and I realized he didn't care. Azriel or no Azriel, he had serious entitlement issues.

"I want you," he said. "Regardless."

"What you want and what you get are two completely different things, Xander."

My heart leapt from my chest into my throat, and I swallowed hard, as if I could force the damn thing back down where it belonged. Xander was everything I should have wanted: gorgeous, powerful, sardonic in that romance-novel sort of way. Figure Ty into the mix, and I was more confused than ever. If Xander had come along a year or even a few months sooner, there might not have been a decision to make. And aside from a past I couldn't forget or overlook, I knew I'd never be anything more to him than a possession, paid or not. And like I'd told him before, some of my services were not for sale. "Do you think you can just snap your royal fingers and I'll fall into bed?" I asked. "You can't have it all. I'm hired to do a job for you and that is all. Period."

"This is about the Jinn," he growled under his breath. "Send him away. It's that simple."

This *so* wasn't just about the Jinn. An image of Tyler's face loomed in my mind, loyal, loving, and glorious. Maybe it was about the Jinn, a little. "I can't do that," I said, putting a good arm's length between us. "I won't."

Xander's body stiffened, his expression that of jealousy and passion. He knocked my outstretched arms aside and cupped my face in his hands, forcing me to look up. He paused and dipped his head. Could I stop him if he chose to follow through? Would I want to? I didn't pull away, but my hand twitched toward the dagger strapped to my thigh. If a poke in the ribs was what it took to get my point across, so be it. But I was saved from any acts of violence when a knock came at the door.

Rather than let me go, Xander held me fast. "I'll send whoever it is away."

"Don't bother," I said, brushing his hands from my cheeks. "I know you're used to getting what you want, *Your Highness*, but not this time. I am *not* for sale."

"Xander," Raif's voice called through the door. "The girl is awake. I thought you'd want to know."

I fingered the hilt of the dagger once more, gave Xander a pointed and meaningful stare, and headed for the door. He managed to secure a grasp on my hand and tugged me back toward him.

"Please," he said. "Don't go."

I freed my hand, and without looking back headed straight for the door.

"Darian." Xander's velvet voice hinted of command.

I pulled open the door and rushed out, closing it before he could employ any more of his seduction tactics. *Jesus*. What had I done to deserve this kind of attention? I wasn't charming by any standards, and my sarcastic quips couldn't possibly be that attractive. I did not have time for these ridiculous, dramatic, soap-opera moments.

Raif gave me a knowing look that I wanted to slap right off his snarky face.

"Has she said anything?" I asked as we walked down the hall, away from temptation.

"Not yet. She's weak. It looks like she was starved in addition to the beatings. There's not much to her—just skin and bones."

"Believe me, there wasn't much to her before she was kidnapped." I listened to the sound of my footsteps on the thin hallway carpet, letting the rhythm pound torturous thoughts from my mind. Delilah needed all the help she could get right now. She needed me. "Are you going to tell me about the Enphigmalé now?" I asked, just as we approached the door to Delilah's room.

"Afterward," Raif said.

I gave him a look that said *You'd better*, and, from the hard expression on his face, I knew he'd tell me. He could taste vengeance, just as I did.

Poor Delilah. I doubt she wanted my pity; she never struck me as that type of girl. But as she lay half-conscious, buried in the heavy blankets of the queen-sized bed, she looked as close to death as she could get. Someone had cleaned her up, and what was left under the crusted blood and grime wasn't much better. Whoever had done this to her had been doing it for a while. The bruises marked her face in different degrees of color and severity. Some had already begun to yellow. But others were fresh, nearly black. One milky eye had started to swell shut, while the other stared blindly at the ceiling. A shudder swept over my body as I watched the barely noticeable rise and fall of her chest and heard the almost-imperceptible rasping sound that came from the involuntary act.

Raif looked down on her with a mixture of bitterness and compassion. Oracles in general weren't exactly on his list of favorite creatures. However, Raif was a warrior right down to the tips of his toes. A warrior's job, first and foremost, is to protect those weaker than himself, and you couldn't get any weaker or more helpless than Delilah. He stood for about as long as he comfortably could before leaving. "I'll wait for you outside," he said as he pulled the door closed behind him.

Just as Raif left, the bathroom door swung wide and Tyler stepped into the room. I thought of Xander's earlier play for my attention, and guilt swept over me. Clearing my throat, I tried to banish the feeling that I had somehow betrayed him. He looked my way briefly before moving to Delilah's side, where he placed a cool cloth on her forehead.

"She'll be all right," he said, as if he'd been repeating the mantra since she'd been brought here. "Anya says she'll be in and out of consciousness for a few days, maybe, but she'll live. You know"—Ty gave me a bitter smile—"in the all the years I've known Delilah, this is the first time I've ever seen her helpless."

"How did you two meet?" I asked, wanting to take his mind off his sorrow.

"We traveled in the same circles. The older supernatural community tends to stay close. The world is constantly changing, and life can get lonely when you live so long. It's nice to have something or someone to ground you. We all sort of keep in touch. Delilah and I would run across each other every twenty years or so. I was living in upstate New York in the eighties. She was hanging out with a CIA contact I'd done some freelance work for."

"CIA? What's that all about?" I couldn't help my wry tone. Good lord, Ty had played with some *big-time* heavy hitters.

He laughed. "I could tell you, but then I'd have to kill you. Delilah's the one who convinced me to move to Seattle. She was headed out this way, and she told me that my future awaited me here." His expression was heated as his eyes bore in to mine. "I guess she was right."

"I'm going to find whoever did this," I said, speaking more to Delilah than Ty. "And when I do, I'm going to kill every last one of them."

Tyler's head snapped up and he stalked around the bed. He grabbed my upper arm, giving me a little shake. "You are *not*, under any circumstance, going after whoever did this. Do you understand me?"

Did Xander and Ty share a brain or something? Since when did I become the damsel in distress anyway?

"Who are you to tell me what I can or can't do?" I said, none too calm. "I'm not that breakable, Ty. I can't sit here and do nothing."

"I care, okay!" Tyler's voice was rising to the point that every Shaede in the house would hear our conversation. "I don't want you to get hurt, or worse. It would kill me if something happened to you."

Literally, I thought. If this was about saving his neck, then I could fix that problem with little fuss. "If you're worried about yourself, *Jinn*, I can release you from whatever bond we have right now. You won't need to die for me or anyone else."

Tyler's face went blank and he looked at his feet, shaking his head. When he looked up, his eyes met mine with a fierce intensity. He grabbed both of my arms just below the shoulder and gave me a rougher shake with each word, "I. Love. You!"

"Shut up!" I said, not caring who heard our exchange now. "Shut up, Tyler! You have no idea what you're saying."

"Keep telling yourself that, Darian. Do whatever you have to do to keep from feeling what you know is there. Play your games with Xander, run from the truth, put yourself in danger. Kill every last thing on the fucking planet if you think it'll keep you from the truth. It's not going to change anything. It's not going to change how I feel. And sooner or later, you're going to have to admit that you love me too."

His words were flavored with something I didn't recognize, couldn't understand. He trembled with emotion. I don't know what he wanted to do—hit me, kiss me, or maybe take me outside and throw me off the balcony. My arms tingled, his tight grip biting into my skin, cutting off the circulation.

"Tyler." My voice had grown quieter, but I couldn't do anything about the hard edge. "You've known me for a long time. I'm not made for that. *Love* isn't in my vocabulary. I don't even think I really know what it is. You're not doing yourself any favors by trying to convince yourself otherwise."

I broke free from his grasp and paused at Delilah's bedside, putting my lips to the one tiny spot on her forehead not marred with cuts or bruises. "Don't worry; I am going to kill the bastards that did this." I shot one last murderous, albeit confused, glare at the back of Tyler's head, and left.

"Let's go," I said to Raif, closing the door behind me and walking down the hall.

"Where?" he said, trying to keep up.

"Anywhere but here. Is there someone who can look after Xander while we're gone?"

"I've got a detail posted outside his suite and I doubled the personnel around the perimeter of the house. He won't be going anywhere tonight. The place is in total lockdown."

"Good," I said, and bounded down the stairs, straight for the front door.

"What the hell is it with men, anyway?" I asked Raif over the music and chatter as I settled onto a chair in my favorite corner of The Pit. "Do you guys have some kind of internal wiring problem, or what?"

"I take it you're talking about my brother and his competition?" Raif laughed and then looked around. "Do you actually *like* this place?"

I quirked a brow. *Competition?* "There's no contest. Besides, it's just too strange. I feel like I have the starring role in some Arthurian poem or Greek tragedy or something." If the situation was so obvious to Raif, everyone in Xander's inner circle must've known about our little . . . *situation.* I wanted to gag. "Is it all about wanting what you can't have? The thrill of the chase? Or what?"

"Darian." Humor lingered in Raif's voice. "Time means something different to us. You're still young, but you'll soon understand. Xander is more than four hundred years old. You can live many lives in the course of a lifetime that spans so long. What does he care who you chose to spend your nights with a century ago? He's still a man, and you're still a beautiful woman."

Oh, so now this is my fault? I wasn't getting the cool-headed logic I'd expected, but was instead getting the runaround from him too. "Okay, fine. All of this is because I'm just so goddamned irresistible. It must be my shining personality and lighthearted spirit. I feel so sorry for them both."

Raif laughed good-naturedly, at once an awkward and icy sound. But now, in our camaraderie, I found his laughter comforting. He didn't offer any further commentary, which was just fine by me. I was sick to death of the whole situation, and I didn't care if I saw either one of their sorry asses ever again. I was in the mood for a fight, and Raif would help bring one to me.

"Enphigmalé," I said, slapping my palm down on the table. "I want to know everything."

Raif stood and took up his chair, spinning it around and scooting it close to me. He straddled it and rested his arms on the high back. An expectant gleam, the bloodthirsty sort, shone in his eyes, and I waited for him to speak.

"As the legend goes, when the British Isles were a wild, nameless place and the human race was in its infancy, the land belonged to the extraordinary. Change came, as it always must, and the human population exploded. We hid ourselves as best we could, but even then there were humans who could see us for what we were. Sometime in the years before Christ's teachings, I believe, it's said that a group was gathered and formed. A collective to . . . police the supernatural community, and keep the natural order, you might say. They called themselves the Enphigmalé, which, to tell you the truth, doesn't mean much to me, but it could have meant something then.

"Anyway, the stories say they were a ruthless bunch of bastards, and even took it upon themselves to regulate us as they saw fit, if it seemed like our populations were increasing to an *uncontrollable* number." He snorted in disgust. "They had a full arsenal of members: theologians, scholars, warriors, high-ranking politicians, and influential businessmen. A mixture of human and nonhuman members, from what I've been told. Their reach was far, and there wasn't much they didn't have at least a finger in."

"The Lyhtan said, 'The Enphigmalé will see to the end of your kind,'" I reminded him. "What do you think that meant? That they're planning on exterminating us?"

Raif shrugged. "Your guess is as good as mine. Lyhtans aren't exactly eloquent speakers, as you already know."

"What about Azriel, then?" I tucked a leg up underneath me and leaned forward, resting my chin on my fingertips. "He has to have *at least* a finger in this. Could his ambition to seize Xander's throne have to do with the Lyhtans *and* the Enphigmalé? And what about Delilah? How does she fit in to all of this? Shit is raining down on us. There's no way it's not all connected somehow. But . . . why beat the shit out her and then dump her in the middle of a supernatural political rally? Why not just kill her?"

Raif shook his head in that disappointed-father way that always drove me crazy. "Why kill her?" he asked. "She has value."

"As what?"

He raised a brow.

"An Oracle," I said, answering my own question.

"Perhaps."

"So apparently they weren't willing to make the sacrifice to buy Delilah's services. From the looks of her, they decided to beat a vision out of her. Maybe they didn't see anything at all," I said, more to myself than to Raif. "Maybe the Lyhtan was just blowing smoke—or propagating something."

"Could be," Raif agreed.

"What else do you know about them?" His little story couldn't possibly be all there was to the elusive group. There had to be more.

"Stories, for the most part," he said. "Conjecture,

guesses. Faerie tales passed down from one generation to the next. They're a tight group and very secretive. Not much is known about them. Over the years the legends change; their role increases or diminishes. Who's to say if there's any truth to the tales at all?"

"What are the other versions of the stories?" I asked.

"I've heard some say the Enphigmalé aren't human at all. That they're something else entirely, and the stories of secret societies are nothing but a smoke screen meant to scare the supernatural community. Boogeymen. It was once rumored that they were the guardians of something. Something so ancient it predates history."

"Like what?" I could barely contain my curiosity. It burned like a forest fire, to mingle with my rage and need for vengeance. "What could they possibly be protecting? And what are they? Do you think they're like us?"

"No, not like us. But who knows? Maybe they're something dark and evil—a creature that answers to a specific master. Maybe the group itself is named after the animal that served them."

"I don't exactly consider us bringers of the light," I said ruefully. "Would you?"

"Since when is everything black and white, Darian?" Raif asked in a reproachful tone.

Since when . . . I was the self-proclaimed Queen of Gray. Black and white had no place in my world. Since when, indeed.

"You're forgetting another important question," Raif said.

I raised a brow in question. *Am I?*

"How do *you* fit in to all of this?"

I suppressed a shudder. Somehow, I *was* a part of this, though I had no idea why. Azriel wanted me . . . for something. But what? "Will you help me?" I asked, already knowing the answer.

"Find them?" Raif said. "Yes. And kill every last one."

I smiled. Finally, someone who wasn't insisting I hide and protect myself. "And what about Azriel? Are you certain he's orchestrating all of this?"

Raif smiled back. "I hope so."

Chapter 21

I'd stopped at my apartment to grab a few things for the night, fully intending on returning to Xander's to help Raif stand guard. Somehow the thought of being housed up with Tyler and Xander, not to mention the reminder of poor Delilah and her battered body, slowed my efforts. I wasn't afraid of the danger. Cutting your eyeteeth in battle has a way of making a person swell with pride. And truth be told, I'd have much rather gone one-on-one with an enraged Lyhtan than spend the evening in the company of Xander, Tyler, or both. Hell, even Anya would have made a better companion, as far as my current circumstances were concerned. I just needed some time to clear my head. Get my shit together. But rather than think about anything, I curled up in a ball on the couch and fell asleep.

It must've been around midnight when I sensed a disturbance in the air behind me. I lay suctioned to the surface of my couch, barely breathing. I refused to wish for help. More than capable and deadly, I wasn't about to go down without a fight. I tried to calm the shallow drafts of breath, slow the brisk thrumming of my pulse, as I waited for my guest to formally make his presence known.

"Hello, my love." That cool, seductive voice snaked into my soul, pulling me unbidden into memories I'd tried to banish. He'd found me. I hadn't been able to track him down, not for decades. And he'd found me. I hoped Azriel hadn't come to kill me, because despite my claim of strength, I wasn't sure I could kill him.

My voice froze inside my throat. Words formed on my tongue, but something prevented me from pushing them through my lips. My heart hammered inside my chest, and I suddenly felt the urge to swallow more than usual. I had often wondered how I'd feel if I ever came face-to-face with him again. Well, in this case, face to back of couch, but his voice was enough to send me over the edge. My nerves crumbled like dry bread, and I tried to make myself believe he'd leave if I could only manage to stay still for a moment longer.

Azriel's soft laughter rippled over me like rings on a pond. I tried to clear my throat in an effort to jump-start my vocal cords, and the sound came more like a whimper than anything with force behind it. Still, I couldn't bring myself to sit up.

"I was expecting the Big Bad Wolf, and instead I get Red Riding Hood. I have to say, Darian, I thought I made you tougher than that."

I tucked up my knees closer to my chest. As if that could save me. I took three deep breaths, the kind deep-sea divers take, and I pushed myself to a sitting position. My back was still turned to him, and I felt more than heard the rise and fall of his chest behind me. His presence burned like an open flame in the center of my existence.

Turn around. Just turn around, Darian. Fuck. My brain was working, so why wasn't my mouth or why weren't my feet, for that matter? Why couldn't I just turn around and face him?

I thought of leaving my corporeal form, but knowing it wouldn't do much good, I remained frozen where I sat. Left with no choices, it was either turn and face my maker or sit like a mute fool and wait to die. With considerable effort, I stood. And even though I felt like I was standing on a metal floor in a pair of magnetic boots, I shuffled my bare feet against the hardwood, inch by inch, until I turned to face the man I'd been hired to kill.

The moment my eyes met his, every memory of our time together crashed over me like a tidal wave. *Every* moment. Every kiss, every touch—all of it.

He smiled and his eyes wrinkled at the corners, sparking to life with the light that had stuck in my memory over the many lonely years without him. He rested his right hand over his heart and rocked back on his heels, putting me instantly under his spell.

"If it's possible, you're even more beautiful than I remember," he said.

"You left me," I blurted like an idiot. At least my mouth was working again.

He laughed his cold and humorless laugh, causing a dread chill to race down my spine. I'd never understood just how much power he held over me—until now. Because I had the strange feeling that I'd leave with him in a second if he asked me to. I'd forget my promise to Xander and disregard every sweet word from Tyler's mouth for an ounce of affection from him.

"Azriel," I choked, as if the word burned my throat.

"Darling," he answered.

I was in trouble. Big trouble.

And then . . . I remembered myself. *Bullshit.* He was nothing but a low-life, lying piece of shit. Savior or not, he was dangerous, a threat to my existence. I shouldn't have been thinking about where we could run away together. But I should have been counting the steps from me to my sword. What was wrong with me? I'd succumbed to the glamour of my own kind for the last time. Azriel had tried to have me killed, or at the very least poisoned by his Lyhtan lackeys. Not to mention the fact that he'd dropped me cold, leaving me alone with nothing but lies to structure my existence. Screw him and his perfect *GQ* face.

"I'm going to slice your sorry ass into little, tiny pieces," I snapped. I wasn't completely confident I could kill him. I hated being on the defensive. My plan had been to ferret him out, bring the fight to his door. Start with the ball in my court. So much for planning.

Azriel threw his head back in a burst of chilly laughter. "There's my girl," he said. "You had me worried for a second."

"I have nothing to say to you." I matched his tone in temperature. "You're a dead man."

"I only wanted to see how you were doing." He smiled another model-worthy smile as he walked around my couch, closer. Too close. "Not too bad, from the looks of it." The heat from his presence bathed me in balmy air. I was suddenly overcome with a desire to reach out and touch . . .

"What brings you here?" I asked, turning my gaze from his glowing features. "Haven't had a good ass beating in a while? Feeling suicidal? I can take care of that for you."

"Ah, but I'd rather die by your hand than live by anyone else's," he said, laughing at his own lame attempt at humor. "I think you said that to me once, if I'm not mistaken."

"I wouldn't know," I said, lying through my teeth. "I've forgotten everything about you."

"If you say so." He laughed and plopped down on one of my chairs like I'd invited him to settle in.

"I hear you've gone into the business of waging war against your own people," I said, inching closer to the kitchen, where I'd left the katana.

"And I hear you're shacking up with the king," he said. "Doesn't that make him sort of like your grandfather or something? Pretty sick, Darian."

"Oh, I've already done pretty sick—about a hundred years ago." I couldn't let him get the upper hand. I knew too well that I could easily succumb to his charms. He'd kept me under his thumb once, but it wouldn't happen again. "Are you disappointed your Lyhtans didn't finish me off the other day? I owe you one, you know. Actually, if we're getting down to business, I owe you two or three."

"I didn't come here tonight to fight you, Darian." He said my name with such ease, something I couldn't bring myself to do. His name was like poison on my lips, a curse.

"I suppose you didn't." I was within feet of the katana now. All I needed to do was shed my corporeal form and I'd have it in my hand. "You came here to kill me, quick and easy. But that's not going to happen tonight or any night."

Azriel laughed, and the sound of it tore at my heart. The pain of him leaving me was as fresh as if it had just happened.

"Are you in league with the Enphigmalé?" I asked. "Should what happened to Delilah fall on your shoulders?"

His eyes danced with mischief. "I never wanted to leave you, you know."

It was the wrong thing to say. The anger rose in me and I'd made my decision. He was going to die—right here, right now, in my living room. I'd worry about cleaning the carpet later. "Liar. You intended to leave me just like you intended to lie to me. Why? You didn't need to keep me in the dark. Why keep the truth of my existence from me?"

He looked sad, if only for a fleeting moment. It wasn't enough to soften my hard-boiled soul. "My hand was forced. The less you knew about yourself, the better. And after a while, I liked it that way. You were my secret and mine alone. If my father hadn't exiled me, we might have conquered him together. You could have ruled at my side. But it's too late now. What's done is done, and now that you've been found and others understand the importance of your existence, there's no going back. You can't run from Fate. I might not have you at my side, but you'll still get me what I want."

What a load of bullshit. I felt my body drift into shadow, and as I became solid, my hand wrapped around the grip of the ancient katana. I freed it from the scabbard with blurring speed, but before I could put the blade to good use, Azriel had passed into shadow and was gone.

"Fuck!" I screamed, slicing through the air.

Sleep would've been impossible after Azriel's visit, so I strapped the katana to my back and headed out in search of trouble. The Pit seemed as good a place as any to start, and with only a few more hours to go until closing, I'd be able to pin down Levi for a minute to talk. At the very least, he may have heard a rumor or two that could come in handy. Either way, I didn't want the night to end without a little bloodshed.

The club smelled like stale alcohol, cigarettes, and sweat. I wrinkled my nose in disgust and walked through a couple groups of drunken slobs, parried a few friendly hands, and kicked one brave soul in the shin after his palm made contact with my ass.

It was unusually crowded for so late in the night. The counter was strewn with discarded glasses that Levi and a cocktail waitress were hurrying to throw in the dishwasher while wiping down the bar and restocking the bowls of peanuts, popcorn, and other nasty-looking snack foods. The TV was tuned to ESPN, and a few guys were catching up on scores from throughout the night while their dates crowded together and whispered in a tight circle.

Levi steered me in the right direction. "See that girl over there?" He pointed to a petite blonde, standing alone and swaying her hips in time to the music. "She's just what you're looking for."

I tipped him a hundred-dollar bill (it was worth it), and made my way through the die-hard partiers to where the girl danced by herself. She couldn't have been taller than four-eleven, and her long blond hair looked wild and un-combed, swirling in a knotted mass to almost her knees. Her eyes were closed, and in a dreamy sort of way she rocked to and fro, her arms waving like tree branches in a strong breeze. She seemed completely oblivious to every-thing around her. Only the music held her attention as the haunting beats dictated the sway of her hips back and forth, back and forth, like the tide washing up on shore.

I recognized her as a Sylph, an air creature, to be more exact. She bore a striking resemblance to the woman seated next to Xander at the Summit earlier that day. Raif had pointed her out to me. The energy coming from her didn't surround me like the bubble of pressure a Lyhtan's presence caused. And unlike the hum that had come from the Fae, her energy was more like a soft wind caressing my face. I was quickly learning to identify these inhuman creatures by the way they felt to me, rather than the way they looked.

I cleared my throat, but I doubted she heard me above the music, so I tapped her shoulder. She opened her eyes in a languid motion, like she was just waking up. Her thin lips turned up in a Mona Lisa smile, and she continued to sway. "You're a pretty Shaede," she said before twirling in a circle. "Wanna dance?"

I wondered if I came across as the kind of girl who let loose on the dance floor. She looked me up and down and gave a small shrug of her tiny shoulders. "No, but I thought I'd ask anyway."

Whoa. That's new. "I guess people have to be pretty careful around you, don't they?"

"What do you mean?" Blondie replied, her eyes drift-ing shut again. "Because I can hear your thoughts?"

"Uh, yeah." I watched her sway and twirl, and the strange flow of air that came off her sort of lulled me, momentarily confusing my purpose in being there. I blinked back a sudden wave of lethargy and tapped her shoulder again.

"I know you're, um, busy dancing and all, but someone said you might have some information on where I can find the Enphigmalé."

She twirled again before peeking out at me through one eye. "When night becomes day and day becomes night, the nine will come to claim their right. When darkest soul meets lightest love, her blood will play creator's role, and from stone release their souls."

I didn't expect her to go all rhyming and poetic on me. Not to mention that none of what she said made an ounce of sense. She spun again and ignored me completely while the music absorbed her attention. "You want to elaborate on that?" I asked, grabbing her by her arms to stop her. I was getting seasick from all the rocking.

"Marked as creator, but no one's maker. No mother, no father, they surely will take her," Sylph Girl said.

"What are you talking about? The Enphigmalé? Whose souls?" I gave her a little shake. "Hey! Snap out of it! What the hell are you talking about?"

Her head lolled back and a deep, throaty laugh bubbled up through her mouth. It drew the attention of a small group, and one of the guys came over to see what was so funny.

"You girls want to go to a party?" he asked.

The Sylph smiled and broke free from my grasp, turning to the guy, who would've been better off minding his own business. She pulled him down for a kiss, which didn't get weird until he started thrashing and fighting to get free. You wouldn't think something that little would be so strong. But all ninety-eight-or-so pounds of her held on to that big guy, and she kept a lip-lock on him like a sailor home on leave. His efforts became weak, and then she just let him go. He fell to the floor, dead.

"That was fun," she said with a giggle, and resumed her dance.

Levi jumped over the bar and rushed right into the

action. "You'd better get out of here, Darian. This isn't good." He turned me around and gave me a little push. "There's something wrong with her; she might've taken something. Human drugs and Sylphs don't mix. That, or someone's really fucked her up. She shouldn't be doing this. Go."

Doing what? Sucking guys dry and dropping 'em dead on the floor? I didn't get the chance to ask my question, though. Levi gave me a harder push this time, and I moved to the darkest corner I could find, passing into shadow before the bar flooded with a stream of Sylphs, armed and ready for a fight.

I didn't think my presence would make anybody feel at ease, so I watched from the shadows. One of them pulled Levi aside, and a discussion ensued that I couldn't hear over the music. While they spoke, the others tried to break Little Miss Dance Machine out of her weird groove. She smiled sweetly and ignored them for the most part, stepping over the body of the guy she'd just killed like he was an obstacle on a hopscotch court. Levi tried his best to evacuate the bar of its human occupants while the Sylphs worked on restraining the girl, whose dancing had increased to a frenzied tempo.

Dancing turned to spinning, and spinning to jumping. The jumping quickly changed to trembling, and the girl shook from head to toe before freezing in her tracks. She bent her head low before a scream broke loose from her chest. Glasses shattered, and the few humans who remained fell to the floor, writhing with hands clutched over their ears. Levi ran for the door but didn't make it before he collapsed, one hand just over the threshold. Still, the girl screamed.

The piercing sound wasn't without its effect on the nonhuman occupants of the club. Sylphs dropped like flies, grabbing their heads between their hands and calling out for the girl to stop. The sound magnified in my own ears; I didn't think I'd be able to take much more before my head exploded. It was as if the howling wind itself blew inside my brain. A few of the humans closest to the screaming girl had begun to bleed from their ears, and I made a decision. It might have been rash, but I'm a woman of action.

With each step closer, the force of her scream seemed to blow me back like a strong gust of wind, and I had to fight to gain ground. The katana was firm in my grasp. I made my way to the girl, who continued to scream, her eyes rolled back into her head. I looked at her face for only a moment, shuddering at the awful sight of those blank white eyes and gaping mouth. I pulled back and with a scream of my own, ran the blade through her chest. The terrible screaming ceased, replaced with an odd and ugly gurgle as blood welled up in her lungs and throat. She grasped at my arm, blood trickling from her mouth.

"You are marked," she said. "They're coming for you."

The blade resisted as the suction from her body held on, but I pulled it free and she tumbled to the floor, her eyes staring at nothing, her last life breath trickling from her chest in a wheeze.

A woman screamed, and the people who had fallen scurried about like frightened mice. Levi looked okay as well, helping the others out the door and cautioning against saying the wrong thing to the wrong person. Gang wars, he'd informed them. The Sylphs stood one by one and circled around the dead girl, their heads bending collectively in a solemn show of grief. The entire scene seemed surreal to me, too strange to be connected to the reality I'd known. But it was, and apparently I'd become a marked woman.

Just like I'd wanted, the night had ended in bloodshed.

Chapter 22

I went home and looked over every inch of my body in the mirror. No marks. Not a birthmark, a mole, or even a scar or discoloration. Screaming Girl must have been mistaken. Her weird little rhyme played over and over in my head, though, as well as her assertion that "they" were coming for me.

I hadn't allowed myself to slow down for weeks. Since Xander's appearance in my life, I'd been kept so busy, I hadn't had much time to consider my situation. But as I crashed down on my bed, I finally let myself think.

Xander. Had he really wanted me? Or was it just another of his tricks to keep me tied to him? I had my own personal wish granter, for who knows how long—and he hadn't even had the decency to ask me how I felt about it. And then there was Azriel. My former lover and maker who'd left me alone and uninformed had returned—for what? To conquer a kingdom? To take some kind of revenge on his own father for sending him into exile? And what was it he wanted? A crown? Me? And last but not least, the "marked woman" thing. Marked how? Where? Why? The whole damn thing made my head ache.

Only one of my boots had the chance to clunk to the floor before I passed into a deep and dreamless sleep.

I woke well into late afternoon, one boot still on my foot. My hair engulfed my face in a snarled mass, and by the look of the twisted mess of covers, I guessed that I'd tossed and turned for most of the morning. My eyes felt a little too puffy when I rubbed the sleep from them, and my mouth dry and sticky. It was like waking up to realize you've partied way too hard the night before. But, unfortunately, my night had nothing to do with fun.

Coffee was my first order of business, followed by a bowl of cereal. The normalcy of my actions both comforted and disquieted me. My spoon circled a bowl of Honey Nut Cheerios as I replayed the previous night's events in my mind. I'd never allowed my conscience to dwell on death. I was a killer. I wasn't so foolish as to try to convince myself otherwise. I'd killed humans, but never anyone who didn't deserve it. Evil people with not even enough moral fortitude to fill the spoon I swirled in my bowl. It was all part of the lovely gray area that freed me from guilt. Last night, I'd killed a girl, a Sylph, and I had not been paid or directed to do so. She wasn't evil. Out of her mind, sure. But I don't think she would have done the things she'd done if something hadn't been seriously wrong with her. If I'd let her continue, she may have killed me, Levi, a handful of her own kind, and a few more humans too. Maybe. Maybe not.

Was I getting soft? The block of ice that encased my heart had begun to melt by slow degrees, and I wondered whom I should blame for that. Tyler? Xander? Both?

Raif would need to know about the Sylph and her strange prophetic announcement. Oh, and the fact that I'd killed our only lead. I paused, the spoon of floating rings hovering in front of my mouth. He'd need to know about Azriel as well. My stomach soured at the prospect of telling him I'd failed in killing the sonofabitch. Holy fuck. I did not want to tell him that.

The grating buzz of my intercom gave me a start. Most of my visitors didn't bother with the formality. I went to the lift and pushed in the button by the speaker on the wall. "What do you want?"

"It's Tyler. Can I come up?"

He never rang. Ever. "Why'd you ring?" I softened the hard edge of my voice as butterflies took flight in my stomach. "You always just come up."

"I was worried when you didn't come back to Xander's last night," he said, and then added, "I thought you'd appreciate the fact that I'm trying to respect some boundaries."

He'd already tried that act and bombed. What made him think I'd appreciate a repeat performance? "Well, you thought wrong," I said. "Come up."

I let go of the button and went back to my bowl of cereal, now too soggy to eat. I put the bowl in the sink and filled it with water just as the lift came to a halt. Tyler stepped out, a grim look on his face.

"How's Delilah?" I asked.

"Asleep. She still isn't talking. Mumbling a little, but nothing coherent. I needed a break, and she's well guarded at Xander's."

My stomach gave a flip at the sight of him, and settled into a warm glow. "What are you doing here?" I wanted him to know that I felt better having him close. That everything wrong in my life had become just a little more right because he was here. But I kept my mouth clamped shut, the words trapped behind a hundred years of practice in keeping my emotions locked down—tight.

"I told you. I was worried. I wanted to see you, make sure you're okay." His voice sounded soft, steady. Not the usual overconfident Tyler. He still wasn't smiling.

"Well, here I am," I said, spreading my arms wide.

He walked toward the kitchen like a reluctant kid, staring at the floor. He opened his mouth, clamped it shut, and ran his fingers through the thick waves of his hair. While he wrestled with what he wanted to say, I held my breath and waited for the blow.

"I came here planning to tell you that if you don't want me, I'll leave you alone. You can break the bond and be free of me and I'll bow out. You can be with Xander."

His words slapped me right in the face. "Ty," I began, wrestling with my own words. "I don't know what I want. You know how I am. I'm not a share-my-feelings kind of person. I'm just—I'm . . . I *don't* want you to leave me alone."

"Do you love him?"

Xander was frustrating more than he was endearing. If love meant that I wanted to gut punch him and kick him when he was down, then, sure. I loved the shit out of him. "No. I don't. He's a royal pain in my ass. But he's a link to my own kind, and I've been alone for so, *so* long. Tyler, why are you putting so much pressure on me?"

Tyler rapidly closed the distance between us. I stepped away from the counter, ready for anything and prepared for nothing.

"He wants you," he said low. "He made it sound like you had feelings for him, too. Told me if I didn't make myself scarce, he'd have Raif chop me up into little bite-sized pieces."

I opened my mouth to protest. I couldn't imagine Xander behaving in such an impetuous way. Not the cool, detached king I knew.

"I thought about it for about half a second. Leaving you. But then I realized something . . ."

I took a deep, long breath. "What's that?" I whispered.

"It's gonna take a lot more than Xander's petty threats to keep me from you."

"Oh." Was it really my voice that said the tiny word? I looked up at him and he smiled.

"I love you. You don't have to say it back. You don't even have to love me back. But I love you. I *love* you, Darian. Till I die, I'll love you."

"I wish I could say it back," I said, honestly sorry. If anything, he deserved reciprocation. "But—"

Tyler took my face in his hands and lowered his mouth to mine. His cool lips caressed mine tenderly at first, but soon the urgency of his actions transformed his kisses into something altogether more forceful.

I should have stopped him, but when his tongue slid against mine, I couldn't remember why.

He didn't waste any time letting me know exactly what he wanted. My head swam from the intoxicating taste of him, and while my own hands were busy slipping under his shirt to explore the muscled expanse of his chest, his were working their way up my back to unhook the clasp of my bra. From there, my shirt made its way up and over my head, landing on the floor in a heap, followed a second later by the bra.

My breath came in a gasp as he pulled away from my lips to leave a trail of cool kisses down my throat, to my shoulder, and across my collarbone. He bent me back, just a little, and ventured farther down, taking my breast in his mouth and sucking deeply before pulling back at my nipple. My body became alive with sensation, the pleasure of Tyler's touch that I'd denied myself for far too long. A soft moan swelled from somewhere in my throat and I guided him to the other breast, where he went willingly, teasing the flesh into a taught peak with his teeth.

The sun descended in the western sky and the muted orange glow filtered in through the skylights to bathe Tyler in a diffuse light. I pulled the buttons on his shirt and raked it over his shoulders, mingling with my own discarded clothes. His exposed chest flexed beneath my fingers as I explored his smooth skin, his heated gaze laying claim to every inch of my body. I kissed his neck just to the side of his strong jaw before running my tongue along his ear. Taking his earlobe in between my teeth, I sucked before returning to his mouth so I could savor the sweet taste of him once again.

He led and I followed. We had eyes only for each other and couldn't bother ourselves to watch where we were going. Stumbling as we went, our hands and mouths greedy for the other's flesh, it took just a few awkward steps before we made it to the foot of my bed. Fingers shaking, I grappled with the button on his jeans, while he cupped my breasts, teasing my nipples with his thumbs, his teeth grazing the flesh at my neck. I jerked his pants down and he maneuvered them to his ankles, kicked them off, and tackled me in one fluid motion. I fell to the downy surface, and he kissed me with a starved passion, his tongue intertwining with mine. He pulled back and unfastened my pants, pulled them off with my underwear, and threw them behind him. His eyes raked me from head to toe, and a jolt of excitement coursed through my body, settling and throbbing between my legs.

Tyler's chest rose and fell with his breath as he continued to stare at my naked body. "I've walked the earth for thousands of years and I've *never* seen anything as beautiful as you," he said before kneeling where my legs dangled over the edge of the bed. I ran my fingers through the silky strands of his hair as it brushed my thighs, and I couldn't suppress a shudder when his mouth latched on to me, tongue flicking out, caressing the most sensitive part of me. I gasped at the sensation, the coolness of his mouth where it met my heat. There wasn't a single inch of me his mouth didn't explore, and I arched my back, hips pressing me against his mouth. I couldn't get enough, starved for the pleasure he gave me, and by the time he made it back up to my lips, I was crazy with desire for him.

"Ty," I said breathlessly. "Oh, God, Tyler. Please . . ."

He braced his arms on either side of me and I reached down, stroking the hard, satin-smooth length of him. *Wow*. A low moan was all the encouragement I needed from him—it almost sent me over the edge—and I guided him into me.

Tyler lowered himself, wrapping me in a tight embrace. "Darian!" he breathed close to my ear. The sensation of his breath mixed with the scent of me on his lips sent another hot electric rush through every nerve ending, and I met the movements of his body with an insistence that he matched with enthusiastic fervor. My nails dug into the skin at his shoulders and I wrapped my legs around him, urging him deeper inside me. Why had I fought this moment for so long? It felt so right, so perfect. We moved together, one body, one breath, joined together in a way I'd never known. Tension built within me as I ground my hips hard into Tyler. I cried out as, deep in my core, the pleasure exploded in myriad lights and tingling sensations. I arched against him, swept up in the pulsing waves that went on and on until Tyler's entire body shuddered as he pressed deep into me. An incomprehensible sound escaped his mouth, and he relaxed against my body, placing languid kisses along my neck, up my jaw, and ending at my mouth.

I lay still, enjoying the pulsing aftershocks that continued to rock my core, while Tyler slowly moved against me. I held on to him, keeping him right where he was so he wouldn't pull away. He stayed, allowing me to enjoy the feeling of his full weight against my chest as I took in shallow gulps of breath.

We lay wrapped together for another moment or two before I finally let him roll away. He gathered me up in his arms, and I rested my cheek against his chest.

When I turned onto my back, Tyler shifted to his side and began tracing lazy patterns with a finger around my belly button. My body trembled and his deep, throaty laugh stirred the glowing embers of passion that hadn't yet cooled.

"Leave with me," he murmured. "It's not safe here. Things are getting worse."

"You know I can't do that," I said.

"War is just around the corner." He rose to plant a kiss on my stomach. "This isn't just about some bullshit job. Azriel is the least of Xander's problems. It's something worse. Something altogether bigger than a feud over his crown."

"I know that," I said.

Tyler looked up from his trail of kisses, an intense expression on his face. "What do you know?" he asked.

I proceeded to recount the events of the previous night, starting with the discussion I'd had with Raif and ending with the point of my sword exiting through the poor, screaming Sylph's back. He listened with interest, offering comments when it seemed pertinent. It appeared that he knew what I knew—the Enphigmalé might be a bigger threat than we'd thought, and though he hadn't outwardly admitted it, Azriel was involved in whatever it was they had planned.

"What do you think she meant?" I asked, referring to the Sylph's strange proclamation.

"I don't know." Tyler sighed. "But I don't like the sound of it."

"Me either." Admitting it to Tyler felt strange, but for the first time, I realized that the idea of being anyone's sacrifice scared the shit out of me.

"I guess as long as you're not staying for him," Tyler said, running a hand along my thigh, "I can live with any other reason."

I didn't say anything right away. In a sense, I *was* staying for Xander. I'd made a deal; money had been exchanged. I had my pride and professional reputation to consider. And what I'd told Tyler earlier was true: Xander connected me to my own kind. He'd rescued me from obscurity. But there was also Raif. I felt a strange allegiance to him, and I'd promised to avenge Delilah. I would never back down from a fight, sacrifice or not. But I wondered, as Tyler nuzzled my neck, *Could I leave even if I wanted to?* In too deep already, I'd been sucked into a world that might not let me go. After hiding out under everyone's noses for decades, I'd been found. It was too late. I wasn't going anywhere.

"You . . . *aren't* staying for him, are you?" Tyler asked.

"Xander?" I asked. "No."

"You paused," Tyler said, sitting up beside me.

"So?"

"So . . . you paused. That means you had to think about it."

What happened to you don't have to love me back? Just having a moment of personal thought evidently made me suspect in his book. I sat up beside him. "Listen, Ty." I stared right at him to get my point across. "I thought we understood each other. Whatever my reasons for staying, they're my reasons. That should be enough."

Tyler looked away.

I ran my fingers up along his arm and around his shoulder. I paused just below his shoulder blade and caressed the muscles there. "Ty, *this* wouldn't have happened if I were staying for him."

He lifted his head and a lopsided grin made a welcome appearance. "I meant what I said. You don't have to love me back. But you will eventually." He looked so confident as he leaned over and kissed me. "You'd think things like jealousy wouldn't matter after so many centuries of existence. I'm sorry." He kissed me again. "I'm sorry. I didn't mean to ruin a perfect moment."

"You didn't ruin anything," I said, feeling a little more mushy than usual.

"So you agree it was perfect?" he asked, smiling as bright as the midday sun.

"Well," I drawled, reaching down to caress him. His body responded immediately, tensing and hardening in all the right places. I licked my lips, the thought of tasting him rekindling my own desires. "I can think of one thing that would make it even more perfect."

"What's that?" he practically growled.

"A repeat performance," I said, tracing his lips with the tip of my finger.

Wrapping his arms around my waist, he spun, settling

me on top of him. I moaned as his fingers and mouth searched and teased. If it were possible, he was better the second time around.

Tyler never disappoints.

I woke before sunrise. Tyler lay next to me, snoring softly. I didn't want to wake him, so I dissolved into the welcoming darkness. I drifted, enjoying the feeling of being free of my corporeal form, and within moments stood on the roof of my building. I remained a shadow. I didn't think the world needed to see a naked woman on top of a building, and, besides, it protected me from the late-winter breeze drifting across the city.

Somewhere, Azriel was raising an army of Lyhtan warriors.

Somewhere, the Enphigmalé made their secret plans.

In the midst of it all, the Shaede Nation, a society in and of itself, waited for attack from all sides.

And then there was me, sitting in the eye of the storm.

A voice whispered on the wind, and I strained to hear the words that ran together like a sigh. "Why don't you show yourself, cousin?" it asked.

"You first," I said.

The breeze increased in force to stormy wind and finally to gale. The gale transformed into a funnel cloud—not large; a few feet or more—and as it died away to again become a gentle breeze, the Sylph appeared.

"Your turn," the girl said.

"Not to be rude, *cousin*," I said, "but I'd rather not. I'm a little on the naked side. So are we actually related, or are you just being nice?"

The Sylph giggled. "Our kind can be traced to the beginning of your lineage. Our ancestor and yours coupled and created the Shaede from that union."

Lyhtans. Sylphs. Talk about your strange relations. I wondered what that family reunion might look like.

The Sylph shrugged and smiled—I supposed at my

thoughts, as if to say she hadn't thought about that. "You killed my sister," she said.

Not the best conversation starter. She didn't mince words, though, so I owed her a likewise frank response. "Yes."

"It was the only way," she said in a high and trilling voice that reminded me of wind chimes. "We hold no grudge."

I remained silent. What was I supposed to say? *Wow, that's a load off my mind?*

"If the Enphigmalé get you, the world as we know it will end."

"What makes you think I'm the one they're looking for?"

"You are marked," she said.

"You know that for a fact?" This all seemed too orchestrated. "Oracles are supposed to be the future seers, not Sylphs."

She laughed, and a breeze kicked up around me. "We are not the future seers, but sometimes prophecy is whispered on the wind. And you have been chosen."

"What's your name?" I asked.

"Sybil," she said in her wind-chime voice.

"Well, Sybil . . . I checked every square inch of my body and there's not one mark. No tattoos, no moles, scars, birthmarks. I don't even have a pimple. So maybe you guys have your facts wrong."

"Not wrong," she said. "You're the one. The Enphigmalé are dark and dangerous, and you will free them from centuries of imprisonment."

Hmm. Cheery. "How do you know I'm what they're looking for?"

Sybil laughed and the wind gusted, increasing in force with her laughter to once again become the swirling funnel cloud. It broke apart and Sybil was gone, dissipating in the air.

Shit.

Chapter 23

"Where are you going?" Tyler asked sleepily, leaning up on an elbow.

"I need to talk to Raif," I said, strapping the katana to my back.

I didn't ask him if he was disappointed, or even if he cared. His opinion was not a requirement. He knew the rules and he knew my mind.

"I'll come with you," he offered, scooting to the edge of the bed.

"Nope. No way. No how." I couldn't risk the resulting friction if I showed up with him following behind. Especially if what he said about Xander was true. I cared about Ty, and I refused to bring him onto the king's home turf. He'd be outnumbered, and we couldn't afford *another* fight. My romantic life—if I had one—had to take a backseat for now. "Ty, stay here for a while. Sleep. You've been up with Delilah and you've got to be exhausted. I just need to talk to Raif and I won't be in any danger. Okay?"

"It's almost dawn," Tyler argued. "What about the Lyhtans?"

"Well, that's what this is for," I said, brandishing the bottle of Raif's shadow-sludge I'd finally had the good sense to arm myself with.

"What is it?" he asked.

"Lyhtan mace," I said, beaming. I hustled toward the lift, out of earshot, before Tyler could get a word in edgewise. "I'll call if anything comes up. Otherwise, I'll be back soon."

"Darian." My name on his lips implored me to stay.

"I wish Tyler would stay in my apartment through the rest of the day," I whispered.

Whether or not he tried to protest, I don't know. Because I passed into shadow and left.

Though I wanted to relay the events of the prior night to Raif, I took a few detours on the way. I became corporeal before the sun rose in a glorious blue sky, casting shadows on the sidewalk where weeds pushed and strained through the cracks. Traffic zoomed by in the morning rush, and I suddenly envied the humans I'd studied like lab rats over the years. Why couldn't I be so blissfully unaware? Then again, I might've been if I hadn't spent the better part of a century dealing out death for a buck. Not exactly lying low. As I retraced my steps to The Pit, I thought again about Azriel's visit. He'd always been one for dramatics. And his appearance was a carrot dangled in front of my nose. Meeting resistance when I pulled at the door, I looked up to find a sign that read: CLOSED FOR REPAIRS. "If by *repairs*, they mean 'blood cleanup,' " I muttered. I'd been looking for Levi and a little more information, but that angle had officially become a dead end.

I whiled away the morning, dissecting the dead Sylph's riddle and her sister's warnings. But I didn't know enough about myself, let alone the rest of the preternatural world, to make any headway. What the hell made me so special? Marked how? And chosen for what? As morning gave way to afternoon, I made the trek to Xander's house, a sense of unease growing with each impatient step.

"It's about time." Raif met me at the door as if he'd been waiting for me all night. "Where have you been? I was just about to go out looking for you."

Oh, hell, I thought. He *had* been waiting for me all night. All day too. In all the excitement, I'd overlooked the fact that I'd been AWOL for the past twenty-four hours. I'd have to work on not becoming so easily sidetracked.

He dragged me through the threshold by the elbow and kept right on dragging me through the house. Down into the bowels of the mansion we went—Raif silent and serious as ever, and me tripping on my own feet to keep up. "You should know that the Oracle left sometime after Tyler yesterday," he said as we walked. "She slipped out when no one was watching, and we have no idea where she is."

Wonderful. There wasn't room for another thing on my plate. I couldn't worry about Delilah right then. I had Azriel and my own neck to think about, and I had to assume she'd left of her own volition and on her own two feet. Maybe she'd called Tyler. Maybe she'd run far from this war that I wished I could run from as well. "I have something to tell you," I said as I negotiated the stairs. "I killed a Sylph last night, and another came to visit me just before dawn."

Raif grunted in response, and didn't even turn to acknowledge me.

"She said—the one I killed, I mean—she said something to me. It was a riddle. *When night becomes day and day becomes night, the nine will come to claim their right. When darkest soul meets lightest love, her blood will play creator's role, and from stone release their souls.* And then she said something about being a creator but no one's maker. And something else about being marked and not having a mother or a father."

Raif stopped dead in his tracks and I ran straight into his back. "What did you say?"

I repeated the Sylph's strange prophecy, but Raif had already turned around and resumed dragging me down the long hallway to Xander's council room with increased speed. "What do you think it means?" I asked.

"The plot thickens," Raif said with a sarcastic edge as he stepped into the room.

Seated at Xander's council table was a Lyhtan, and by the way it was bound, I had a distinct feeling it wasn't an invited guest. The cords securing the creature to its chair looked strangely familiar, and I stuck a hand in my coat pocket, instinctively gripping the bottle of shadows. Black and inky, liquid in quality, the ropes marred the Lyhtan's skin at its wrists and ankles. I had a sudden mental image of Raif blowing gently on our guest's wrists, and shuddered. It thrashed about and spit at us as we entered, and I had to jump away to avoid being struck with a rather large gob of gooey, green spit.

After the dramatic display, the Lyhtan paused and looked me over from head to toe. It screeched and cackled wildly before saying, "You are marked! The Enphigmalé will see to the end of your kind!"

Lovely. That sentence must have been the equivalent of a Lyhtan secret handshake.

"We've been questioning him for the last few hours," Raif said.

I wondered how Raif knew he was a he. Maybe he lifted the tuft of fur dangling from its belly and checked.

"What has he told you?" I asked.

Raif gave me the gravest of looks before pushing me back out the door.

"You are marked, Shaede! You will free them, and you will all die!"

The door closed, effectively blocking out the seething sound of the Lyhtan's laughter and cackling proclamation. I wish I could have blocked it from my mind just as easily.

Raif led the way to a small office down the hall and slumped in one of the high-backed chairs. He looked me dead in the eye. I wasn't going to like what was coming.

"I checked," I said, trying to curb the path Raif's mind had assuredly taken. "I looked over every inch of my body. No marks. He's wrong."

"No," Raif said. "He's not."

Panic welled up in me, threatening to bubble right out of my mouth. I swallowed against the bile in my throat and focused on keeping a calm facade. Inside, I was screaming.

"No," I said. "No marks. I swear. Raif . . ."

"I should have made the connection sooner."

No. No, no, no, no, no. If I could think the word enough, I could make it true.

"Xander," Raif sighed.

"What? Xander? What does he have to do with this?"

"He knew, I think. He's known. For a while now."

"Known what?" The panic I was trying to keep a handle on flew out of control. "*Known what*? Fuck, Raif. What the hell is going on?"

"You'd better sit down," he said.

"No! Tell me. What's going on?"

Raif took a deep breath. Not a good sign. "It doesn't mean *marked* marked. It wouldn't be visible."

Gulp. My worst fears were about to be confirmed. "What does it mean?"

"You are *marked*, meaning 'different. Unique.' "

I stared at Raif and he stared right back. I wasn't unique in any sense of the word. I wasn't even a Shaede by birthright. My human life had been stolen and I'd been cast into this new form. Others like me existed. Two, to be exact. So I could admit to being a rare breed, but not unique. "No." The word barely issued from my lips.

"I've heard the whisperings of such things for years but never believed in them," Raif said more to himself than to me. "The Lyhtan said the eclipse was the key."

"It's not true," I protested with everything I was worth. "Azriel made me. He told me. The Sylph didn't say anything about an eclipse. Maybe the Lyhtans are lying, trying to throw us off the trail."

Raif gave me a pointed look, silently imploring me to stop lying to myself. Azriel's words from the previous night floated through my mind; he'd kept the details of my existence a secret even from me.

"I always knew there was something . . ." Raif said to himself. "Why Azriel was so intent to return here. Xander couldn't have kept him away. Nothing could have stopped him from coming back here for you."

The gears clicking away in my brain came to a grinding halt. "What are you talking about?"

"And you . . ." Raif continued, nonplussed. "Something just not right, not like *any* of us. The way you smell things, the way you sense the energy of others . . ."

I didn't wait for Raif to finish his train of thought. I rushed up the stairs, taking three at a time, crossed the first floor, and continued my flight to Xander's suite. I didn't knock, and I wasn't about to simply let myself in. I kicked the damn door right off the hinges.

"You lying sonofabitch!" I screamed.

Xander looked up from the sheaf of papers he'd been studying and regarded me with mild curiosity. "Hello, Darian."

I drew the katana, letting it sing as I ripped it free. Swinging it toward Xander's head, I stopped short and leveled it at his throat. "I'm going to ask you a few questions, and you're going to answer every last one," I said. "And I *dare* you to lie to me again."

It was right about that time that I felt cold steel poking into the back of my own head. *Anya. What a bitch.*

"Lower your blade, or you're as good as dead," she ordered in a self-satisfied tone. "I wouldn't even think twice before ridding the world of you."

I laughed. Serious, stomach-cramping, suffocating laughter. "What do you think, Xander? Should I take her threats to heart? The sun is about to set. Could she do it? Could she take my head off my shoulders before I take yours?"

"Anya, leave," Xander said, no longer amused.

"B-but, Your Highness," she stammered.

"Get out!" he shouted at the top of his lungs.

I turned to see Anya drop her blade to her side, cowering as she backed from the room and out of sight.

"Sit," Xander said.

"No." I was damn tired of being told to sit.

"I said, sit." Xander's tone was not in the least bit playful as he directed his finger in a downward stabbing motion. I perched on the edge of a chair and leveled the tip of the sword blade until it hovered in line with the hollow of his throat.

"The last time Azriel tried to stage a coup against me, he came to me himself. He didn't bother with any envoys or Lyhtan lackeys. He claimed he'd acquired a rare and valuable possession, and said once she came into her true power, he'd finally have my throne. Always one to brag, Azriel went on and on about how he'd stumbled across an anomaly. Apparently, you'd begun to shed your humanity before he'd met you, and he sensed that change, though you did not. A Shaede, created, it seemed, from her own will, or perhaps chosen by Fate for a far greater purpose. He told me he'd killed your abusive husband, thereby earning your undying loyalty and trust. No one would find you, he said. He'd taught you to hide, and he planned on keeping you tucked away until it was time for your existence to be known. My first thought was that he intended to use you as a weapon. I wasn't willing to chance anything with him, and I refused to risk my kingdom. I had him taken into custody immediately, and I sent him as far away from me as possible."

"How did it happen?" I asked, my voice quavering with emotion. "How could I possibly change myself?"

"I do not know," Xander said. "I told you that it is possible to change a human when shadows dwell in her soul. I assume your soul was so shrouded in darkness that, unconsciously, you sought the change without even knowing what you were evolving into. Perhaps you were tied to us, through your bloodline somewhere. But of that, I have no knowledge."

I shot from the chair and began to pace. I looked back in memory, to hazy remnants of a human life I had put behind me nearly a century ago, for an answer or at least a clue to confirm the truth of Xander's words. Emotions that I'd locked away like old clothes in a trunk burst out to torment me. The anxiety, pain, and fear choked me with an intensity that ridiculed my usually defiant outlook.

"And what about me?" I said, turning my back to him. "You knew about me all along, and you just let me roam the city like a stray dog?"

Xander sat stoic and silent.

I whipped around to face him. "Answer me! Are you frightened of me? Is that why you exiled Azriel and abandoned me? Why hire me to kill him? Maybe you should have just killed *me*."

"Honestly," Xander sighed, "I don't know how to kill you."

I'd quit paying attention, and continued my rant. "*Oh, Darian,*" I said, mocking the eloquent bunch of lies he'd told. "*If I'd only known about you. I would have fetched you away from your miserable existence years ago. You poor, stupid, pathetic creature. Let me take you under my wing. I want you so badly*— Wait. What did you just say?"

Xander gave me a sad and wan smile. "I don't know if you *can* be killed."

I walked straight up to him and slapped him so hard across his face that my hand burned and stung. He took the blow and didn't do anything to retaliate. "I suppose I deserved that."

"What you deserve is a lot more than that," I said.

"No more games, Darian. I'll tell you everything I know," he said, reaching out to take my hand.

I took a step back. No way was I going to let him try

to soothe and seduce me with his gentle charm. I sat back down on the chair, sword in hand and ready to strike.

"When Azriel came to me, I didn't believe him at first. It was unheard of, a human making the transformation on her own. But I sought you out shortly after and saw you with my own eyes and knew from that first moment that what Azriel said was true.

"You were a new and unique member of our kind, and your nature might have been as unpredictable as your evolution. He claimed that Fate had plans for you. He spoke of revenge and scores being settled. He'd lost his mind. Azriel had been convinced you were meant for something far beyond our scope of understanding. Something ancient and secret. Fear prompted me to sever his ties with you, and I made sure no one besides the two of us knew of your existence."

"Raif?"

"Knew *of* you, but nothing more. I didn't divulge the entire truth of it to him until recently."

I could deal with the fact that Xander was scared of me. Right then, I was scared of myself. And Raif had been left as much in the dark as I. But more questions were being raised than answered, and my stomach convulsed as I fought another crippling wave of anxiety. "What about Azriel? Why do you really want him dead?"

"I think he's discovered a truth I'd never bothered to find. I think he's ambitious and mad for power. He'll kill me if he gets the chance. Then what will become of my kingdom? My people? What power will the Lyhtans have over our kind if he's allied with them? Innocents would be steeped in war and death. He's calculating. Formidable. Azriel has been biding his time, and I think he's spent his years in exile doing what I should have been doing for all those years."

"I saw him two nights ago," I said. "He came to my apartment."

Xander nodded, momentarily lost in thought.

"Would you care to tell me what he's been doing that you should have been?" I asked.

Xander sighed, and the phrase *heavy hangs the head that wears the crown* came into my head. He looked at me. "He's been learning all about you."

Something in that simple and yet unthinkable statement sent me into a rage the likes of which I had never felt. I stormed from Xander's room, back down the stairs to the main floor, and past two Shaedes standing watch at the doorway. From there, I ran down into the bowels of the house, past Raif, who stood gaping, and into the council room. I stepped inside, coming to rest at the clawlike foot of the Lyhtan still secured to the chair, cackling wildly in the empty space. I grabbed it by its lanky hair that felt remarkably like corn silk, elastic and fragile but at the same time not. Fighting the urge to cringe, I jerked its head back so it would look me straight in the face, and I snarled the words, "Who is your master?"

The Lyhtan continued to laugh, the sound crawling up and down my spine like a thousand tiny insects. It spit and coughed, spewing a fowl-smelling gunk on my shirt. "I will walk proud in the light of day and laugh as we wipe your kind from the face of the earth!"

The time for talk had long passed, in my opinion. I felt the setting sun with a clarity that I had not recognized before. Every facet of my being tingled with the approach. Twilight was upon us, and, particularly, the gray hour that I longed for. I released the Lyhtan, who laughed hysterically again, drooling all over itself, rocking back and forth against its shackles. I pulled back and waited until I felt the sun pass below the horizon, as if I had plunged to the other side of the earth. With all my strength, I cut down with the blade. The Lyhtan's laughter stopped. Its head rolled toward the door, where Raif stopped it with his foot.

"I take it we're done with him?" he asked.

"Him?" I snorted. "How could you tell?"

Raif graced me with a humorless laugh. He rested an awkward hand on my shoulder. "What did he tell you?"

Of course, he meant his deceitful, high-handed brother. "Nothing worth a damn," I said, leaving the Lyhtan's body and the council room. "We're in deep shit, Raif. This is bad."

"Tell me," he said, low and dangerous.

I didn't have much to offer, save a few threads of thought I could not weave together. I relayed everything I knew, starting with my supposed making and ending at Xander's revelation that I was neither made nor born, but a creature of my own creation. Raif already knew almost everything else, and the things he did not know didn't garner much surprise. He was a pragmatic man, a skilled warrior, and one of the few I counted as a friend. I didn't leave out a single detail, and I spared no one's feelings, least of all his in offering my opinion of his brother. The corners of Raif's mouth twitched and he shook his head.

"It's hard, Darian, to rule. Xander protects his people the best way he knows how. If he must lie and cover things up to do so, then so be it. I am sorry that much of it was at your expense, but you've got to accept these things, get over them, and focus."

"On what?" I asked.

Raif's eyes glowed with bloodlust. "Battle."

Chapter 24

"I'll be there in fifteen minutes."

"No, you won't," I said into my cell.

"Bullshit. You're going to need me. I'm coming."

I wondered what it would take to keep him at my apartment. I couldn't focus on protecting my own neck if I was too worried about protecting his. I was officially in deep shit, and there was no way in hell I would risk Tyler's safety. If anything happened to him—especially in the course of protecting me—I'd never forgive myself. *Eternally gallant* described Tyler to a tee. I didn't want to do it, but perhaps another wish was in order. "Tyler, please . . . do as I ask."

"Dar—" He started to argue back, but the next thing I heard turned my warm blood to ice. A scuffle, shouting, and several loud crashes. I held the air in my lungs and didn't dare breathe as I listened to sounds of Tyler's assault, followed by a furious roar that could only have come from an animal. Raif peeked around the corner from the next room and froze, watching with suspicion. I returned his regard with my own expression of urgency, and he left his comrade in midconversation. He stood at my shoulder—and waited.

I heard the sickly rasping of breath before it actually spoke. The same wave of terror raced down my spine. The war had begun.

"We have your pet, Shaede," the voice said. "If you want him back . . . unsullied, you must turn yourself over to my master."

"How do I know you won't kill him anyway?"

The creature laughed—a sound I had come to hate—and said, "How, indeed?"

"Tell Azriel and your Enphigmalé I'm not afraid of them," I said with as much defiance as I could spare. I'd almost reached my quota for one night, and I needed to save a little for later.

Again the creature laughed. I'd begun to think it was the only sound their race could make. "You'll come, Shaede. Because if you don't, the Jinn will die."

Could I wish Tyler out of this very dangerous situation? It might work. He was my genie. If I made a wish, he had to grant it. Right?

"Well," I said aloud, as if I were actually contemplating letting them have Ty, "I'm not sure that's a fair trade. A magic-wish granter in exchange for a girl? Seems like you're getting the shitty end of that deal."

More laughter. The first thing I planned to do when I got my hands on this particular Lyhtan was rip out its vocal cords. I'd see if it found that funny.

"Come and trade yourself for him, or he dies."

I sighed. "Do you know what I wish—?"

"Don't say it," the Lyhtan hissed. "Make a single wish, and we tear the Jinn's throat open."

They wanted *me*. Period. And to get me, they'd taken the only thing on this planet I cared about. Shit, how could I have been so *stupid*? I should have handcuffed Tyler to me, begged him to come with me, rather than wish him confined to my apartment for the day. I couldn't lose him. I refused to let him die in my place. Azriel was a shrewd sonofabitch. Leave it him to know my Achilles' heel: affection.

"Fine." The word sounded as final as death. I put my finger to my lips as Raif opened his mouth to protest. "Where and when?"

"Dawn. At the domed fountain."

The domed fountain. I knew of only one in the city

that matched the description. "I'll be there," I said, and the call disconnected.

"Where are you going?" Raif demanded.

"The Seattle Center. They want to make a trade."

Raif glared and shook his head as if he felt sorry for my simple stupidity. "The Jinn for you—am I right?"

I nodded. Tyler's smile, his homey smell, the warmth that blossomed within me every time I saw him . . . The growing lump in my throat would undoubtedly betray my bravado if I spoke.

"They'll more than likely kill him anyway. You know that, don't you?" Raif was as cool and detached as anyone could get. I envied him that.

Laughter bubbled up from my chest. I thought of the insectlike creature holding Tyler's phone up to its . . . ear hole? I couldn't help myself. The sound sputtered from my closed lips and quickly turned into an all-out guffaw. Raif looked at me like I'd finally lost my mind, and for a moment I would have agreed with him. Tears rolled down my cheeks as I continued to laugh. My stomach ached from it. But slowly the laughter transformed into something altogether more hard and angry. It ended in a slow, building scream that sent my mentor back a pace or two.

"Out!" Raif commanded, and every soul in the room vacated the main floor in a dusting of shadow, the compression of which nearly forced the air from my chest.

I doubled over, drawing as much oxygen into my lungs as I could. Shaking with rage and fear, I stayed bent over for a long time, unable to meet Raif's gaze. A quiet moment passed, and I focused on the sound of my breathing until Xander came rushing down the stairs.

He was geared up for a fight. His mode of dress wasn't unlike Raif's, though it lacked the elfin flair. With a sword on one hip and a dagger at the other, he reminded me of a medieval knight, complete with chain mail. Xander's was a little more modern—shiny and somehow glittering in the faint artificial light. His boots looked like military issue to me. I wondered if a Shaede among us ever considered using a gun, but I assumed a bullet to the chest would not be nearly as effective as a clean cut through the spine.

"What's going on here?" he asked his brother.

"I think she's finally cracked," Raif said.

I would have laughed again, but I was afraid of another hysterical fit, so I kept my amusement to myself. I straightened and stared Xander down. "None of your business—that's what's going on."

"She's agreed to give herself up in exchange for the Jinn," Raif said. "The Lyhtans have taken him."

"Don't be a fool, Darian." Xander said, as if I weren't allowed to do anything of the sort. "Raif will send a party to retrieve your pet. There's no reason for you to stick your neck out for him."

"I'm going, Xander," I said. "They're going to kill him."

"No," Xander said. "You're *not* going after him by yourself."

"But, Xander," I crooned, my voice dripping with honey, "don't you want me to do my job? Don't you want Azriel to shut up once and for all? It would be a win-win for you if I go, wouldn't it?"

"Darian." Raif laid a hand on my shoulder, and I shrugged him away. "We need to strategize, collect ourselves. Forming a plan will serve Tyler better than charging off like this."

"We don't have time, Raif." I tried to keep my voice level, controlled. But it quavered with anger and fear. "They'll kill him. He's bound to me, and it will be *my* fault if he dies. Mine!"

Xander brought his fist down on an end table near the foot of the stairs. The wood splintered and cracked, sending a vase of flowers spilling into the foyer. "This is ridiculous!" he bellowed. "You. Can. Not. Go! That is an order from your king."

"You are not my king!" I walked right up to him, my head held high. "And I am *not* yours to command."

"Darian—" Raif tried to interject, but I ignored him, my anger focused solely on Xander.

"I'm going to go get Tyler. Then I'm going to find Azriel, and I'm going to kill the fucker. And after that . . . you can go to hell."

Raif's fingers grazed my shoulder as he tried to stop me, but he was too late. I had already passed into shadow.

The beveled-dome fountain at the Seattle Center looked different in the dark. A bit surreal and almost magical, it appeared to hover over the pavers. Round lights ringed the dome, illuminating it from beneath, making it look like a flying saucer. Water sprayed in a tall plume from the top of the dome, while smaller jets fanned out from the base. The Space Needle loomed in the background like a sentinel watching over the city. I wondered if it watched over me.

Staying in the shadows, I crept along the buildings, making sure to blend in with the scenery. I felt the energy of unrest all around me, my assassin's senses alert and tuned in to the faintest sound or movement. Azriel had taught me to be stealthy, but Raif had taught me to be deadly, and I didn't plan on going down without a fight.

The area usually swarming with people resembled a ghost town this early in the morning. Even the usual scattering of the homeless had taken their leave and found another place to haunt. The Seattle Center Monorail sat dead on its track as it waited to take the normal rush of tourists and travelers to their destinations. I missed the whooshing sound of its motion among too much silence. A strange and unwelcome stillness settled over me, and the peace did little to encourage my hopes that this would all end well. I tasted danger, smelled it as it raced to me on the blossoming wind, and felt it all the way to my bone marrow.

As the sky began to lighten, I left the cover of shadow and paced around the fountain, edging the wet pavers heel to toe, heel to toe, keeping my path confined to the dry area that marked the boundary of the water jets' reach. Stealth would do me little good once the sun rose. The Lyhtans wouldn't come until the sun peeked over the eastern horizon, thereby securing a weakened Shaede. Keeping myself hidden would only help so much, and if it came to a fight—which it assuredly would—I needed to be in an open enough area to properly defend myself. Sybil's rhyme looped in my mind as my hand relaxed and clenched around the hilt of my dagger. Her words taunted me with newfound meaning and renewed confusion. Once alienated from the world, I'd been gathered into the folds of my own kind, only to be cast out and marked as something else.

I must have been on the home stretch of my fiftieth lap around the fountain when the first reddish streaks blazed a path across the sky. I stood at the ready, no longer an assassin stalking the shadows for her prey, but as a warrior, proud and facing battle head-on. Through the quiet, a sound raced to me on eager wings. The many-faceted voices of Lyhtans echoed across the empty space, many more than I'd ever heard. One by one, they emerged from behind buildings and sculptures, out of the cover of darkness and into the unforgiving gray morning. They kept their distance, wary of me while the sun still hid behind the horizon, but with every passing minute, they closed the gap.

"Where's Tyler?" I called out to the group at large. My heart thumped so hard against my ribs, I thought it might burst right through my chest. Adrenaline coursed through my body, rushing outward toward my limbs, shaking with every movement. "You offered a trade," I said. "So here I am. Where is he?"

As dawn burst upon the world, I feared the worst. One by one, the Lyhtans' laugher rang out, thousands of tones surrounding me in a cacophony of assaulting sound. The morning became brighter, and with it the Lyhtans' skin glowed and shimmered and some became less solid as they joined with the light, while others shrank to the ground as glimmering insects. I knew, though, that the ones I should fear had chosen to remain in their true forms. I looked around me, spun to guard my back, and drew my sword in one hand, my dagger in the other.

I heard the sound of a scuffle somewhere behind me, shouts that seemed friendly, though I didn't have time to identify the voices. A heavy-handed blow came out of nowhere, and the skin above my eye split. A trickle of thick warmth ran into my eye, blurring my vision in a haze of red. I stabbed with the katana and followed through with a slicing motion of the dagger. The pained shrieks of the Lyhtan cut through the morning air, its rust-orange blood running in rivulets down the grooves in the pavers.

Shouts from my left mingled with Lyhtan screams, and I recognized the sound of battle. Leave it to Xander to always have his way. He'd had me followed, and those Shaedes were going to suffer for nothing. We were outnumbered by at least ten to one, but I didn't have time to count my backup, as a clawed fist came whirring toward me. Another strike and I reeled backward, pain exploding behind my cheekbone. Cowardly bastards didn't even fight fair. Something knocked me from behind, and then something to my side. A rib cracked, and my stomach heaved in retaliation. A battle cry erupted from my throat and I lashed out, thrusting, slicing, stabbing. I watched a few of the bastards drop to the ground, but for every one I injured, two more took its place. Something rammed the back of my thigh and I buckled, falling to my knees. I tried to fend off the blows, protect myself from the impact. I reached for my pocket, for the bottle that was my only defense. But before I could wrap my hand around it, something struck the back of my head and an unwelcome darkness swallowed me whole.

As I came to, visions of Henry floated through my consciousness. There'd been several times when he had knocked me out cold, and every time I woke, I felt like I was fighting my way back through a murky sludge to awareness. Soft swaying soothed me, and I almost succumbed to the darkness once again before awareness took hold. The deep, hollow sound of waves lapped against the hull of a boat, and the clean scent of water carried on the morning breeze. Bound at the wrists and ankles, I'd been rendered completely helpless, my face pressed uncomfortably into a prefabricated floor. The vinyl had been fashioned to allow for sure footing and the sandpaperlike surface scraped against my swollen cheek with every lurch of the boat.

I sensed someone or something, unlike anything I'd felt before, with me. A slow burn deep inside my chest, I could almost taste the sensation, acidic on the back of my tongue. My stomach heaved, and I quelled the nausea before the bile could make its way up my throat.

I blinked my eyes, crusted with blood, and the details of the boat came better into view. Midday sun shone straight down on my face, and my eyes watered. From what I could tell, the boat was maybe fifteen feet in length, a small recreational fishing vessel with an outboard motor. Wedged between two bench seats, I was invariably drawn to the center of the craft, where the two halves met in a V. I tried to turn so I had a better view of my captors, but thanks to my bound state, I could only stare at their feet. Their voices carried, more than three, and they spoke low in a strange language resembling Latin in many ways, though I couldn't interpret a single syllable.

Helpless, I was pressed deeper into the boat by the sun, which beat down, mocking me with the weakness its presence caused. Moments passed, and the metallic echo of lapping water turned into the hard scrape of the hull against a rocky shore. The boat came to an abrupt halt and I slammed into one of the benches, adding to my collection of bruises.

The boat was pulled higher onto the shore, and my captors stepped out. Hands, small and with thin fingers, reached over the edge, wrapping around my arms and legs. I didn't expect the strength that lifted me like a feather from in between the benches. They dumped me unceremoniously onto the wet, sandy shore. I squinted into the light until four bodies leaned over me to block out the offending sun. The burning pressure in my chest intensified.

Two boys and two girls who appeared no older than fourteen or fifteen stood above me, studying me like I was some alien life form that landed in their backyard. Their black, feathery hair curled around their pale, cherubic faces, and their amber eyes stared at me with a trace of innocent wonder. Their strength belied their slight bodies and thin, bony arms. My hands were untied and resecured in front of me, and like a fresh kill, I was hauled through the trees and foliage toward some unknown destination and, perhaps, my death.

Chapter 25

If my captors' strength had been surprising, then their stamina was an absolute feat. They carried me for what felt like hours, weaving their way through boulders, stepping over fallen logs, and negotiating streams. At least they were kind enough to lift me high so my head wouldn't submerge or bang against some obstacle. I supposed they were keeping me unscathed so they could kill me properly later.

"Hey! Aren't you late for the prom or something?" I shouted, if only to hearten myself. "Shouldn't you be off buying acne cream? When I get out of these ropes, you're gonna get more than a fucking time-out!" They ignored me. My world was topsy-turvy as they carried me like a hunk of meat. I dropped my head back to discern my surroundings when we entered a large clearing.

The grass appeared manicured. Like a carpet of artificial turf. Its shape reminded me of an arena. I felt a sense of reverence deep within me, and I realized we must have come to an ancient, sacred place where rituals had been held for centuries. I fought against my bonds, twisting and arching my back. The creepy adolescents moved forward, unconcerned with my struggles. A gray figure caught my eye, and I twisted my head to get a better look, noticing first the large stone feet and then the bodies of nine statues. Almost as large as mature bulls, and much more menacing, the beasts stood at attention with claws dug into low stone pedestals, as if waiting to pounce. Snarling mouths gaped wide in a silent roar.

Tongues curled in frozen waves within their mouths. Gargoyles, ferocious and ghastly. They faced the clearing, bent toward its center, watching with vacant, staring eyes the size of softballs. Their batlike wings wrapped protectively toward their bodies like billowing capes, and sharp, fanglike canines jutted down from their jaws. In groups of three they spanned the clearing, leaving an opening between each grouping.

In the first of the open spaces sat a large cage, and inside paced a huge, golden-furred bear. The poor animal bellowed to the sky and thrashed its head wildly before snorting and pawing at a large metal collar secured around its neck. It took two long paces back and rammed its massive shoulder into the cage before flopping to the ground, tucking its muzzle beneath its paws.

The second space was occupied by a low stone dais. Moss grew up the sides, covering three-quarters of the table, giving it the appearance of an ornate and wonderful bed. I could picture a faerie princess sleeping there, her silver hair flowing to the green earth.

In the third space from where we'd entered the clearing stood a bower of willow branches growing up from the ground, bending over one another to construct a green, leafy archway. Like a gaping black hole that opened to nothing, it was something I could neither see through nor beyond.

My kidnappers tossed me to the ground and stepped back a few paces, and the burning sensation in my chest eased. Relief washed over me until a new sensation took its place. I found it difficult to draw a breath with the invisible Lyhtan spectators weighing down the atmosphere around me. Slowly they took form, their glistening, praying mantis bodies leaving the light, becoming solid. I'd never seen the creatures en masse to this extent. Not even by the fountain did I feel their presence as severely as I did now. Their wide smiles and drooling mouths watered in anticipation of bloodshed. Looking me over with greedy eyes, they sniffed the air with anxious noses and fought among themselves. Several of the snarling creatures left the clearing to lick their wounds. The air tasted of violence.

A breeze cleansed the awful Lyhtan smell from my nostrils and replaced it with a welcome, comforting aroma. A scent that spoke to my soul filled me with emotion I didn't understand. My chest swelled, and I said a silent prayer of thanks, my spirits instantly bolstered.

Tyler never disappoints.

He walked into the clearing of his own free will, and my heart, which suddenly floated near my throat, dropped into the pit of my stomach.

"What's going on?" I said, slow and disbelieving, as my brain struggled to keep up with my eyes.

"I'm sorry," he said, walking past my child guards to stand before me. "I had to."

My body grew cold and I felt like I wanted to throw up. I'd been betrayed by everyone in my life. My parents when they'd dumped me on Henry. And, of course, by that same human husband, who'd used me as his personal punching bag. Even Azriel, who'd once claimed to care for me, and Xander, who'd proclaimed his desire for me, had both used me to suit their needs. But not *him*. God, please, not Ty. Not the one person I'd grown to trust. Not the only man on this earth I didn't think I could live without. "You used me?" I choked on the words, forcing them past my lips. He'd professed his love, tended my wounds, and bound himself to me just so he could . . . kill me?

A dark, black hole opened in my heart, emptying a place I never realized existed. He said he loved me. No man had ever said those words to me before. I couldn't help but remember how it felt to have his hands on my skin, caressing me, giving me pleasure. The connection, the sense of rightness between us, as if it has always been meant to be. I thought we'd joined on a level that transcended the physical. Tyler made me feel safe, protected. For the first time in my life, I'd felt complete. My soul ached from his betrayal. I rose on my knees, and Tyler ran his fingers through my tangled hair. I couldn't bring myself to look into the hazel eyes that had so easily fooled me. Instead, I reached out and swung at him with my bound fists, catching him in the ribs. He grunted, rocking back on his heels before standing straight and taking a cautious step back.

"I'm sorry it has to be this way," he said. "But we've waited for you a long time. Xander made sure that no one would know about you, but he couldn't keep you hidden forever. Lucky for us, you're ambitious and easily bored."

"You bastard!" I screamed. "This was a setup all along?" I tried to stand, but my bound ankles tripped me up and I fell to the soft grass. "So, what? You're in league with the Lyhtans and whoever this Enphigmalé is? What about Azriel? Is he hiding around here somewhere too?"

Tyler laughed. It sounded so out of character, hard and unfeeling. "Azriel did what was asked of him," Tyler explained. "He was easy to manipulate. I've promised him Xander's throne, once the king and his brother are dead. He's been in exile for years, and I guess he's tired of being overlooked."

"What are you going to do with me?" I felt like I had a right to know.

"Nothing, yet," Tyler said. "Stone will become flesh, but not until light becomes dark. You'll just have to wait."

He motioned to the four teenagers. They took me up again and carried me to the large cage, where the bear had resumed its pacing. Two of them used iron prods to keep the bear at bay, while the other two opened the door and tossed me in. I landed squarely on my face, and blinding pain stole my breath for a moment. When

I managed to sit up, blood ran warm and sticky from my nose. I scooted to the far corner of the cage, away from the bear, which sniffed at the air before licking his lips in a disturbing and hungry manner. I shrank as tightly into the corner as I could. The bear snorted again—a snuffling, cute sound—and padded toward me with slow and measured steps. I jerked back, smacking my head smartly against the bars, and I closed my eyes for a moment, sucking in a lungful of air through clenched teeth.

The bear's warm breath blew in my face, and I have to say it had a surprisingly pleasant odor. A large, wide tongue flicked out and licked my nose, cleaning the blood away, before going the extra mile to wash the rest of my face. I peeked through one eye and then the other. The bear retreated, giving me a view of his backside, not to mention gender, before curling up in a ball in the corner farthest from me. He sighed heavily and rested his chin on his huge paws, now and then whining like a nervous dog.

I pulled up my knees and examined the rope around my ankles. I'd been bound with Lyhtan hair, so freeing myself was out of the question. As for the cage, I kicked against it again and again, but after my tenth attempt, I threw in the towel. Like the rope that bound me, the cage held against my preternatural strength.

My cellmate stood, turned in a circle, and lay back down. He looked at me with a sad, hopeless expression, and a mewling sound escaped his vibrating lips. Once I was pretty sure he wasn't going to eat me, I actually felt sorry for the poor thing. "What do you think they're going to do to us?" I asked. He snorted and pawed at the grass.

The bear lumbered over to my corner of the cage and rubbed his cold, wet nose on my cheek before settling down beside me. I placed tentative fists on top of his massive head, bigger than two dinner plates set side by side. He sighed, and I wriggled my fingers free enough to scratch behind his ears.

While the two of us sat—me contemplating my current state, and the bear contemplating whatever bears think about—I took in my surroundings with perverse interest. This was the place where I would more than likely die. Maybe for good. If I wasn't a run-of-the-mill Shaede, I doubted I could expect to pass into beautiful shadow for all eternity. So maybe my death would be better, or worse, depending on the circumstances. I hoped they'd kill me quickly, maybe a knife to the chest or an ax through my neck. I didn't know if I could take a slow, painful death, and my pride demanded that I stand brave no matter the situation. I wanted to die like a warrior. A death Raif could be proud of.

From this far inland, the water was no longer visible. I smelled it all around me, a clean smell. Crisp. More like freshwater than the briny scent of Puget Sound. The landscape seemed as unnatural and out of place as I was in the human world. Set apart somehow, it reminded me of tales of Avalon. From the misty air surrounding the forest, I expected King Arthur himself to emerge, Excalibur in hand. Were we somewhere in the middle of Lake Washington? Mercer Island, maybe? Or had we, in fact, crossed through the mists to a different realm entirely?

I didn't see the dark-haired teens again. But from time to time, I caught a movement in the corner of my eye, so quick that even with my superior sight, I couldn't identify what had flitted past. Gone, too, was the foul stench of Lyhtans, as well as the bubble of space that usually pressed against me when they were near. I did, however, feel Tyler's presence. And though I didn't see him, I felt him as strongly as if he were sitting right next to me. I'd always been able to pick him out of a crowd. Perhaps he was somewhere near—watching and waiting.

With my back to the bars of the cage, I brought my

bound wrists up to my forehead, massaging as best I could with my thumbs to ease the throbbing ache that refused to go away. All of the Lyhtan attacks, the threats, the taunts, and esoteric mentions of masters . . . Tyler had been behind it all. But why? It's not like he'd had to chase me down. I'd been right by his side, ready and willing to do whatever task he laid out for me for five goddamned years. Not exactly hiding out. Or running away. And aside from the fact that Xander believed I was unique, the only Shaede ever to make the transformation by sheer will, I couldn't think of any reason why Tyler would plot and plan. Coerce me into caring for him. And then take me prisoner.

What did he have to gain from all this? The Lyhtans were crazed, violent, jealous. Easy to manipulate. He'd no doubt promised them the moon in exchange for their services. It's not like he could buy them off. Levi said Lyhtans didn't have any use for money. So he'd made promises. Chaos, war, and the total annihilation of their enemies in exchange for a ready-made army. He was obviously using Azriel as well. If I had to guess, he'd lied to him too, promising things he had no intention of delivering. But what could Azriel deliver in exchange for Xander's crown? The only answer made my stomach twist into knots. Perhaps Azriel had found me, kept me safe, and then led Tyler straight to me. Despite all of my speculation, I still didn't have the answer to the most important question buzzing in my brain: What part was I to play in all of this? I had a feeling I didn't really want to know.

Sitting in my cage with the large golden bear at my side, I watched the shadows I loved so much creep and crawl across the clearing as the sun traveled through the sky. Morning quickly turned to day and afternoon to twilight, making me anxious and terrified all at once. What would happen once the sun set? My answer: absolutely nothing. When night finally swallowed up the last trace of light, I hoped against hope I could become one with the darkness. But the Lyhtan hair that bound my wrists and ankles dashed any upbeat thought I might have had. Bound to my solid form, I was forced to sit and wait . . . and wait . . . and wait.

Only barely awake and still groggy, I noticed how content I felt. Like I was wrapped up in a fleecy blanket, I snuggled deeper toward the warmth, letting it banish the cold night air. As I became more aware, I realized the blanket was more furry than fuzzy, and then that my blanket rose and fell beneath me, beside me, all around me, really. Then my blanket snored, and I became more than fully aware that my cozy blanket was alive.

I stayed very still. One of his paws rested across my waist. I was caught in a real-life bear hug. Night had become morning once again. A light frost dusted the grass in the clearing like powdered sugar on a cake, but thanks to my living bear-skin rug, I hadn't even noticed.

How long was I to remain a prisoner? Almost twenty-four hours had passed since my abduction, and I was still just as clueless about my fate as I had been yesterday. Where were the strange kids? Where were the Lyhtans? And, more important . . . where was Tyler? I almost hoped someone *would* come try to kill me. At least it would break the monotony.

The bear rolled away from me, and though the freedom of movement was a welcome relief, I would have liked for him to leave his pile of fur on top of me. He was waking as well. Perhaps he was wondering how much longer he had on this earth, just like I was.

The chill in the air burned off by slow degrees, and my black clothes drew the warmth of the sun. Signs of life— besides my furry companion—appeared minutes later. The fair-faced youngsters had returned.

The four that had hauled me here were accompanied by an additional five, and the significance of the number was not lost on me. Nine strange kids, guardians of nine gargoyle statues. I looked at the bear and jerked my chin in their direction. "Maybe they should just sacrifice those weird little things and let us go?"

The bear snorted, as if laughing at my attempt at humor, and then cried his mournful bear cry. "Yeah, I know," I said. "Wish in one hand . . ." My furry friend gave a very pointed stare, as if saying, *Couldn't hurt.* But my wish granter had betrayed me. I didn't have much hope that the bond between us still held. If there ever was one to begin with. Even so, I decided to give it a shot. Anything was worth a try at this point. I closed my eyes, the words waiting on my lips and . . . *Clank, clank, clank.* My captors circled the cage, running sticks along the sides like bored children before cable television and video games. *Pissed* didn't begin to describe the angry sensation boiling over my skin. "How about some breakfast?" I shouted out to our jailers, rather than follow through with a wish I knew would not be granted. "Or is that what I'm in here for?"

They turned as a collective body. One of them smiled. And as the same collective body, they turned and walked away.

As the day wore on, the heat increased to a sweltering temperature. The Washington area wasn't exactly a tropical climate, yet the air was warm and humid. Lucky for me, I didn't mind the heat, but the bear lay panting and stretched out. "We need water!" I shouted to no one, and was answered by the frantic chatter of some kind of squirrel or bird. My throat burned with thirst, and I could only imagine how my furry friend was faring.

I longed to stand up straight. Stiff from lack of movement, my feet and hands constantly tingled. But every time I tried to rise, I tripped on my own bound limbs and tumbled without the use of my arms to break the fall. I tried to uncross my feet in their fetters, but the Lyhtanhair rope held tight, and I was unable to loosen them even a little. Frustrated, tired, hungry, and parched, I let out a wild and primal scream that echoed all around me, bouncing back to my ears, taunting me with the helplessness of the sound.

The bear cowered away from me in his corner, and I laughed long and loud. I guess I was scarier than I thought.

The air began to cool with the setting sun, and my anger turned to despair. I was about to mark the passing of another day of captivity, having no idea how many more were to come. Tyler had betrayed me, lured me with love and devotion, and I had eaten every spoon-fed bite of it. Truly alone in this world, I had nothing more than a wild animal for company. I scooted closer to him as the sky darkened, more afraid of the loneliness than I was of being eaten. He didn't protest as I cuddled deep into his shoulder, but sighed contentedly and licked the side of my face. I hoped he wasn't just sampling the dinner menu.

Creatures stirred around us, both supernatural and natural. An owl landed in a tree branch above the cage, and I trembled, thinking of the bad omen it presented. In just the short time since my capture, a new and disturbing feeling had begun to take root deep in my soul. I was possessed with the feeling that every particle of my being had begun to shift, transform. The presence of this process frightened me more than the prospect of the coming hours, days, or weeks. The Sylph had been right. Xander's fears of revealing my existence were well founded. Something *had* happened to me.

I was changing.

Chapter 26

I'd lost count of the days. For some reason, I thought I'd been locked up for three or four, but I was so weak from hunger and thirst that I merely passed the time slipping in and out of consciousness. Was Tyler really here, holding me prisoner? I held on to a small glimmer of hope that I was dreaming—or dying, and that the final, dark end would come soon.

At least I wasn't alone. I had the strange, docile bear that shared the cell with me. He seemed to have taken up the habit of watching over me, and whenever I managed to wake, he'd be next me, mewling and worrying and rubbing his warm, soft face against mine. My world had been reduced to the cage. And, like my beastly companion, I had been reduced to a kept thing, ignorant of my purpose or fate. My entire existence was made up of ignorance, and I found myself laughing and crying hysterically in the moments before I succumbed to the welcoming void of darkness once again.

I dreamed. More than I ever had. Or maybe I just remembered the dreams more now than I had in the past. Fleeting images like a slide show floated through my subconscious, a montage of my past, present, and, perhaps, my future. I dreamt of Henry, handsome and cruel, beating me into a state of despair and loathing so intense, I found myself longing to become invisible. I wanted to melt into the dark places of night and remain there—strong and safe from human harm. I dreamt of Xander, beautiful and aloof. But rather than pull me toward him, he pushed me away, proclaiming my mere existence a threat to everything he held dear. I dreamt of myself, free from captivity, walking in the sunlight that permeated my skin, sparkling and luminous, until there was nothing left of me at all. And I dreamt of Tyler, again and again, drawn to him like a magnet. Wanting him no matter how he'd betrayed me.

Those hours of unconsciousness mingled with the days of wakefulness. I passed the time like a moth in a chrysalis, waiting to emerge as an evolved species. Change swirled within me, and though I was aware of it, I thought on it little, until the first time I recognized the transformation from day to night as a physical sensation. With almost perfect detail, the changing time washed over me. Its scent a mixture of rain and diminishing sunshine, twilight had become a woolen blanket—warm but rough as it scratched against my skin and rustled over my ears. Like a living clock, I marked every second, felt every hour. The clarity of it astounded me. The passage of time came to me as a living, breathing thing. I'd been in my cage for eight days, twelve hours, and forty-seven seconds.

A pair of small, bare feet came to a halt on the other side of the bars. I tried to lift my blurry gaze to see the face that went with those feet, but I was so weak. I reminded myself I didn't need my eyes to see, and I closed out the graying world around me to feel the being standing before me. Heat grew from the center of my chest, and I drew a shallow breath. One of my nine young tormentors belonged to those feet. The burning intensified as another and yet another approached. I curled into a tight ball, unable to bear the sensation of so many of them standing close. The bear pawed at me. He whined and sniffed my hair before giving me a nudge with his giant head. I panted through the pain, so intense it blazed a path through my body.

"Neither Shaede nor Lyhtan be. Mother, creator, the blood will see."

"I need water," I croaked, surprised at the sound of my own gravelly voice.

The teens giggled, their euphonious laughter like a thousand bells clanging in my ears. I pulled tighter into the protective ball. "Stop!" I cried, hoping there was some small fraction of force behind the word. "Stop it! I need fucking water! And food. Untie me! Get me the hell out of here!"

"Soon, Mother," one of them said. "When night becomes day and day becomes night, the nine will come to claim their right."

Mother. The word sounded foreign to my ears. "Please," I sobbed, "untie me."

"Soon, Mother," a young voice said again, and they left. The burning receded from the center of my chest.

By slow degrees I lost my drive and the fight melted right out of me, pooling into submission. Time taunted me with its presence, and now the only escape I sought was sleep. Again I dreamt of Tyler. He lay next to me on a soft bed of grass, his naked body entwined with mine. A cool breeze washed the remnants of passion from our skin, and his soft kisses sent a trail of chills across my shoulder.

Bound to the moment, to the dream, to Tyler—I couldn't escape.

"I love you," he whispered, his voice becoming one with the wind. "I will protect you until I breathe my last breath, and love you beyond my life."

I fought against the feeling that his words pulled from my soul. It swelled from the cold void of my heart and bloomed outward to overwhelm me with the strength of pure, untainted emotion. I'd been caught in my own sick fantasy. I tried to yell out, to scratch and claw my way to reality, to the real me waiting outside this time warp I was stuck in. Though I tried to speak, the words refused to come, and I averted my gaze, rolling my head away from him.

"Darian ..." He whispered against my ear, "Darian ..."

Something poked uncomfortably against my back and brought my body awake and back in touch with my mind. I moaned, the agony of my reality crushing the ecstasy of my dreams. Prodded again, I rolled over, shaking and barely able to support the weight of my body as I lifted myself to a kneeling position. It wasn't much, but I was *up*. My head lolled, drooping in front of me. I tried to open my mouth, and my too-dry lips cracked and bled. My tongue, which felt like it was covered in scales rather than soft flesh, flicked out in a vain attempt to moisten my lips, and my stomach heaved at the coppery taste of blood.

"Wake up, Mother," a singsong voice called out. "It's time."

"Eight days, twenty-two hours exactly," I said, borderline delirious again. "Five seconds, six seconds, seven ... eight ... nine ..."

"Yes, nine!" The voice interrupted. "The nine are waiting. Come, Mother, and give them life!"

The door to my cage swung open, and I tried to focus my blurry vision. Was the bear still there with me? Or was he a figment of my imagination, a companion created by madness?

The burning in my chest intensified as the teenagers entered the cell. I blinked and squinted to bring their young, lithe bodies into focus. Six of them circled me, and with great care, they cradled me in their tiny arms and carried me from the cage.

"No!" Every movement became dreamlike and weak. I felt the sun as it continued its arc in the sky, and also something else. The moon—I shouldn't have been feeling it then—but the moon as well was traveling in its own arc toward the rising sun. "Night becomes day and day becomes night," I whispered.

The will to live crept into me like a tiny point of light

in a dark cave. Barely there but growing as I forced myself to consciousness. I couldn't let it end this way—alone, betrayed and used. To better *feel*, I kept my eyes shut. I sensed my surroundings better this way, and I recognized the bubbles of pressure belonging to many Lyhtans before their stench reached my nostrils.

A Shaede stood nearby as well. Azriel. I thought of his cruel, sparkling eyes and seductive smile. Aligned with them or in charge of them—it didn't matter. He was there, playing a part in my impending death. I reached farther, sending invisible feelers out around me in search of other creatures. I sensed something familiar, someone I thought I knew.

I was lowered onto a spongy surface, and I opened my eyes. Three of the menacing kids stood at my head and three at my feet, where they worked the fastenings of my bound wrists and ankles. On the moss-covered dais, they secured my limbs to each corner of the rectangular stone. At least it was a different position.

Come on, Darian. Keep your shit together. No matter what, I needed to remain lucid. I couldn't let the lack of food, water, and comfort lull me into a submissive state. They wanted me dead or worse, but I refused to make it easy for them.

I silently counted the minutes, my new internal awareness marking not only the time, but also the path of the sun and moon across the sky as they traveled toward one another. It wouldn't be long. In as few as sixty minutes, on the ninth day of my captivity, the moon would pass in front of the sun, and nothing good could come of it.

I lifted my head, searching for the cage. The bear had been removed and stood at the center of the clearing, a thick length of chain fastened at one end to a stake and at the other to the wide iron collar at its neck. The chain clanked and clamored with the thrashing of the bear's head. He pulled against the restraint as he tried to slip from the collar. His gaze locked with mine and he froze before throwing his head back. The sound that issued from his mouth was a combination of fierce growl and vengeful bellow. As if he called out to me, the sound shouting my name, begging me to forgive him for not being able to save me.

I know how you feel, buddy, I thought as I lay my head back down against the cool stone of the dais.

Two shrouded figures approached the dais, and a feeling of familiarity rippled over me. I never wanted to see either one of them again, and at the same time, I hungered for one last glance. The painful emotions tore my composure to shreds. Quite a pair, the two of them made.

Looking like druids or mystical priests of a long-forgotten religion, they stood near my head and waited as the clearing became a stage. Around that stage gathered the many witnesses to my sacrifice. Lyhtans, each and every one. Their proximity pushed the breath from my chest as if a giant boulder had been suddenly rolled atop it. I estimated their numbers in the hundreds, and their many-voiced murmurs came to me as a dull roar.

The raven-haired teens entered the clearing next. Four boys and five girls dressed in deep crimson robes with hoods pulled back, serene smiles painted on their Michelangelo faces. The short, curling locks of their baby-soft hair, like raven feathers, shone against their fine porcelain skin. They chanted in their strange language, and each carried a shallow bowl. I wondered what they intended to fill them with—and fought a wave of pulsing nausea.

A stillness settled on the clearing, and even the bear stopped his wild thrashing and listened. My breath sped in my chest and I fought back the fear that threatened to drive me once again to the brink of sanity.

"Are you afraid to look into my face when you kill me, Azriel?" I directed my words to one of the hooded figures. The open confrontation bolstered my courage and helped to slow my racing heart. "Don't tell me you've come this far only to hide behind a blanket when you do the deed."

His icy laughter trickled from deep within the hood, and he reached back to pull the cowl from his dark head. He gazed down at me and smiled.

"Is this better?" he said, his voice as cold as his laughter.

I wasn't sure it was. Maybe it was better to be killed by an anonymous stranger than someone you'd known in the *biblical sense*. "What about you, Tyler?" I asked, letting my bravado wash any trace of fear from my voice. "Why stop now? Let's get this all out in the open."

Strong and proud in his crimson robe, he lifted his hands to the hood and pulled it back. I tried to suppress the tears pricking behind my eyes, but I was too late, and pain won out over strength.

"Tyler," I implored.

He stared off into space, eyes straight ahead, seeming to focus on nothing, and his mouth curved up in a handsome, detached smile. The bile rose in my throat, burning, nearly choking me. The bear snarled from the center of the clearing, echoing my rage and frustration at being duped by someone I'd cared for.

"It's almost time," he said.

"You asshole," I said through clenched teeth. "How could you do this to me?"

"The nine must be set free," he said, cut-and-dried. "When day becomes night, you will turn stone to flesh and the Enphigmalé will be free."

Anxious murmurs ran through the crowd of Lyhtans, and I sensed an escalation in their excitement. Azriel smiled.

"Looks like your army is assembled and ready to go to work," I said in an effort to buy time. "What's your plan? Kill me, bring these statues to life somehow, and make war with Xander?"

"Why stop there?" Azriel asked. "A wrong must be

righted, and the Enphigmalé will claim their rightful place. The true natural order will be restored. We will hold dominion over every creature, including the humans. And those who have wronged us will die."

"I'm going to kill you," I said, my voice as calm as an ice-covered pond. "And I'm going to take my time."

Azriel chuckled, replacing his hood—a little like rewrapping a present, in my opinion—and stepped away from the dais to take his place beside the bower. A light breeze stirred the willowy green, leafy branches that swayed above his head, framing him like a living portrait.

The seconds ticked away inside me, and I looked to the sky. Sun and moon were nearly touching now. Inching together like lovers joining in slow motion, night and day would soon be one. I'd never believed in prophesies before, but as I watched the joining of heavenly bodies, I would never doubt one again.

Nine guardians chanted, oblivious to their surroundings, lost in the moment and the coming ritual like enthralled youngsters at their favorite concert.

The collective rasping breaths of the Lyhtans converged into a single sound, no longer seething and evil, but almost lulling, melodic. Nature thrived around me, the energy of many creatures swelled within me, and my death loomed before me. My eyes threatened to drift shut. I was so tired. So *done* with all of it. I wanted to sleep forever, to rid myself of all the emotion that seemed to be only a hindrance. Tyler had ruined me. I was irreparably damaged, and though I wanted to hate him with everything I was worth, the pain of his betrayal tore at me like barbed hooks in my heart.

As if the eclipse took place within my own body, I felt the moon begin to pass over the sun. I became hot and cold all at once. Every cell within me tingled. And the change I had felt coming throughout my days of imprisonment swirled within me, bringing me close to fainting.

A surge of energy flowed through me and I lurched, arching my back against the moss-covered dais.

Tyler went down on his knees. I felt his once-cool breath now warm on my face, and I turned away, forbidding myself from taking in a single detail of the features I had grown to cherish. "I love you," he whispered, though he still refused to look directly at me. His cold, indifferent stare seemed to pass right through me, as if I were invisible. The sob I tried to suppress broke free from my throat. I shook my head in denial.

"Your soul was the blackest hole until you met me. Admit it, Darian. You didn't know love until I showed it to you."

I shook my head and bit down hard on the inside of my cheek so I wouldn't be tempted to answer. Fresh blood welled up in my mouth, and I gagged as it trickled down my throat.

"Your love will free them. And your blood. You have to understand."

"Tyler," I gasped, desperate to shake him out of whatever influence held him. "You don't kill someone you love to bring something evil to life. These creatures are pure hate—I can feel it. How can love breed something like that?"

He kissed the top of my forehead, and I recoiled. It felt wrong somehow, that physical contact. "Don't do this," I said, pulling against my bonds. "Please, Ty, you don't have to follow through with this."

"Say you love me," he said. "Let it flow through you, Darian. You can't fight this any longer. Say it."

I shook my head. He knew what he'd done to me. As sly as any hunter, he'd crept undetected beneath my skin. I took a deep breath, desperate to inhale the sweet smell of him, but the scent was gone, drowned in a sea of Lyhtan stench.

The teens continued to chant, and one by one they left their posts beside the gargoyles, falling into a single-file procession, walking clockwise around the grassy clearing to end at my feet.

Tyler placed lazy kisses along my forehead before running his fingers through my knotted hair. He hushed and soothed me, and the soft, chanting voices of the teens comforted me. The moon continued its path before the sun, and the light slowly seeped away like water sucking down a dark drain, to bathe us in a gray combination of both.

Pulses like the ticking of time pounded in my chest. I felt every fraction of every second and fought again against the eclipse of my own soul.

"Say you love me, and I'll end it quickly," Tyler crooned. "Isn't that love, Darian? Sparing you from further pain? Say the words and it will all be over."

The moon moved its last little bit, passing completely in front of the sun. A halo of light shone out from the empty black disk, and I knew I would never be the same. *Why not say it?* I was tired of this existence, tired of pretending I didn't care about anything. The gray had swallowed me whole, and I yearned for a little clarity. Black, white, light, dark. I no longer craved obscurity. I could try to lie to him all I wanted, but I could no longer lie to myself.

"I love you, Tyler," I said through my tears. "Damn you to hell for making me love you."

Chapter 27

Another pulse of energy rocked my body. Tyler looked to the sky and pulled a shining, blue-steel dagger from the folds of his robes. With surgical precision, he sliced one and then my other wrist. I didn't feel a thing; my circulation had been cut off from the rope that held me down. A sliver of red flashed against my skin before pouring from the cuts.

My captors, the creepy poster children for birth control, broke their ranks and split to either side of me, filling the bowls with the blood that carried some magical connection to my heart. Not the beating lump of flesh that pumped the sticky red stuff from my wrists. But the essence of every feeling, every emotion that resided in the secret parts of me that I had hidden away for so long.

Tyler walked around the dais and knelt near my shoulder. I turned and stared straight into his eyes, hoping he saw the defiance burning in my own. Again his gaze seemed to pass right through me. He brushed his lips against my forehead one last time, and I screamed with as much force as I could muster. *Thrump-thump, thrump-thump*, the soft pounding of my heart echoed in my ears, and the blood gushed in rhythm with each pumping sound. My eyes drooped as I focused on the beat, like the new internal ticking that marked the passage of time inside me, and I felt a surge of peace. I floated in nothingness for a brief and pleasurable moment. I wondered if I'd go to heaven when I died. No tunnel of heavenly light appeared to welcome me. I was

more than likely headed somewhere considerably
warmer. I didn't bother atoning for my sins. What was
done was done, and it was too late to consider making
amends with God or anyone else.

Tyler's face loomed in my memories; that last look
into his eyes frozen in finite detail. His breath no longer
cool, but *warm* against my skin. And then, as if I'd
dropped from the sky, I no longer floated in a state of
death-bliss. A throbbing from my hand drew my thoughts
to the ring circling my thumb. I'd always wondered why
the symbol on the ring that was supposed to guarantee
my protection had looked like some prehistoric buffalo.
I mean, why not something *huge*? Something fierce, with
vicious claws and weight to throw around. An animal
with thick, warm fur and impenetrable skin. A beast
worthy of the term *protector*. The ancient animal carved
into the silver *was* fierce and large; a hulking beast, but
no buffalo. My eyes opened wide in pain, and, finally,
recognition. A Lyhtan's scream pierced the air, and Tyler
cocked his head toward the sound. The movement was
almost . . .

"You're not Tyler!" I gasped, struggling against the
rope restraining my bleeding wrists. "Who are you?" I
spit at the cloaked figure and kicked my legs. "Who the
fuck are you?"

The teens had filled their bowls with my supposedly
magic blood and filed in a respectful line, walking the
clearing counterclockwise this time. Each took up their
former positions in front of his or her corresponding
statue. Each dipped a finger in the bowl of blood, and, in
turn, anointed the forehead of the statue with a long,
bright-red smear.

A cool breeze stirred from the center of the clearing,
from where the bear had been chained, and hit me full
in the face. The sweetest smell permeated my senses,
and for a moment I could almost taste his cool kisses.
Tyler was here, right under my nose the entire time,

watching over me. How could I have let my eyes trick me so easily?

The furious chanting of the dark-haired guardians drew my attention. Their ritual had begun. One of the girls raised her bowl and paused. The moon pulled away from the sun, and a sliver of light shone onto the clearing. I observed the whole gruesome scene, noticing hundreds of details in a space of time no longer than a single second. . . .

Azriel stood, proud and smirking, at the bower, watching with sick delight as my blood drained from the gashes at my wrists.

The Lyhtans, worked into a frenzy, cried out in myriad voices for killing, for revenge, for retribution.

Nine teens stood before nine gargoyle statues, chanting in low, melodious voices, bowls poised above gaping stone mouths.

The moon traveled, undeterred by the events taking place below it, to reveal more of the sun's glorious warmth.

Tall grass swayed, the short grass of the clearing quivered, and a breeze whispered through the trees, sounding like crumpling tissue paper and soft applause.

And at last I locked my gaze with the bear, pacing and pulling at his chain, desperate to free himself. I looked hard and deep into those eyes for the first time and noticed the beautiful hazel color, green with an almost-brown star blooming from the pupil. I'd had to learn so much in such a short time, I'd forgotten Xander's Genie 101. . . . *They possess a very powerful magic and can change shape and form, but only when their charge is threatened. . . . The shape they choose is the physical embodiment of their protection.* It must have happened when the Lyhtans attacked him. A knee-jerk reaction, because he knew they were after me. All this time, *my* Jinn had been protecting me, and I'd been too stupid to realize it. But why remain in animal form?

Did it make him stronger? More capable of keeping me safe?

"Tyler!" I called out. "I wish Raif were here! I wish he were here now! Please, Tyler!"

Tyler's bear lips quivered and he mewled in answer. I turned to the imposter standing beside me. "Why don't you show your true face, coward?"

The blood loss had begun to take a toll on me. My breathing was labored as I tried to focus on saving myself. There was fight left in me, and I wasn't about to go out flat on my back.

As the moon finished its passage across the sun, the clearing filled with blinding sunlight. I realized as the rays poured down on me that I had become something more than I had been, and with the passage of the eclipse, that transformation was complete. I thought about the cuts on my wrists, bathing the lovely green grass in crimson red, and I visualized the cuts healing more quickly than even my supernatural body allowed. *Close,* I told the cuts. *Heal. Stop bleeding.*

A chill ran the length of my arms and snaked around my wrists like bracelets made of ice. The sensation intensified, and though I couldn't see the wounds, I felt my skin pull together, sensed the bleeding as it stopped.

By small degrees, my strength returned and I pulled against the Lyhtan hair binding me to the stone dais. My right ankle and then the left broke free, and I rotated the stiff and nearly numb extremities until I was certain I could move. I pulled with my arms and they broke the Lyhtan hair as if I'd been tied down with merely a thread.

The imposter Tyler flinched, taking a cautious step back. Indecision marred his features as he looked back and forth from me to the kids, who carried on as if nothing disturbed their moment in time. My body tingled in the sunlight. A faint glow burst from my skin, filtering all around me, but I had little time to contemplate these changes. I had to do something to stop the insufferable teenagers, who proceeded as if the world held nothing more enchanting than these nine horrible statues and the bowls of my blood.

The first of the nine lifted her bowl above the gaping maw of the snarling gargoyle. She poured the blood into the mouth of the beast, draining every last drop into the lifeless statue.

A vicious snarl cleaved the air, and the earth shook beneath me. I looked wide-eyed to the first gargoyle and watched in horror as it sprang from its perch and mauled the girl, tearing at her flesh with razor-sharp teeth. It no longer resembled hard granite; the gray flesh appeared smooth and supple. The sinews of its body flexed, and its wings beat slowly, stretching a body frozen in stone for ages. Its dull skin quivered as it lapped at the torn and bloody body it held in a clawed grasp. And the tongue that had once been curled inside its gaping mouth flicked out, forked and seemingly as sharp as a whetted blade.

Tyler's stolen form shimmered for a moment, a wave of clear energy reminding me of a mirage. Or a glamour. A clever creature, indeed, but no Shaede could change its form to that extent. I leapt toward the imposter and tackled him to the ground, surprised at how easily I managed the feat.

I wrestled the dagger from his hand, still dripping with my blood, and held the tip to my would-be killer's throat. "Show yourself," I said.

The mirage flickered, and dull, expressionless eyes transformed to a milky blue. His head deflated and became small and girlish, fragile even, framed with mousy brown hair. The masculine frame grew more female and much more delicate. I stared at the tiny woman beneath me with disbelieving eyes. All at once, the truth seemed stranger to me than the illusion.

"Delilah," I said.

"There's nothing you can do!" She seethed. "It's already begun, and once the transformation is complete, the Enphigmalé will be free!"

I looked up as a second guardian emptied his bowl, mimicking his neighbor's actions. He fed the blood into the gargoyle's mouth and it sprang to life, devouring his body in large, crunching bites.

"Why?" I had a hard time wrapping my mind around her decision to see this awful thing through. She was Tyler's *friend*. I thought she'd been mine. What was her motivation? What could have filled her with so much hate?

Surrounded by enemies, I tried to assess the risk to myself and my only ally. The bear, or, rather, Tyler in bear form, pulled against his chain, but he was safe. And the third guardian of nine emptied the last of my blood from his bowl. Azriel stood guard at the bower, frozen by fear or wonder as he watched the grisly scene unfold. And the Lyhtans . . . they were so entertained by the violence, they'd forgotten about me altogether. But that would last only so long.

"They awaken," Delilah said in awe. "The Enphigmalé will mete out death to those who imprisoned them. And for my part, I'll finally have revenge."

"Revenge?" Good lord, what kind of grudge could Delilah be harboring to prompt her to set these events in motion?

"Do you know how long I've waited?" Delilah wailed. Her eyes darted from side to side, making her look on the verge of madness. "What I had to do to orchestrate it all? It will all be worth it. Once he's freed from his beast, those who've wronged us will pay. He promised me!"

Christ, she wasn't making an *ounce* of sense. I debated a course of action. Listen to more of Delilah's incoherent ramblings, or shut her up once and for all. With a heavy-handed swing, I knocked her out in a single punch. Taking a chance, I cut several strands of my hair with her dagger, using them to secure her wrists behind her back and her ankles. I plucked her from the ground and tossed her down on the dais, leaving her until I could decide what to do with her. In the meantime, I had a ritual to stop and a bear to set free.

Three of the kids were in the process of being devoured by the living Enphigmalé. Their batlike wings flapped in the breeze while they enjoyed their meals.

I crept slowly to the center of the clearing where Tyler had been chained. His purpose seemed pretty clear now. He was meant to be dessert.

He leapt and strained against the links in an effort to pull himself loose. Grabbing a section of chain in his mouth, he shook his head back and forth, gnawing down again and again, but the links held. He paused, panting, and changed his course of action, clawing at the spike protruding from the grass instead. Breaking into a run, I dropped to my knees and wrapped my hands around the spike, pulling with all my strength. The ground released its hold and I yanked the spike from the dirt with ease. He couldn't run or fight while dragging the long rope of links behind him, though, and so, with a pat to his large, furry head, I braced one hand against the collar and pulled the chain with the other. I strained and groaned, yanking as hard as I could without hurting Tyler. The link at the collar weakened, and it pulled away by small degrees.

"Come on," I said as I pulled. "Just a little bit more."

Tyler dug his furry heels into the grass and leaned backward to help. The chain gave more with our joint effort, and I'd managed to separate the link enough to free it from the collar. A movement from the corner of my eye caught my attention, and I buried my hands into his furry side, shoving at Tyler's massive form. "Run!" I shouted.

He took off with amazing speed for such a lumbering creature. I rolled in the opposite direction as one of the

Enphigmalé landed in the very spot we'd occupied. Its tail swished from side to side, cutting into the soft grass with ferocious force, throwing pieces of turf flying this way and that.

I trained my eyes on Tyler, and he stared straight back. "We have to take out the kids before they wake any more of them up!"

His head bobbed up and down and he took off, circumventing the living gargoyles and the bower where Azriel stood, eyes wide and mouth agape, unable to do anything but gawk like an idiot at the havoc he'd helped to give rise to.

Armed with nothing but Delilah's dagger, I was at a disadvantage. I looked around for anything that might pass as a weapon, but the closest thing I could find was the cast-aside chain. I reached out, snatching it back to me like a whip.

Menacing silver eyes glinted from the dark gray, monstrous head of the Enphigmalé, and its tail jerked to and fro as it studied its prey. I stole a quick glance behind its shoulder, watching as Tyler successfully tackled one of the boys, bringing a swift and seemingly less-painful end to his life. A moment later, one of the girls met the same end. But four remained, and one had already tipped her bowl to the gargoyle's mouth.

I looked back at the beast whose wings flapped like great paper kites to stir up a balmy wind. When I shut my eyes against the dust and bits of grass flying at my face, it took the opportunity to attack and leapt toward me. I felt a rush of energy as it came at me, and I twirled the chain in a frantic circle and let it fly, striking the gargoyle in the face and knocking it to one side.

A Lyhtan spectator cackled wildly at the entertainment, drawing the Enphigmalé's attention from me. It charged, head down, straight for the Lyhtan. His—or her—screams pierced the sky before it fell under the pouncing beast. The Lyhtan screamed in horror while the gargoyle clawed and bit chunks from its segmented body. Wary, the crowd of Lyhtans began to disperse as shouts of alarm rang out around them. It seemed they'd just begun to realize that this little scene wasn't going down the way they'd expected.

Tyler had tackled kid number five before she could drain her bowl into the statue's mouth, and I looked to Azriel, who remained stock-still at his post beside the bower. As seconds continued to tick away inside me, the changes became more pronounced, and I noticed again how time meant something completely different to me now. I moved quickly, and I noticed so much more and processed the information, while the outside world continued at a much slower pace. I studied the bower and the black space beyond it, finally recognizing it for what it was: a portal.

I'd first been brought into the clearing through the bower. Perhaps this place *was* like Avalon—another realm, unseen in the middle of a bustling city or peaceful lake. The bower was the entryway to this place, and Azriel stood guarding it—or waiting to let something out of it.

Knocked off my feet, I tumbled to the ground in a tangle of hair and limbs and claws and tough, leathery wings. Another Enphigmalé had finished snacking on its sacrificial lamb and turned its hunger on the closest thing—which happened to be me. I placed both feet against its belly and shoved, tossing it away before its jaws could clamp down on my arm. It rolled once and regained its bearings, shaking its massive head and charging again. With one swift movement, I rolled onto my back and kicked, thrusting myself to a standing position. I braced myself, holding the chain in both hands, ready to defend myself in any way possible.

Tyler made short work of the remaining teens, enraptured by their sacrifice, and only four of the nine gargoyles had been awakened. Three had scattered among the Lyhtan ranks to enjoy fresh kills, and the remaining one was hunting me.

It circled me like a stalking cat, placing one giant, clawed foot over another. A low, thunderous rumble erupted from deep within its throat, and its silver eyes glinted in the waning sunlight, a reflection of death incarnate. It studied me, tilting its head to the side. I danced in time with the pursuing creature, mirroring its every movement. Its presence came to me in a wave of heat, and rather than concentrating on a specific region of my body, it hit me full on, like a balmy tropic breeze.

Without warning, the beast leapt. It caught me off guard—I'd had no time to react, and I recognized something happening to me that shouldn't. A shimmering light burst from my skin, and my corporeal form faded away. I had become one with the day and with the sun. Like my Lyhtan enemies, I had drifted into light.

My disappearing act confused my attacker, and it twisted in midair, landing sideways to its original target. I moved fast—faster than I ever had—and was gone in the blink of an eye. I appeared safely at the other side of the dais, where Delilah had regained consciousness. She thrashed about, consumed by madness, crying and screaming to no one but herself.

Adrenaline-infused shock burst through my veins, and my entire body began to shake. I crouched low, still partially melded with the rays of light, and tried to calm down while watching as the Enphigmalé turned circles and sniffed the ground where I should have been standing. It threw its bullish head back and roared in frustration, but soon gave up its search and joined the others in the Lyhtan ranks.

We had four living, breathing gargoyles to contend with, and they were wild, hungry, and dangerous. Too many variables remained, preventing me from forming a rational plan of attack. And though *I* could elude an attacker, what about Ty? Was he even in his right mind? And who, if anything, controlled the Enphigmalé?

A few more Lyhtans had fallen to the ravenous hunger of the attacking Enphigmalé, but most of them had decided the time for sitting on the sidelines as spectators was over. "Betrayed!" one of them shouted. "Used!" said another. "The Oracle lied to us! Azriel tricked us!" The rage and confusion in their many-faceted voices rose to a din. "They brought us here to die!" Some passed into the light, appearing to me as nothing more than flickers in the rays of sun. My own body shimmered, fading in and out of corporeal form, a mirage of quavering light.

"See her!" A Lyhtan seethed and spit as it changed course from its hasty retreat, its shimmering form becoming solid. The others followed their comrade's gaze, momentarily distracted from their flight. A collective screeching of voices reverberated through the clearing, giving even the feeding Enphigmalé pause.

Oh. Shit. For some reason I felt like I had more to fear from these thinking, slavering creatures than I did the mindless beasts running ravenous through our ranks. And then the reason hit me—well, that and a half-ton bear.

Tyler knocked me to the ground, and my corporeal form returned completely. I looked up to see a wall of golden fur. Standing over me with all four legs braced apart, Tyler snarled at the creatures that stopped to gawk. He knew they wanted me too.

Lyhtan by day and Shaede by night, without the ugly exterior to keep me in hiding, I'd evolved into everything they wanted to be and more. It seemed like I was the hot commodity of the day, and as the Lyhtan army drew near, I appreciated just how sticky our predicament had become. We couldn't fight four hungry, out-of-control Enphigmalé while at the same time keeping the Lyhtans away as they sought to take me.

"I think we're screwed no matter what, Ty." I tried to twist so I could look into his face, but he pressed down like a mother hen, keeping as little distance between me and everyone else as possible. "Maybe we should run for it." A coward's exit, but considering the circumstances, I wouldn't last long in a fight. "I think that bower's a portal of some kind. All we have to do is get past Azriel. Whaddaya say?"

Tyler made his nervous-bear noises, I hoped because he was thinking over what I'd said. Escape was our best and only option, no matter how much I wanted to fight. His fur rippled from his chin to his backside, and his tensing limbs signaled that something was about to happen. Lying there, with nothing but a landscape of fur to stare at, I closed my eyes to better feel the circumstances.

In my mind's eye, our fate was painted out for me in varying degrees of sensation. Like I'd been equipped with infrared vision or sonar, I recognized the shapes and positions of every creature in the clearing—and they were moving in on us.

The Enphigmalé gnawed the bones of their Lyhtan kills at the edge of the clearing. Azriel, who had shied from his post, crept closer to where Delilah lay bound by locks of my hair. And the Lyhtans—who numbered exactly 230—continued to close in on us, their many voices making them seem like an army of thousands. I sensed Tyler above me, his fragrance so close and so sweet, I wanted to cry. He wouldn't leave me. He'd be the first to die, and my heart nearly broke as I thought about what they'd do to him before they laid their collective hands on me.

"Ty, run away," I urged. "Don't worry about me; they can't hurt me. Just go before they tear you to pieces."

He snorted, which I interpreted as either a burst of laughter or bear talk for *Hell, no.* I thought, *Stubborn ass.* I pushed at his stomach, and he pressed down harder in protest. Twenty yards, maybe a little more, were all I needed to clear the crowd of Lyhtans. *Easy*. I pressed my palms and the bottoms of my feet against his belly and chest. Gave a little, bending my arms and knees, took a huge breath, and forced my limbs to push and spring out at the same time.

Tyler flew away like he weighed nothing at all. He landed in the taller grass outside the clearing, and it rustled as he thumped to the earth and rolled, finally coming to a stop. *Hope he's not too mad*, I thought. *Or too hurt*. And jumped to my feet.

"Look how strong," a Lyhtan whispered as it crept steadily toward me.

"And see her skin in the light of day," said another.

"We'll take her and tear her apart in little pieces until we discover her secret!"

That didn't sound good at all. I had no intention of being torn into pieces large, small, or any size in between. On the flip side, I had no idea how to escape the circling Lyhtans, whose segmented insect bodies jerked and twisted as they studied the object of their desire—a creature with their strength, minus a very big weakness.

Tick, tick, tick. Time sped away from me, thundering in my ears, chest, and soul. I counted the minutes until twilight, when at least a portion of my enemies would be vulnerable. Exactly twenty-five minutes and fifteen seconds ... fourteen ... thirteen ... twelve ...

I gave myself a mental shake. It was hard not to become wrapped up in the passing of time when it felt like it passed through me before breaking out on the world. I wouldn't last twenty-five seconds, let alone an entire half hour. Searching for Delilah's dagger, I patted my waistband and then my coat pockets, and felt a bulge. I'd completely forgotten about the contents of my pocket. I reached in, closed my fist around the bottled shadows, and smiled.

Patience is not one of my many virtues, but the situation demanded it, and I waited as the horde of Lyhtans came closer. The timing had to be perfect, and since I didn't know how or even *if* the gooey black stuff would work, I had to try to take out as many of the bastards as I could. It was the only way we'd have a fighting chance.

Closer and closer, *tick, tick, tick*, the moment crept on with a sluggishness that only I felt. The Lyhtans could have been running at me, for all the difference it would have made.

The grass where Tyler landed began to stir. It was now or never, and so I pulled the bottle from my pocket and held it before me. Pausing, my fingers resting on the cork stopper, I considered my new circumstances. I had become one with the light—would I share in their fate?

Fifteen minutes and two seconds until twilight, but what did it matter now? My enemies were many, and I was only one woman with no weapon, no sword with which to strike them down. They would either have to be killed, or they'd do worse to me before they were done. If I died with them, so be it.

I moved quickly, and my foes slid toward me like an ice floe. Again, I reminded myself to put the amazement on the back burner, and I plucked the cork stopper from the thick glass bottle. I didn't breathe. I didn't blink. I didn't move a muscle.

Tiny tendrils of the inky black stuff seeped out from the mouth of the bottle and slid to the ground like many cobras escaping a basket. Toward my feet the black threads crept, twisting and writhing near my ankles. But rather than continue their twining search, the dark strings paused, like a dog sniffing, at my feet and continued searching outward.

The first Lyhtan screams were terrible. With a languid slither, the sludgy shadows entwined their bodies, constricting and sinking into the greenish-tinged flesh of my attackers. They fell to the ground, shaking and jerking, trying in vain to pull away from the shadows permeating their skin, right down to the brittle bones that broke and splintered as the black cords pulled and tugged their bodies in ways they weren't meant to bend.

Raif's soul shadows had killed fifty in all, but it wasn't enough to level the playing field. The contents of the bottle had been enough to protect me in the event of a chance meeting or minor ambush, but not in a full-scale attack. I threw the useless bottle to the ground, hoping Tyler wouldn't gallop out of the grass until after they'd killed me. Maybe then he'd do what I asked and save himself. I stood proud, pushed my chin up a notch or two, and waited to die.

I didn't think much of it when the first cries sounded from the rear of the Lyhtan ranks. I assumed the Enphig-malé had become hungry again and were seeking new prey. But soon a feeling of joy and salvation filled the darkest and most hopeless parts of my soul. My wish had been granted, and I didn't have to see him to know that Raif had finally come, and death came swiftly on his heels.

Chapter 28

The next few moments passed in a haze. Raif had brought a small army with him, and the many Shaedes filtered in through the black space beneath the bower like ants fleeing their mound. Behind Raif charged the king himself, hacking through the crowd of Lyhtans, his sword bright with rusty orange blood and cutting a path to the center of the circle—cutting a path to me.

Tick, hack. Tick, slash. Tick, ring. I stood there, my body nearly limp, my jaw slack and my eyes wide as time marched to its own beat, alternating with the sound of each sword's stroke. *Seven minutes and twelve seconds till twilight.* Until then, my allies were weak and our enemies strong.

Lyhtan and Shaede alike lay bleeding and screaming. Raif, Xander, and a few others had broken from the masses, continuing their charge to the center of the circle. I looked frantically toward the dais, where I'd left Delilah. Between the battling bodies, I caught a glimpse of an empty stone table.

Coming to my senses, I pushed the sensation of passing time from my mind—*four minutes, forty-four seconds*. Shoving and ducking, I fought my way in the direction of the dais, determined to keep Delilah and Azriel from escaping.

Xander saw my struggle and immediately changed his course. With wide-armed swings, his blade cut the air and struck down a Lyhtan; blood gushed from the stump of its arm where the king had severed it at the elbow. He jabbed another straight through its distended stomach and another through the throat. Their wounds were healing fast, though, and if twilight didn't hurry the fuck up, we'd be screwed before the fight was fair.

A Lyhtan grabbed me by the ankle just as I was about to break through the crowd to the granite dais. I was strong, but it held fast and pulled me close to its sharp-toothed face. "How did you do it?" the Lyhtan de-manded, giving me a hard shake. "How do you join with the light and the shadow? Tell me!"

My teeth chattered in my head as the Lyhtan shook me again, and its clawed hands bit deep into my arms, piercing the skin. I waited for the debilitating effects of its poison to kick in, but to both of our surprise, it had no effect whatsoever. I had become immune.

The Lyhtan gave a screeching cry, drawing the atten-tion of the others. An instant shift took place as the bat-tle swung in my direction, the Lyhtans making their way to their prize while the Shaedes sought to impede their progress. And I was caught, kicking and yanking my arms free, with one single-minded mission: find Delilah *and* Azriel.

Two minutes and five seconds. If the Shaede army could hold off for a little more than one hundred sec-onds, they'd be safe and the Lyhtans would die. I pushed the thought of time from my mind, though I felt its rhythm soft in my chest. A vicious screech pierced my ear drums and the Lyhtan who held me clutched at its neck, cut deep and squirting blood. Its grip on me slack-ened, and Xander stepped from around its writhing body to scoop me up in a strong embrace.

"Are you all right?" he asked breathlessly, his face buried in the tangles of my hair.

"Yes," I said, but I couldn't have been further from fine. "I need to find Delilah and Azriel," I said, pulling away. "They're here somewhere. She's the one." I shoved against him. "She's behind it all. I have to—"

Tick—three, *tick*—two, *tick*—one ... the sun dipped into the west. My knees buckled beneath me as the rush of change to the gray hour swelled in my body, filling me with a dizzy, drunken sensation. The earth seemed to slant beneath my feet, and my head spun. I slipped from Xander's grasp like wind through a net and he jumped back, shock showing on his strong and handsome face.

No longer light or dark, the scope of my evolved abilities became obvious to me now. I was not restrained by anything. Time did not matter. The sun, moon; the absence and presence of both swayed me. No longer a slave to my corporeal form at any hour, I had become one with those hours. I had, in essence, become time.

"What's happened to you?" Xander asked.

I didn't have time to give him a sufficient answer, because Tyler's bear cry tore through the air, stealing the breath from my lungs.

Delilah had to take a backseat to a more important crisis. The Shaede army was making short work of the Lyhtans, whose power had diminished significantly once the sun had set. The injured were dying; the dying were now dead. And fresh blood flowed at the hands of Raif and his companions as their swords met little to no resistance. But one formidable enemy had been forgotten in all the chaos. More dangerous than Delilah, more devious than Azriel, and more deadly than the most vicious Lyhtan, the Enphigmalé had joined the fray.

As if he knew my thoughts, Raif paused and caught my eye. He ran his sword through his opponent's chest and pulled a scabbard from around his shoulder. With a great heave, my katana soared above the heads of the fighting armies, and I dug my heels into the ground and took off at a run. I leapt as the katana arched and came down, and caught it in a swift and fluid motion. Ripping the blade from its protective sheath, I discarded the black scabbard and ran through the ranks of allies and foes alike, my form nothing but a passing breeze.

Three of the four gargoyles had converged on Tyler. Bright teeth flashed in the graying light and claws dug into his golden fur. He bit and fought, twisting and swinging with his massive paws, but the tables had turned against him, and he was losing. Blood trickled down his face, and the fur around one shoulder was matted where the flesh was torn. I saw his composure falter, and his glistening nose sniffed the air for barely a moment. He made eye contact, and before he swept his foreleg at a biting mouth, he thrashed his massive head as if to tell me to keep my distance. An Enphigmalé seized the opportunity of his distraction and sank its teeth deep into Tyler's throat.

He should have known I didn't follow directions well. Panic surged within me as I put Raif's training to good use and jumped right in the middle of the feeding frenzy. Tyler had slumped to the ground; I didn't have time to gauge whether he was conscious or not. My only thought centered on keeping him safe. I kicked at the beast whose jaws snapped repeatedly, trying to finish what it started. The force of the impact sent it flying a good twenty feet or so, and it barreled into a Lyhtan trying to flee the melee. It made a quick and easy meal for the insatiable Enphigmalé that gobbled its prey like it hadn't already glutted itself for hours.

I swung with the katana at the second gargoyle, who tried to flog me with its great, leathery wings. I cut through the skin-covered appendage and the beast swung around, snarling and snapping, grazing my arm in the process. I jerked back and stabbed high, piercing one of the glowing silver eyes. The creature reared and stomped down, shaking the earth with the movement. It pawed at the bleeding hole in its head, thrashing and whimpering as it bucked and jumped away.

Twilight faded into ever-darkening night, and the Shaede army continued its efforts against the Lyhtans, who refused to surrender despite their vulnerable state.

A flash of red leather caught my eye and a long braid whipped through the air as Anya spun and danced in battle. She flashed a wicked smile in my direction, the exulting rush of battle lust flushing her cheeks, and the joy of victory glowing in her violet eyes.

The other Shaedes had twenty-seven minutes and nine seconds before they could pass into shadow, but I was not held by such restraints. I passed into the gray again and again as the Enphigmalé tried to make purchase on my twisting form. I cut and stabbed, sliced and jabbed, protecting Tyler the only way I could, while he lay bleeding and damaged. One of the braver gargoyles charged, and I rammed the katana into the earth as I waited for the charging beast. My breathing slowed, my focus sharpened, and I stood my ground. Its progress came slow and measured in my new and heightened sense of time. I reached out, and my palms wrapped around the beast's face. As I jumped to the side, avoiding its charge, I twisted with all my might, groaning under the tremendous force. Its strength was immense, more of stone than flesh. I jerked *hard*, and after hearing the snap of its neck, I released my hold. The Enphigmalé continued in a skid across the clearing until its progress was stayed by a rather large tree. The great gray beast slammed into the trunk, twitched, and let a loud snort from its wide nostrils before becoming still. It did not move again.

I pulled my sword from the ground and charged another, leaping onto its expansive back. It turned circles, trying to throw me off, but the movement seemed so slow, I barely felt it. I raised the katana high and stabbed down through the flesh and bone, deep into the creature's skull. I wrapped both hands around the hilt and twisted the katana. The gargoyle crumpled in a useless heap and jerked once, twice, and died.

The last of the gray hour melted into night. Screams echoed in the clearing, the sound of the injured and dying lingering on the wind. Raif turned his force's attention to the Enphigmalé, they joined my efforts to eradicate the ever-starving beasts before they could do any more damage.

Leaving the battle to skilled warriors, I turned my attention to Tyler. I gripped the wide collar in my hands and pulled with all my strength, forcing the heavy clasp until it broke under the pressure. I threw it to the side, and, within moments, the bear's form shrunk and faded away. In its place lay a bleeding, naked man, his breath rasping in his chest.

"Ty, can you hear me?" I said close to his ear. "Hold on. Don't leave me yet." I threw off my coat, then ripped the sleeve from my shirt and wrapped it around the gaping wound in Tyler's neck.

His eyes fluttered and my heart mimicked the act. *Not dead.* I sighed.

"Raif," he said, barely a murmur. "Is he here?"

"Yes," I breathed. "My wish is your command, right?"

He gave a wan smile. "Exactly."

Around me the Enphigmalé snarled, Lyhtans screamed, and Shaedes cheered. But in front of me, Tyler lay dying. I didn't care about any of those other things if I couldn't fix the only thing that mattered. "Tyler," I said. "I wish—"

"No!" he said, forceful for the first time. "Don't say it, Darian. You can't."

"Why not?" I asked, trying to keep the desperation from my voice. "If I can't use my wishes to heal you, what good are they?"

"My life is yours, not the other way around. You can't wish the dying back to life, remember? I love you, Darian. All that matters to me is you're safe. If I have to die to make sure that happens, so be it. We have to follow the rules."

"Fuck the rules," I said through my emerging tears, "I don't give a damn about your rules! I wish you were better. I wish you were healed."

His eyes drifted shut, and I gave him a shake. "I wish

you were healed! Damn it, Tyler. Don't do this to me! I wish you were healed!"

A sudden wave of energy left me like air from a vacuum. I slumped over, my breathing heavy for the first time in this long and seemingly ceaseless day. The wet, slurping sound of Tyler's breathing didn't slacken despite my urgent wish. I retrieved my black duster and draped it over him, whispering the words over and over. Wishing, *willing* him to live. "Don't leave me," I whispered over his chest. "Please, Ty. *Don't leave me.*"

In a gust of warm and fragrant air, Raif came to stand beside me, placing a reassuring hand on my shoulder. I wanted to shake him off, to refuse the comfort he offered as I allowed myself to deny the fact that there might soon be reason for me to grieve.

"One of the beasts ran," Raif said, with a mixture of anger and regret. Blood stained his shirt from a cut to his forearm, and his face was beaded with sweat. "But the remaining three are dead."

"What about the Lyhtans?" I asked, combing my fingers through Ty's hair.

Raif laughed. "No contest there—almost a disappointment. Most of them are dead. The others fled."

"And ours? How many gone?"

His voice became thick. "Eleven."

"Anya?"

"Alive."

Oh, well. You can't win 'em all. Really, I could have cared less if she lived or died. The *only* thing I cared about was bleeding away on the grass.

"Azriel is gone. The Oracle as well."

My shoulders slumped. Leave it to the snake to find the quickest way through the grass. He couldn't hide forever, though. And when I found him, he'd pay in spades. "How did you find me?" *And how do we get back?* Could we get back?

"I just knew," Raif said. "It was the strangest thing. One

moment I was scouring maps, trying to pinpoint locations that they may have taken you, and the next moment, I knew where you were and exactly how to get here. I assume that was your Jinn's doing. Very clever, Darian."

Sounds drifted to my ears—the running of a great beast through the woods, the last, sighing breath of the dying, and solid pats on the back as comrades-in-arms congratulated one another. The night progressed and time marched on, the cadence of which had not left me and probably never would. For the umpteenth time, I tried to ignore the sensation that the world spun within me, outward.

"We should take him home," Raif said, placing his other hand around my opposite arm to encourage me to stand. "We'll do everything we can for him."

Several branches were brought and bound together with vines. My duster was thrown over the makeshift cot. And though I insisted Tyler would be no burden for me to carry, Raif insisted just as sternly that he be transported with the least amount of jostling possible. I reluctantly agreed and followed behind, as the remaining members of Raif's forces, led by Xander, made their way to the bower, and, one by one, stepped through the gaping black portal.

When we emerged on the other side, the blinding sunlight threw me for a loop. Raif shielded his eyes from the offending glare. "When we arrived here, it was the dead of night. Imagine our surprise to walk into that opening and come out in the light of day."

I didn't have to imagine anything; I was surprised enough. We loaded Tyler onto one of two large pontoon boats. I raised a questioning brow to Raif.

"What? They were the only vessels I could find. How else would you expect me to transport so many after daybreak?"

I allowed a subdued laugh. "No wonder it took you so long."

"What do you mean so long? You've been gone for only twelve hours."

My jaw dropped a little. Time had become a different thing entirely on the other side of the bowered portal. Hours had become days, and no one was the wiser. No one but me.

"Not that it would have mattered," Raif continued. "You could have taken them all single-handedly. I'm impressed, Darian. You're a true warrior."

He inclined his head respectfully and left me at the bow of the sluggish boat that chugged us from the island to the mainland. Tyler remained unconscious, lying in the shade of the awning. I wanted to be at his side, but I needed to be alone, to feel the wind in my face, whipping my hair. My eyes stung as unshed tears came to the fore, finally spilling over my lids and down my cheeks. I swiped them away, swallowing against the grief that threatened to consume me. I didn't think I could live without Tyler. I sure as hell knew I wouldn't want to. I breathed in deeply, letting the cool air clean the stench of Lyhtans, death, and betrayal from my memory. If only it could erase the memory of change.

A warm body pressed against my back and I closed my eyes. Still on the edge of violence, I could easily lay my fist to the softer parts of his face. But despite everything that had passed between us, I knew somehow that Xander held an inexplicable magnetism. I was drawn to him, no matter how many times he'd burned me. He'd tried to protect me in his own way. And like a nagging child, starved for attention, he made sure his presence was known.

"You are different," Xander said. The King of Obvious, among other things.

"Yes."

"You have made yourself yet again. How did it happen?"

I sighed. The last thing I wanted to do was satisfy Xander's sick curiosity. His ambition knew no limit. "Would you lock me up and try to discover my secrets?" I asked, my voice broken and weary. "Do you share your enemy's desire to be both light and dark, free to roam unseen in the night or day? Would you take the gray as well and make it your own at my expense?"

"I would take you and keep you safe," he said, bending to lay his cheek against the top of my head. "I would take you and make you mine if you would only let me."

"That's not going to happen," I said, refusing to turn and look at him.

"Maybe not now," he said, confident as he ever was, "but someday."

"Raif said Tyler would be taken to your house," I said, ignoring his romance-novel spiel. "If you don't want him there, I understand."

Xander turned, and as he walked away his voice carried to me. "The Jinn is welcome. He saved the woman I love."

If anyone loved dramatics more than me, it was Xander.

Chapter 29

A mournful air hung heavy throughout Xander's house. Lives and friends had been lost on the island. Enemies as well had slipped through our grasp. Tyler had been cleaned, his wounds tended, though they refused to heal, and his care knew no limits.

Curious stares and whispers followed me wherever I went. An oddity, something to be pointed at and talked about but never to. Some avoided me altogether after tales of the clearing became more widespread. No one dared speak about it in the presence of the king, as it was well-known I was far and above his favorite. *Alienation* took on an entirely new meaning as I wandered the halls of Xander's house, looking for any diversion to take my mind off Tyler, who still hadn't regained consciousness.

Hours passed to days and days to weeks. Raif had formed reconnaissance parties whose sole mission was to flush Azriel and Delilah from hiding. They'd been unsuccessful.

I'd been given my own suite of rooms; I hadn't even stepped foot in my own studio since our trip across the lake, and I was comfortable enough. Though the house lacked the privacy I craved, it held Tyler, and he held my heart.

I'd been alone for a century and then found and cherished. But now I was alone again, the only one of my kind, sticking out rather than belonging. Time marched on, and I felt every second of its passing deep in my soul.

The sun rose and set, and the moon inevitably came to take its place. I felt all of it, my form ever changing from light to gray to dark and back to gray again.

I stood on my balcony, listening to the sounds of the city mingle with the sounds of nature in the strange area where all manner of lives and lifestyles converged. The comfort I gleaned from the never-changing bustle of Seattle was the only thing I had in a life that felt too full and too empty all at once.

"How've you been?" A cool voice asked out of nowhere.

Past shock of any kind, I merely smiled, remembering Raif's words: *Be patient, and your prey will come to you.* "What are you doing here?" I asked. "Shouldn't you be running from Raif?"

"I should," Azriel said in a very cavalier, very *him* manner. "But I wanted to see you before I leave for good."

"For good—or for a while?" I asked.

Azriel's laughter lent to the chill of the night air. "Maybe a little of both," he said. "I doubt I'll stay away for too long."

"You've always needed to be in the spotlight. I can't imagine this worked out the way you expected it to."

"We wouldn't have killed you," he offered, as if I cared.

"No," I said. "You would have just thrown my scraps to your Lyhtan dogs."

"A ruse," he scoffed. "We needed their help, nothing else. No one but Delilah and I know your true purpose. But it will come out"—he laughed as if sharing a private joke—"in time."

"Oh yeah?" I said, sarcastic as ever. "Sounds like this had less to do with me and more to do with revenge. For Delilah, at least."

Azriel shrugged. "True. Delilah has a score to settle. And she's not particularly fond of Shaedes. Well"—he smirked—"one in particular. But wouldn't you seek revenge if someone dear to you had died needlessly?"

I gave him a you've-got-to-be-fucking-kidding-me look. Azriel had more balls than sense to say that to me. The only person I'd ever truly loved *was* about to die needlessly. And you could bet someone was going to pay for it.

"So you can hardly blame her for her actions," Azriel said. "She's actually quite brilliant. And an Oracle is always handy to have around. She put all of this together, you know. With a little help . . ."

"From you?" I asked.

"Wouldn't you like to know?" Azriel laughed. "She sent me to you in the first place. Told me that through you, I'd gain my father's crown. I imagine she sent your Jinn to you as well. Or at the very least, pointed him in the right direction. The way I see it, Darian, you owe her a debt of thanks. She did set the two of you up, after all."

"Jealous?" I asked.

"You have no idea," Azriel said, and for a moment, he almost sounded sincere. "But the Enphigmalé would have never awakened without your little romance. The odds were one in a million that you'd wake them. Curses are funny things, Darian. To break one, you need all the elements that made it to begin with. In this case, it took an act of deep, abiding love to break the curse. Well"— Azriel flashed a secretive smile—"love, and the blood of a fated protector."

My heart ached. Swelled to bursting with love for Tyler. And Azriel was right: I would have done anything to protect him, though I don't know that made me a fated protector. Could it have been that simple, though? What made me valuable to Azriel and Delilah was the fact that I'd fallen in *love*? "What about the eclipse? I suppose my new and improved physical state was just a happy accident? A side effect from being in the right place at the right time?"

Azriel laughed in earnest. I guess I was a regular fucking comedian. "You could have been asleep in your bed, ignorant as ever, and the change would have occurred. The eclipse was just the catalyst. That eclipse—with a little help from Fate—made you stronger. And for the trials you've yet to face . . . you're going to need it."

What a load of bullshit. Azriel was nothing more than a liar. I couldn't trust a single word that came out of his mouth. All he was doing was buying time, cleaving to every extra minute he had on this earth. He'd told me one too many tall tales for me to believe anything he said.

"Instead of trying to pass off more of your stories as truth, shouldn't you be worried that I might kill you right now? I could do it, you know."

"I have no doubt," Azriel said. "But you won't kill me, just like I didn't kill you. You're too special for a paltry death."

"Give me a break." The effect of his dramatic flair had definitely worn off. "I can't let you go. Not after what you've done."

"I was afraid you'd say that. And after everything we've been through . . ."

I looked at him incredulously. "Exactly."

"Aren't you scared of me?" His arrogance was laughable. "It's the gray hour, and I was once Raif's best student."

"What do I care about that?" I could be arrogant too. I had a right to be. "I have no more restraints, and you're not the only one who's spent quality time with Raif. Surrender now, and I'll go easy on you."

He looked to his feet, his expression contemplative. But I knew his little act was just that. Lunging toward me with immeasurable speed, he struck, his fist catching me high on my cheekbone. I spun from the impact and he used the opportunity, flinging himself from the balcony. He landed soft and soundless on the grass below.

Blood trickled from the split on my face, the skin tightening and healing instantaneously. I leapt over the railing, landed on Azriel's back, and sent him sprawling face-first to the lawn. A low growl rumbled deep in his chest and he rolled, spinning his legs in a scissor kick, and knocked my legs out from under me. In a misty cloud of gray, I disappeared, regained my footing before he could stand, and kicked a booted foot hard into his ribs. The satisfying *crack* made him double over in pain.

Azriel didn't go down without a fight. His fist made contact with my stomach, knocking the air right out of me. Gasping for a decent breath, I tried to stand tall. Without pause, he struck again, this time dagger in hand, and ran the blade along my thigh before bringing it up in a swiping motion, catching me along my hip. Inhaling lungfuls of air, I gained my wits and spun, joined with the gray twilight, and appeared at his side, my own dagger gripped tight in my right hand. A quick stab caught him just below his lung, and another made contact with the fleshy part of his side. He crumpled but continued to lash out with the weapon, catching my calf on the backswing.

"I'm done with this shit," I said between gritted teeth. I doubled my fists, still wrapped around the dagger's grip, and brought the pommel down on Azriel's head. He fell to the grass at my feet, and I stomped a booted foot down onto his neck.

"Raif!" I called toward the house. "Get the fuck out here!"

"He's secured for now," Raif said, dark and serious.

I pushed myself from the table where I'd been pretending to eat. Xander remained in his seat, a dark look of regret marring his handsome face. He scowled and threw his fork across the dining room. It stuck in the wall just to the right of Anya's head. It just seemed I couldn't catch a break.

Azriel could have run. But instead he'd waltzed right into the lion's den. He had no choice now but to face the consequences of his actions. "I want to see him."

"I thought we'd let him stew for a while," Raif said. "*Then* we'll pay him a visit."

"Don't do anything without me," I warned, and took my leave.

The quiet dark of Tyler's room seemed appropriate. I thought he'd like it that way, for some reason. I should've let the light in every once in a while, but for the life of me I couldn't bring myself to pull the curtains aside. I wanted him back. Now. Awake and smiling and filling me with comfort I hadn't dared to feel. Henry had left me craving affection, and Azriel had led me around by a ring in want of it. But Tyler had given it freely and without anticipation of anything in return. He'd bound himself to me, tied his life to my very existence, and had never held that fact over my head. Unconditional—that was Tyler. And when I didn't think I was worthy of love, or contained the capacity to feel it, Tyler had taught me that I'd been wrong. I loved, deeply. I loved him.

"You know," I said as I planted myself in a chair beside his bed, "I really want you to wake up so you can explain your little animal act to me." I'd taken to talking to him, whether he was awake or not, hoping I could coax him from whatever held him. "Have you always been able to do that? Xander says that Jinn can change shapes, and it embodies their protection. The bear suited you. You could have saved me a lot of trouble, though, if you'd stayed in human form. Did you even think about that, Tyler? You are such an idiot!"

His wounds refused to heal, seeping blood and pus, infection pulling him closer to death every day. Rage and frustration blossomed from the pit of my stomach. I kicked the side of his bed, jostling his body. "Wake up!" I stood and leaned over him. "Wake up, damn you! Don't be so fucking weak! Get. Up!"

"Darian," Raif's voice called from the doorway. "Maybe you should take a few days away from here."

I spun around, mad as hell and ready for a fight. "He can wake up! He just won't! Why the hell not? What did I do?"

Raif came to me and laid a comforting, albeit stiff, hand on my shoulder.

"Fuck!" I cried. "What the hell is wrong with me?"

Raif laughed quietly. "You're feeling something," he said. "I know you think you're immune to such tender things, but you're not as damn hard as you've convinced yourself you are."

"I love him," I whispered.

"Yes," he said. "I think that's pretty obvious. I'm going down to Azriel. Are you coming?"

I paused, looked back at Tyler's still form on the bed.

"Let's go." He tilted his head toward the door. "Don't go easy on him either."

The corners of my mouth tugged into a reluctant smile. "Don't worry," I said. "I won't."

Indignant and full of fire, Azriel laughed in our faces. He'd been afforded better treatment than his Lyhtan associates, given a prince's imprisonment in a huge suite of rooms.

Though my wounds had healed since our fight, Azriel's were still fresh. His wrists had been bound with silky strands of Lyhtan hair and tied behind him. Raif may have treated him like a prince, but he was still a dangerous prisoner. "You think this is over?" He laughed, spitting blood from his cut lip. "You think because only one of the Enphigmalé lives and the others are either dormant or dead that this is the end of it? You're wrong."

I didn't need to hit him again, but I wanted to. It made me feel better to rattle his brain a little. Besides, I had a month's worth of built-up tension to release. "That one's for Tyler," I said, shaking out my hand.

"The iron collar did the trick, didn't it? Kept him locked in his animal form. He was with you all the time, and you were too stupid to see it. You actually thought *Delilah* was him!"

I backhanded him, nice and hard.

"Hit me again," he said, "and again and again and again! It won't change anything. It won't change who or what you are! It won't change your purpose."

"Don't speak unless you have something worth saying," Raif snapped from near the doorway. "Repent now, Azriel, and perhaps this will end well for you."

"This is only the beginning," he said. "My father can't stop it, and you can't stop it either, *Uncle*. The floodgates are open. And if you think Delilah's failure is the end of it, you're wrong. She has more reason to hate you than I do."

Raif shrugged, quirked a curious brow.

"Why did my father send the pair of you to deal with me?" His voice became cold, detached, hollow. "Not man enough to face me himself, I suppose. I'm insulted, actually, that he sent his servants to clean up *his* mess."

Beating him wasn't going to do any good. Keeping him captive seemed futile as well. He'd gone mad with his need for vengeance and power. A need founded from years alone, separated from his own people. I knew just how he felt. He'd done the same to me. "I'm surprised at you, Darian," he said, spitting more blood. "This is the thanks I get for everything I did for you. You would have remained a human punching bag if it hadn't been for me. I *saved* your weak and sorry ass."

"Get out, Raif," I said, low.

"Darian—," he warned.

"Now. You don't need to be party to this. Leave."

I waited for Raif to close the door, which he did reluctantly. I'd been paid to do a job, and it was *finally* time to go to work. "Listen, you slimy sonofabitch. I don't owe you a fucking thing. You got that?"

Azriel gave a crooked, swollen-lipped smile. His eyes narrowed in calculation, and that was enough to earn him a black eye. I shook out my fist, looked at the tiny cuts on my knuckles, which closed before the blood could spill over my skin.

"Delilah left you high and dry," I said. "Your little coup failed. You're all alone, and it's time to settle your tab."

"Do you want me to beg for forgiveness?" he asked, his voice turning seductive and sweet. "Is that what you want, *love*?" He approached me slowly and warily, his eyes roaming hungrily over my body. "Well, it's not going to happen. I refuse to beg *him* for anything!"

Jesus, I wish he'd shut up. How I'd spent twenty years in his company, I'll never know.

"You're still as stupid and ignorant as you ever were. You and Raif. Serving my father like his lapdogs." He snorted in disgust. "But he'll trip up sooner or later, and you'll both regret your allegiance. Fools, both of you."

At least now I knew where Azriel had gotten his dramatic tendencies; seems it ran in the family. My fingers caressed the dagger's hilt, protruding from the sheath at my thigh, and my conscience hitched for a brief, intolerable moment.

"You can't talk your way out of this one, Az." I wondered what could have made him hate his father so much, what skeletons lurked in his closet. "Besides, I don't give a shit about Xander's kingdom. When I finish this, I'm done with him."

Azriel laughed again; his rope was *seriously* unraveling. "You know, now that I think of it, I should have killed your little pet. He fell hard for you, though I don't blame him. You are extraordinary. But you—you surpassed my expectations. Delilah knew your love for him was deep, and I doubted it. You were right—I *am* jealous. You certainly didn't love me as much. How's your true love doing, by the way? Not much of a wish granter anymore, I hear."

I never said my moral compass pointed due north. My own skeletons needed a walk-in closet. I'd been paid, plain and simple, and I always followed through on a job. Always.

The dagger slipped from the sheath, quiet as a lover's whisper. I choked up on the grip, the guard biting bitterly into my skin. Twenty years I'd spent with him. He'd seduced me and I'd thought I loved him. He could have been honest with me. If he'd told me the truth all those years ago and defied Xander, I would have taken his side. I would have followed him anywhere, and we might've been happy. Looking into the cold light of his eyes, though, I saw the truth. He wanted me dead. Me and every last person who'd wronged him. He could never be stopped or restrained or imprisoned. Raif was right. He was simply too dangerous, and I held to my standards: Never kill the innocent. I sucked in a breath, looked deep into the fathomless depths of his black eyes, and reached behind him, my face brushing his as I cut the Lyhtan hair with my dagger, freeing his hands.

"I'd rather die by your hand than live by anyone else's," he said, almost too low to hear. He reached for his boot, for the knife I'd seen hidden there.

Mercifully quick, I stabbed at his jugular, severed the carotid artery.

Bright crimson gushed from the wound, and the air tinged with copper. Eyes large and disbelieving, Azriel stared. He twitched, bent forward, and lurched upright. "That's . . . my girl," he said in a gurgling breath. The spark drained from his eyes, and he slumped to the floor.

I stumbled and found my back against the far wall. Sliding to the floor, I sat with my knees drawn up and the bloody dagger dangling from my hand. I'd always thought he was dead. And now he was. Once and for all, Azriel was gone. And my hand had dealt the blow.

Anya rounded the corner at a full sprint. She wore a canary-yellow jumpsuit in her signature leather. I wondered how much I'd have to pay her to get her into a nice pair of cotton Dockers. "What happened?" she asked, curiosity watering down her usual condescension. "I've never seen Raif so unsettled."

"It didn't go well," I said, using the wall as leverage to push myself from the floor.

"You think?" She motioned to the door.

Three Shaedes entered, looking more afraid of me than the mangled and bloodied body lying on the floor. They skirted me by way of the opposite wall, and I did them a favor by getting the hell out of there.

Not confined to time of day, I became one with the very air and appeared at Raif's back as he hurried toward the second flight of stairs. I drifted into my corporeal form and laid a hand on his shoulder to stop him. "Raif, there wasn't any other way for this to end. You know that, right?"

"Do I?" he said, taking my hand and removing it from his shoulder. "I'm not so sure. Do you think he was telling the truth in there?" He jerked his head toward the stairs. "I always knew that Azriel had designs on Xander's throne. But more than that? 'This is only the beginning.' That's what he said. I was stupid to hope that merely killing the fool would put an end to this. And, frankly, I don't need the headache."

"Azriel was a liar. We both know that. There's always hope, Raif," I said.

"Oh, really?" His jaded tone screamed hardened, battle-weary warrior. And, perhaps, *grieving* uncle? "Do you have hope now? You've been wandering around this house for weeks like some sort of damned ghost, waiting for Tyler to wake up. Is that hope? Knowing there's not a single thing you can do for him, but staying here anyway—is that hope? Living for a dead man—is that hope? Or is it just pathetic?"

Ouch, Raif. He'd stung me with his words, but deep down I knew I wasn't pathetic. I did have hope. I hoped that Azriel's plans died with him. I hoped we'd have some peace and quiet for a while. And I had to hope Tyler would be okay. And as Raif's words came back to me, my hope transformed into a plan.

"I'll show you what hope can do." I disappeared, and like the ghost they all thought I was, drifted up the staircase to Tyler's room.

I burst through the door and knelt beside him, put my mouth to his ear. "Tyler, I'm not letting you leave me. I've been alone for too goddamned long, and I refuse to allow you to break our bond." I'd told Delilah, disguised as Tyler, that I loved him. But had I told the real Tyler? "You said I didn't have to love you back, but I do. I love you, damn it. I love your smile and your smell and the annoying way you follow me around. I love that you love me despite my faults, what I've done, and who I am. And I love that you're not afraid of me." I laid my lips to his temple. "I. Love. You."

If anyone was going to drink my oh-so-special blood, it was going to be Tyler. It had turned stone to flesh, and what I wanted right now was less a feat than that. He'd bound us by magic, perhaps something deeper still, and I was going to bind us by blood. I could heal almost instantaneously. Could my blood heal Tyler as well? I took the dagger stained with Azriel's blood. I wiped it clean on my shirt and swiped it across my pants for good measure. Drawing a breath, I sliced the blade across my palm and waited for the ribbon of blood. It welled up and I made a fist, holding it over Tyler's mouth, which I pried open with my other hand. Crimson droplets splashed against his teeth and dripped into this throat.

I healed so much faster now, I had to reopen the wound three times. Squeezing my fist each time, I willed every drop I could, and it came faster, running in a tiny stream. I didn't know how much to give him. I wasn't even sure if it would work. A few seconds passed, and I pulled my fist away and watched as the wound closed before my eyes. I marveled at the changes in me, but I didn't have time to worry about it. I closed Tyler's mouth and massaged his throat to aid in swallowing. I said a silent prayer, and then I waited.

Maybe I needed to chant a set of magic words, or something. My love for Tyler had been the ingredient needed to create life. Surely my love for him now was all I needed to save his. I sat for what seemed like an eternity, but nothing happened. He lay still and peaceful, his chest rising and falling as it had every day for weeks.

"If you don't wake up in thirty seconds, I'm outta here—for good," I said.

Turning on a heel, I walked toward the door, my steps in perfect time with the passing seconds. *Three ... two ... one ...*

"Is there anything in your wardrobe that isn't black?" Tyler's voice was little more than a whisper, calling out from behind me. "Don't get me wrong. You look great. Sexy in a badass sort of way."

My heart swelled in my chest as I turned to face him. I smiled, finally *wanting* him to see the trace of warmth his nearness caused in me.

Tyler never disappoints.

Amanda Bonilla lives in rural Idaho with her husband and two kids. She's a part-time pet wrangler, a full-time sun worshipper, and only goes out into the cold when coerced. When she's not writing, she's either reading or talking about her favorite books. For more about Amanda, visit www.amandabonilla.com.

Read on for a peek at the next novel
in the Shaede Assassin series,

BLOOD BEFORE SUNRISE

Available from Signet Eclipse in July 2012.

"*What are you looking at?*"

I tore my gaze from the delicate curve of the dagger's blade, my eyes drawn to Azriel's dark, handsome face like a magnet to metal. "Nothing," I said, though that wasn't entirely true.

"Ever lacking patience," he said with humor. "You'll never make it as an assassin if you can't wait more than a few minutes to get a job done."

True enough, I supposed. I liked to wait about as much as I liked to be doused with gasoline and set on fire. "Lorik's late," I said. "It's not like him."

Azriel stroked his finger along my jaw and his eyes burned with an intensity that had nothing to do with business. "It matters little to me if he shows or not. Either way, my night won't be wasted."

I flushed at the innuendo, knowing all too well where a jobless night would lead us. Not that I'd complain . . .

An engine growled in the distance, followed by the squealing of tires. The Cadillac LaSalle Roadster came to a halt inches from where I stood, and the driver's expression was full of adrenaline-infused excitement. Lorik loved flashy cars, and despite the fact that he needed to lay low, he could never resist showing off. What's the point in not putting that engine and sleek body to use? He'd consider it a waste. Besides, I had a suspicion that the combination of fancy car coupled with his pinstriped suit and fedora pulled low over his brow made Lorik feel like he'd just pulled a bank caper. Driving into the sunset and im-

mortal glory would be the icing on the cake. And I'd be willing to bet a Chicago typewriter rode shotgun to round it all out. I mean, what self-respecting gangster didn't have a machine gun in the front seat?

"Looks like your clothes will be on for a while longer, my love." Azriel leaned down and pressed his mouth to the pulse point just below my ear.

I shivered at the contact, suddenly not caring whether Lorik's life was in danger or not. Though the guy's father did pay our bills, I supposed I could put my erotic thoughts on hold. But if he didn't get down to business—and soon—he could rot in hell for all I cared.

"What are you looking at?" Tyler asked again, his tone bemused when I didn't answer him right away.

"Nothing," I finally said as I stared at the spot near the alley where that LaSalle had come to a skidding stop all those years ago. "Not a damn thing."

God, I hadn't thought of that crazy Armenian in decades. He had to have been dead for a while now, if someone hadn't managed to do the deed in his youth. Lorik had been the closest thing Azriel had to a friend. I always wondered about it, the comfortable way Azriel had with him. Usually we lay lower than low, but with Lorik, Azriel had allowed us to let our guard down a bit. Maybe I'd do some digging just for shits and giggles. Find out what really happened to him after he went off the grid. Because I had *so* much free time on my hands these days.

My annoyance wasn't so much about memories of Lorik—and Azriel—intruding on my thoughts. Or even my lack of actual downtime. Rather, it was due to the fact that I stood at yet another dead end. It's damn hard to catch someone who's always one step ahead of you.

And chasing an Oracle is like chasing the wind.

I drove my katana into the scabbard at my back. Yet another close call, and the bitch had slipped right through my fingers. You wouldn't think someone as blind as a bat could escape so easily.

But she had.

For months.

Time and again.

A discarded can nudged at my toe and I kicked it, sending it sailing down the sidewalk toward the street, narrowly missing a parking sign. I was beyond frustrated, and my agitation settled as a knot between my shoulder blades. I stretched my neck from side to side in a futile effort to ease the mounting tension. Raif, my mentor and the best friend I've ever had, laid a comforting hand on my shoulder. "Don't worry," he said. "We'll get her."

Tyler took a step closer, his body touching mine in more places than was appropriate for work hours. He snaked an arm around my waist as he brought me against him, his eyes narrowing in Raif's direction. *Jeez, touchy much?*

Raif shook his head. He looked at me, his expression saying, *Is he for real?* I raised my brows, which was as good as a shrug. I had no idea what had gotten into Tyler, but I could almost hear the predatory growl, the low rumble of a wary bear. "Relax, Jinn," Raif said, tucking a dagger into a sheath at his side. "You look a little wound."

"Not hardly," Tyler said, his tone just on the edge of becoming hard. "In fact"—he lowered his face to the top of my head and nuzzled my hair—"I'm pretty damned relaxed right now."

Again, Raif gave me a look. And again, I gave him the equivalent of a facial shrug. Hell if I knew why Tyler was acting like a high school jock facing off with the opposing quarterback. Maybe we all needed to take it down a notch and hang it up for the night.

As if he'd read my mind, Raif gave me a playful knock against the shoulder, eliciting another grumble and glare from Tyler. "I'm calling it a night. See you tomorrow?"

"You know it." There was no way I was letting up anytime soon. I'd search day and night until I found that mousey pain in the ass Oracle. "Meet me at my place."

Raif's brilliant blue eyes glowed against the backdrop of night as he gave Tyler a last questioning glance. He flashed one of his deadly smiles. "Tyler," he said with a nod, his tone dry. He scattered into a dusting of shadow and left us alone in the alley.

I turned a caustic eye to Tyler. I hated it when he got all territorial on me. It made me feel like a bone—and tonight, Ty was definitely the dog. He put his lips to my forehead, ignoring my accusing glare. Apparently he didn't think his behavior was as juvenile as I did. That was saying a lot, considering Tyler had centuries on me in the age department.

Hunting a mark had never been enjoyable. Exciting, sure, but also a necessity. Going out with Tyler put a whole new spin on "job perks." As my Jinn, my personal genie and sworn protector, he made it his business to have my back. But as my boyfriend, it was a pleasure to have him along. Although the word *boyfriend* didn't do justice to Tyler's role in my life, I thought he might appreciate the more modern reference. He might have had centuries on me in age, but he was a modern guy through and through. I doubted a word existed to describe what Tyler was to me. More than simply my lover, and definitely more than a friend, he had captured more than just my heart over the five years I'd known him. Tyler had claimed my soul.

He'd been out combing the city with me every night this week, staying out even after Raif abandoned the hunt. I guess Ty was the only person with the stamina to keep up with me. And believe me, his stamina wasn't something I was about to grumble over anytime soon.

"We might as well call it a night too," he said, giving me a squeeze. "I think we should try Idaho again. Maybe next week. I know a lesser Seer in Coeur d'Alene who might be tempted to shelter Delilah—for the right price."

Idaho again. We'd already searched most of the panhandle, and I doubted another go around would produce better results. "No," I said, leaning into him so I could feel his muscled chest against my shoulder. "I don't think she's that far away. Don't ask me why, but I can't shake the feeling that she's staying close to home. Delilah has unfinished business, and she never struck me as a quitter."

"Darian," he said, his fingers stroking up my arm, "let's go home."

I melted against him, loving the way my name rolled off his tongue like a sacred word—or a prayer. It never took much for Ty to break down my defenses, and the thought of spending the rest of the night naked and twined around his magnificent body beat the hell out of standing on the cold, rain-drenched street for another second. He placed his lips against my neck, his tongue darting out to trace my flesh. Chills rippled across my skin from the contact. Oh yeah. It was time to go home.

Side by side, we walked through the Queen Anne District just like any human couple would. Though nothing stopped me from becoming one with the shadows and traveling under the cover of darkness, I liked walking with Ty. As we headed down the street, the black tails of my coat floating out behind me, I was just a woman, one of thousands inhabiting the city of Seattle. It made me feel just a little less like a freak of nature, and more like the person I used to be. Night, day, dawn, or twilight—I could now pass through the world without the hindrance of being corporeal no matter the hour. I had to admit, it was a nice perk, though the means to that end had been anything but pleasant. I never used to believe in prophecy or rituals until I'd been the focal point of both. One attempted sacrifice and an eclipse later, and I had a whole new perspective on life.

Though months had passed since my transformation, it seemed only a matter of days. My former lover and supposed maker, Azriel, had made an alliance with the Oracle Delilah and a small army of nasty Lyhtans—violent praying mantis–looking bastards who hold a serious grudge against any Shaede—to bring down Xander Peck, the king of the Shaede Nation. The fact that Azriel had been Xander's son made the situation that much worse. Hungry for power, he'd had designs on Xander's crown for centuries. And he'd been willing to do *anything* to get it. I'd been the pawn in their little power struggle. A creature created by her own will and my super-special blood used to awaken the Enphigmalé, hideous gargoyles with a serious binge-eating problem. But since I was alive and well, and Azriel had gone into the shadow forever—meaning, I ran my dagger across his lying, traitorous throat—it wasn't hard to tell who'd come out on top in his little coup.

Delilah had been the one loose end I'd failed to tie up—so far. According to Azriel, she'd had more reason to hate Shaedes than anyone, though for the life of me, I couldn't guess why. She'd proved to be more slippery than I'd given her credit for, however. And that was a sharp thorn in my side.

Night wrapped me in its warm embrace, tickling my senses. I grabbed on to Tyler's hand as we continued walking at a steady pace. I liked the feeling of being *real,* substantial and not just a whisper of something too foreign for even preternatural creatures to comprehend. The glorious anonymity of my life prior to my transformation was gone. Up until several months ago, I'd thought I was the only Shaede in existence. Part of Azriel's lie to keep me good and hidden. It's hard to hide under the cover of darkness when shadows are watching, though. Alexander Peck—Shaede High King, or to me, just plain Xander—had been watching me for a while. Once he plucked me from obscurity, there was no going back.

Splinters of muted silver moonlight shone between

the taller buildings, casting shadows on the rugged, handsome lines of Tyler's model-worthy face. My pace slowed and I released his hand as a strange urge pulled at my center. *Turn here,* intuition called and, as if I had no control over my limbs, I obeyed.

"Darian?" Tyler said. "What's up?"

I ignored his question, my mind too focused to answer. My legs followed a path down an abandoned side street, the stench of ripe garbage wafting from a nearby Dumpster. Clearing my mind of conscious thought, I moved on instinct alone, allowing the strange feeling to guide me past a fire escape toward a gaping door where the street dead-ended.

"Darian!" Tyler's tone sharpened as something close to a growl rumbled in the lone word. A warning. He was my bound Jinn, a mystical protector, and his Spidey sense must have been tingling. I held up a hand to quiet him as much as to reassure him. I wasn't in any danger. At least, not yet.

I walked through the opening, surprised to find a storage space large enough to park a car in. From the look of it—not to mention the stale smell—no one had used the space for a while. Through the dark I perceived the presence of another, and the feeling in my stomach tugged lower, like a rope drawing me to the floor. Squatting down, I roved the space with my eyes, grateful for the ability to see through the dark, marking a path of dirty blankets and discarded food containers. And at the end of it all, a body sat huddled in the corner, knees tucked up and head hidden beneath thin, bony arms.

"Hello, Delilah," I said. "I've been looking for you."